HOME WALTZ

HOME WALTZ

G.A.Grisenthwaite

Palimpsest Press
1171 Eastlawn Ave.
Windsor, Ontario. N8S 3J1
www.palimpsestpress.ca

Book and cover design by Dawn Kresan. Printed at Rapido Books in Ontario, Canada. Edited by Jamie Tennant. Palimpsest Press would like to thank the Canada Council for the Arts, and the Ontario Arts Council for their support of our publishing program. We also acknowledge the assistance of the Government of Ontario through the Ontario Book Publishing Tax Credit.

LIBRARY AND ARCHIVES CANADA CATALOGUING IN PUBLICATION

Title: Home waltz / G.A. Grisenthwaite.
Names: Grisenthwaite, G. A., 1959– author.
Identifiers: Canadiana (print) 20200279890
Canadiana (ebook) 20200279971

ISBN 9781989287644 (softcover)
ISBN 9781989287651 (EPUB)
ISBN 9781989287668 (Kindle)
ISBN 9781989287675 (PDF)

Classification: LCC PS8613.R646 H66 2020
DDC C813/.6—DC23

To three strong women (my grandmothers)
who helped me in almost every way imaginable:
Margaret, Vera, Hazel

"Home Waltz? I dunno how to explain it to you, Constable Bailey, really. I mean, any slow song can be the Home Waltz. It's never the last song of the night, but always the last slow one. And not everyone gets one, even when the band plays it. And I should know, I never get one.

"It's hard to watch all them couples practically doing it to each other on the dance floor. And I don't even know why they call it the Home Waltz, cos most of 'em just jump into the backseat and hump each other's brains out. Sick."

FRIDAY

UNGODLY HOURS

So, my dead cousin Erica walks into my dream again, pulls the covers off me doing it to a girl, Bernie, I think. My spaeks? shrivels. Goosebumps rise on my arms and legs. Erica's arms flap and wave like wind-ripped clothes on the clothesline. She yells but her words only spit a little cold wind. Bernie crumbles to dust in Erica's growing shadow. Erica only visits my hot dreams, so she visits me way, way more now than she ever did in life. Her visits leave me sad.

Erica, always a little chubby, liked her chips and Pepsi for breakfast and then got the diabetes. Till the day she died she'd gone with a séme? called Johnny Smith, a walking venereal wart of a kid who came to town with his parents, from somewhere out east.

The Smiths, as white as Aunt Polly's fence, claimed that their Great Maker commanded them to come here and open The Groovy Grub, one of those weird, hippy-dippy food stores. They came to save us with their so-called health food, and save us with their trans-mental, ram-a-lam-a ding dong stuff. Almost no one bought anything from the Smiths. Would you buy raw peanuts and herbs and powders that smelled like ground-up gym socks? They kept the store open about a year. They had a going out-of-business sale and couldn't even give away any of their rotten food. Even Crazy Thom, a guy who drinks gasoline for beer money, wouldn't eat it.

Erica and her mom, my Auntie Lois, took in all the Smith's Great Maker stuff to cure Erica's diabetes. But she got sicker and sicker, and then a Big Town doctor told her he'd have to chop off one of her legs. Besides Erica and her mom, only some hippies who ran away from the Vietnam War to squat in the bushes outside of town bought the Smith's stuff. Them hippies live in one of them communes, where, they say, everyone does drugs and has sex orgies all day and night. But Skinny, JimJim, Cody, and I never seen one, and not one single naked girl. Bimbo says he sees them every time he goes over. He says you just need to know where to look but he won't tell us his secret place and won't go over there with us.

I'd just turned nine, the last time I saw Erica, almost sixteen, and, according to her, the oldest, least-liked girl in Grade Nine. Friday, the fifteenth of June, just after school. We had no classes cos of Sports Day, a form of organized torture, forcing you to run and jump under a hundred degree sun, but not over stumps or creeks, or other cool, useful stuff. Us Intermediates had to run every event, even shot put, discus and javelin, like the Juniors. I even got a ribbon—third in long jump. One ribbon from eleven things. Skinny got eleven ribbons, all first place, except a second for shot put, and a third for the relay.

All sweaty and miserable about getting only one ribbon for all my work, I bought myself a bottle of Orange Crush. On my way to Yéye?'s, I startled Erica, sitting in the shade of an old shed at the end of town. She sat next to an ugly patch of prickly pear, a bottle of wine on a blanket beside her. Doctor told her not to drink pop or booze, cos it would kill her.

I pointed my lip at the wine, Asti Spumante, not just booze but sweet, fizzy booze. "Hey, cuzzy, what's up?"

"Nothing," she said, all stiff-necked and swallowing hard. "Just waiting for Johnny."

"O?"

"Yeah, I and him's havin' a picnic."

"Can I come?"

"No, you. Just go away. Sheesh you, stop bothering me."

"I'll tell."

"You tell and Snk̓ẏép gonna gechoo. Grab you by the tongue and fling you into River."

"He won't."

"If he don't, I will. Now just go," she said. "And don't tell no one. It's our secret, okay?"

"Okay," I said. The weight of other people's secrets always pulled my dreams into Nightmare's black mud. They got lost there.

They found her a day later, laid out like a body in a casket. So perfect. So peaceful and almost beautiful, even with Death's blue on her. Funny how the ants and other critters hadn't gotten to her before the searchers.

Her mom went all bat-shit when Erica didn't make her 9:00 curfew. She went to the Smith's and practically melted when Johnny'd said he hadn't seen her since he'd dumped her the day before. She totally broke when Bailey told her they'd found Erica dead. They sent her straight to a rubber room at a mental hospital near Big Town. They kept her for the better part of a year. They kept her so drugged-up that she couldn't go to Erica's funeral. Auntie Lois came home a different person. Not better.

Everyone in town goes to every funeral. Almost everyone. Some people, like Cody, won't ever go to a suicide's funeral. Cody even skipped his older brother Francis', cos he'd shot himself in his garage, leaving his body for his wife and daughter to find.

Erica killed herself a long time ago and I'm still mad at her for making me keep her secret. I still can't go near the place she chose to die. That spot is cold all year round and makes my skin crawl. I guess that cold spot has trapped Erica's spirit, or she keeps hanging around cos she's mad at me for keeping her secret, or not keeping it. She killed herself but didn't leave a note, and didn't tell anyone, even Johnny—who should've known—and kinda made it my fault, cos I should've seen what Erica was up to and stopped her, or called someone who could. No one knows I saw her last. Blabbing my secret now would open up shame in me deeper than Canyon, and harsher than the shame inside me now. Could I grow to hate myself as much as Erica hated herself? As much as she probably hated me?

Twice a year—on Erica's birthday, the sixteenth of September and fifteenth of June, the day she died—I go not to her grave, like a normal person, but near the cold spot that swallowed her soul, and ask her if I should've stopped her and whether she'd have listened if I'd tried to stop her. I cry when I'm with Erica but not for her. I cry for myself, cos I'm the one who has to live with our secret: I killed my cousin by leaving her alone to die. I tell her I'll never let anyone die like she did again.

I wish she would answer but maybe the way she always barges into my hot dreams to yell at me is her answer.

11:30 AM

The clock's second hand ticks backwards. The clock stops dead at half past eleven. From behind, Cow Petersen, girls' gym and everyone's math teacher, could pass for human. She scratches gibberish onto the blackboard and drones on about something. She may as well speak Greek, for all the sense she makes. Cody drops his pencil in the aisle between us. Cow gorgons Cody. Skinny, JimJim, Bimbo, and I whiten up like marble. I can't breathe. No one wants a mad Cow, especially on the Friday of a dance weekend. Her white chalk looks like a lipstick inside her chalk holder. It has more colour than her skin. She points it at Cody.

He raises his hand.

"Well?" she says.

"Excuse me, Miss Peterson," he says. "My pencil fell."

"Did it?"

Just two small words but they crush us like a building falling on us.

"Yes. I apologize for interrupting you."

Except for Wind tapping pebbles and grains of dirt off our classroom's windows: silence. I stare at my text, its gobbledygook about lines, segments, and points. Cow might chalk a line between Cody and detention, and make me a point folded into his punishment cos she can. A year or so ago she ran to Principal Fish and put assault charges on Tommy John. Could she do it to us, too, so I won't get my Home Waltz? I ache for a drink. All week long I've behaved like a kid working to stay off Santa's naughty list, and even finished my French homework once. I need everything to go right, so all week long I've slept with my brand new rubber, dance ticket, and all of The Footnotes' 45s under my pillow.

Cow snorts then says, "Pick it up."

Cody taps my shoe and flashes a perfectly square note tucked into his palm. Cow waits a full hundred heartbeats before going back to scratching her lesson on the blackboard. Every tick of the clock, every beat of my heart, adds to my fear that Cow can get us locked up for the weekend, and gnaws at my hope of having my first Home Waltz.

11:35 AM

The clock, trying to tell me only five minutes have passed, ticks back to life. Eyes front, I slip the note into my desk, carefully unfold it, and then press it flat on my binder:

(9–12 Ashcroft girls + 4 dozen beer) ÷ {4} 5 horny guys = fun for all.

Bimbo gawks, whispers, "Hey, lemme see." His voice is the one that tries to wake up that drunk sleeping under your porch. "Lemme see next, 'kay?"

Cow stiffens and sucks in a harsh breath. I crumple the note into my pants pocket.

"I expect more from you, Thaddeus," Cow says.

"Yes, Miss Peterson," he says. The five become four as I split Bimbo's image in half with a thick black line.

Her snake eyes and snake hair slither all over me. "See what, Mr Bob?"

"I dunno," I say. "Ask him."

Her eyes coil around my throat and squeeze. I sink into my seat and wait for her to order me to detention right at 3:00. Anger sets my face on fire.

Bimbo, like the dumbest kid to make it out of kindergarten, says, "I wanted to see his answer. See if I got it right. I don't think I'm getting it."

"What makes you think he has an inkling about slopes of lines if you can't grasp the concept?"

"Well, I guess he has to get lucky sometime. I thought I'd give him a chance."

Sniggers rise like ice cracking on River. Cow smiles. "Considering the fact that he has already failed this class twice, one might assume, however unreasonably, that he might have absorbed some of algebra's basic concepts."

Everyone says she's failed me so many times cos she has a crush on me, then they start calling me the granny porker all over again. You make one (big) mistake and no one ever lets you forget it.

"But we are talking about Squito," Bimbo says.

Sniggers become laughs. Elizabeth, who thinks sitting in front of me is punishment for getting only 99 in math on her last report card, glares at me like I've just snapped her bra again. I force a smile and mouth a laugh, my eyes squinted to hide the murder in them.

"Enough," Cow says. Instant silence. "Thaddeus, show us your solution."

Bimbo holds his notebook up in front of his face.

"On the blackboard. Come up here and draw it for us."

Bimbo drags himself to the front of the class and copies Cow's graph and line.

As he heads back to his seat, she says, "Now explain to us how you arrived at your answer."

Except for the shifting shades of red painting his throat and face, Bimbo freezes. His Adam's apple bobs like a feeding chicken's head. Then he stammers and stutters a parroted explanation.

In blue chalk, Cow draws a new line over Bimbo's. "Following your logic, Thaddeus, your solution ought to look like this." She stabs the blackboard. Shards of blue chalk crumble. She smiles the smile that says checkmate. Bimbo flinches. She draws a yellow line over the other two. "Had you paid attention to what I demonstrated, your solution would've looked like this one. Correct."

"Yes, ma'am," Bimbo says. He zips back into his seat and buries his face in his text.

Bimbo's screw-up has eaten almost ten minutes of class time.

"Next time," Cow says, her words a rifle shot. "Next time any of you need clarification, ask me, a mathematician." She aims her lipstick-chalk at me: "And not that."

I wish I could make her words bounce off me and stick to her.

NOON

The clock starts ticking backwards as it closes in on lunch time. As dorky as it sounds, about two minutes before the bell rings I start sprouting a hard one, just thinking about all them Ashcroft girls camping at Auntie Max's. I drink in a long look at Cow, the next best thing to jumping into an ice-filled bathtub. The snakes on her head transform to dicks, leaving mine like a roadkill snake in my pants.

The Footnotes have three different Home Waltzes. Their oldest ones belong to CCR: "Long as I Can See the Light" and "Who'll Stop the Rain." Their newest melts every girl on the dance floor, and I guess everyone else. The Stampeders "O My Lady." It gets to me and I sorta don't care who knows it. When I dream of my Home Waltz, it's "O My Lady," but the girl changes from the impossible Bernie Paul to the last girl I saw before passing out. But "Angie," that new song by The Rolling Stones, moves me too. I made the hotel coffee shop juke play it three or four times in a row the first time I heard it. Just as the last play started, Agnes, the day waitress, went and unplugged the juke, saying she didn't care if she never heard that song again.

The bell finally rings. No one moves. My brain has already left the building but my body waits for Cow to let us leave.

And waits.

The hall empties. Everything's quiet, except for squeaking seats, and someone's growling gut. After ten minutes as long as God's first six days, Cow rattles off a list of chapter exercises she wants us to have done by next day—it's enough homework for a month of math classes—and then she begins to dismiss us.

First, she frees all the girls. Elizabeth sticks her tongue out at me as she walks out. I wish I could get girls to love me as easily as I get them hating me.

One by one she frees us boys, all of the səmséme except Bimbo, first. Then the residential school boys. When it gets down to Skinny, JimJim, Cody, Bimbo and I, we look questions to each other and shrug back answers.

She shuffles papers.

"Miss Peterson, can we please go?" Bimbo says. He doesn't exactly say *bitch* but you hear it anyway, and by the way Cow goes all stiff and even paler than the palest pale you can get and still have something like colour on you, she hears it, too.

Skinny flashes a fist Bimbo's way. Cody, who's unlucky enough to have to sit behind Bimbo, punches him between his shoulder blades.

"Ow," Bimbo whines, spinning around in his seat. "Stop it."

Cow stink-eyes me while she dismisses Skinny and JimJim. Dance magic—and it will be magic, with Fast Freddy and the Frivolous Footnotes playing—is the only thing keeping me from telling her exactly what I think. Another thing, almost more magical, is all the buses full of senior girls from the other schools in our district that will be in town for the senior girls volleyball tournament. Most of them səmséme, so almost none will be relations, raising my chances of scoring a Home Waltz, and the sex and stuff that always follows it, cos up to twelve of them will billet at Auntie Max's. I have a real chance for my first Home Waltz.

"Have a good, safe weekend, Quick Sky Bob," she says, mispronouncing my name the way she has since forever. Just 12:15 and it feels like I've lived through an ice age.

"Thank you, Miss Peterson." I guess I'd rather die than wish her a good weekend too. I scoop up my binder and head out in an orderly fashion, without looking anywhere near Cody and Bimbo.

After locking up my books and grabbing my coat, I head to the coffee shop. If that Cow wanted me to do her homework she should've asked nicer. One more *F* from her can't hurt me, and maybe that idiot guidance counsellor will finally pull his head from his butt long enough to put me where I belong, in Industrial Math.

12:20 PM

Agnes puts Skinny and JimJim's large fries and gravy and a big basket of onion rings on our table just as I get there. My gut growls.

"You like how that Bimbo got us a detention?" JimJim says.

I slide in beside him and grab one of his chips.

"You shoulda been more careful with that note," Skinny goes.

"Not my fault the kid's got eyes in back of his head," I say.

"Whatever. Anyways, it wouldn't a been a problem if Principal Fish hadda screwed her right this morning."

"Hey, you, watch your mouth," Agnes snaps, "or I'll wash it out with soap and kick your bony arse outta my café."

Skinny turtles and mumbles a hundred apologies. Agnes is Skinny's Kryptonite and she shrinks him down to a size I could stomp as easily as I could stomp Bimbo.

"That's better," Agnes says. "And that goes for the rest of you. I don't want no bad talk from none of you."

Her glare stiffens us up like soldiers sitting at attention. We *yes ma'am* her until she nods and heads toward the kitchen.

"She needs a good swift kick in the twat," Skinny goes, in a voice as soft as thought.

"Agnes?" I say.

"No, you moron, the Cow," Skinny goes. You have to wonder which woman he really meant.

"'Course. Stupid me," I say.

JimJim pipes in, "Yeah, stupid you. I dunno. Maybe she just needs to go ten rounds with the big stick."

"No way, José. There's no effing way I'm sticking it to that Cow," Skinny goes, far too loudly.

"Look at you. Thinking yours is the only big one around," JimJim says. He's one of a few people who can talk to Skinny that way and not get beaten to death. I'm not one of them.

"No, not the only big one," Skinny goes. "The biggest one."

Skinny puffs out his chest and sits a little taller. Skinny's not bragging cos what he's saying is true. It's not as if I like thinking about another guy's spaeks? but Skinny's belongs in the Guinness Book or something, everyone says so, and that's why he calls his the Golden Sceptre. Skinny's dad used to drag him into the pub and measure it in front of all kinds of guys. It started back in Grade Seven, when most of us were still looking for the first of our pubes. You'd think having a bunch of old drunks gawking and pawing at your dick would've embarrassed him but no, he'd come out waving a wad of singles, sometimes as much as ten dollars, smiling as big as someone who'd just gotten laid. Skinny's dad probably made a ton of money betting on the size of his son's dink, maybe not enough to pay the rent and stuff, but his winnings had earned him a lot of drinking money. You could offer me a cool million dollars and it still wouldn't be enough to get me to whip out my little chief for anyone to gawk at. Skinny's happy to show his to anyone who asks to see it and even those who don't.

Agnes puts a coffee in front of me and hands me a menu, a gentle reminder that during lunch they charge a two dollar minimum to sit in a booth. Then she punches Skinny's shoulder.

He looks up at Agnes, all hurt, a little surprised, rubbing his shoulder, and says, "Holy! Jeez you, how'd you learn to hit like that, anyways?"

She cackles.

"That wasn't even my best shot. Keep talking that rude and you'll see how hard I could hit."

She laughs. JimJim laughs. Skinny says, *ha ha ha.* I thank her for bringing me coffee, but not for the menu. Getting ready for the weekend cost me just about all the money I'd saved. Putting a minimum charge on booths at lunch ranks as one of the cruelest things Alister "Sinister" Snook did to us since he took over as manager of the hotel, and he's done a lotta bad things.

"Could I get a cheeseburger with chips and gravy?" I say.

"What else?" Agnes says, a glint like a bit of sand in her eye. Her face wears a smile.

Skinny and JimJim laugh their arses off.

"You guys wanna go in on a large onion rings?"

"You blind? Can't you see we already got one?" Skinny goes.

I blurt a weak laugh. "O, yeah. Guess I forgot." For a second there I want to hit him square on his beak.

Skinny and JimJim get away with murder and Agnes makes me order the minimum booth charge. Why does she hate me so much? Skinny swears and does other bad things. JimJim's just JimJim, so I can sorta see why Agnes would go easy on him.

The last thing I need is so much food in me that I have no room for all the booze I'm about to drink. I need to eat just enough to coat my stomach so the booze doesn't eat my gut. I know everything on this menu, and in all the years I've eaten here, only its prices have changed. Agnes has served me so many times that she knows what I want before I even ask for it, just like she does for Fat Elvis and everyone else who eats here.

"Maybe a large onion rings?" I say. She scruffs my hair and laughs. It sounds like choking.

"Don't worry about the booth charge. No one really gives a care," she says. She winks. "This time, I mean."

"K^{w}uk^{w}scémx^{w}," I say, "but I think I'd like them rings anyways."

Agnes walks away cackling like a witch on laughing gas.

"Shoulda seen the look on your face," JimJim says.

"You're such a sucker," Skinny goes.

"How would I know she's joking me, hey? When does she ever joke?"

"All the time. I guess you're just too thick to get it," Skinny goes.

We talk about class and what a douchebag Cow is. Cody knows better than to set Bimbo off, especially in Cow's class, so who can say what crawled up his butt this morning. It could be Bimbo-being-himself stuff but I doubt it cos in some ways Cody's as cool as Skinny.

But Bimbo.

Trying to figure out what happens inside his broken brain makes algebra seem easy. I guess I coulda passed Cow's class if I liked her, and wanted to try, but she has a way about her that makes you not want to do anything for her cos she's mean and has snakes for hair. Funny how she let us go like she did today. She always punishes us for something one of us may or may not have done. Like two weeks ago, when Cow caught JimJim spitting a chew into the garbage can. He hadn't hawked up a pound of lung-butter or anything super gross, just a ton of tobacco-spit, but it did sorta looked like he'd puked into it. Cow showed the garbage can to Principal Fish and then told a story so gross, even my stomach got all grumpy. Fish threatened to strap each of us but changed his mind and gave us a week of detention. He made us wash every garbage can in the school. To add to our misery, that a-hole janitor Mister Geordie made us paint the bottoms of every one of them. Five days of hard-labour cos one kid spit a little tobacco juice into a garbage can.

No matter what happens this weekend, I will have the flu or something Monday morning.

12:45 PM

Skinny rests his back against the wall, stretching his legs out along the bench, not something any of us do, especially during Agnes' shifts.

"I'm killing that Cow," Bimbo says. He's burst-vein red. "C'mon, Skinny, move your damn feet."

"But nah," Skinny goes. He takes a bite of a huge onion ring and crunches it all cow-like, then flashes Bimbo a chew-and-show. "Sit your sorry butt at the counter."

Bimbo huffs a bunch of nasty words to himself then turns his whine on me. "Slide your fat ass over."

I don't budge. Bimbo reaches for one of JimJim's onion rings. JimJim grabs Bimbo's thumb and yanks it backwards hard enough to buckle his knees.

"Keep your greasy mitts off my food," JimJim says.

"It's just one onion ring. Christ Almighty, you're the cheapest asshole around."

He cradles his thumb like it's a wounded bird. I stand, a full head taller than Bimbo, and look down at him. He grows redder and squirms like a wormed-up dog.

"What?" he goes. "What?"

"Slide your skinny white arse in," I say.

"Screw you. I'm not sitting in the middle."

"Well, you could always take a stool at the counter, hey?" JimJim says.

"Yeah," Skinny goes. "Sit down and shut up before you get us kicked out of here again."

Bimbo slumps into the booth and slides into JimJim.

JimJim punches him. "You homo, watch it."

My elbow clips Bimbo's fat head. "Oops," I say. I reach over Bimbo and take another one of JimJim's rings. Bimbo, all fish-faced, says, "Hey, why you let him take one?"

"Cos he's not you," JimJim says.

Skinny sits proper and Cody plops down next to him, way quieter than usual. Sinister Snook has snuck in and sneers at us as he pours himself a coffee. Agnes hands Bimbo and Cody menus and pulls out her pad.

JimJim slides his basket of chips toward Cody. "Chip?"

Cody takes one and says, "Just a coffee for me, Agnes."

She points her lower lip at the two-dollar-minimum-between-eleven-and-two sign. "Sorry."

Cody slumps into himself, like his head suddenly gained a hundred pounds. "O, guess I'll just wait outside. Excuse me."

Skinny mouths *what?* and watches Cody leave.

"I'd've paid for his meal," Skinny says.

"Coulda said something before he left," Bimbo says. "Anyway, you could pay for mine."

"You could lick my bag."

Agnes, all grr-faced, says, "I already warned you once about using that potty-mouth of yours in my café. One more word and you'll be barred, Bernard Paul."

"Shit, Agnes," Skinny says.

"That's the word. Pay up and leave. I won't be disrespected."

Sinister smiles a Snidely Whiplash smile. Hands on his hips, he straight on stares at our booth.

"Yes, ma'am. I'm sorry, Agnes. Really. It won't happen again."

"It will. But not for the rest of today. Let's go. Now."

Skinny grumbles as he slides from our booth.

"C'mon, guys. You heard the lady. Time for us to go."

"Just you, Bernard."

Skinny's face and shoulders scream, *Well, let's go.*

I slip into Skinny's vacated spot.

"In a few. I'm still waiting for my meal."

"Just get it to go. C'mon."

"I won't be long," I say.

"Right behind you, buds," JimJim says. He punches Bimbo's shoulder and then slides out. Bimbo bites his lip and grumbles some sorta crybaby gibberish. Skinny taps Bimbo's shoulder and nods toward the door.

"Not yet," Bimbo says. "I haven't eaten anything all day."

"Like it's my fault your mother starves you," Skinny goes. He sighs. "Just eat. Who needs you around, anyhow?"

I hate to-go food from the coffee shop cos it's always cold and soggy, no matter how fast you get to it. They say Gladys the cook lets it cool before wrapping it up, that she does it cos she wouldn't serve food on paper plates to dogs. Jonathan Delorme, after he lost his dishwashing job, said he'd caught Gladys peeing on a takeout order. Gladys runs her kitchen like one of them fancy big-city kitchens. She's worked at the hotel longer than Agnes, some say since they rebuilt after that last fire, maybe thirty–forty years ago. I don't think anyone believed Delorme, that filthy-rat-outsider-from-somewhere-down-east, anyway. Gladys caught him stealing food more than once, but what else would you expect from a guy who stole a job from one of us guys, or might have, if Sinister thought enough of us to give us jobs.

Skinny and JimJim leave me alone with Bimbo. He orders a deluxe burger with an extra patty, a fried egg and extra cheese, with onion rings instead of chips, and a bottle of Coke, and, as usual, grumbles about the hotel not having fountain Coke. Agnes sighs, *whatever*, snaps her book to a new page and writes up Bimbo's order. Two dollars and fifteen cents, for a meal they don't even have on the menu. Only someone like Bimbo could even think to ask for anything special. And only someone like him would expect to get it, too. For a complete idiot, Bimbo does have smart moments.

"Listen," Bimbo says. "I'm a couple a cents short. Could you lend me half a buck?"

"If you cancel it now, Agnes might not kill you."

"Don't be an a-hole," Bimbo says. "I got to eat or I'll get sick."

"Why should I?"

"Cos I'd do the same for you, if you needed to eat."

"Would not."

"Would, too. C'mon. Please."

I smile, big and toothy. He squirms, eyeballing the kitchen, jumping at every little sound. Instead of his usual splash of reds, he whitens, and sweat bubbles up along his hairline and on his nose. He shivers.

"What's wrong with you?" I say.

"Nothing," he stammers. "I didn't get to eat breakfast. I'll be okay after I get some food in me."

Crap. Crap. Crap. I pull out my skimpy roll, peel off a single and slide it across the table. Bimbo looks at it but I don't think he sees it. My appetite is gone and I ache for a drink. Agnes brings my food. I plop my burger onto my rings and shove the plate of chips and gravy at Bimbo. He inhales them, chewing like a thresher, and doesn't even use the fork. I focus on my burger. I wolf my food down, making double sure not to make disgusting noises while I chew. Bimbo will probably puke his meal up like a snake spewing a rat's carcass as soon as he takes his first drink. Still, hearing him puke won't gross me out as much as his eating. He slurps grease and gravy off his fingertips. Even with my eyes tightly closed, I see him eat. I wipe my face and fingers with napkins. I'll need to wash my hands in Varsol to clean off the grease, just the way I like it.

"Ah," he says. "That feels so much better."

I ask Agnes for my bill and head for the till.

"Hey, where you going? I still need to eat," Bimbo says.

"Funny, I just finished, and I'm outta here. See you around, clown." I chuckle all the way to the till.

I tip Agnes fifteen cents. It's a lot, and I've already lost a buck to Bimbo. Unless I get super lucky, I'll only have enough cash for one meal tomorrow, but none if I need to buy a bottle from the bootlegger. Thinking about all the money I don't have makes my stomach roil.

Skinny and them have disappeared. They're not in the alley, or between the pub and Groovy Grub, that stupid hippy food store that sells raw peanuts. Raw. Birds won't even eat them raw.

Bimbo taps on the coffee shop's front window. He looks at me like a kid abandoned at a Greyhound station. I laugh and head to our drinking hole above the CP tracks, probably where I should've gone in the first place.

We claimed that spot for ourselves but cops or CPR yardmen always chase us off of it, like they got nothing better to do. Losing them lazy cops in the bush is easy but it's no fun watching them pour out our bottles when they find them. Scroungers always comb our spot for empties, forgotten bottles, and lost money. As a joke we sometimes fill a whiskey bottle with piss and hide it good. Skinny's figured out a way to peel off a bottle's seal in such a way you couldn't tell anyone's messed with it. You can reseal it after topping it up with your pee. None of us has ever seen anyone drink from one of our pee-whiskey bottles and no one's ever admitted to drinking from one. But we keep filling and hiding them anyway, wondering how drunk a guy could get drinking a drunk's pee. Bimbo says that's how you get pissed. But he won't say how he knows.

I've found partially filled bottles of whisky, rum, gin, vodka, and even anisette a time or two, but I just smash them, all of them, especially the full ones, cos you never know if someone else has bottled up their pee, laced it with LSD, or some other evil drug. I mostly find just enough shrapnel to pay for a cup of Agnes' coffee, and every once in a while, a whole meal. But I'm not a scrounger. I just have a crow's eye for finding cash.

1:15 PM

The guys belt out the Lulu song so loud that Darnel Corbin the CPR yardman could probably hear them over his grinder. I skitter across the tracks, then slink into the bushes.

"You guys making enough noise?" I say.

"Not noise," Cody says.

"Beautiful music," JimJim says.

"Yeah, man," Skinny goes. "Music. We just made a new verse for that Lulu song."

"I heard, and so did everyone inside of ten miles of you."

Skinny snorts. His laugh is all I-spit-on-you. He takes a long pull from a mickey of navy rum, wipes his mouth with the back of his hand and hands it to me. I take a small drink and pass it to Cody. He takes a big drink and passes it to JimJim.

Skinny sneers.

"You enjoy your meal?" he says.

Shrugging, I say, "You know. Just the usual."

"Stuffing your gullet's more important than your friends, i'nit? You prefer all that greasy food to us?" Skinny goes.

He pastes on a crazed axe-murderer smile. Cody and JimJim look away.

O crap, he's gonna beat me into next month. He stands. I brace for a shit-kicking. Skinny slaps my shoulder and laughs.

"Where's your sense of humour? Jeez you, I'd've finished my meal if you was getting the boot. I'nit, JimJim?"

"Prob'ly. Yeah. And so would I. How bout you, Cody?"

"Course I would. A man's gotta eat."

"But seriously, Squito, it's good to see you've grown a pair. I couldn't be prouder of you."

I feel like the only thing I've grown is a nervous stomach. Skinny snatches the rum, raises it, and toasts me before taking a bottle-draining pull. He tosses it into the bush behind him. The trick is to toss dead soldiers as far away from you as possible without breaking them. If the bottle breaks, you get two in the shoulder, sometimes from everyone. It can hurt a lot. Skinny's bottle shatters. He looks me square in the eyes as I wind up. He cocks a fist and shakes his head slowly.

I take a deep breath and tap his shoulder twice with my reluctant fist. Skinny laughs, rubs his shoulder.

"Ow!" he goes. He laughs. "So not ow. Fly farts got more power than your punches. Hey, you hiding a pussy where you spaeks?'s s'posed to be?"

Next thing I know my three friends have me pinned to the ground and pantsed. Skinny tells me he's gonna piss all over my underwear before giving it back to me. The little bit of my nuts that hasn't shrivelled up in the cold shrivel up so much that my balls bump into my stomach and twist my guts up so tight they suck all the colour from me.

"Ha! Hey guys," Skinny goes, "He thinks I'm a really gonna piss on him."

Silence.

Eyes creep over me like ants. My own, even tightly closed, see only Skinny's spaeks? hanging over me like a wind-bent lodgepole pine. Skinny's pulled stunts like this before but you never do stuff this sick to friends. Well, not close friends. At least I wouldn't.

"Put that cock a yours back inside your pants," Cody says. "Hawk's gonna swoop down and fly off with it."

"Or haul your bony ass to jail for indecent exposure," JimJim says.

Skinny folds his Sceptre up and stuffs it back inside his pants. "You mean decent exposure."

"Nope," JimJim says.

Skinny snorts. He dangles my underwear just outside my reach. I grab at it. He laughs and yanks them away. Skinny shoves them down the back of his pants, lifts a leg, and cuts a fart louder than a revving Harley.

"Oops. Think I got a little poop with that one."

My brain yells at my body to move but my body freezes in place, just like it would if a big old black bear stood over me. Skinny presses a knee into my throat, just hard enough to cut off my air off and make my brain set up the movie of my short, miserable life. I suck in a quick, dirty little breath as he pulls my underwear over my head. Then he's off me like Wind grabbing a sheet of foolscap. I squeeze my lips and eyes tightly closed and keep that last tiny breath.

So glad I remembered to put on a fresh one today.

1:20 PM

Almost naked and wearing my underwear like a ski mask, there's no point in trying to cover up, so I lay limp and spreadeagled, letting my little chief shrivel up in this chill November afternoon. Except for Wind, and Skinny huffing, mumbling, pacing, and pounding his thighs with his fists, the place has grown as quiet as Cow's classroom before she hands out a test. I can't see my other friends but I feel their eyes skate over me. Feet swish over pine needles. Someone takes a loud drink. Pine needles and what-not dig into me like scabies. My gut aches for a drink.

Skinny yanks the underwear off my head, whips them at my crotch, and says, "Put them pants back on or I'll piss on you."

Once more he unreels his spaeks? over my head like a fire hose. Nothing about the way he looks at me says he's joking. If he pisses on me I'll have no choice but to scrap him and die. I'll put everything I have into grabbing him by his Golden Sceptre, and I'll squeeze, twist, and yank on it like a thistle bush. He will kill me but he'll never forget me, or how I crippled his dick.

"Stop it. The kid's had enough," JimJim says.

"Yeah, c'mon, Skinny. It's gone on long enough. Leave the kid alone," Cody says.

Skinny looks at them, smiling like a flying monkey. He stuffs his dink back into his pants and offers me a hand up, but not his dink hand. He doesn't take me in his usual car-crusher grip.

More like Father McNaughton's, all clammy and soft.

"I guess I got carried away," Skinny goes.

After a pause long enough for me to get all them pine needles off my butt and then slip back into my pants and shoes, he says: "Sorry."

All red-faced, Skinny looks at his shoes instead of into my face.

"Muriel and me got into it and now she says she's not going to the dance with me."

"You two break it off again?" says JimJim.

"I dunno. I guess so."

"Why this time, hey?"

"She didn't want me going to Max's tonight. Said I was only gonna get me some white meat."

"It's true, i'nit?"

"That's not the point," Skinny goes, his eyes punching JimJim, as he hammers his own thigh with a fist.

JimJim pulls a mickey of Five Star from his boot, cracks the cap, and tosses it over his shoulder. Instead of taking the first drink, he hands it off to Skinny and says, "Easy, buds. No point in getting mad at me, too. Just forget about it."

Skinny tips the bottle JimJim's way and then passes it to me without taking a hit. I take a good swig and pass it to Cody. I don't feel much like talking to any of them and I sure can't look them in their eyes. If they weren't my best friends I'd up and leave them here in the bush, go off and drink with someone else, not that anyone except the pub regulars would be drinking this early in the day, not that anyone but these guys would even think about drinking with me. We sit close enough to pass the bottle to each other and drink without speaking. Cody pulls a mickey of vodka from his pants as soon as JimJim's whiskey's gone. He gulps down the first drink and passes it to me, reversing the order. He chuckles when I pass it back to him and nod toward Skinny.

"Sorry," I say. "My hand's trained to go the other way."

Skinny laughs. He secures the bottle between his legs and slaps his thighs like I've just said the funniest thing ever. He seems happy again, like the sun has just decided to burn a hole through the clouds and shine into our drinking hole. We laugh and act out my wrong-way hand.

No words, just four clowns clowning, laughing and drinking.

You always hear Bimbo from a mile away, no matter what he tries to do. He crashes toward us and we laugh even harder.

"What's so funny?" Bimbo says. He gawks at the vodka. "Gimme a taste?"

Skinny reaches for the zipper of his jeans. Bimbo turns instantly red and then white as the noon sun when Skinny starts pulling it open. But it doesn't go too far this time. I kinda wished they'd pants Bimbo and really pee all over him and his underwear. I doubt I could piss on him, cos my pee stalls if I even hear anyone around me, even at Yéye?'s. Skinny hands Bimbo the vodka, who wipes its lip on his sleeve before taking a chug and then hugs the bottle to his chest.

With his eyes closed he looks toward the sky, smacks his lips, and lets out an "ah" almost as long as "In-A-Godda-Da-Vida."

"Man-o-man, that sure goes down good," Bimbo says. He takes another big swig.

"Hey, pass it on," JimJim says.

"In a sec. In a sec." Bimbo takes another shot, then wipes his lip on his sleeve. He downed almost a third of it. He pulls the bottle to his lips to take another swig. A gang of Indian eyes kick the crap out of him.

"What? What?" Bimbo clucks. "What'd I do now?"

Cody turns into a sneer and doesn't even waste the breath to chew out that Bimbo, his coal eyes as silent as the dead's.

"Think maybe you had enough," JimJim says.

"No fair. I gotta catch up. You guys already drunk, what, three bottles? Four?"

"Could be one. Could be a hundred. It don't matter, cos it's our liquor."

"Yeah," Skinny goes. "Ours. As in not yours."

He snatches the vodka. Some sloshes out, spilling onto his hand. Skinny licks it, madmonkey eyes ripping into Bimbo.

"Speaking of yours," JimJim says, "it's your turn to share."

Bimbo squirms. His hands twitch like a magician about to pull a bottle of whatever cheap crap he conjured from his father's liquor cabinet. Always the cheapest stuff, liquor that tastes like rebottled piss, or muscatel at sixty-cents a bottle and so vile you can only take it with 7-Up or ginger ale. Such cheap stuff from a guy who could afford to fill his liquor cabinet with the best booze cos he must make a fortune working for the village. We never ask Bimbo to go first cos you need time to numb your tastebuds before drinking any of the crap he brings. But they say the same about me and my lemon gin.

"Sorry guys, I couldn't find a runner. You could front me till later on?"

"You mean your father finally locked up his liquor?" I say.

"Naw. His mother must've finally got fed up and threw it all out, hey?" JimJim says.

"Screw you guys. Nothing wrong with the booze Dad buys."

Bimbo hunches into a pout. Skinny apes him, adding a foot stomp.

"It's always later on with you, i'nit?" Cody says.

"Do you even have any money?" says JimJim.

"'Course I do."

"Show me it," Skinny goes.

"Well, it's not on me. I had to use most of what I had to pay for my lunch. Which I had to eat alone. Screw you very much."

"Yeah. I had to give him a buck," I say.

"A loan. You just loaned me a dollar."

Sneer. Bimbo's idea of a loan is anyone else's idea of a gift. He flinches but no one hits him or bitches him out. He relaxes a bit after a second or six. "I have to get more from Dad. He gets off work at four. He promised me a sawbuck. I can pay you then."

"Right," Skinny goes.

My lemon gin's stashed a ways into the bush, under a hollow log. It's a spot the cops and scroungers have never found and I hope they never do. I'm pretty good about disguising it, too, like covering my tracks the way Uncle Walter's shown me. My trick is to only go to it twice: Once to stash my bottles and once to grab them, cos after a few, a guy can get sorta careless. I haven't even told my friends, not that I think they'd scoop my booze, but who knows what anyone'll say or do after they've had a few.

"It's okay. I'll get this one," I say and start to stand.

"Don't bother," JimJim says. He laughs. "I already got it for you."

He reaches behind him and pulls up my lemon gin. Both bottles, still sealed.

"You leave a trail even Bimbo could follow. Good thing you're the only person in the world who likes this piss-water, hey?"

JimJim laughs again as I take them. I crack one and hand it back to JimJim. He takes a good, long drink and then passes it to me. I take a swig, swill it around my mouth, swallow it a little at a time. Bimbo wipes the bottle's lip before taking a small drink. His face screws up and he gags.

A little spit dribbles onto his chin.

"Ugh. Tastes like piss," Bimbo says. His face is all twisted and his whole body shivers.

"How you know what piss tastes like? You drink a lot of it?" I say.

"No, it's just that this crap tastes like piss smells."

"O," I say. "Just go and sniff pee then. You don't have to drink it. Leaves more for us."

"Jeez, you, it's just booze. Anyways, a buzz is a buzz," Cody says. He curls his lip like Elvis and shakes his head.

"You're gonna have to get something at the bootlegger's," Skinny goes. "We could stop by her shack on the way to Max's."

He passes the bottle to Skinny. "But she never has Bacardi. I need my Bacardi. And she charges way too much. There's no way I can get enough."

Everyone laughs. Bimbo's actually had Bacardi only once. He'd stolen it from his dad's liquor cupboard. His mother called the cops on us and tried telling them that we'd coerced her son into taking the rum. We'd said we didn't and Bimbo agreed with us. Also, it helped that no one saw us around the Bimbo house.

Skinny passes the bottle to Cody.

"Shoulda thought about that before. It's kinda late now," JimJim says.

"You suck. All of you," Bimbo says.

"And you swallow," JimJim says.

"No," I say. "Only good people swallow."

Bimbo becomes a fresh-caught fish.

We laugh.

Bimbo shrinks into himself and makes me reach over him to pass the bottle to Skinny.

Skinny snatches the bottle and whaps Bimbo across the knuckles with it.

"Just cos you screwed up's no reason to take it out on us," Skinny goes.

Bimbo rubs his knuckles and watches us drink.

It takes a while to kill my smooth, sippable, lemon gin. I figure that the guys like its taste more than they would ever admit, sorta the way most of us watch *The Edge of Night* but never mention it to each other, even after one of the girls asks us if we caught the latest episode. Whiskey and dark rum might go around twice, three times, tops, but my lemon gin can go around as many as six times. They say

I drink it so I don't have to share. That can't be right, cos if I didn't want to share I'd come to the circle with nothing but the cheapest of cheap booze and whiny excuses. Besides lemon gin's taste and its smoothness (you never need a mixer or ice with lemon gin), I get it cos I like it. They say lemon gin will make you go blind and I tell them I'll only drink it till I need glasses. But that cheap booze is a poison-tipped arrow in your liver, and there's no coming back from that.

We have some good people looking out for us. People who run for us and always get us exactly what we ask for. My friends like to use my Uncle Angus cos he won't even take a dollar for his trouble, and his old smʔeméc̓e, my Auntie Elizabeth, is the best, cos when she's around, she just gives me whatever I ask for. My father charges two bucks, unless he's desperate for me to be gone all weekend, and he's usually desperate. The worst runner has got to be my cousin Sam Johnny. He charges a deuce, too, but we only go to him if there's no one else or it's getting late. Even then, there's a better-than-even chance he'll just go to the pub and drink your booze money. Nothing you can do about it. Everyone will say you should've known better. If you make a stink about getting burned, no one will run for you cos they sure don't want the headache.

On my next turn, I hand the bottle to Bimbo. He takes it between his fingers like it's a steaming turd and cranes it to Skinny.

"You remember your hand drum this time, Skinny?" Bimbo says.

Skinny fires a throttling glare, strong enough to rock Bimbo off his puny white butt.

"What? What'd I do this time?" Bimbo says.

"I never bring it drinking."

Bimbo opens his mouth to peep, thinks better of it, then turns his pout back on. Skinny smiles, and not his leering-monkey grin, or his you're-about-to-die-a-slow-and-painful death one. His grin, pointed at Bimbo, is about as plastic as a doll's, and catches us all in its chill.

After a sliver of eternity, JimJim says, "Want to practice, in case they ask us to sing later?"

Skinny puffs his chest. "You know they will."

Bimbo slurps his lips. "And think of all them Ashcroft girls, just itching to do it to us afterwards."

"Not if Max has anything to say about it," Cody says.

Skinny winks. "She won't be a problem, i'nit JimJim?"

After they've had a few drinks they'll demand us to sing for them. People only like us when we sing together. When we sing they see us as a group, not a gang, but we *always* see ourselves as a group, not a gang. Skinny thinks we could be the next Three Dog Night, but Not Four Dogs and a Pussy, like I suggested.

JimJim laughs and winks at me. He says, "Maybe after we get some more beers. Throat's all ratty from that gin, hey?"

"See," Bimbo says. "Everyone hates that pig piss you drink. Right?"

"Enough!" Skinny blurts, and Bimbo stops dead, mouth hanging open.

I need to stash my gin before we head into town. If the cops stop us, and they will, they'll snatch my bottle and probably toss me in the drunk tank for the weekend. I say I've got to pee. They laugh at me.

"Gonna hide your gin, hey?" JimJim says.

"Why bother?" Bimbo says. "You could leave it on a stump and no one, not even Crazy Thom, would touch it."

"I said enough," Skinny hisses. Bimbo sucks in a breath harsh enough to suck his stupid words back into his head.

So stupid, lying to my friends, but I do it from habit, not cos I'm trying to fool them. I have this other stash in an old cottonwood that's maybe three feet across, with two branches forking about twelve feet up it. I shove my lemon gin deep into the crotch of those two branches and cover it with some dead leaves and stuff. When I get back the guys are looking at sheet of foolscap Skinny's holding.

"It's 'Four Years Older Than Me,'" Skinny goes. "You know it?"

"Yeah," I say. "It's a good one. Yeah, pretty good."

"Good. I think we should do it," Skinny goes.

"Me, too," says JimJim. "It goes real good with the drum."

"Could I sing lead on this one?" I say. The words just popped out. Now I know what the deer feels like just before the lights that hypnotized it grind it into asphalt.

"Lead? You?" Skinny goes. I flinch. He half-smiles, devil dancing in his eyes. He shrugs. "Maybe it could work. Sing it."

"Now?"

"Of course now."

I swallow hard and picture me putting the record on my grandmother's Seabreeze; clap twelve beats and sing with all the heart I have when mostly sober. Skinny shushes me after the third line.

"Whadya think, guys? Could I sing lead on this one?"

Right away, Bimbo says, "No!"

Cody and JimJim mumble, "I dunno."

Bimbo thinks he should be our lead singer, not fifth lead. He thinks he has the best voice around, and unlike me, he doesn't have to be half-cut to sing, though when his part's too big, he loses his voice and ruins the song by going all Tiny Tim. He only ever practices when we practice together. Even Cody, who doesn't like singing much, practices almost every day, and I practice all the time, mostly at Yéye? 's, and always when no one's around. Yéye? teaches me our family's old songs and she even lets me use her grandfather's hand drum, but she won't let me take it out of the house and she won't let me near it when I've been drinking. She says I should never sing the songs she's taught me when I've been drinking. I haven't sung any of them songs, or played my great grandfather's hand drum, since I started going to dances.

2:30 PM

Wind pushes a storm toward the canyon, darkening the sky, and perfuming the air with the threat of snow. O, xeʔłkʷúpiʔ, keep the roads clear. Bring Fast Freddy and the Frivolous Footnotes safely here.

We head to the pub.

Stanley August's boss '64 Merc—a real beaut: three-on-the-tree, Thunderbird engine, and chrome dual exhaust pipes, like a semi's, running up the back of the cabin—takes up two stalls in front of the pub. He lives out Four Mile, in a hand's shack near Auntie Max's. Skinny, at the Ladies and Escorts door (the old guys call it the Indian door), pokes his head inside and calls Stanley out.

Stanley, his face a mess of scars and pockmarks, wears a wooden leg. They say he'd played goal for the Penticton Vees a long time ago and was so good that Chicago drafted him. But he never got to play cos he had a bad wreck—rolled his car nine times, leaving his leg and career with the 'Hawks on Highway Three, ten miles west of Trail. But you never see him anything but laughing and smiling.

He staggers past Skinny, leans against the wall next to us, one hand inside his vest. His mouth—but not his eyes—smiles, as big and welcoming as usual.

"You boys ain't after money?" he says.

"No, Uncle," Skinny goes, "just wondering if you could give us a ride to Max's."

"Right now?" Stanley slides a glass of draft from inside his vest. He takes a taste and passes it to Skinny. "Maybe after I lose the table, but I'm shooting good today, so it could be a while."

Skinny, about to hand the glass to Bimbo, stops dead when Stanley sneers, slowly shaking his head. He snatches the beer from Skinny, tips it at Bimbo, then downs it, his eyes strangling Bimbo. Bimbo squirms. Stanley leans against the tailgate, beams a summer sun-coming-out-from-behind-storm-clouds smile, and places the glass in his pickup's bed. "Hey, hey, hey. One more and I got a full set."

Cos of Bimbo's mom, Stanley lost all of his kids to white welfare that one year the lice got really bad, back in Grade Two, the year the Bimbos moved to town. She raised such a big stink at school after her son came home with a few critters that white welfare came to town with some cops and took away a bunch of kids. Even Uli Wasserman lost his five kids, then his wife—she stabbed him in the eye with a railroad spike one night after he had passed out. Uli had nothing, didn't even own his house, so the town had to pay for his burial. They locked his wife in a rubber room instead of a jail cell.

He walks past us, stops at the Indian door, pulls it open, then looks over his shoulder at us.

"Anyways, if you still need a ride when I'm ready to head 'er, I'll drive you."

"Thanks, Uncle."

He shoots another nasty glance at Bimbo. "Even the séme?."

None of us move. Stanley's smile broadens. He lets the door glide closed and hobbles back to us.

"Hey, I ever tell you about the rattlesnake I bagged last summer?"

Whether he's told you this story once or a hundred times, he'll tell it again, and I guess it gets better—longer, anyways—with each telling. Hearing it again would be the cost of a ride out to my aunt's. When he played goal for the Vees, he helped them win the 1955 World Ice Hockey Championship. The team bought him a '55 Chevy Nomad, his dream car: "Something I could use to drive Mom and them to town Saturdays and look good doing it, hey?"

He wipes his cheek with the back of his hand. All tight-lipped, he nods long and slow. Grunts softly. "Yeah, they coulda gived that car to Billy for scoring just about a goal a game in that tourney. But they gived me it, I guess cos I only let in six goals in sixteen games. And them Blackhawks drafted me. Barely eighteen and had the world by the balls. Coulda come up with the likes a Bobby Hull and them."

But driving back to Penticton after beating the Trail Smoke Eaters, Stanley hit a patch of black ice a little ways west of Trail and rolled his car, totalling it. He lost his left leg, and his career with Chicago cos he was too proud to take the team bus. Then, one day last summer, out chasing stray calves, he got too close to a rattler. It struck, biting into his wooden leg—he calls it his tree. Instead of panicking, he stood his ground, set his rifle's muzzle level with the snake's head, and then blew its head off when it struck at his gun.

"Anyways, the old lady makes up a wicked rattlesnake stew and I'm one skin closer to making me a pair a rattlesnake-skin boots. That's right, I'm gonna make myself a pair of rattlesnake-skin boots." He grabs his belly and laughs. "And I'm gonna put in salmon skin inlays, tool 'em to look like sockeye jumping. Gonna use moose hide, too. Snake, fish, and moose boots. They'd be one of a kind." He howls a wheezy laugh, rolling his eyes skyward. "O, no, tha'd be two, hey? One for each foot."

He leans against the wall and laughs so hard tears roll down his cheeks. "Two of a kind. But I could just make two left boots, cos I don't really need one for my tree, hey?"

He wipes his eyes, then wipes his hands on his thighs.

Bert Macpherson stands in the Indian doorway: "Hey, Stan, you're up. Take your shot or give up the table."

"Thought I already cleaned you out. Gimme a minute," Stanley says.

He waves, walks off, laughing at some private joke.

"You think he'll be long?" JimJim says.

"Who knows," Skinny shrugs. "Hot stick'll cool off sooner or later. Still a little early to head to Max's, so we could wait."

Us four pile into the Merc's bed. Bimbo sits on the bumper. He says he doesn't want to catch our lice. None of us has had them since third grade. But that's just stupid Bimbo. Skinny shoves a hand down his pants, roots around a bit before he pulls it back out, thumb and pointer nails pinching down on nothing.

"No lice here. But I hear you like seafood so I got you some crabs."

Skinny flicks the nothing between his nails at Bimbo, who shrinks away like an ant in acid.

"Screw off. Keep your stinking bugs offa me."

We laugh ourselves into coughing fits. Bimbo leans against the pub's wall, arms crossed over his chest. He could be crying, and if not, he ought to cos of what his mother did.

"We'll get busted for loitering if a cop catches you standing there. If we get tossed in the 'tank, lice'll be the least of your worries," JimJim says.

Bimbo sneers but doesn't move.

After a bit of forever, he mummy-shuffles toward us and plops onto the Merc's bumper, his back to us. So typical.

When the Bimbos first moved to town we'd sometimes go up and play at their place. Missus Bimbo would make us empty our pockets before we left, and if we had any money on us, she asked where we'd stolen it. You get used to old people acting weird and hope you don't turn into one of them, if you even live that long. She always talked slow to us, always preachy. (She still does, if she bothers to talk to us at all.) Every time she gave us any kinda food, even an apple, she'd say, "We always wash our hands before eating," and then she'd scrub our hands at her kitchen sink. She had a way of making you feel you weren't part of her we. And really, what eight year old doesn't know to wash his hands before eating? Knowing is one thing, remembering's another. Bimbo almost never looked at anything but his feet with his mother around, except when she'd make him sing some lame kiddy song or do a ballet dance. She called her son talented but really any puppet could do what Bimbo did, if you pulled its strings just right.

At least Bimbo has turned back into his abnormal self. Cody snarls and shrugs. Skinny and JimJim roll their eyes. I guess if you can have a best friend, you can have a worst. Bimbo's my worst friend. Easily my worst friend. I sigh and promise not to let that kid ruin my perfect weekend. We settle in to watch nothing happen all around us.

2:40 PM

Maybe five minutes pass before both the pub's front doors burst open, pouring everyone, including the bartender, Margaret Starr, onto Front Street. Old guys scrap less often now than they did in the old days. Back then most of them brawls started when someone crossed the line separating the white and Indian sides of the pub. Sometimes the fight would start inside and explode onto the street. Them old-guy scraps can be brutal, and we have a great view from Stanley's truck. Instead of circling around a pair of scrappers, though, the mob follows Crazy Thom Thomas, a Welshman who says he's Tom Jones' older brother and a bard, whatever that is. He lives in a driftwood and tarpaper shack that's more like an abandoned beaver lodge, in a dried up ditch above River's high-water line. Crazy Thom's a scrounger.

Crazy Thom leads them to the Shell station a half block west of the pub. He stands between the pumps, holding a nozzle over his head.

"Gentlemen, who among you will pay a quarter, just twenty-five measly pennies, to witness me imbibe a glass of the Queen's petrol?"

I'd have paid two bits to see that. We've talked about drinking gas sometimes, not to earn beer money like Crazy Thom, but to see if that's the secret to lighting farts. We've all tried and none of us can, not even JimJim, whose farts wither outhouse walls. All them guys toss shrapnel at Thom. He watches the coins fall around him, wearing a big, black smile. Margaret hands Thom a glass. He pours a bit of gas into it.

"You crazy bastard, what you trying to pull? That's not a full glass."

"Right you are, sirrah. Shower me with encouragement as I fill my glass."

More shrapnel tinkles at Crazy Thom's feet.

"Think he'll do it, JimJim?" Skinny goes. He's leaning on the cab roof. "JimJim?" We've paid so much attention to Crazy Thom that we lost sight of what was happening around us.

JimJim's disappeared.

"Think Sasquatch got him?" Skinny says, looking real worried.

"Maybe," I say.

Bimbo, now leaning on the cab roof with us, says, "There's no such thing as Sasquatch."

"Shows what little you know. Idiot. Sasquatch watches us from his place in the bush. He eats kids sometimes. If you don't watch it, he'll snatch you, too."

"C'mon, what kinda idiot do you take me for? If Sasquatch got JimJim, we'd have seen it," Bimbo says.

"And smelt it, too," I say. "He reeks like your skinny white butt times a hundred."

"Ten thousand," Skinny goes.

"Screw you guys. My ass smells better than your breath," Bimbo says.

"That's something you'd know, all right," Skinny goes.

Bimbo's jaw works but his words are balled up like phlegm in his throat. His face goes red from his shoulders up, bit by bit, like a thermometer dipped in boiling water.

"O, well. He'll be mad he missed this. Think drinking that gas will kill him?"

"Course it will, but not right away," Bimbo says. "He'll go like a dog after drinking antifreeze."

"Know-it-all," Skinny goes. Bimbo beams like he's won some kinda trophy.

The crowd cheers. Thom holds an empty glass over his head.

"Darn. We missed it," I say.

Cody elbows me in the ribs and points toward the pub. The door has swung open wide enough to let JimJim's head poke through it. He flashes a half empty glass of draft. He smiles huge. Cody slips into the pub.

"I got ten bucks says you can't drink a glass of premium now," says Reggie Aleck.

"Well, sirrah, I see the colour of your money and I accept your challenge."

Thom snatches the bill Reggie holds out and then pours himself a glass of premium. The men bubble and joke. Thom smiles like he's just won the Irish Sweepstakes. He holds up his glass and starts singing a song that sounds like "Truck Drivin' Man" but the words are wrong.

"Shut up and drink," says Reggie.

"Where's your sense of drama, good sirrah? You're about to witness a feat of daring not unlike the great Harry Houdini's most spectacular escape. Enjoy the show, for you may never again witness such a momentous event in your hollow, little life."

"I'm paying you good money to drink gas, not spew it. Shut up and drink, clown."

Some guys side with Reggie. Some with Thom. You hate to see a guy kill himself trying to scrounge up a few bucks for a drink but Thom drinking gas is one of the craziest things I've ever seen.

"You're lookout," Skinny goes, "Let us know when they start coming back."

"'Kay," I go. Skinny sneaks into the pub, leaving me stuck alone with Bimbo. Again.

The old guys bicker, bitch, and laugh. Crazy Thom's accent thickens as he drones on about his great show. Can gas evaporate in cold weather? Does he hope to bore the old guys into walking away so he doesn't have to drink the premium? How lonely would it be inside

Crazy Thom's brain? Could a guy walk far into it without falling into one of the pits drilled by all the booze and drugs he's taken?

"Screw that, I'm not getting stuck out here with you while they're in there having all the fun," Bimbo says.

"Whatever," I say, following Bimbo to the pub. He goes inside and I take a spot under the pub entrance's overhang, back far enough to be mostly invisible to a bunch of drunks watching an old scrounger drink himself to death. My hands ball up and my body tenses and vibrates. You stupid, stupid kid. Why you let them run off and have all the fun, hey? What's wrong with you? Thing is, that brain voice sounds more like my father than me. Part of me wants to ditch them, hide across the street, and watch them all catch hell from Margaret and the drinkers. I'd get the crap kicked out of me later on but it'd almost be worth it, just to see the looks on their faces. JimJim says I should speak my mind more often. I tell him that I do but they just don't hear me. And he just walks away like no words at all have tumbled from my mouth.

Crazy Thom falls silent, drops to his knees, and horks all over his money. The crowd of men jumps back two or three steps. The ten dollar bill, buried in slop, lays on the pump island. The premium floats atop the pukey cash.

From his knees, head down, a chain of slobbery goo stretches from Crazy Thom's mouth to the pump island. Guido Abandonato, the Shell station manager, yells harsh Italian words, probably swears, blasting the pump island with his high-pressure hose.

Thom waves a hand and says, "No refunds, sirrahs."

He heaves another hork, so harsh I feel razor wire shooting up my throat. Is the guy dying right here right now? Most of the old guys look away, their faces white, their cheeks swelled out, like they're about to puke, too.

Reggie, his words as acidy as Crazy Thom's puke, says, "Aw, just keep it, you old fraud." Or did he say *old frog?*

My stupid brain never remembers homework, fails to remind me about dumb chapters I need to read for English, Social Studies, and Science, but it won't let me look away. It watches intently, painting pictures and making notes. So what test is this on, xeʔłkʷúpi? Why do I need to know what a dead man breathing looks like? One of the things I love about lemon gin: no matter how much I drink, if I puke at all it's cos of the mix, especially soda water.

They crowd breaks up.

I open the door a crack and whisper, "They're coming."

The pub's empty.

The bar clock reads 3:10, but it's always fifteen minutes fast, so they can roust the drunks out quicker at closing time.

I scan the pub one more time.

My friends are nowhere.

Margaret Starr's the first one of them back. She looks at me like I'm up to no good. I smile.

"I'm looking for Uncle Moses. You seen him?"

"Not yet," says Margaret. "I don't want you loitering in front of my pub."

"Yes, ma'am. You'll tell Uncle I'm looking for him when you see him?"

"Sure. Now go on."

I climb back into the bed of Stanley's truck. Them guys all say hi as they traipse by, most of them still all *wow, can you believe what that crazy old coot'll do for a dime?*

Crazy Thom, now all alone on his hands and knees between the Shell's gas pumps, scoops coins into his glass, that ten dollar bill in his mouth like a pirate's knife.

Guido watches over Thom with his hands on his hips, shaking his head and bitching him out in Italian.

Margaret bursts through the doors and yanks me by the back of my collar from Stanley's truck.

"Where is it?" she goes, shaking me like a crying baby.

"Ow, stop it." My brain jiggles. Margaret's eyes punch me stupid, her mouth all foam and spraying spit.

"Where's what? Stop it. You're hurting me." My brain shouts, *Blame Skinny and them for whatever happened in there.* If I say anything like that I'll have no friends at all. None. Cos no one likes a rat fink. With no friends, I'll be slightly worse than dead.

"Empty your pockets. Now."

"You got to let me go first. I can't reach it."

She shoves me into the side of the truck. I empty my pockets. Aside from my dance ticket and some lint, they're empty.

"Now your shoes and socks."

"Why? Geez, Margaret."

"You can empty 'em for me or for the cops. Your call."

"Fine."

"You wouldn't have crotched my money, would you?"

"Sick," I say. "I'm not letting you look down there."

"Your puny boy bits don't interest me at all," she goes. *Puny?* Now I sorta feel I have to show her.

She pulls my eyes to meet hers.

"Were you in my bar while we were out?"

"No, ma'am."

"What about those friends of yours?"

"Maybe they're in there now," I shrug. "They ran over to the Shell to see what you guys were doing. Haven't seen them since."

"And you decided to stay in Stan's truck all by yourself?"

"I had to."

"It's here all day, every day, with no one in it. What's so special about today?"

"He's taking me to my Auntie Max's."

"You can walk. It's only four miles."

"Sure. But I hurt myself in gym. So walking for a long time really hurts."

"So you didn't steal any money off of my tables?"

If I answer no, does this mean I'm saying I stole her money, or does yes mean I stole it? How are you supposed to give a clear answer when the question's messed up?

"I didn't take it. How could I? I was out here the whole time watching Crazy Thom drink gas," I say.

A good chunk of that cash now belongs to me, if they were stupid enough to take it. I've earned it.

"It took you long enough to answer. Last chance. You take it or not?"

"I said I didn't. I didn't. Why don't you believe me, hey? When have I ever lied to you?"

"There's always a first time. I'm not done with you. Remember that."

"Yes, ma'am."

Now most of whatever they took belongs to me. I doubt Margaret will call the cops. She'd have to explain how a bunch of idiot kids got into her pub in the first place, and then Alistair "Sinister" Snook would fire her for leaving his pub unguarded and it's not as if there are that many jobs in this town. She could easily take me out back and work me over, or have someone else thump me. Stuff like that happens quite a bit.

Maybe the guys should give me all of what they took. Not that it would pay for the doctor, or my funeral.

Anger burns away my buzz. I could waste even more of it looking for my friends, or sit in the back of Stanley's truck and wait for them to come and get me. Wind tears off all of the straggling leaves and whips them around like murder balls before smashing them into the dust. I huddle in the bed like a snoozing bandito, trying to keep

Wind from kicking dirt in my face. *To hell with you, all of you.* I look Wind in the face and belt "Four Years Older Than Me."

Wind-blown grit nips my face like flea bites. Before I get to the first chorus, a thunk as loud as a dog bouncing off the truck's fender jolts me from the song.

"Hey, Squito!" Cody says. "Hey, whatcha doing? C'mon." He slaps the side of Stanley's truck again. I scowl, thinking murder. "We been looking for you."

My eyes cuss him out. "Looking for me? I haven't moved from where you left me."

"Mmm," he says, his eyes casting about as if looking for words to make their a-hole moves okay. "Sorry 'bout that. We had to. You'll see. We gotta hurry, though, before someone sees us."

"Why?" This had better be good.

"Never mind. C'mon."

A fenced-off patch of weeds sits between the Indian door and an old room attached like a porch to the side of the laundromat. Cody leads me toward it. We squeeze through the gap between the last fencepost and the hotel wall nearest the Indian door and sneak to the porch.

The fence only went up after they'd found Justine Thomas dead in that grass, naked. Cops said she passed out trying to pee and died of exposure but Joe Henry found her pants in a ditch about ten miles southwest of town. Cops said they didn't belong to Justine and whoever owned them must have stolen her ID. Them cops threatened to charge Joe with possession of stolen property and then they tried to convince him he had stolen it from her dead body. Joe shut up about what he'd found pretty quick, mostly, they say, cos his wife Hazel told him to keep quiet.

Justine's story ended there.

The guys laugh low and talk a little lower. The three of them squatted like toads behind the driers, pulling on sweaty bottles of Old Style.

Skinny nods, points his smiling lower lip at the beaten, old cement wash tub in the corner behind me.

"Shoulda seen it, Squito," Skinny goes. "Shoulda seen all them ice cold cases of beer stacked almost to the ceiling."

He smacks his lips.

"If you was there, we coulda walked out with a whole bunch more than we got," Bimbo says.

"Bull," JimJim says. "Total bull and you know it."

"Nah, we only took two so they wouldn't miss 'em."

Cody hands me one. Unopened. I point it back at him and count the white rabbits hidden on the label.

"What?" Cody says. "What?"

"Could you open it?"

He snatches the bottle from my hand, puts it into the corner of his mouth, bites down on it, hands my beer back to me, then spits the cap at my face.

Wiping his mouth, he says, "Such a baby, you. You got to learn to open your own."

Every time I have a bottle opener on me, a cop takes it from me, telling me it's a concealed weapon, telling me if he catches me with another one, he'll send me to juvey till I turn twenty one. Bimbo has a bottle opener on his keyring and not once has a cop taken it away. I can't open bottles with my teeth like the other guys. I tried it once and broke a molar but, lucky for me, it was just a baby tooth. Cody, JimJim, and Skinny can open a beer with just about anything from a wrought iron fence to a claw hammer.

"You guys find anything else," I say. "Like cash money?"

Cody, JimJim, and Skinny look at me over their bottles. Bimbo goes red and stuttery, even though his lips don't move.

"Yeah," I say, aiming my words at Bimbo. "Yeah. A stack of bills. Margaret thinks I took it. And she's not letting this one go."

One by one, the guys look at Bimbo, now the colour of a marshmallow strawberry.

"How much you scam," Skinny goes. He squares off against Bimbo. "We told you to leave their money alone."

"It was just a few bucks. I didn't think anyone'd miss it," Bimbo says.

"You should leave the thinking to people with brains, idiot. Now hand it over."

"Finders keepers," Bimbo says.

"Losers weepers," Skinny goes. He punches Bimbo in the belly. Bimbo folds up like a lawn chair. His beer spills and he cries. "Now hand it over or I'll really give you something to cry about."

Bimbo hands over a small wad of bills, all except a single are folded in half lengthwise. Skinny counts twenty-seven dollars.

"This yours?" Skinny goes, holding up the wrinkly one-dollar bill.

"Yeah," Bimbo says. "I was getting more from Mom."

"Thought you said it was your dad bringing you money after work. You got no drinking money, no dance ticket, either, huh?"

Bimbo says nothing. He sucks a drink from his bottle.

"We can't just give back that money. They prob'ly know there's beer missing by now. We'll be in big trouble. They'll prob'ly call the cops and everything," JimJim says.

"We're always in trouble, anyways," Skinny goes.

"Not always," I say. "And I'll be the one they send away for this one."

"It's about time you got a stay at the Crowbar Hotel, anyways," JimJim goes. He laughs. "Become a real juvenile delinquent, like the rest of us."

"Hey, don't include me. I'm no JD," Bimbo says.

At twelve I thought it would be cool to be sent to youth jails like PG or Brannen Lake. I thought girls would want me. I thought I'd be feared and respected by everyone in town. But guys who come back from juvey always get harassed by cops—even more than us—and the girls they get aren't exactly the kinda girls I want wanting me. So a few years ago I decided I'd be cooler if I did nasty stuff in such a way no one ever knew, but until now I hadn't done anything more than roll a drunk now and then, and sometimes at school I'd cheat on a test or hand in an essay I'd borrowed from someone else. O, and lift candy and stuff from Major's General store. Stuff like that's not really a crime cos everyone does it or has done it.

"You haven't included me. None of you has," I say, my words as sharp as a skinning knife.

"So why should I take the blame and be sent off to juvey for something you did?"

"No one wants you to go to jail, Squito," Skinny goes. "But it's gonna happen just the same. Either juvey or adult, it'll happen to each of us."

He socks Bimbo in the gut again. Bimbo melts to the floor, crying. "But what do we do about this idiot?"

"Which one?" JimJim says. "Margaret's the bigger idiot. She left the bar wide open and unguarded. Really, it's her fault that money and beer walked outta her pub. Hers and no one else's."

I'd already figured that one out and didn't think it worth mentioning. Once again, I guess I thought wrong.

Snivelling, Bimbo moans and pulls himself to his feet like a cowboy who's just been shot and doesn't realize he's already dead. He takes a loud pull of beer and wipes tears, beer foam, and snot from his face onto his sleeve. That kid's so sick.

"I never thought of that," Skinny goes. "They'd be stupid to call the cops."

JimJim snorts and says, "It won't stop them from taking us out back and kicking the crap outta us."

Skinny points his lower lip at Bimbo and goes, "O-well, then. We'll just tell 'em the truth. You can't leave anything unguarded with a thieving séme? around. Them buggers'll take anything that ain't nailed down."

Taking a step toward the door, Bimbo says, "We learnt stealing from you."

Cody sniggers, puts his beer on the folding table, and says, "Prob'ly true. Yeah. But the way I see it, stupid-arse here'll be bumming off us all weekend, unless we give him that money." He takes a drink. "But no one's gonna run for us cos they'll all be mad about being rolled. So he'll end up with the money, no booze of his own and still drinking ours all weekend."

"Not rolled. It's not our fault they left their cash unattended, i'nit?" Skinny goes. "But, nah. You're right, they'll find a way to make it our fault. They always do."

Skinny wallops Bimbo upside his head. "Gimme one good reason not to stuff that money down your throat and hand you over to Margaret and them."

Bimbo drops to his knees. He doesn't cry out but real tears gush. I want to kick him to Cache Creek and back and then dump what's left of him into River. Picturing him dead doesn't make me feel even a little bad. My beer sours in my belly.

"We got plenty enough to drink for everyone already," Cody says, "So I was thinking we just split up the money the a-hole took between the four of us and call it even."

"You mean five," Bimbo says. "There's five of us, 'member?"

"Shut up," Cody says. "You don't count."

Bimbo slams his beer onto the folding table and whimpers, "Yes, I do."

Instead of becoming big and angry, Bimbo's turned into a ghost, nothing more than a puff of a draft seeping under a door.

"That works for me," Skinny goes.

"Yeah, makes sense," JimJim says.

"I got blamed for taking it, so I should get it," I say, and bite my lip, too late to stop my thought from bleeding into my friends' ears.

"Hola. Selfish guy," Cody says.

"O, no, he's right, " JimJim says, "He should get all of it. Forget all the times we paid for him to drink, hey?"

Skinny goes, "Ha. Good one. You know, if a few bucks means more to you than your buds, then I say go ahead, take it."

What kinda idiot you take me for? That line didn't work on me at lunch, so what makes you think it'll work on me now?

He shoves the wad at me. I don't reach for it. Maybe I am greedy but I sure don't want to look it. Anyways, I don't want to wind up impaled on Skinny's fist and crying like Bimbo.

"It's fair, i'nit?" I say. "I mean they think I took it and I'll get whatever they're gonna do about it."

Skinny taps the wad under his chin and thinks a bit. Bimbo sets his jaw, head bobbing with the money's movement, like a mesmerized chicken.

"I need a dance ticket, too," Bimbo says.

"Jeez, you. It's just a few bucks. Let them babies have it all," Cody says. He chucks his empty at the far wall. Bimbo flinches. Some glass sprays off his back.

Bimbo squeals, "Hey! You coulda hit me."

"Sorry I missed."

"Watch the noise," JimJim hisses. "We don't want anyone catching us back here. You want them catching us?"

Cody pops the cap off a beer and Frisbees its cap into Bimbo's face. His beer foams like a bottle of champagne in a movie. The cap bounces off Bimbo's forehead. He doesn't even seem to notice it.

My eyes loosen their grip on Bimbo's money. The more I think bout it, the less I want it. Say Margaret, some of the regulars, or a cop catches me with it. Then what? Cops get madder when they catch someone in a lie (and to them, lies account for seventy percent of what they hear), and get way, way madder when they catch an Indian in a lie (and to cops, that's a hundred percent of what they hear from us). For all I care they could burn it, just as long as Bimbo doesn't get a single penny. But really, I guess I want it, and I sure could use it. That stack of cash is more than I make in a month from all three of my paper routes.

"You know what?" Cody says. "We should talk about something important, like our beer. It's warming up fast. Maybe someone should run out and get a bucket of ice."

"Just run down to the general store and grab a bag," JimJim says. "O, wait. It's fricking November, so their machine'll be empty."

"Then we just drink faster, i'nit?" Skinny goes.

"Faster than I cut a beer fart?" Cody says, and rips one that echoes all around us. "Ah," he sighs. "Catch a whiff of that one, hey?"

JimJim gags then says, "Crisakes, kid. You trying to kill us all?"

"Point taken," Skinny goes. "There's that ice machine in the hotel, upstairs. I could sneak up there and grab a bucket. But we need to deal with this money first."

Skinny looks each of us up and down before slapping his full attention on Bimbo.

"I guess we could split it evenly between the four of us, like Cody said," I go. "It's not like I did anything more than I'd have done anyways, right?"

"Four? Like I said, there's five of us, dick-breath," Bimbo says, almost reaching for the wad.

"You don't count," Skinny goes. He sets aside the crinkled single before dealing out the others into four equal stacks. "That's six skins each, boys. With two left over."

He studies the piles, scratching his chin. With his lips pursed, he peels two bucks from each stack and puts a single on Bimbo's one and then the rest on the fourth pile, making it a rich, thirteen-dollar wad.

He hands me that big one. Cody and JimJim each grab a four-buck stack. Skinny unfolds his stack and crumples each bill. So do Cody and JimJim.

"You should, too, Squito," JimJim says, "unless you want them thinking you stole it."

"Thanks," I say. "Like they don't already." And crumple my cash before putting it into my wallet.

Skinny says: "Just so you know? You'd have gotten that much anyways. We appreciate what you done for us out there."

Yeah, right. JimJim nods. Cody sneers and lets out a spazzy, "Ha."

"Now we can get to the very serious business of drinking our faces off."

All slack-jawed and pouty, Bimbo fondles his two singles.

"Now I can't buy any booze," he says. "None. Not even a mickey for the dance."

"Shoulda thought of that before tonight," JimJim says.

"But I don't get my allowance till tomorrow."

"I thought your old man was giving you money after he got off work. What happened there?" Cody says.

"Yeah," JimJim says.

Skinny goes, "You wanna get your story straight in your own head before you shoot your stupid mouth off?"

"I guess I forgot. And now it's too late. He's probably already home," Bimbo says. "Could you pass me a beer? Hey, Cody?"

"Get your own."

"But you're closer."

"I wouldn't pass you a fricking beer if I was sitting on them," Cody says. At Skinny, he says, "What about that ice, there, buds?"

Skinny taps my shoulder. "Right. Ice. Gonna need your expert help."

“’Kay. Just let me pound this one back.” I chug my Old Style and bullfrog a belch. It bubbles out my nose. Maybe my best beer-belch ever. I puff out my chest and beam.

Skinny burps out *a* through *f* and moans, *ahhh!* Then JimJim croaks out *g* through *l*.

Show offs.

Cody lifts his leg and blasts a poison gas fart.

“Sick, kid,” I say. He laughs and wafts his stink my way.

Skinny tries to part Cody’s stink cloud and gags as he takes a long-legged stretch through it.

He steps behind the driers. Bottles clatter and roll. One smashes.

“Oops. Sorry,” he says. Glass tinkles.

3:30 PM

Skinny jimmies the delivery door and opens it wide enough to let his shadow-thin self slip inside.

"Listen," he says, "I need at least ten minutes to get the ice and get out."

I freeze at the lobby doors. Skinny'll need way more than ten minutes if he expects to sneak past a gang of cops. And not our cops, either. Out-of-towners, all of them, and not at all friendly looking either. Then again, the only friendly looking cop I've ever seen is Sheriff Andy Taylor.

Six cops I've never seen before stand at Sinister's desk. All cops look like trouble but two of them, one with his hand on his revolver's holster, and the other fiddling with his nightstick's leather strap, look as bad as our own bad constables: Spotface and Howe. Sinister looks like a mouse at a gathering of mountain lions: his little nose and fake little moustache twitching, his little hands fidgeting, his little eyes dancing from one big man to the next, as his little mouth "yes sirs" and prides itself on being the most well-equipped little hotel this side of Big Town. Hand-On-Holster asks about room service and twitchy Sinister goes as still as a pigeon trying to transform into a rock.

"What sorta room service did you have in mind, officer?" He fusses with the little bell he keeps on his desk, the one he has warned us never to ring.

In a big, slow voice, Hand-On-Holster says, "Room. Ser-vice. I call the desk, order a meal and something to drink, and someone brings it up to me. Room? Service?"

"I am a professional hotelier, sir," Sinister says. "I know what *room ser-vice* is. Our clientele have no use for such amenities as *room ser-vice*, sir, so we do not normally provide it. However, we shall endeavour to accommodate you to the best of our abilities."

"That a yes or no?" Hand-On-Holster says.

Sinister flinches and shrinks back a step as he says, "I had assumed policemen would have a solid grasp of English and its nuances."

"Nuanced language usually hides something. You hiding something?" Hand-On-Holster turns, winks at Nightstick. Right then, he catches sight of me and waves me inside. My Home Waltz spreads its wings and flies south. My butthole does, too.

Nightstick and Hand-On-Holster meet me near the door.

Nightstick sniffs the air around me, "Smells like you've *chugged* back a few." All them cops laugh, even Bailey. Snook turns his head and fakes a cough. When my butt jumps off and bounces safely away, I break that turn-the-other-cheek-rule. My dance ticket sprouts wings and floats heavenward, like Sylvester the cat after Hector snuffs his ninth life. Hand-on-Holster clamps my shoulder and squeezes. Constable Howe grabbed me like that once. With the fingers of his other hand gouging my shoulder blade, he told me how he could rip my arm off at the shoulder with one little tug. He said he would. I believed him.

Hand-on-Holster loosens his grip a little. Nightstick slips between me and the door. Will Sinister bar them for making me bleed all over the lobby carpet? I only have my school ID, with its gruesome picture and hand-written name, address, and birth date. Hand-on-Holster could claim it an invalid ID and lock me up for the weekend. Howe's done it. Spotface has done it.

Bailey says, "Make sure to carry your ID on your person at all times. We can hold you without arrest forever under the War Measures Act if you don't have proper ID."

He said it had to do with hippies or someone with bombs. He said it kept citizens safe. I'm a threat to citizens? I'm not a citizen?

He didn't say that it had stopped in 1970 though. I guess I learnt something in Social Studies 10, after all.

Hand-on-Holster could use my school ID as a reason to take me up past the dump and rip me apart.

If I look scared he'll think I'm hiding something and harass, then arrest me.

If I look cool he'll think I'm hiding something and harass, then arrest me.

I swallow hard, "You know, one day I hope to be a cop."

Hand-on-Holster lets go of me, turns me to face him. In a low growl, he says, "Like they'd ever let a goddamned prairie nigger into the academy."

Again the cops all laugh. Even Bailey. We live on the plateau, not the prairie; everyone knows that. Sinister tenses up. He cradles the phone real loud. He waves the piece of paper the cop handed him.

Dry-mouthed, I squeak, "No. I mean me."

The cops laugh louder. Nightstick grabs his belly. Hand-on-Holster shakes his head, throws up his hands, and says, "See? See? They are so fucking thick-skulled they don't get it."

Sinister harrumphs real loud. "Excuse me, officer. There seems to be a problem with your chosen method of payment."

Hand-On-Holster huffs under his breath, "O, for fuck-sake."

Nightstick hands me my wallet. "Get outta here. Don't let me see you again tonight. Get me?"

"Yes sir."

Skinny wouldn't stick around if he saw them cops. I wish I hadn't.

So I try jamming my wallet into my back pocket as I stumble to the café. I probably look drunk, and not the sort of I-know-you're-cops-but-you-don't-scare-me banty stride I'd hoped for. Just great. I do cool like Crazy Thom does sober.

3:50 PM

Some time ago, I lost a whole night to drinking, just one of those things that happens when you mix wine and hard stuff. I'd woken up in the Brown's house all naked. My spaeks?, all covered in guck, looked diseased. I thought maybe my friends had pantsed me and instead of painting my nuts with shoe polish, they'd painted them with wood glue. My clothes made a trail to my dream girl Mavis Brown's room. She lay on the bare bed, naked and more beautiful than any sorta heaven you could imagine. I thought that Mavis had taken my boy cherry. I tried to remember what had happened but them beautiful memories kept repainting themselves into something ugly.

Her aunt, Delores, just as naked as Mavis—but so old she went to school with the Virgin Mary—slept in the room across from Mavis'. They say she had done me, that she rode me like a barrel race horse, that I had told that old woman I loved her and wanted to go with her, and she laughed and said *like I would even want to go with the likes of you, ugly halfbreed.* So ever since that night with Delores, Bernie has called me Loverboy. At first Stupid Me thought she'd meant it.

Bernie. Bernie Paul. Bernadette Louise Paul. Bernie, as tiny as a chickadee, with boobs that would make Cyndi Wood, the most beautiful *Playboy* centrefold girl of all time, jealous. Boobs that make Raquel Welch's look like Twiggy's. She smiles a smile bigger than her perfect boobs and bright enough to light up a dark room. Back in Grade Four I drew her name in the margins of my scribblers, even though a Grade Sevener would never go with a Grade Four. I only stopped drawing Bernie's name cos Mavis Brown joined our class. Her whole life, Mavis' beauty stole my tongue, my voice. before I got to say more than hi to her. Eventually I forced myself to say more than hi to Bernie. It's taken a long time but she's become about as much of a friend as I can hope to have, even though last year, in Grade Nine, on a dare, I tried to put my hand up her top.

They told me that all girls with big tits loved to have them grabbed, and grabbing Bernie's would let her know how much I wanted to be with her. I jumped at the chance and Bernie socked me on the jaw so hard I flew backwards at least two feet. She punched me again, knocking the wind out of me. I fell onto my butt, dizzy and breathless, but not the kinda dizzy and breathless I'd hoped Bernie would leave me.

Laughter everywhere.

She stood over me and I saw her white panties, as bright as her smile, between her dark thighs. Such a beautiful sight, it drowned out my laughing friends' laughter.

"Stop looking at me, you perv," Bernie said.

I, all red, stammery, and wobbly between the ears, drank her in: her black mini skirt that let me see her strong, smooth, curvy, sports-star legs and white panties. Then her ruffled white shirt, sort of like Laurie Partridge's, but more see-through, showing off her dark skin and white bra. And her face: the not-smiling mouth and seriously kissable lips, eyes hinting laughter underneath the murder in them. Her black hair, all big and poofy, hanging past her shoulders, around her face like a black silk kerchief.

And her boobs. Her boobs.

Even though my jaw stung like it had caught a line drive, I couldn't pull my eyes away from her. She wound up to kick me. I pointed my eyes where she wasn't. I believed she would've kicked me to death, cos she reminded me of my grandmother, a big storm in a small package, but generous enough to give me a chance to leave in one piece. I shuffled to my feet and looked past her.

"I'm sorry, Bernie, really, I am," I mumbled as I slithered past her. But she didn't stay mad long, and ever since that Delores Brown thing, has called me Loverboy.

And now, a year later, Bernie spins around me with a deluxe burger with fries and clubhouse with fries and gravy in her right hand and a fries and gravy in her left. The gentle smell of her patchouli tickles me in my underwear as she swishes by, heightened by the beautiful stink of fresh chips and grilled bacon.

"Coming through," she says, "hot stuff."

I can't tell from her grin what she means. Is she hot stuff? The steaming food? Me? I wish! I'd rather she call me hot stuff instead of Loverboy. I'm almost four inches taller than I was in Grade Nine but still three years younger. Girls still don't look at me with love in their eye.

Watching Bernie dish out meals is enough to make me crazy. She smiles. She jokes. She catches up on *The Edge of Night* and the fate of Adam Drake. In the next instant she gets all dreamy over Keith Partridge. Most of the girls say Jeremy from *Here Come the Brides* is better but Bernie sticks up for Keith. She jokes about fighting for her man while she wipes a table. I want her to fight over me—*as if.* A guy can dream, right? Just as she starts to write up Fat Elvis' bill, Agnes John zooms from the kitchen and beelines in to cut her off. Fat Elvis wants us to call him The King, cos it's like his name, and we do, but only to his face or if Agnes is around.

"Qʷóqʷésk̓ iʔ Bob, you put them eyes back in your head and close that mouth of yours before it draws flies," Agnes says. She fumbles with her waitress book and looks at Fat Elvis all the time she writes up his bill. He looks right back at her, a fat old man with teenaged lust in his voice, while Elvis sings "Love Me Tender."

"You still here?" Bernie, goes. "You want something?"

I'm breathless.

"Jeez, you," she says. "Am I gonna have to beat you again?"

"What? No. I mean, I'm sorry. I… I just forgot my head for a minute."

Damn my eyes. She laughs and puts a hand on my shoulder. *Wow! Melt! Swoon!* and every other lame romance comic idiot-in-love word whips through me with enough force to lift me off the ground.

"If you were three years older, I'd be all over you, Loverboy," Bernie says. She smiles. Winks.

"See you later, Squito."

She blows me a kiss. And then I'm alone in crisp November air, except it's springtime where I stand. I give my head a shake—Bernie had to be joking around, just joking to get me all hot and flustered, cos no way a girl like her could like me, right? I head to the laundromat, my brain tearing petals off of daisies: she loves me; she loves me not….

4:10 PM

Only four pm and Crazy Thom, soaked from head to toe, lies passed out on the sidewalk beside the pub. He's lost his socks and shoes, probably took them off and flung them at his invisible enemies, or ate them for a glass of beer. You can never tell with that guy. He should have a lot of shrapnel in his pockets, and maybe his tenner, or what's left of it—unless he's stashed it somewhere: he gets rolled all the time, even though he doesn't have much, so he should've learnt to keep just enough on him to pay for the day's drunk. At least that's what I'd do. I've rolled him a time or two, when he'd passed out on one of my paper routes, if you could call taking a buck or two rolling a guy. I could go through his pockets pretty quick but Front Street gets busy on Friday afternoons and getting busted for rolling Crazy Thom is the last thing I need. Maybe later. Maybe he'll have enough cash on him to pay for a meal tomorrow.

It sorta feels wrong to leave Thom on the sidewalk without checking his pockets at least, but not as wrong as spending dance weekend in the drunk tank. Anyway, would Bernie think me a sleaze if she found out that I'd paid my bill with money I'd taken from Crazy Thom? I think I need to be a better guy if I want to get Bernie. Maybe she would start to see me as mature enough for her and forget our age difference if I didn't roll drunks for a little extra cash. Nah, just another stupid thought from my stupid head. But Bernie did call me Loverboy.

A beer will clear my head.

At the laundromat, the guys drink quietly. Only Skinny seems to notice me.

"Look at you," he says, all lazy-eyed and sneery.

What I do wrong now? Ah, let him down again, I guess. "What?" I say. "You saw them cops, hey? Nothing I could do. Sorry."

He shakes his head. Laughs. "That? You did good. Handled them porkers better than I coulda, that's for sure." Then, in a loud voice, he says, "Look at him. He's got love in his eye. Musta been one a them outta town cops, hey? Which one? The short fat one with the grey hair—you do like 'em old, hey?"

Here it comes. The Delores Brown jokes begin now. I paste on a frown but my smile bursts through, "I guess I did, i'nit? You see the look on Bailey's face when I told that big cop I wanted to go to cop school after grad?"

"Yeah," Skinny goes. Nods. Sips his beer. "Yeah. The guy took you serious but he thinks you need help counting your papers."

Skinny sniggers. Then says, "O, and then what'd that one cop say?"

"Your boyfriend?" Go screw yourself, you boney piece of crap.

"As if. No, the fat one, Hand-on-Holster, says, 'like they'd ever let a prairie nigger into the Academy—'"

"Then," Skinny says. He holds his breath until the snicker passes. "Then you go: 'no, I mean me.' And all a them bust a gut laughing, looking at you like they never seen anyone so stupid in their lives."

JimJim says, "An no one plays stupid better 'en you, i'nit, Squito?"

Skinny laughs. Beer shoots from his nose. Playing stupid is way easier than playing smart but almost as hard to pull off, except with cops and teachers, cos they already think we are.

Except for Bimbo, everyone laughs. Turning his back to Skinny, he says, "Eww. I think I'm gonna puke."

Skinny, as red as embarrassed-Bimbo, puts his beer on the table, doubles over and wheezes. He looks like my grandfather just before he died, only younger. Except for the dread clawing its way through my guts, I can't move. JimJim goes to slap Skinny's back but Skinny waves him off, coughing out words that sound a little like, "I'm all right." He sucks in a harsh breath, then another, then hops onto a washing machine. I take a shaky drink, wipe the dribble away with the back of my hand.

"Must a went down the wrong tube, hey?" Skinny goes. He reaches for his beer and then pulls his hand away.

"I don't get why he called me that," I say. Better they bug me about not knowing what a prairie nigger is than humping old Delores Brown. In his please-the-Cow voice, Bimbo says, "You're a prairie nigger as long as you got one single drop of Indian blood in you."

"Not," JimJim says.

"Yeah, not," Cody says. "First off, we're plateau Indians, not plains."

"Doesn't matter," Bimbo says. "Plateau, saulteaux, desert, or plains, you all look the same."

"Says you, the half-blind séme?," I say.

"Yeah, says me and just about every other human in the world, you quarter-blind halfbreed."

JimJim seems to double in size and in a Hulk-smash-like voice, says: "How about I rip out your stinking tongue and hang you with it?"

JimJim never gets mad, or never shows it like Skinny, leaving me scared, even though I stand outside his grim shadow. Skinny, as wide-eyed as I feel, steps between JimJim and Bimbo, arms extended and palms up. "Whoa, guys. We're all friends here, right?" He faces JimJim. "Listen. It's just Bimbo and his stupid mouth. No big deal right? Right?" Skinny nods long and slow. JimJim, still as stone, eye-chokes Bimbo.

JimJim sucks in a deep breath and slowly shrinks back to his real size. Bimbo, either sweating, crying, or both, wipes his face with the back of his hand. He looks a good two-inches shorter—a few more scares like that and he'll be the same sorta mouse on the outside as he is on the inside. Skinny wraps one of his spaghetti arms around

JimJim's neck and guides him behind the driers. Almost as soon as they disappear around the corner, a thunderous, metallic wham, and a monstrous *Fuck!* explode, echoing through the room. Three quick *WHAM! Fuck!* combos pound our eardrums. Me, Cody, and Bimbo jump out of our skins. My breath, trapped behind the heart in my throat, stalls. Bimbo has shrunk another inch or so; he'll soon be able to slip under the door and scurry off into the night.

"C'mon, guys," Cody says, "That noise'll have Snook and them cops here. Then what?"

Skinny pokes his head around the corner. "We know. We know. Just a sec, okay?"

When JimJim joins us again he looks as if nothing's happened, a huge smile on his pumpkin head. He hands me and Cody a fresh beer, opening mine with his Zippo. Bimbo starts to make a little noise but instead slips behind the driers to get his own.

"So," Skinny goes, "getting excited about them Ashcroft girls?"

"Foxes, all of them," Bimbo says. "Not a skag among them." He beams.

"And you know that how?" Cody sneers.

"Um, like I go to Ashcroft every week. I see those girls. I even know a few of them. They're my friends."

"Friends?" JimJim says. "You want us to believe that you know foxy girls and you're just telling us now."

"Yeah," Skinny goes, "what's up with that?"

I smile. Idiot kid's caught in another lie.

Without stammering or turning a hundred shades of red, Bimbo answers: "If I told you before, you'd have wanted to come out there with me. All of you. I didn't want that."

"You can't handle one girl. What the hell you think you could do with nine."

"Not nine. Three. And one likes me as much as I like her."

"O, yeah?" Skinny goes. "What's her name?"

Without hesitating, Bimbo says, "Ingrid. And she'd go with me if I lived closer to her."

"As if," Cody says.

"No, it's true. I swear it."

Bimbo truths, and double-takes and silences surround him. Ingrid stands a head taller than Bimbo and he says she doesn't mind short guys. Bimbo likes slow dancing with her cos he can stick his face between her boobs. He can't say for certain when and where they danced, or how good her boobs feel on his face.

"Sometimes you just know how good it will be," he says. "When Fast Freddy does the Home Waltz, I'll disappear between them. Wait and see."

"And you'll bang her right there on the dance floor?" Cody says.

"Don't be stupid," Bimbo says. "We'll go someplace private. Some place nice."

I laugh. "Like the backseat of your car? Back to your house?"

"I might get us a room at the Welcome Inn."

"With that crumpled single you got in your pocket?" Cody says. "You'll wind up trying to sneak her into your bedroom, i'nit?"

"Like his mom'll let him bang a chick in his bedroom," Skinny goes.

"Why not? Ingrid's nice," Bimbo says.

"And white," JimJim says.

"'Course she's white. What's that got to do with anything?"

All monkey-faced, JimJim, Skinny, and Cody scratch their heads and whoop like the Indians in that Peter Pan cartoon.

Bimbo, in high-whine, pouts, "I'm sick of you guys always trying to wreck everything for me."

Even though his lips barely move and he stands stone still, you can see his lower lip dangle to the floor, hear his foot slap the ragged lino. How can such a baby in teen's clothing have a real girl lined up for the weekend? It can't be a white thing, cos almost every other séme? is better than Bimbo. And who knows if the thing he says he has with Ingrid lives outside his dreams.

Like the thing he wants to have with Bernie, a goofy fantasy love affair that he invented way back in the Sixth Grade. Maybe no different from the one I have with her, I guess. But she calls me Loverboy.

Letting my little chief think for me again, I blurt: "You think I have a chance with Bernie? I mean like a real chance?"

Skinny laughs a single, acidic, "Ha!" and JimJim rolls his eyes and groans, "Christallmighty, not this again."

Cody shakes his head.

Bimbo says, "Go near her and I'll kill you. Kill you dead."

"Then what'll you tell your precious Ingrid?" I say.

"Shut your yap, Bimbo, or I'll shut it for you," Cody says.

"Yeah," JimJim says. "And you too, Squito. She's way outta your league."

"What? She—" Skinny punches Bimbo's shoulder, shutting him up.

"No," I say. "I mean she called me Loverboy and said if I was just three years older—"

"You got a thing for older women, i'nit?" Cody says. He laughs a humourless laugh.

"Stop," Skinny goes. "Don't get your panties up in a bunch over her. She's nice but she's teasing you. Just teasing. You do know that, right?"

"She was three years older than me," JimJim sings.

"Had the biggest dang boobies you'd ever seen," Skinny and JimJim sing.

"But it sure didn't seem to matter, she made me so crazy that I threw my love at her," Skinny, JimJim, Bimbo, and Cody sing.

"And got shot down, cos she belongs to me," Bimbo sing-says.

I guess it's stupid to think a girl like Bernie would ever want anything to do with me in that way, and even stupider to think I could talk about it with my friends and not get teased about it.

"I don't think we should change the chorus like that," I say. "Especially Bimbo's lame line."

"What's wrong with it? I got just as good a chance of nailing her as any of you," Bimbo says.

"Next time I see her, I'll ask her what she has to say. Then we'll know for sure, i'nit?" Skinny goes. The devil himself can't smile as sinister as Skinny and no one's ever looked as scared as Bimbo.

"I dunno," JimJim says. "Take the Bimboness out of it and it could work: So I threw my love at 'er and I missed. Whadya think?"

"But is it a wild pitch or murder ball?" Cody says. "And if you miss, how could she give you 'the best piece of cake you ever had?' Losers never get the prize, i'nit, Bimbo?"

Instead of deep-voiced authority, I kazoo, "But that's not the way Dr. Hook sings it."

"Shut up," Bimbo says.

"I think we should change the chorus, just for tonight," Skinny goes.

"Yeah. Show the world you can laugh at yourself," JimJim says.

"You can't beat 'em, so you may as well join 'em. I mean everyone laughs at you all the time, anyways," Bimbo says.

Skinny, his words pure hydrochloric acid, says, "But not as much as we laugh at you."

Bimbo slouches into himself, head tucked into his chest, arms crossed over it.

"You know what, I think we should do it. Yeah. And if Bernie shows up, we should sing it to her. I'll even dedicate it to her. Like Elvis live in Memphis," I say. Butterflies try pulling the beer out of my gut. I can see how singing to Bernie this way would make everyone forget about my night with Dolores Brown. *The Hope Standard* headlines will read: BOY STOMPED TO DEATH BY ANGRY WOMAN. *Idiot Boy's Homicide Ruled Justifiable. Bernadette "Bernie" Paul Awarded Medal of Honour for Ridding Town of Loser.* Of course my friends like the idea.

I don't see how a whole song about Bernie's boobs—the twins—and us doing it will make her fall for me for real. I can't see her liking it at all but I can see singing her this song killing any real chance I might have had with her. And maybe killing me for real this time. But the guys tell me she's proud of the twins—proud, maybe, but she's all *don't look* (too long) *and do not touch*. The guys also say girls with big boobs like it when you say good things about them, like that thing with Bernie never happened. Maybe for some girls but not Bernie, not with me anyway. I doubt she'd call me Loverboy after I sing her this song. I don't want that to happen.

Skinny goes, "So let's give it a go with our chorus, 'kay?"

Along with the other guys, I say, "Sure." My brain slaps my stupid tongue around and tells me to kiss any chance of going with Bernie goodbye.

"You know, this got me thinking," Skinny goes, "we got this whole falling in love thing going on and chicks dig sappy love songs, right? So we should sing our sappiest songs tonight. Whadya think?"

"Maybe too much?" JimJim says.

"Can't ever have too much of a good thing," Bimbo says. "Anyways, how many white chicks ever heard 'Fais-Do?'"

"Shut your hole," Cody snaps. "Everyone, and I mean everyone, loves Redbone."

Bimbo raises a pointer finger, opens, then closes his mouth, then huffs a harsh breath out his nose and lowers his finger. He nods.

"Maybe you're right," he says in a low voice. "I hadn't thought of it like that."

Cody grabs our beers and scoots behind the driers. Just as Bimbo goes, "Hey!" we hear why; outside the laundromat, three guys are talking about busting some heads: cos of Bimbo, probably ours. They're angry drunks and they're coming our way, at least two of them. We're dead if they think we lifted their cash and they'll blame me, cos of Margaret. And they'll thump us all.

"I'll look in here. You guys head up the station house." It's my Uncle Angus. I'm pretty sure he won't beat me but he'll be pretty mad just the same.

He was another one who lost all his kids to the lice lady. They say he hasn't been the same since. His real name is Alexander but they've called him Angus for so long it's all anyone knows him by. They call him Angus cos he's as big as a bull and he's not only as big as a bull, but full of it, too. Uncle Angus says he's one-hundred-percent-pure beefcake. I guess girls think so, too, cos you never see him without one and they pretty much line up to go with him.

"O," Uncle Angus says, "It's just you boys." His smile turns into a snarl when he sees Bimbo and his eyes, for an instant, become a double-barrelled shotgun. Bimbo squirms like a worm you just split in two with a shovel and starts for the room behind the driers but Skinny grabs him, holds him in place. Uncle Angus pastes on a Hollywood smile.

"How long you been in here?"

I say, "Hey, Uncle. A while. What's up?"

"Seen anyone from outta town? Looking for a coupla səmséme? driving that Caddie parked in fronta the Chinaman's. One's under a black Stetson and the other's wearing a bone and quill choker. Fuckin' séme?! Playin' AIM."

"Haven't seen no one. Why you want them?" I hope he says he thinks they're the ones who took their money.

"They beat up my friend here," he says, stepping aside to let a little white woman in. Except for some blood and dirt stains on her ripped shirt and torn pants, she didn't look like she'd been beaten up at all. "This is Melanie. She's up from Big Town. Come all the way up for the big dance tomorrow night. The bastards dumped her in a ditch outsida Kanaka."

After dumping Melanie, he says they went to the New Fu Manchurian but snuck out after he, Bobby Alphonse and Kermode Jack slashed their caddie's tires and ripped out its distributor cap. If I had those three guys after me, I'd run fast and far and never look back. If those two outsiders can't get out of town, they're gonna wish the cops had found them first.

"O, sorry. I haven't seen anyone since Thom drank that gas."

Uncle Angus burst into laughter. "That crazy séme?! You got to see him. He'll do fuckin' near anything for a drink." He chuckles and elbows her in the ribs. She buckles and yelps like a wounded puppy. I guess she took body shots, maybe hard enough to crack her ribs. I feel real bad for her now. There's not much worse pain than walking around with a cracked rib or two.

"Hey, Uncle, she been to Saint Jude's? Maybe the nurse should have a look at her?"

"She's fine. Ain't you, babe?" Melanie nods but I don't believe her. "Throw back a coupla beers and life's good again, hey?" He kisses the top of her head and wraps an arm around her, one of his huge hands cupping her butt. She winces and moans.

"How you doing for money, Nephew?"

"O, you know me. Rolling in it. The usual." I laugh. Fibbing makes me laugh but not in a happy way. It also burns my face.

"No reason to be ashamed. Least you're working hard for what you got. You keep working hard and more will come your way."

He lets go of Melanie's bum and reaches into his inside breast pocket. He pulls out a mickey of whiskey. Breaks the seal and tosses the lid toward the garbage can. He watches the lid bounce off the floor. Shrugs. Takes a long pull. Melanie shakes her head when he offers her a swig. He passes it to me and I take a good swallow. It wants to come back up. Everyone laughs when I gag. I'm not man enough for whiskey, I guess. I reach over Bimbo and pass the bottle to Skinny.

"It's okay. I don't mind that little shit drinking my booze," Uncle Angus says.

"But I do," Skinny goes.

"So, Thaddeus, you still think you're too good to drink with our kind?" Uncle says.

Bimbo stammers something about it being his mother's fault, not his. We laugh and drink until the whiskey's gone. Cody hasn't shown his face or made a sound. Bimbo sulks, his heels thumping the washer he sits on. After taking the last drink, Uncle Angus hands the bottle to Skinny, who puts it in the garbage. Melanie shivers. She's a white shadow held up by a wall and not much else.

"Know what, kiddo? I think Mel here should see that nurse. You mind running her over to the hospital? I need to find the cocksuckers who did this to her."

"Sure thing, Uncle. I could do that for you."

"Good boy." He stops in the door. Laughs. "Almost forgot."

He buries a hand in his front pocket and pulls out a mound of coins. Dumps them into my hands. It feels like twenty dollars. I feel rich and rich feels good.

"Sorry. All I got's shrapnel. Some bastard stole my cash. But I guess it serves me right for leaving it on my table, hey?" Uncle Angus points his shotgun eyes at Bimbo. I wish I could pull the trigger. He laughs again and then he's gone. Bimbo sneaks behind the driers, returns with four beers, and chirps, "Who wants a cold one?"

The guys each grab a beer, open it, and then flick their caps across the room. Bimbo pushes the last one toward me. I point my lip toward Melanie, shake my head, and open the door.

Melanie can barely walk. She smells like an open wound and all sexed up after a three-day drunk. Even so, I put my arm around her and hold her close. She goes stiff and jumps away from my touch.

"Don't," she says. "Please don't."

"Sorry," I say. "I just thought—"

"I know. But I'm fine, really."

She winces, then stumbles. She wraps her arms tightly around herself and takes tiny steps, each one making her moan. Even a slow walk is too fast for her. I walk with my arm extended behind her, thinking I could catch her if she falls, and hope I'm fast enough to catch her if she falls forward. The three short blocks to the hospital feel like a twenty-mile walk to Spences Bridge.

From habit, I almost tell the nurse Melanie had fallen down the stairs. But after my brain and mouth finish fighting, I tell her what my uncle told me. Melanie says nothing. The nurse asks if Melanie has some place to stay cos there won't be anyone to take x-rays until Tuesday. Melanie cries a little. We're choked by the kinda quiet that fills a room before your teacher hands out the final exam. The nurse excuses herself. She comes back some minutes later, pushing a wheelchair.

"Constable Bailey has asked me to keep you here until we can get you properly looked at. Just routine, he said." Melanie shivers. If she gets any paler, she'll turn invisible. The nurse nods toward the door. "There's no reason for you to hang around, Mister Bob. I'll see that your friend is properly taken care of. Okay?"

Melanie looks at me. I can't tell if she's scared or asking me to stay or to get her out of there.

She needs to stay. They say a broken rib can punch a hole in your lung. I'd hate for her to die cos she's too afraid to get help. I sorta feel responsible for her and think I should sit with her until she's better. But really, it is dance weekend. On top on that, for the first time ever, I sing lead on one song tonight. Maybe Auntie Max will hear me. Maybe she'll like my singing. Probably not, but… I guess I'll dedicate my song to Melanie, even if it's mostly for Bernie. She nods when I ask her if she'll be all right. I don't feel so bad about leaving her at Saint Jude's. I guess, whether she wants to be there or not, it's the right place for her.

5:30 PM

The sound of the guys singing our version of "Four Years Older Than Me" leaks into the street. One of them plays a washer like a drum. Sinister must be too busy trying to impress those out-of-town cops to chase them out of his laundromat. All these lucky breaks now probably mean something really bad will happen soon, unless we keep our guards up. Maybe even if we keep them up. Dear xeʔłkʷúpiʔ, *keep us safe from harm, from them cops, and get Fast Freddy here safe and sound.* Kʷukʷscémxʷ. I push open the door. The singing stops. Sneakers shuffle. Bottles clank. I smile. They all lean against the two washing machines.

"O, it's just you," Skinny goes. He pulls his beer from inside the washer.

"Look at you, all cazh," I say. "No funny business going on here, hey?"

"We worked on the song. Maybe have some lines that'll work. Wanna hear it?" Skinny goes.

"I could hear it in the street. What you guys thinking, anyways?" I say. Skinny looks at me, his chin pulled back into his neck, his lips puckered up like a horse's ass.

"There's five new cops in town and they're staying here."

"Here," Cody says. "Right here?"

"Yeah, I told you that already."

"Here? In the laundromat?" Cody laughs.

"No," I say. "Upstairs. In rooms. Like normal people."

"O, so we aren't normal?" JimJim says.

"Jeez. You know what I meant."

JimJim, smiling wide, pats my shoulder. Bimbo skitters by us then disappears behind the driers. He returns, hugging five beers to his chest. He puts them on the folding table. The Bimbo I see is not the Bimbo I know. Part of me wants to touch him to see if he's real but a bigger part goes all ewwww! Bimbo slips a church key from his back pocket and opens all five bottles, then hands them around.

"Why?" Skinny goes. "Why you acting so weird?"

Bimbo shrugs. "Can't a guy be nice once in a while?"

"'Course," JimJim says, "but it's you, not some guy."

"Look," Bimbo says, "I'm sorry. Sorry for being a dick about the money. Sorry I took it."

Stone silence. Blank stares. "No, really."

It's hard to hate the kid when he acts almost human.

Skinny tilts his head, points his lip at his beer, and says, "Yeah, sure. Why not?"

We drink wordlessly for a while. JimJim, head bobbing slightly, taps out beats on his thigh.

Cody seems to scribble words onto the air with his fingertip, face screwed into a frown. Skinny stands, one hand deep in his pocket, thinking or not thinking about something. Bernie grooving to my singing fills my brain with balloon hearts.

"So," Skinny goes, "What happened with that chick, anyways?"

As if wakened from a dream, I jump. I say, "You mean Melanie?"

"Angus' jump?"

"Melanie. She wasn't my uncle's jump. He just helped her out. She's in pretty rough shape, so they had to keep her in. So rough, they'll probably send her to Royal Jubilee."

"Why? What happened?"

"I dunno," I say, "Uncle and them pulled her out of a ditch. Figure it out."

Silence.

Then I tell them what I know happened at the hospital. I count my pocketful of shrapnel. Uncle had handed me almost twelve dollars, too much change to carry around. I could change it for bills at the coffee shop. That would give me a wad almost as thick as Fat Elvis', my pocket full of bait, or I could spring for chips and gravy and onion rings. Maybe even tip Bernie a silver dollar. But maybe she'd expect a huge tip every time she served me. I would hate her to think I'd let her down or teased her with one big tip.

"Watch the door, hey," Skinny goes, drunk—almost stupid-drunk—but not falling-down drunk. It usually takes him longer, being tall and more hollow-legged than most. He sprays, *shhh*, and then pees in the drier. It hammers the drier's drum. It echoes. He must have gallons of pee inside of him. As he goes, he tells us about the time he and one of his cousins snuck into a guest ranch outside Ashcroft and pissed on the sauna stones. He says a sauna's a little like a sweat bath for white people. When them rocks got hot they gave off such a stink that a bunch of nearly naked people rushed out of the sauna like it was on fire. They blamed racoons for the mess.

The way Skinny tells it, watching them nearly naked people scream and jump into the swimming pool beside that sauna was funnier than The Three Stooges Show. But here and now, I have to make sure Yéye? never uses that drier again. I have to make sure I put my father's clothes in it, though. So what if he beats the crap out of me again and I smell like a piss-pants drunk; it would be a small price to pay to see my father's face when he opened up that bag of clean clothes.

"You know what?" I say. "I think we should have something to eat before heading to Auntie Max's. I'll buy you all a chips and gravy. Maybe some onion rings?"

"Everything's onion rings with you, i'nit?" Cody says. "You're gonna turn into one. You know that, right?"

"I think he takes 'em home and humps 'em," JimJim says.

Skinny laughs. "That's putting the *o* in *o, baby!*, hey?"

We laugh. My brain plays a short movie of me sticking it to an onion ring straight from the deep frier. I flinch.

"Even me?" Bimbo says, almost in time to save me from feeling the pain my brain has painted on me.

"Yeah. Even you," I say. He's my worst friend but still a friend.

Bimbo closes in on me: "Think you could spot me a fiver. For a dance ticket and a mickey, I mean?"

I say, "Maybe" but it sounds like my father's: just a coward's *no*. So, I swallow hard, and say, "Yeah," even though I know the only way he can get hard stuff now is to lift it from his father's liquor cabinet and we leave him enough cash to pay for his ticket.

5:50 PM

Agnes snake-eyes Skinny. "Lucky you, it's tonight. Not today." She cuts a cat-dying chuckle. Skinny beams at her. She winks at him. She fills our coffee cups. She takes our order, too: four chips and gravy, and a small onion rings. Bernie runs back and forth between the formal dining room and the kitchen and doesn't even seem to notice us. I can't tip her for serving everyone but us, so I give Agnes the silver dollar tip. When you get right down to it, she treats us as good as my own aunt.

"What's this for?" she says.

"You," I say. "Just cos." Agnes smiles, and it looks like she's wearing a stranger's mouth, but underneath of it, you can see her heart.

6:15 PM

Back at the pub, Stanley's truck is gone. He must have forgotten us—something that'll happen after you've had a few. It happens to everyone, so I'm not mad. After all, it's only four miles to Auntie Max's not much longer than an hour-or-two walk: time we could use to warm up our voices and maybe get "Four Years Older than Me" down. I sure need the practice. But Bimbo whines, saying the walk will kill him, give his toes frostbite, and make us miss out on something.

"If you shut your yap and walk, we'll be there by seven. No one shows up to these things till at least nine," Skinny goes.

"Or ten," JimJim says.

"The real cool guys don't show up until after last call," Cody says.

"I'm gonna be banging a foxy lady way before last call," Skinny goes.

"Just one?" Cody says. "Those Ashcroft girls are so hot to trot, they'll probably want to jump us two at a time."

"Sick," JimJim says. "You're talking about being gangbanged by girls?"

He freezes, mouth open. His mouth transforms into a wide grin. "O," JimJim sorta moans. "Gangbanged by girls. Let's get going, hey?"

Mac Mackay, cussing up a storm, tries to figure out how to tow the Caddie with its four slashed tires. Angus and them pass a brown-bagged bottle around and watch Mac work like Highway guys patting each others' back around their patched up pothole. They don't offer to help Mac, even though they slashed the Caddie's tires. We stand on Front Street and watch.

Mac takes off his hat, scratches his head, then takes the bottle Angus hands him. "Don't have a cocksucking clue how I'm gonna get this cocksucking piece of suck-cock-shit car to my yard. Who'd do something this cocksucking stupid? Cocksucking cocksuckers."

"Just tow the cocksucking thing on its rims," Angus says, his face a devilish smile.

"Might have to, at that. Any cocksucker can afford a caddie, can cocksucking-well afford new rims and tires."

Angus holds the bottle up to the light. "Hey, neph, come have a snort."

"Can't, Uncle, sorry. We got to head out to Auntie Max's."

"Fine, then. Say hi to the old girl."

"O, Uncle," I say. "You checked on Melanie yet?"

"Who? O, the séme? chick? No. She all right?"

My body twists into an I-don't-know shrug.

"Find them a-holes yet?"

He mimics my shrug. "Still looking."

Mac drags the Caddie away. Its tires flap. One tears free, shedding chunks of rubber, the rim grinding sparks up the street. A couple of guys gab outside the Ladies and Escorts door. A few more lurk in front of the main entrance. Crazy Thom has disappeared. Five kids pester the drunks to run for them. They're like crows fighting over a roadkill rat. Young kids these days just don't have the same respect for runners as us. If they don't smarten up, they'll ruin it for all of us.

Well, for themselves, cos they have longer to wait till they're legal. When I'm legal, I'll probably run for my cousins and stuff, but I wouldn't want it to be the way I make my living, even though it would be a pretty good one while it lasted.

We head toward Auntie Max's. As soon as we get to the bridge, Skinny belts, "Ain't nothing like a gangbang. Ain't nothing like a gangbang. Ain't nothing like a gangbang to blow away the blues."

The song belongs to The Sensational Alex Harvey Band. I know some of the words, mostly from listening to Skinny sing it to us.

The SAHB are from England and almost no one in town's heard of them, except maybe Skinny. He always brings new music to us and I have no idea how he finds it. People usually only want songs they know, so there's no way we'd sing any of their songs at a do. It just wouldn't work. But we join in, screaming out the chorus, and shuffle dance to the beat we clap out.

"You know, we could do this song," Skinny goes. "It'd be real boss. I could make it work with just our voices and everyone will dance like they do to our other stuff."

JimJim says what I think: "I'm not so sure. It's not the kinda song everyone'll love."

"Nah. We're doing it. They'll love it," Skinny goes.

I almost tell him that there are lots of things I love that do nothing for anyone else. We might love singing this song but I'm pretty sure almost no one will like hearing it. The girl in "Gang Bang" asks for it—not the passing-out-at-a-party kinda asking for it, but for real. For whatever reason, she likes a bunch of guys at once. She's not the kinda girl I ever want to know. I can see guys digging this song but not many girls at all. Yéye? would hate it. She calls lots of music I listen to ugly and whenever she hears me singing an ugly song, she asks if I would give it at a gathering. Would I sing "Gang Bang" to Yéye? and the other grandmothers and grandfathers? If I say I would, she'll ask me why and she'll make me give her a real answer, the kinda answer that rips at your guts like a knife wound. If I say no, she'll ask me why I'm wasting my time singing a song I wouldn't give to anyone else. Sometimes I think she's just trying to boss me around, or she's just not with it, but mostly I think she just wants to make me a better person than I am. If Skinny sets his mind to adding "Gang Bang" to our set list, I'll go along, not cos I want to, and hope an older person pulls us aside and tells us it's not a good song. It'll have to be someone Skinny respects, like his great-grandfather. I wonder if he'd have us sing "Gang Bang" for his great-grandfather. I should ask him but don't.

6:45 PM

By the time we get to Two Mile, my throat's scratchy. We finished our beer about a mile earlier, so I have nothing to soothe my cranky vocal cords. Stanley's parked his truck in a ditch again. It looks more like a sloppy parking job, or he forgot to set his emergency brake, than had an accident. He probably stopped to puke or something and forgot where he'd parked. We call out his name. He doesn't answer. It's already nearly freeze-a-drunk-to-death cold. Anything standing still for too long could get frostbite in weather like this. Skinny's wearing a white tee shirt and black leather vest. He's too cool to get cold. I'm not. I wish I had gloves and a toque and a way heavier coat than my jean jacket.

Candace Steward-Day is our bootlegger. She was kicked off the res and then kicked out of town for selling booze. She has a shack about a half-mile into the bush, an old ranch hand shack that Derek Palmer rents to her. No one can do anything about her cos his land's not in town and not on res. I guess the cops could shut her down but everyone, including the mayor and Constable Howe, buy from her.

You have to be pretty desperate to walk all the way up to her shack and back and pay her prices. She sells warm half-sacks for five bucks, mickeys of whiskey for seven and her home brew for three. I guess her prices are so steep cos on top of being barred from living in town or on res, she's barred from the liquor store here, so she has to drive all the way to Kamloops to get her booze. They say she does a good business, especially after the pub and Legion close, and Sundays. I don't go to her cos I can't afford her prices and she doesn't sell lemon gin.

She and Stanley hump each other sometimes. You have to wonder what's so wrong with you when you can't get a girl of any kind and a guy like Stanley can have a sm?eméc̓e and a woman on the side. Candace is not a going-steady kinda girl. Yéye? says Candace hates men and that she may have good reason, too.

Everyone's heard Candace's stories at least once. If you're around her for more than a few minutes, especially after she's had a few, you're in for an earful. So far, every man she's been with, except Stanley, has done horrible things to her. She says she's never done anything to deserve her bad treatment and has always been the perfect wife, girlfriend, or jump.

"We better make sure my uncle's okay," Skinny goes.

He and JimJim head into the bush. They're real hunters and find Stanley's trail right away. Skinny points out a snapped twig here, a scuffed leaf there. A footprint stamped in moist dirt. A little rock kicked from its bed. A still steaming puddle of piss. If deer left trails like a drunk man, and I could actually shoot it, I'd be one of the greatest hunters around. Uncle Walter has tried to teach me how to track an animal in the bush but I'm not all that interested. I might be more interested if I could shoot straight but I can't. I don't know what it is, I can't hold my rifle steady, even when my breathing's right and I picture my father in the scope.

We find Stanley, sitting on a log, mumbling bad words, his mud-caked wooden leg across his lap.

He looks up at us. The front of him covered in muck.

"My tree," he says, "it went timber. Then down I went, right after it. Flat on my face. Slipped on some mud, I guess."

He laughs. Then turns stern and points two fingers at us. "What you boys doing out here, anyways?"

"Saw your truck in the ditch, Uncle. Just wanted to make sure you were okay." Skinny goes.

"I didn't put her in a ditch." He sits up straight and scratches his head. "Did I?"

"Yup."

"She okay?"

"Yup. She looks okay."

"Can you pull her out? Park her proper? Back her onto the shoulder and put my keys under the seat. I don't want no hanky-panky. You hear?"

"Sure thing, Uncle," Skinny goes. "I'll put her on the shoulder and leave the keys under the seat."

"You better or I'll kick your arse all the way to Hell's Gate and back."

He looks each of us in the face, an unfocused drunk look that could be funny. Then he pisses himself and doesn't even seem to notice. A little part of me wants to laugh but mostly I'm sad for him and grossed right out. Stanley's a good man, a smart man, but he's now just a piss-pants drunk who left his truck in a ditch. I'd rather be dead than that kinda drunk. I doubt I'll even live as long as Stanley has, so I don't really need to worry about it. Much. We look at each other. None of us wants to see what Stanley's become. Not even Bimbo, who's at his best when someone else is at their worst.

"You got your keys?" Skinny goes.

Stanley says nothing. Leans back and falls off the log. Skinny, JimJim, Cody, and I try to pick him up.

"Get the hell away from me," Stanley says. "I don't need no one's help. You hear me? Hey? Well, do you?" JimJim, Cody, and I surrender and back away from Stanley.

Skinny, standing on Stanley's legless side, stays put. "Yes, Uncle. But let me give you a hand up. It's pretty slick."

Stanley mutter-cusses, grabs hold of Skinny's arm. From where I stand, Skinny lifts his uncle, one-armed, as easy as picking up a sack of potatoes. While Stanley fishes for his keys, Skinny, holding his uncle up by his belt and shoulder, says, "JimJim, grab his leg and wash it over at the pump, hey?"

JimJim scoops up Stanley's wooden leg and drags it to Candace's well. Skinny points his lip in the direction JimJim's gone and hands Cody Stanley's keys. Unlike his normal self, Bimbo, a disgusted look pasted to his face, has all but disappeared. I could grow to like him if he stayed this quiet.

Stanley lets me take his other arm. He hops between me and Skinny, chuckling to himself. Candace opens the door as we near the stoop.

"You got to get them clothes off him," she says. "He can't come in my house like that."

Stanley takes a swipe at Skinny, knocking the three of us off balance.

"Smarten up, old man," Candace says. And just like that, he snaps to. Candace undresses him: first his shirt and undershirt, and then his pants and underwear. He hops naked, shivering, me holding him by one shoulder and Skinny the other. Candace, a full head shorter than Stanley, slips under Skinny, wraps an arm around Stanley's waist. She piles his filthy clothes beside the stoop and tells us she'll clean it in the morning.

"I got him," she says. Skinny and I let Stanley go but we stay close. "C'mon. Let's get you inside and cleaned up. What got into your head? Coming up here when it's so ugly outside."

"Just had to see you, Babe," Stanley says.

"Had to get one last drink before bed, hey?"

"Sure," Stanley says. "That too."

Stanley, mud-faced and more naked than a man ought to be around anyone, leans on the door and says: "I'm coming right back. Just got to get some whiskey." He winks and puts a pointer finger to his lips. "Shhhhhh. We can't tell no one where I got it. Okay?"

"Yes, Uncle."

"Hey," Candace says. "Let's get you inside."

She plops Stanley onto a chair. It screeches as she pushes him tight to her kitchen table. She comes to the door and takes Stanley's now clean wooden leg from JimJim.

"You boys run along. Stan's all right now."

For a woman who hates men, she sure takes good care of Stanley.

7:00 PM

Skinny's the only one of us who can drive a stick. The four of us grab a place and lean into the grill and push hard. The truck doesn't budge. Skinny pokes his head out the window: "Hold on. I can't get her into neutral." The gearbox clunks and tings. The old truck groans.

Finally, Skinny yells, "Aha! I got it."

Again we push. This time we rock the truck forward and back but seem not to move it much.

"Ah, shit," Skinny goes. "Forgot to release the emergency brake. Sorry."

Thunk. Stanley's truck lurches forward a good foot before squeaking to a stop.

JimJim pounds the hood: "What the hell! You trying to kill us?"

"Yeah," Bimbo says. "Let me drive or we'll be here all night."

"Drive this," Skinny says, jamming up-yours fingers against the windshield. Bimbo returns the sign, mumble-cussing like Stanley.

Cody says, "Just fire her up, put her in reverse, and back out."

"Already am," Skinny goes.

He gets the truck started without flooding it or running us over. It rolls forward, and if it rolls too much more, it'll get hung up by its driveshaft and probably have to be towed out.

"Push," Skinny shouts. He guns it, spraying the undercarriage with pebbles and dirt. The truck fishtails some. We push and little by little get the truck onto the shoulder. It feels like forever passes before we get her parked.

JimJim looks at Skinny and Skinny looks at the truck, then goes: "You know what, boys, I think we could borrow her. Drive ourselves to Max's. Whadya say?"

"Stan'll kill us," Cody says.

"If he kills anyone, it'll be me. Do I look worried?" Skinny flashes his insane monkey smile and we laugh.

"What the hell," Bimbo says. "We wasted the better part of an hour making sure he wasn't dead in the bush. It's the least he could do for us."

Cody frowns, slowly shaking his head. My brain paints pictures of us all crushed under Stanley's truck. But Bimbo's sorta right, we have spent a lot of time taking care of Stanley and his truck.

"How you gonna get her back?" Cody says. Skinny shrugs and cups his mouth and chin in a hand. "I guess we could get Max to drive back with us. Think she'll do it, Squito?"

"Not if them Ashcroft girls are already there. She has to watch them. And not if she's had more than two beers."

"Then we'd better hurry, hey?"

We climb into the truck: Skinny behind the wheel, JimJim riding shotgun and me, Cody and Bimbo in the bed. Wind reeks with the promise, or threat, of Winter's first snow. I hope not, but it could blow cold and hard so them Ashcroft girls will have to snuggle up to us, real cozy.

7:30 PM

Only Auntie Max's '62 Flareside Ford and Uncle Keith's '66 Malibu SS 396 stand in the driveway. Both vehicles were something in their day. Auntie's Ford is a work truck—rusty, dented, its paint peeling like a sunburned séme?. Back in her rodeo days, she used it to tow her horses to competitions. She was a champion barrel racer and has seven silver buckles to prove it but she had to quit cos her back couldn't take the pounding any more. She still rides around her ranch, just not much more than a lope, I guess. And she sometimes trains young barrel racers, usually family members, but not everyone who asks. She'll watch you ride and if she doesn't like the way you sit on your horse, she'll say you're not ready to be a barrel racer and refuse to teach you. She's honest and kind but honesty can make you cry just as hard as a mean crack. She faces crying girls—even relatives—every month. Last week she had to say no to my cousin Alice cos they pretty much had to strap her to the saddle to keep her from falling off. Alice cried and begged her stepdad, a nice séme? from Big Town, to make Auntie teach her. He just thanked Auntie for taking time out of her day to give Alice a chance, then took his stepdaughter for ice cream or something.

Alice's mom, my aunt Mary—but I'm not sure how she's my auntie, cos she's not one of Yéye?'s daughters—screamed bad things right into Auntie Max's face. Aunt Mary's a town girl and just talking about doing chores exhausts her; she's the exact opposite of Auntie Max. Auntie can scrap, too. In her day she had the reputation as a brawler. Uncle Walter says, "Max is strong as a bull but she ain't no cow." So she could've pounded Mary into the ground like a fence post.

Instead, she asked: "Would you rather have a wheelchair-bound gimp for a daughter? And yeah, a good rider could end up crippled up like that too, but Alice is too afraid of the horse to have any control. Anyways, she needs to learn to ride before she can race."

Auntie Max isn't happy about refusing a kid but she'd rather say no now than scrape her broken body out of the rodeo's ring. She and Uncle Keith never had kids of their own. If she talks about not having any kids at all, she shrugs and says, "I guess all that hard riding scrambled my eggs."

Uncle Keith named his Malibu "Boo." She was the fastest car in the Canyon but now sits in the driveway, as dead as Uncle himself. He would hate seeing Boo like she is now, in her final resting place, up on blocks, under a tarp, and rammed hard against a skinnier pine tree than the one Uncle had crashed into. Even though Auntie lifted the tarp and waxed her once a month, Boo should've had a nicer end. Auntie told everyone, including Uncle's family, how Boo had to live out her days. Auntie often sits beside Boo with a jug of wine and talks to Uncle Keith long into the night. All year long, but not so much in winter, guys driving flatbeds pull into Auntie's yard and offer to haul Boo away, free of charge. Auntie tells them no and they all ask Auntie to take their phone number and call when she's ready to let go of Boo. She tosses all of those numbers straight into the fire pit.

Uncle had babied Boo and kept her as shiny as the day she rolled off the assembly line. He drag raced her often but never on dirt roads cos he didn't want any pebbles dinging Boo's paint, and he didn't want a rooster tail of dust and pebbles scatter-gunning everything behind him. The one time he agreed to race on a gravel road, he died, crashed to a halt by a forty-foot Ponderosa pine. They say his last words were: "Fuck, Boo, Maxie was right. You done killed me." They say Auntie wanted to put those words on his gravestone but the funeral guy said no way.

Auntie Max stands on her back stoop. She watches us pull up beside her Ford.

"What you doing with Stan's truck? Where is he? You boys better not have stole it," she says.

Skinny tells her what happened and how he thought he'd just done Stanley a huge favour, keeping him from driving off a cliff or something. Auntie Max buys none of it.

"We were kinda hoping you could follow me back to Candace's and then give me a ride back," Skinny goes.

"You could hope to win the Irish Sweepstakes, too. In fact, you got a better chance of winning them Sweepstakes than you got of me driving to Candace's right now," she says. A whip cracks under her words. I flinch, even though it's aimed at Skinny.

"You heard her. C'mon guys, let's get going," Skinny goes.

"Screw that," Bimbo says. "It's cold and it was your brilliant plan. You go. I'm staying right here."

Cody and JimJim head inside. Cold, and in need of a beer, I inch toward the house. After all, I need a good buzz on before singing in front of everyone. Skinny clamps one of his giant paws on me and goes, "C'mon, Squito. It looks like it's just me and you."

Like a guy on death row, I climb into the passenger seat. But maybe it won't be so bad, a little walk might kill the butterflies and I almost never see Skinny without JimJim at his side.

Skinny badmouths Auntie Max all the way back to Candice's. He thumps the steering wheel with the heels of his hands and loses control of the truck, just for a second. It's long enough for the passenger side tires to slide onto the soft shoulder. We fishtail. It feels as if we're out of control forever and my life, not bright enough to flash, flickers past my eyes. Dead at fifteen and practically a virgin. Skinny laughs.

"Whoooo hooooo! That was great, hey? Can I drive or what?"

"What?" I say. It was supposed to come out *or what!* But some of it got drowned in the stomach juice pooled in my throat. Skinny repeats himself.

"Yup. You're the best driver I know," I say. One hand has a death grip on the door handle, the other squeezes the edge of my seat. Both my feet are stomped on the place they should've put the passenger side brake.

Some few minutes later we see Stanley staggering our way. He has a half-sack under one arm and a two-six in his hand. He yells at us to stop after Skinny's already pulled over.

"'S about time you showed up. I been walking for hours, you little prick," Stanley says.

"I'm just gonna find a place to turn her around, Uncle. I'll be right back. Okay?"

"Be quick, goddamnit."

We drive to Henderson's ranch, about a quarter-mile up the road. Their driveway's long and wide. Except for grinding off most of reverse and first's teeth, Skinny has almost no trouble turning Stan's truck around.

Stanley has on clean clothes that fit him pretty good. He looks a little less drunk than when we left him at Candace's. He wants to drive. We tell him that it's better if Skinny drives us back to Auntie's. We guide him into the passenger seat and almost as soon as his door's closed, he's snoring, head resting on the side window. He jolts awake when Skinny twists off the whiskey's cap, mumbles something about killing anyone who touches his bottle, and just drops back into his drunken sleep. We each take a good pull. I hop into the pick-up's bed, Skinny takes the wheel. Stanley lives in a ranch hand's shack on Dermot Kelly's land, across from Auntie Max's.

We get Stanley inside and onto his bed. I think I'd rather hog-tie a mad bull than get a comatose drunk out of his boots and into bed.

We pile blankets on top of him. His place is heated by a woodstove and there's no way we're leaving him alone with a fire, no matter how carefully it may be built. We each take a beer from his half-sack.

"Taxi fare," Skinny goes. He pockets one more. We have a good chuckle and I take another one, too. It's a long, thirsty walk back to Auntie Max's, all five hundred feet of it. It may have been fair to take Stan's beer but I put about two-fifty in change on the table beside his remaining beers, cos I don't feel absolutely right about taking his booze. He can't drink my money but I hope those two beers and the rest of his whiskey are enough to help him wake up when he wakes up. The money I leave isn't enough to cover what he'd have paid Candace but it's enough to get him a case from off sales at the pub.

Skinny puts Stan's keys under the driver's seat.

7:40 PM

The rumble of heavy wheels on gravel. A school bus, too short to be one of ours, turns into Auntie's yard. My heart pounds in my ears and crotch. I jump to my feet, ready to run after the bus like a dog. I skip into a trot. Auntie's will soon crawl with girls and I need to make sure I get one. Skinny grabs my shoulder and spins me around.

"Tapper cool, kid!" he says. "Tapper cool. You run in there oozing desperation like that and them girls'll run from you like you're diseased."

"I'm cool," I squeak.

"Nah, if anything, you're uncool. But with some help you could maybe fake it long enough to snag yourself a fox. Do what I say and you'll do okay."

I never ever thought myself cool, but uncool? What could be worse than uncool? Even not cool is realer, like Bimbo—someone who sits in the bottom of a deep pit drilled into cool's basement. I'd figured I'd earned a place in cool's front stoop, at least; Cody maybe on the tenth; Skinny and JimJim had penthouses. Uncool puts me in a pit inside a pit under Bimbo's. Just when you think you know your place in the world, something comes along and undoes it.

"*Un*cool? What's that even mean?" Like I really want to know. Maybe it's not as bad as it sounds.

Who'm I kidding?

"Well," Skinny goes, "when *Cool* walks into a room, he don't walk, he struts, his head held high, his chest puffed out. Not all old guy sucking-in-his-gut-puffed but—" Out his chest goes and he grows almost two inches taller, then he struts four steps away from me, spins and struts back. "And you don't walk. No, no, no. You swagger. Like

Jagger. And them girls'll fall at your feet. You try it."

I feel like a world-class dope. My body doesn't have a clue how to swagger like Jagger, or anyone else, except maybe a two-year-old in a poopy diaper.

"Christ. All. Mighty. You walk like you got a hot load of crap in your pants. Just relax. Think confidence. It's easy."

I suppose it is easy if it comes to you naturally but for me? Not so much. He swats my butt and then my chest.

"Stand like a man. Not some Homo Erectus," Skinny goes. He practically doubles over with laughter. "Ho-mo. E-rect. Us. Well, not till you bagged your fox, then you can go all homo erectus on her." He thrusts his hips, shouts *Sproing!* and madly humps the night.

He opens his other beer with his teeth, spits its cap into the air. It arcs like a perfect hook shot and then it's swallowed by night. Instead of heading to Auntie Max's, he pulls up a stump and sits, legs fully extended and spread wide.

"What about the girls?" I say.

"Girls don't want a guy who runs after them like a drooling puppy. You gotta make 'em think you don't even care they're around."

"What?" No. I got to be first in line for one of them, before a better guy comes along. How else they gonna notice me?

"Sit. Relax. Have a drink. We know where they are. They know we're coming. Let 'em wait. Remember, just swagger like Jagger." He takes cool to a new level, stretched out all long and thin on that stump—King Cool—especially next to me, all hunched over like a toad on the stump across from him—King *Un*cool. Instead of relaxing, my mind plays movies of me as Jerry Lewis in *The Bellboy*, except I don't stumble into love or anything good. My brain's practically convinced me I could wander into the bush and Sasquatch wouldn't take me as either mate or meal. I will dive into the bottom of my bottle and drink myself to death. Who needs girls anyway?

What a stupid question. I do.

"So how you like 'em?" Skinny goes.

"Like who?"

"Girls, you simp. You like 'em tall? Short? Thin? Chunky?"

"I like them all, except the mean ones."

"They're all mean. You got to know how to tame em's all."

"No, they can't all be mean. Can they?"

"Yup. They are, unless they want you or something you have." Skinny cups his crotch. "With me, all they want is my Golden Sceptre. And I don't care, cos that's all I got to give 'em."

"At least you got that." Way more than I have, just a soon-to-be-dropout-with-three-paper-routes. I suppose Creator put prostitutes here so guys like me could rent love now and then.

"So what about Bernie? You real like her?"

"Yeah," I say. "I think I could go crazy for her."

"So what's keeping you from going for it? What's the worst thing that could happen?"

"What if she shoots me down?"

"So, what? She shoots you down, you get up, wipe the dirt off your ass and ask her again. A different way. Once she sees you're serious, maybe she starts taking you serious, too."

"But, you guys said it would never happen."

"Teasing. Just teasing. You got to learn to take a joke. When you can laugh at yourself the way we laugh at you, you'll find your cool."

Or a jail cell, cos I'd killed someone after taking one joke too many. Or a rubber room in Riverview, cos I was laughed at so much it broke my mind.

"My cool?"

"Yeah. Your cool. Steve McQueen has his own cool. Jagger has his. Paul Newman. Elvis. All the greats have their own cool. I guess they were born that way but the rest of us? We got to work at it. We got to practice till it fits us better than our own skin."

Skinny tosses his bottle into the bush behind him. I place my empty near my stump, beside its twin. We swagger like Jagger—strutting like this does not feel like me—to Auntie Max's back door. Skinny swings the door open like he's Clint Eastwood's character in *A Fistful of Dollars.* Besides a blast of light and warmth, we're greeted by The Stones blaring "Brown Sugar" and the voices of o, so many girls. I've followed the light and now I'm about to enter Heaven.

8:00 PM

Nine Ashcroft girls. Tall and white. Short and white. Chunky, thin, and white. Three blondes, five brunettes, and one green-eyed, freckled, redhead. I see why Charlie Brown went crazy for his little red-haired girl. Her super-tight tee shirt, cut low enough you can see a lot of her fat little boobs. Her nipples poke out like Cyndi Wood's. In fancy letters, shiny as fish gills, her shirt front shouts out that this fine little redhead is a *Foxy Lady.* But she doesn't need a tee shirt to tell you. She is. I have instant wood for her. Well, my heart beats heavy inside my pants. I slip my coat off and hold it over my front, just in case.

She zooms straight to me, her tiny, perfect hand slips into mine like a knife into its sheath, and all angel-voiced, she says, "Hi. I'm Pixie Holland." I sigh. Every drop of my new cool swaggers off, taking all of my best words with it. A dunce-y grin bubbles to the front of my face and, along with it, every dunce-y thing a guy could say around a girl. One word from my idiot face will drive off Pixie and every girl within earshot. *Come back, cool. Come back.*

I swallow hard and mange to spit out, "Qʷóqʷésk̓ iʔ. Everyone calls me Squito."

She laughs, warm, sweet. Maybe she titters, cos of the way it jiggles her boobs. My want of her is that first swallow of lemon gin after my father leaves for camp. Somehow my mouth finds her knuckles and kisses them, and my eyes hunt for hers. Whenever I think about kissing a girl, I never think of her hand, not cos kissing her hand is gross or stupid, but there are so many other places I'd rather kiss. Our eyes meet and tear each other's clothes off. We swirl into a different universe, one made for just the two of us. The second our bodies melt together, Pixie's ripped from me, and replaced by an angry ogre-eyed girl. Another girl drags Pixie away like a kid having a tantrum in the toy aisle. Pixie turns and mouths something like, *later*. Or *sorry.* Or *I love you.* I blow her a kiss. Even if Bernie shows up tonight, I want Pixie.

The other girls are Angelica Dykstra, Abigail Alfredson, Jeanine Reimer, Jennifer George (I never knew a sémeʔ with the last name of George before), Belinda Jamison, Henrietta la Boeuf, Joanne Yachenko and Ingrid Sorensen. Aside from ogre-eyed Angelica, the one who stole my Pixie right off my lips, they seem pretty nice. And ever snaggable. They hang in the kitchen with Auntie Max. Us guys hover around the record player in the living room but not Bimbo; he sits quiet and alone in Uncle Keith's easy chair, staring at his feet—probably cos Ingrid didn't fall at his feet like a lovesick puppy, the way he told us she would. JimJim flips through Auntie's 45s and stacks them in play order. Skinny runs over our playlist with me, JimJim, and Cody one more time while we move the furniture to make room for a good dance floor.

Skinny slaps JimJim's back. "Hey, JimJim. You gonna put on something groovy? Something that'll get everyone dancing. Know what I mean?"

"'Course." He puts on "Shambala."

Bimbo, from his corner, looking all serious, says, "I been thinking we should settle on a name, cos tonight is our night, if you know what I mean. We're like Three Dog Night, just a bunch of singers, right? So I think we should call ourselves Bimbo and the Four 'Skins. The girls'll dig us."

"We're not foreskins, you a-hole," Cody says.

JimJim adds, "Why should we name our band after you, anyways?"

"Cos Bimbo's got real music to it. And not *foreskins*, you idiot. *Four. 'Skins*, as in *redskins?* Don't you get it?"

Skinny's glare kicks Bimbo in the crotch. Skinny snarls, "What you're gonna get is your ass kicked all the way to Big Town and back. Anyways, what we need a name for? It's not like we're a real band, or anything."

"Skinny," JimJim says, "think about it. We're almost a real band. And he's right, we are like Three Dog Night. We sing good but we don't have our own songs."

"Never thought of it like that," Skinny goes. He taps two fingers to his chin and cocks an eyebrow Bimbo's way. "I guess the next thing you'll do's write some Shakespeare, hey?"

"Ha ha ha," Bimbo says, his face twisted into an angry-hurt-puppy-run-to-mama-pout-snarl. "I'm smart and you can't handle it, can you?"

Skinny rolls his eyes, shrugs, and turns his back to Bimbo. "Who's gonna take a bunch of Indians serious?"

"Look at Redbone," I say. "They made it."

"Right," JimJim says, "We need a name as cool as Redbone. Something that says we're warriors and we're not gonna be messed with."

"But I'm not Indian."

"You saying you don't want to be in the band?" Cody says.

"No. 'Course I do. But I don't want people thinking I'm a fricking Indian."

"Believe me," JimJim says, "No one will ever think you're a fricking Indian."

"Or any other kinda Indian, for that matter," Skinny goes.

"How about The Warriors?" Bimbo says, "A white guy can be a warrior."

"Or The Chiefs? For crisakes," JimJim says, "you want people thinking we're too stupid to come up with an original name?"

"Or an *ab*-original one, hey?" Cody says. "It's too bad we don't have a cool name like Mohawk or Blood or Apache."

"Why do we even need an Indian-sounding name, anyways?" Bimbo says. "I mean I'm as white as sunlight and," he points at me, "dick-breath there's just a half-breed."

"You calling me dick-breath?" I say.

"Must be. Cos you're the one answering to it," Skinny goes. Everyone but me laughs.

"ʔÚu," I say, "how is it you know what a dick smells like?"

Only Bimbo quits laughing.

"Enough," Skinny goes. "I dig the idea of having a name, so let's pick one before we play."

"It's gotta be good. Original," Cody says.

"Why original? We just sing other people's songs," Bimbo says.

In a low voice, Cody answers: "For now. I'm working on some we might do one day."

"Yeah, right," Bimbo says.

Bimbo shrinks before Skinny's words reach him. "Put a sock in it."

"Since when are you a songwriter?" JimJim says.

"Awhile, I guess."

"When were you gonna bring 'em to us?" Skinny goes.

Cody shrugs. "When they're ready."

"Let's work out a name and then give us a sample of what you got. Okay?"

"Sure."

"Hey," I go. "Wolfherder. How about Wolfherder?"

"What a stupid name," Bimbo says. "Who herds wolves? No one. That's who. Anyways, it's *pack* of wolves. Wolf Pack. Wolf Pack*er*. Way too fricking lame."

"I like the sound of Wolf," Skinny goes. "Wolf-something? Something Wolf. Mad Wolf? Foxy Wolf? Hey, Foxy Wolf." He laughs. JimJim snorts. Cody shakes his head.

"Nah," Skinny eurekas, "I got it! How 'bout Howling Wolf?"

"Howling Wolf's taken," Bimbo says.

"I know that. What kinda idiot you take me for?"

"Mad Wolf's got a nice ring to it," I say. "It's a little dangerous. A little heavy metal."

"Yeah," JimJim says. "I can already see our tee shirts. I don't want it howling at the moon, but I do see a wolf man, big muscles. Torn pants. No shirt. Girls'll dig it."

And I can see my Pixie in our tee shirt. And I can see her out of it. ?Úu, can I ever see her out of it. Cody likes Mad Wolf. Bimbo grumbles something. So we're Mad Wolf. I like it.

Cody pulls some beaten up hunks of paper from a pocket, unfolds them, and presses them flat.

He pulls up the top one, written on the back of one of Cow's pop quizzes. He scored a B-. I had no idea he knew math so good.

"This one's new. Wrote it this morning. I call it 'The Wrong Woman Blues.' I guess it's kinda bluesy."

"Would never 've guessed it by the title," Bimbo says.

Skinny snatches the paper from Cody. "Boss title. How's it sound? Can I see?"

Cody snatches at the paper. "Hey." And misses. "Hey. Gimme that. It's not done yet. Anyways, my handwriting's a mess."

"I can read it fine," Skinny goes. His lips, then the rest of him, move as he reads Cody's song. His jaw drops. He gapes at Cody. "You sure you wrote this?" Nodding, Cody steps back.

"Guys, hey. You got to hear this," Skinny goes. "Take a listen:

I know exactly what I have to say
but I can't when you look at me that way.
I know exactly what I got to do
something easy a better man would do.
instead of speaking, I stand in the doorway
like I can block your path and make you stay.
You may be right for me but I'm so wrong for you.
Why does loving you make me so goddamn blue?

"Je-zus-Christ-all-mighty. This could be about Muriel and me."

"Or you and any of your girlfriends," JimJim says.

"That's why they call me the lady killer, i'nit?" Skinny goes. "Cody, you mind me showing your song to Alex and Perry? I think they could do something with it."

"Maybe Cody should show his own song," JimJim says. "Them two don't like you much."

"Meh. They like me fine."

"What about—"

"What about nothing," Skinny goes.

"Suit yourself."

"No, really," Skinny goes, "it was just that one time. That's all."

"Shambala" ends. Aside from the girls chattering and giggling in the kitchen, and the record's *keh keh keh* the house is too quiet to be a party.

Alex and Perry Brown, twins born with music inside of them, listen to a song one time and they know it better than the guy who wrote it. Everything's a drum to Perry. He can make beautiful beats come out of a waterlogged cardboard box. Alex and Perry play together like they think with one brain. They make magic but they're kinda weird cos they don't drink and, except for Skinny, seem to like hanging around us drunks. They could make us a real band; never in a hundred-million years would I have even dreamed about being in a real band—never mind singing lead in front of a bunch of people.

"Jeez, that's intense. You got more?"

"About thirty, I guess."

"You serious? Lemme see, 'kay?" Skinny goes.

"Well, I got another one called 'The Wrong Woman Blues' that I kinda like."

"What the hell? Two songs with the same name? That's pretty screwed up," JimJim says.

Bimbo crows: "Like Cody."

Cody shrugs. "I call all of 'em 'The Wrong Woman Blues.'"

"Why?"

Cody, all cocked .357-Magnum-eyes, says, "It's their name."

He pulls out another sheet of paper, its back all blue-ink scribbles and its front a bunch of quick-written words.

Again Skinny snatches it and reads it, lips moving, head bobbing, foot tapping.

"Man, o, man!" he says. "This one's better than the first. But don't you have any other titles than 'The Wrong Woman Blues?'"

"Love the name," JimJim interrupts. "Maybe we could do a whole album of songs, nine or ten of 'em all called 'The Wrong Woman Blues.' Lemme see."

Skinny spins away from JimJim's snatching claw. "Yeah, I love it. We could call the album 'The Wrong Women Blues."

Cody smiles for maybe the first time all day, bites his lip and rolls his eyes. Laughter.

"So many wrong women, wrong girls," I say, "but you only need one that's right for you."

JimJim says, "Remember, mosta the fun's in the hunt. Hey, Skinny, hand over that song."

Skinny bats away JimJim's grabby paw. "In a sec. In a sec."

"Great name," Bimbo says, "but is there such a thing as a right woman for you?"

Fists raised, Cody says, "What's that supposed to mean?"

"Nothing. Can't you take a joke?"

Skinny snaps a slow four count. "Quiet, boys. Listen:"

Saw her at a party
man she sure looked fine.
I said to myself
that girl's gonna be mine.

So I wooed her 'n' I cooed her
whispering words so sweet
'n' I told my little honey
she knocked me offa my feet.
She ga' me a kiss. She wiggled.
She jiggled. I bought 'er a drink.
Her smile done disarmed me
'er skin as fine as mink
got me all slow 'n' stupid,
'n' thinking with my dink.
She wrapped me round 'er finger,
moulded me in 'er silky hand,
blinded me with promises,
telling me I was her man.
Turns out she had another,
some guy from outta town
Now I lay here crying
like some loser clown.

CHORUS
That girl has got me moaning
that girl has got me blue
so sad I feel like crying
them wrong woman blues.

"So, whadya think, boys. Think we should learn 'The Wrong Woman Blues?'"

Of course we should. Of course we should! But which one, or should we wait till we have an album's worth? JimJim says the same thing before I open my mouth.

We'll only be something if we play originals. That's what Fast Freddy told me. I'm glad Cody can write songs. I can barely write my name. Bimbo can't write anything, unless it's about poop. One time he made up this pretty funny poem about farting, but not Doctor Hook funny. Skinny can take someone else's song and fit new words over it, kinda like slapping Bondo on a rusty fender, I guess. JimJim might not write a single word but he'll make sure we practice hard and he'll make sure we get paid. Well, he'd use his brains and words, backed up with Skinny's fists and feet. Bimbo makes stuff happen, even though it's mostly on accident, so I'm the only one of us who can't do much of anything.

9:00 PM

It looks like everyone in town has spilled into Auntie Max's, filling her living room and kitchen, with a huge crowd around the front yard bonfire. But Auntie herself has disappeared—not in the kitchen, not in her bedroom, not in the living room, not all broody over them Ashcroft girls. So not like her, especially when she has a bunch of foxes to save from a bunch of dicks on the hunt.

Skinny slaps my back, knocking me forward a full step. He practically glows. "Look at 'em all! Must be a hunnerd and fifty people here. This is so cool."

Then he bobs his head and chews on his pinky nail, which now looks like my stomach feels. "You know what, Squito, I been thinking. Maybe we should do 'Four Years Older Than Me' the way Doctor Hook wrote it. Whadya think?"

Skinny just poured a bucket of ice water on my stomach butterflies. My brain screams out: *Wha'd I tell you? You should 've listened to me in the first place!* My mouth stutters, *"You sure?"*

"'Kay. I'm gonna round up the boys. You see if Byron and the Brown boys are ready to go."

The Browns, playing "Your Cheating Heart," stand in the middle of a crowd by the bonfire. I push my way to them as they finish playing and let them know we're ready to go.

Byron looks alone in his truck until I get close enough to see some girl's shiny black-haired head bobbing up and down over his lap. He jerks his thumb toward his shoulder, his face a twisted threat.

"They want us to start singing," I say.

"Five minutes," he moans. "I just need a few more minutes." He sucks in a huge, teethgritted breath. "Now fuck off, perv."

He pounds the steering wheel with one fist, clamps his other hand on top of the girl's head and pushes. He howls. I can't tell whether she finished him off or bit him. Then he flashes me that sly, tired smile. Man, o, man, that Byron's a lucky guy.

No Bernie, at least not yet. My brain sorta tricked me into believing she would be mine tonight, and left me a little sad, I guess, even though I sorta have Pixie now. All them Ashcroft girls have been pretty much trapped in the kitchen, surrounded by every guy in town. Most of them look goofy. Skinny says they're just a bunch of baboons waving their dicks at our girls. When my eyes meet Pixie's, our looks hold each other like Fred and Ginger and dance over those baboon-headed boys.

"You are so in," Skinny goes. "You got nothing to worry about. Let them monkeys dance for her. It's you she wants, you lucky dog." He slaps my back. He walks away singing, "Save the Last Dance for Me." I am King Kong, flipping off all the little monkeys on Skull Island.

At least fifty people have squeezed into Auntie's living room. The space we'd cleared for a dance floor is crowded with kids. Byron—with my cousin Georgina wrapped around his neck like a scarf and kissing him all over his face but not his mouth cos he keeps whipping it from her sucking lips—and his snare drum and high hat take up the middle of the couch, between the Brown boys. We take our places behind them: first Skinny, then just behind him on his right, JimJim and Cody, with me and Bimbo on his left. Some girl shouts "'Smoke on the Water.'" Then some guy calls out louder: "'Wipeout,'" and then, louder yet: "'China Grove.'" Brown boys' songs, all of them.

Skinny cocks an eyebrow, whispers something into Alex Brown's ear. Seconds later Alex and Perry break into "Down on the Corner," and everyone dances, mostly shuffling in place, and breathing as one. When we join Skinny for the chorus, everyone joins in. We rock Auntie's house. The Ashcroft girls don't dance like us. They kinda clunk and clonk along, their feet and upper bodies dancing to different songs. But ever-foxy Pixie's hips hypnotize me and she looks at me like I am her supper. My little chief groans and reaches for her. Not now! Not yet, you stupid. Cow. Cow. Cow. Cow. Cow-Cow-Cow. Cow-Cow-Cow-Cow. Cow.

Just before we sing out the last line, the Brown boys break into "China Grove" and our friends hoot and holler like the Doobie Brothers themselves have just walked into the room. Skinny sings with them. He sings louder. They play louder still. Me and the boys drink and shuffle, scoping the crowd. Pixie, eyes closed, grooves between the two taller girls, Ogre-eyes and the blonde—Ingrid, who seems to eye me up and down with her insanely sexy eyes, but not with love, not like Pixie. Pixie's eyes are wide open and stuck to me like humping dogs. The kitchen monkeys have walled behind the Ashcroft girls but most of the girls ignore them. Ogre-eyes swats my drooling eyes off Pixie, like maybe she wants Pixie the way I do. But even I can tell that Pixie wants me, not Ogre-eyes, and if I can see it, everyone can, cos when it comes to being thick about boy-girl things, I am the thickest. The one thing I am best at, cos no one else wants to be best at sucking at sex. I never had to fight anyone for a girl before, not that any girl ever made me fight to get her, so it has never even occurred to me that I might have to fight a girl to win a girl. On a night of almost-firsts, I can't say I look forward to this one cos I don't hit girls and, even if I did, Ogre-eyes could kick the living crap out of me. But what about Ingrid?

The Brown boys rip into "Smoke on the Water"—another song Mad Wolf never sings together, and a song so long I could walk all the way to Candace's, buy a bottle, and be back here before it ends. It snaps me out of my head and into the party. Skinny whispers something to Alex. They both look at me like I've got a booger dangling over my lip. Alex nods. Skinny and JimJim sing with the Browns. Auntie's house, steaming hot and rocking, bounces to our groove.

It could come down tonight. *The Hope Standard* headline will read: MAD WOLF AND THE BROWN BOYS BRING DOWN THE HOUSE! Them Browns together, a living jukebox, a real music machine, Indian maestros, could play whatever song you requested, and everyone loves every note. We don't know as many songs the Brown boys and Skinny refuses to sing the crowd's requests, cos he says they like a song more when you make them wait for it. Hearing them respond to the Brown boys' music now kinda makes me wonder whether Skinny's right, except they always go crazy when we finally sing. I guess when it comes to how people think and act, Skinny's usually right.

I chug my beer and open another. Me, Cody and Bimbo dance in our places behind the couch. We're pretty much go-go boys and as I dance, my brain paints Pixie dancing with me, and then shows me movies about life with Pixie, a happier-ever-after life. But it gets carried away and makes me start to grow a hard one—not major wood, just a little wood for my little red-haired girl. A woody for my redhead. There's music in them words and not just sappy violins. Maybe Cody could help me write a song for her. I guess he'd have to write it, cos I sure can't.

The music stops. Skinny stares everyone down and person by person the whole house quiets. The room feels like the gym during assembly, just before Principal Fish starts his weekly whine. Skinny, without guitar and drums backing him, sings: "Uh-oh, well I'm falling in love again, uh-oh. Uh-oh!" The Browns join in and almost instantly I feel like one of The Drifters singing a cowboy song. Skinny sings *her greenest of green eyes*, instead of bluest of blue. I feel like the world's greatest doo-wopper and there's no doubt in my mind that the Creator has blessed me with my very own little red-haired girl. Right now we are bigger rockstars than Fast Freddy and the Frivolous

Foot Notes. We feed love to the crowd and they feed just as much love back to us. The four of us dos-a-do behind Skinny. We could squeeze past a fat guy in the aisle of a Greyhound bus more easily but who cares? Pixie, smiling as big as a Cheshire moon, as bright as Sun, dances like we're already humping. I sing to her and her alone, and soon the world becomes just her and me.

We swing right into "Fais-do." Everyone sings the chorus with us. Instead of feeling shy and worthless, I feel like a star: even lemon gin doesn't make me feel this good. We don't sing it like Redbone but like a call answer song—JimJim's idea. Annabelle George two-steps in front of us. She can dance as good as anyone, maybe better than most. She's locked Skinny in her sights. Skinny says there's nothing going on between him and Annabelle but you have to wonder. Annabelle's best friends with Skinny's girlfriend, Muriel. It's their business, not mine. Skinny's always saying he's a one-night stand kinda guy but his only answer to why he goes with Muriel is a shrug. I guess Muriel's okay. She's kinda chubby and a good foot shorter than Skinny and quiet, until she's had a few. Skinny says she loves his Golden Sceptre but he says that about all girls.

Last summer, we're drinking way out in the bush and Skinny turns into a mean drunk, looking for a scrap. He goes all Sasquatch on this poor little kid from Dead Man's Creek—a cousin of JimJim's cousin, or something—and probably would've killed him but Muriel gets up in his face and stops him with a single word as sharp as a faller's axe. A few minutes later, she has him asleep. Alone. Almost anyone as drunk as Skinny would've blacked out. I think blackouts are a trick our brains play on us to keep us from killing ourselves after we climb out of a bender. But sometimes hearing about the shameful stuff you did the night before makes you want to kill yourself anyway. I guess you always pay a price for a good time but sometimes it feels like too high a price. Next morning, sitting around what's left of our fire, passing around a bottle of whiskey, Muriel tells Skinny, in front of us all, what an arse he'd made of himself the night before. He goes all red and stuttery and apologizes to the kid from Dead Man's, and then one-by-one to each of us. He doesn't even blame the booze. When I mess up bad, something I do a lot, I blame red wine. Cos I know what red wine does to my head, I try not to drink it, but after a while, it doesn't matter what's in your glass, as long as it blankets you under its loving burn.

9:30 PM

Near the end of "Come and Get Your Love" Skinny leans into me and whispers, "You ready?"

It's one thing to be with your friends in a laundromat and talk about singing lead and a whole nother to look out and see a thousand pairs of eyes looking back at you, waiting for me to screw up again. Just when I need it most, my brain abandons me like a sack of puppies on Dump Road. I nod at Skinny and draw in a deep breath. I've only had six or seven beers, so I can't even blame the booze for making me mess up.

Skinny pats my back, and says, "Forget about everyone, except Red over there. Sing it straight to her and you'll be fine. 'Kay?"

So I focus on Pixie. Our smiles find each other and sway to their own private tune. If it goes as bad as I think it will, I can blame her, but in a good way: "O, honey, your beauty took my breath away. I am so crazy for you I lost all my words. Except for these ones, I mean."

I miss my cue. Alex and Perry laugh and start over.

Bimbo grumbles, "Effing idiot."

Skinny goes, "Let's take it from the top," and counts me in.

My song fumbles out like a new-born foal. When I think about Pixie, my words paint themselves into pictures my tongue can't read. I guess I trick my brain into thinking I'm back inside the laundromat, cos by the end of the first verse I am the song. Byron even plays dance bells with his snare, so to me, anyway, we sound a lot like Doctor Hook. I'd like to say I have that Jagger swagger. I sing like a kid who wants to sing more than one who can. Really, I'm nothing but a doo-wopper, not a lead singer at all.

But no one boos or throws bottles at me. They're probably just being polite. Whatever, I'm relieved, a little, anyway. JimJim punches my shoulder before handing me a beer. He nods, points his lower lip at me. Butterflies the size of bats ripple my stomach juices. Skinny says we need to take a break but, before he joins the crowd, he puts his arm on my shoulder and says, "I knew you could do it. You keep singing like that and you'll end up taking my job." He laughs and fades into the crowd with the rest of the boys. I scan the room for Pixie and drop onto the couch. Them butterflies have turned my legs to rubber. She, along with the rest of the Ashcroft girls, have disappeared. "Four Years Older Than Me," was supposed to be my snagging song, and I sang it, setting my trapline, but it's empty. I got skunked.

9:35 PM

My heart heaves a heavy sigh and drains my beer. As I place my empty on the coffee table, Pixie bounces into view and, before you know it, she's on my lap. I accidentally push my cheek into her boobs. Her hummingbird heart makes mine stutter. My brain orders my cheek to let go of Pixie. My cheek says, "Screw you. I like it here." Her hands hold each other behind my neck. She leans into me. What if I fill my pants with jizz? I'll have to pee in them to hide it. Stop that stupid thinking; I'll make Pixie spill her beer. Our eyes recite love poems to each other but our lips play dumb. I ache to kiss this girl. I don't know where to start. Or how. I want to take her somewhere private; I have no idea how to get her there. I guess I'm not even sure about how to start anything like that with her.

"Drink?" I go. Idiot me. Idiot mouth. Why won't it swagger like Jagger?

She holds up her beer. "I'm good."

"You're better than good. You're the best." My words gush out like a teeny-bopper talking about Susan Dey. My stupid mouth is gonna drive away my new dream girl. (Not my dream girl: my here-and-now girl.) But she doesn't run. She giggles and turns a sexy shade of red. Her hands are soft on my face. I kiss each hand's heel. But it's her lips I crave. She squirms on my lap. Her fingertips press a little and, I think, she moans. I moan low and dog-like. Our breaths are the only sounds I hear. We've slipped outside of time, into a universe of two. My clumsy hand brushes her boob on its way to her cheek. She doesn't shy away from my touch. She kisses my thumb. Her kiss is a little stiff, awkward, wet and sloppy.

And then it's gone.

"There you are," Angelica says. It's more of a growl. It's ripped us from our private universe and back into a noisy, smoke-filled living room, jammed against an arm of the couch. With no girl on my lap. Auntie's stereo blasts "Chain of Fools." Ogre-eyed Angelica drags Pixie, squirming like a well-hooked trout, through the crowd.

"Let me go, Ang. You're not the boss of me. Let me go, right now," Pixies squeals. She sounds like a three-year old. "Squito, help me!"

"Squito, stay right where you are." This new voice isn't threatening. It belongs to a pair of long legs in tight jeans. It belongs to a belly button peeking out where a shirt should've been. It belongs to a tight little shirt that starts just below a set of tiny boobs. It belongs to a beautiful neck, wrapped in shiny blonde hair. It belongs to a mouth almost as fine as Jane Fonda's. It belongs to a nose as pretty as Cyndi Wood's. It belongs to a set of blue eyes, round, wide and shiny as wet glass. She kneels on me, her hands on my shoulders. She leans into me and our eyes shake hands. She wears Charlie, a smell so powerful they barred girls from wearing it at our school. It's not like the ban they put on eating garlic, cos that was just rank (and a great way to get kicked out of school for a day or so). No, they banned Charlie cos it made us guys so drunk with lust we couldn't concentrate on our work.

This girl's Charlie tries to erase all my memories of Pixie but it fails.

"I'm Ingrid," she says. "In case you've forgotten."

"Hi, Ingrid. Yeah, I remember. We met earlier. In the kitchen. You're one of the Ashcroft beauties."

"You're such a liar. You didn't remember my name, did you?"

"I remember you're one of the tallest girls, and the prettiest."

"Prettier than Pixie?" Her laugh hides a hint of meanness. Or anger. Or hurt feelings, cos I don't recall much about her, about any of them girls, not after seeing Pixie.

"That's not fair. You're pretty in your way and she's pretty in hers.

It's not like one of you is more or less prettier than the other."

She laughs some more. This time it sounds much friendlier. She slides her knees off of my thighs and I am grateful, cos they were about to give me charley horses. My mouth tastes her neck. I like it but I'm not sure this new girl does. She pulls away, cups my chin in her hands.

"So you'll try to jump anyone who comes along? You know Pixie's my friend. What do you think she'll do if I tell her you were putting moves on me?"

"It was on accident," I say. "Anyways, it was your neck touched my mouth. And I guess I kinda forget myself when a girl's wearing Charlie."

"See You Later Alligator" plays in the background. People have moved on, leaving enough space for Annabelle George and Skinny to jive. Those two can dance.

"It can't drive you *that* crazy. You're acting like I'm not even here."

"O, sorry. It's not you. It's them. They dance good. You should watch."

Ingrid moves onto my lap. I'm eye level with her boob. Her shirt's so tight I can see all the hard little bumps around her just-as-hard nipples. It's almost as good as x-ray vision but not as good as having her sit on me like this with her top off. What's Pixie gonna do when she gets back? If she gets back. I was only joking when I said I wanted girls to fight over me. I hope the grandfathers aren't playing some trick on me to teach me a lesson I don't want to learn.

"They can dance. Can you?" She jumps up and tries to pull me up with her. She's strong. Way stronger than me, that's for sure.

"But."

"Butt?" she goes. She shakes hers in my face. I don't know if it's a good one or a bad one. It's just a bum. On a girl I like boobs and smiles and hair and eyes and boobs (I like them so much I have to mention them twice, cos you can't have just one!) Whenever one of the guys says a girl has a nice butt, I look and I try to see what makes it nice. Skinny likes them tiny. JimJim likes them a little bigger. Bimbo, just like my father, says every butt's a nice one. You can't ask anyone what makes a butt nice or not. You're just supposed to know. It's like they give you a tool but no instructions on how to use it. One thing I do know: it never hurts to say good things about someone to them.

"Nice," I say.

"Nice? Just nice? I have the best bum on our team," she says.

"Maybe the best one anywhere," I say.

"Too late. You can make up for insulting me by dancing with me."

Her crooked little smile is warm with just a hint of the devil. I could grow to like this girl. Even though she's almost a little taller than me. The next song is "Save the Last Dance for Me," by The Drifters. It's slow. I hold her close and she pulls me a little closer. My Home Waltz at a party?

"Kiss my neck again, if you want," she whispers. I taste her Charlie, a hint of sweat and something that tastes like more. As I'm already in trouble with Pixie and my night might end badly, I savour this time with my tall beauty, cos this moment might be all I have to remember.

I didn't know girls mowed each other's grass, like some of us guys do. I guess they're just as human and able to make stupid mistakes. It even makes sense that girls can chose who they want to be with; they don't have to wait to be chosen. I mean, two have picked me tonight. Both foxes, one a volcano, ready to explode, and the other one? Well, I'm not so sure what Ingrid's about. So I guess she's my mystery girl. I do like a good mystery. One thing I do know for sure: This girl is all but making me forget about Pixie.

We dance one more song. I would know which one but Ingrid's just asked me to go someplace we can be alone and that's all my brain cares about right now. Well, not just my brain.

10:00 PM

The bonfire's brilliant orange glow colours the night and all of us caught in it, maybe thirty people in all, in groups of two, three, six, and everyone, it seems, talks at once. There's a ranch hand shack off Auntie's horse barn. It's not much to look at and smells like a stall but it has a cot and some old wool blankets. There's even an indoor toilet but at this time of year, there's no water cos Auntie thinks it's safer to shut it down. Auntie will get mad if she catches me and Ingrid in the hand's shack. I'd rather her mad at me than have Ingrid say no cos we had to do it outside.

Ingrid grabs my shoulder and spins me to face her. Scared, maybe confused, or a little hurt, she says, "I thought you were taking me somewhere we could be alone."

"I am," I say. "Just past the fire. You see that shack?"

She nods, squeezes my hand a little tighter, scans the people around the fire and practically pulls me toward the shack.

My little chief starts to tango in my pants.

No tent. No tent. No tent.

My bigger brain paints a picture of Cow in frilly underwear, chasing me. But right now seeing an old woman squat to pee behind the pub would make me grow a hard one, so imagining mostly naked, un-sexy Cow fails to make my hard one wilt, just twitch and squirm like a worm on a hook. All the people around me, snagging or snagged, got better things to do than look at my crotch. All of them, even the girls, will pay attention to Ingrid, not me. And I guess I want all of them to see me sneaking off with this tall, beautiful white girl—my jump, maybe my girlfriend. I want all of them wishing they were me. I want them to cheer me on. I want them to see me with a girl about my age and not some old hag like Delores Brown. Then again, I don't want any of them banging on the door, listening in, peeping through the crack under the door or the old blanket covering the window over the kitchen sink. And then again, they could all see us two sneaking off with each other and think we're gonna do it. But what if I say something wrong and make Ingrid mad or make her think I'm some kinda idiot and then storm off? They'll see Ingrid huff off alone. They'll say, "That kid can't get nothing right. You shoulda seen him, all naked with that tall séme?, and he still couldn't do her."

"We go in through the barn," I whisper. "This way."

I tug her by her elbow.

"Is it really your birthday?" she goes.

"No. Why?"

"Well, you sang that song about it being your seventeenth birthday and I was thinking I might. You know?" Yes, I do know, but why you and not Pixie? I can't ask her that. After all, I am about to put my bird in her bush, or something like that. "I liked you best right from the minute you walked in the door," she says. "But I didn't think you even noticed me."

"O, I sure did, but, you know," I say.

"You went straight for Pixie. Every boy does, you know that? I should hate her but she's like a little sister to me."

"Actually," I say, "she sorta went straight for me. Anyways, Bimbo said you and him had something going."

"You mean Thaddeus? The only thing between that little creep and me is my two fists."

Ingrid stops. She takes my hands in hers and caresses my thumbs. "You have nice thumbs. They say you can tell how good a guy is in bed by his thumbs. Did you know that?"

"No. That's news to me," I say. "How's it work?"

"It's not science, silly boy. This chick I know won't sleep with a guy until she checks out his thumbs." She kisses my thumbnail. "She swears by it, and if anyone knows, it's her."

"It's a quiet place. And warm. Well, warmer than out here, for sure."

"Do you take girls here often?"

"I wish," I say. "You're gonna be the first."

"Of many?" she says. O, I wish.

"Well, hopefully just one," I say.

"Do you think I'm a black widow, gonna eat you after we mate?"

"No!" I say. She's bigger and stronger than me, yes, but it hadn't occurred to me that she'd kill me after she was done with me. She laughs. I need to learn how to make it so people don't laugh at me when I open my mouth. I guess the easiest way would be to keep my yap closed all the time, which I can do pretty well, until after I've had a few.

"You do know I was just joking, right?"

"'Course I did. So was I. Didn't you get it?"

She kisses my cheek. "You're sweet."

Auntie sold almost all of her horses this past summer. Except for some ghosts, her barn stands empty and dark. Its only smells are ghost smells—smells that lived in the barn before she and Uncle bought the place—cos Auntie keeps her stalls clean enough to eat off of, not that you'd want to eat where a horse has pooped. The shack has one room and the john. Except for the fact that its door's at the back-end of the horse barn, it feels more like a motel room than a home. Auntie keeps the door open when she has no help. The shack's key hangs on a hook near the door. I slip it into my pocket. Close and lock the door behind us. Flip the light switch. Dead. Right, Auntie shuts off the power when no one stays here cos it makes the barn safer from fires. Use my Zippo as a flashlight to find the Coleman lantern.

The Coleman takes its sweet time lighting up but when it does, it fills the room with light like a jarred sun.

"I love what you've done with the place. You sure know how to treat a girl," she says. I hold my breath until she laughs.

The bathroom stands where the stall Auntie Max's favourite mare P-41 (Uncle Keith had named her) had lived and died. It has no door now. One night some years ago, a handsome séme? from Clinton—too drunk to open the door, kicked it to splinters. He got himself fired, not so much for wrecking the door, but for calling Auntie and Uncle Keith bad names and blaming them for his stuck bathroom door. After a hard day on the ranch I guess most hands only have enough energy to shower and drink themselves to sleep, and maybe that's why Auntie tacked an old woollen blanket—a drunk tank souvenir—to the jamb instead of putting in a new door.

The shack has one window over the kitchen sink, covered by an old saddle blanket. The rough plank floor, mostly bare, except for an old round rag rug Yéye? had made, has ruts like deer trails to the bathroom and fridge, and a deep one on the fold-down couch. Two deep drawers in the kitchen counter store everything a hand needs: cast iron frying pan, pot big enough to cook Kraft Dinner in, church key, corkscrew—not that anyone bought fancy wine—enamel plate and bowl, some forks, knives and spoons, and an old wood-handled carving knife Uncle Keith had made at residential school. The two-door'ed cupboard over the counter now holds old bridles and other horse stuff. The one under the sink has cleaning stuff, a new bottle of whiskey—Silk Tassel, the good stuff—and a sweating magnum of Baby Duck; so, someone else has already thought about bringing his honey here. All I have to say to that is, Kʷukʷscémxʷ.

We won't need the two rickety kitchen chairs, glued and re-glued after many drunken accidents, that sit at the scarred round table, scrounged from The Princely Sum, the town's fancyschmancy restaurant, the one only tourists and about eleven səmséme ever ate at. Whoever left us the whiskey and Baby Duck also left a pile of firewood, kindling, and a few old Sears catalogues in the firewood box beside the stove. It may not be some fancy city hotel but maybe Ingrid will like it enough to stay all night. He even set out a coupla blankets and lumpy pillows on the lumpy fold-down bed. The couch.

"Nothing but the best for you, ma'am," I say. We can see our breath. I build a fire. The room starts to fill with smoke.

"You forget to open the flue or you deliberately trying to smoke us out?"

"'They said some day you'll find all who love are blind. When your heart's on fire you must realize, smoke gets in your eyes.'" I croon, goofing a shuffle dance as I fan the door until the smoke blows out.

Her crooked smile throws almost as much light as the Coleman. She claps and sways to my goofy tune.

"Bravo. Bravo. I'll let you sing to me all night, after you open the flue."

"O, yeah. I forgot."

She opens the flue. I close and lock the door. She pats a spot on the couch beside her. I keep up the goofy dance all the way back to the Silk Tassel and Baby Duck, then dance them back to her. I never dance. Never.

"O," she says, "expecting company, dear?"

She just called me dear. I'm in. I'm in. I'm in.

"Naw. Just got lucky, I guess."

I pop the Silk Tassel's cap, take a decent swig, and pass the bottle to Ingrid.

"I don't know what kinda girl you think I am, rock star, but I do not drink from the bottle. Find me a glass? Mix mine with ginger ale. And ice, if that's possible."

Two cans of cold Coke, two more of Ginger Ale, and a small stack of to-go cups sit in the stinky fridge. This guy thought of everything except a bag of chips or something else to snack on. He should write a book or something: *Snagging Rights (and Wrongs): or How to Impress the Pants Off Your sm?em.* He'd sell a million copies. Guys like me would eat it up. No one I know drinks Silk Tassel but every guy I know, the ones who get lucky, always gets Baby Duck for his girl. Baby Duck's a new thing, brought back to the village by some girls who stayed in Big Town awhile.

"No ice," I say. "No power for the fridge. I'm sorry. But the wine's still cold."

"You mean the Baby Duck."

"Yeah. It's all we got here."

"You don't fool me, Mister Mosquito. I know you boys call Baby Duck the panty remover."

"Actually, that's gin," I say. But not lemon gin, damnit.

"If I didn't know better, I'd say you were trying to get me drunk, young man." But you already are, right?

"Me?" I say. "That's not my style. I like to let the booze get you drunk."

"O, that's different then. I'll have a glass of that bubbly."

I pop the cork without taking out her eye or anything, and spill next to none of it. I fill one of the takeout cups.

Ingrid takes a small sip and shudders. "Like that fat guy on TV says, 'mmmmmmm, that's good booze.'"

We touch our glasses together and drink. Like Elvis, my words have left the building. I have no idea what to say to this girl. I feel like a faithful puppy waiting for a scritch or a biscuit. I feel like I'll bore her out the door if I don't say or do something smart, and soon. I wipe my chin, checking for drool. After slurping a bit too much of my drink, I say, "How long you played volleyball?"

"Since Grade Seven." She blushes. "Coach kinda made me. I mean, I already played basketball and pitched fastball, but she said I was too tall and too talented not to play volleyball."

She takes a tiny sip of her drink. "You know," she says, nudging me, "I really wish I could play ice hockey. Wish girls were allowed." She sets down her drink and puts both hands on my knee. Yee haw!

"You think that's weird?" she asks. I shake my head and swallow hard without taking a drink, then shift my hips.

"No! I mean, no. Girls should be allowed to play ice hockey." After all, they let me play and I can't even skate.

"You really think so? That means so much to me. It really does." She moves into me and kisses my cheek. Just cos I said girls should play hockey? I don't get it. I just don't get it. And then she starts to talk: She plans to go to college and doesn't understand why I don't. She doesn't know what she wants to be after college. She thinks she might want to be a marine biologist and work with Jacques Cousteau, or maybe the first girl to ever play in the NHL. She wants to work with starving Biafrans, solve world hunger and stop wars. She wants to be the first woman Prime Minister of Canada. She dreams bigger than I used to, not that I've had a dream worth mentioning since my first report card in Grade Two, when I found out I was slightly dumber than a stick.

Ingrid talks more than she drinks and I listen more than I drink.

"I've nearly talked your ears off. So, tell me about you. Why'd your mom name you and what does that even mean?"

"O, my mom didn't give me that name. My Auntie Violet did."

"What," she says. "What did your mom call you?"

"They say she called me bad things. But I don't know for sure, cos I was too young to remember."

"So you had no name?"

"O, yeah. She named me Darryll."

"That's a way nicer name than Squito, you know?" Maybe, but I am Squito.

"I go by Squito. It's short for Mosquito."

"And you like being named after a nasty little bug? Is there something wrong with you?"

"Prob'ly. But they haven't found out what," I say. She laughs.

"No. Seriously. I want to know your name. I want to know all about you."

"There's not much to know. I earned my name when I was eight. I had a broken leg. Walked with crutches and stuff. I took on two big white guys. I mean, old guys. In their twenties, at least. Smashed my crutch on one them and broke his arm. Well, I guess the way he landed on it actually broke it. They tried to kick the crap outta me after that but my Auntie Violet came out and finished them off."

She rubs my thigh. I want to chug back my wine, pour another, and then another. I just told her that I lost a fight and had to be saved by my auntie. Why? Do I want her thinking she's wasting her time on a wimpy guy like me?

"Why'd you try fighting them?"

Instead of a deep breath, I take a gulp of my drink. I can't bring my eyes up to meet hers.

"Cos they were rude, I guess."

"They were rude? That's it?"

"Yeah."

She bobs back and forth, trying to lock focus on me. Her crooked smile is almost a sneer, but it's not.

Next thing I know, she flops on top of me. I'm in bed with a real girl and I'm not so drunk I'll forget what happens between us. Her lips stagger toward mine and we fall into a drunken kiss. Her hand squeezes my crotch, a little harder than I'd have liked, but a real girl has her hand on me and mostly in a good way. My hands freeze. They must be shy and stupid, just like the rest of me.

"You aren't gonna just lie there like a dead fish, are you?" she says.

Girls do that. It's one of the first things Skinny says about a girl who's bad in bed. Has she already forgotten what my thumbs told her about how good I should be? Could be? Her hands, as heavy as irons, plough their way up my belly and chest. They close on my cheeks. She kisses me hard and long. My arms fold around her. We kiss a good long time, not outside of time, as with Pixie, though: I feel every second. It's like counting down those last seconds of your school day. Sexing up a girl is supposed to be different, mad, and crazy-wild, tearing each other's clothes off and then bumping uglies until we become the universe. But here I am, with a pretty girl, on a lumpy, itchy-wool blanketed fold-down bed, under a harsh white light, and the ghostly stink of old horse-pee. We grope and try to swallow each other's faces. She shoves my hands away from her when they close around her boobs.

"Don't," she says. "Don't touch me there." How does she expect me to do it without playing with her boobs? That's just dumb. She sits up and I want to pull her back down to me but I sit up, resting a hand on her thigh.

"I don't usually go off with strange boys, you know," she says.

"So, I don't usually go off with strange girls."

She slaps my chest with both hands, hard enough to drop me onto my back.

"You liar."

"I'm not lying. I didn't say I didn't want to go off with strange girls. It's just that I haven't."

"Have you even been with a girl?"

"I guess there was one time but I'm not sure that one counts."

"Of course it counts. Tell me about it." Really, it don't matter. What counts is right here, right now with you.

"What's to tell. We liked each other. We bumped uglies. The end."

"You're a natural storyteller, Mosquito Boy."

She pats my hand and drags it up her thigh, not all the way up it, just far enough to send a zillion bolts of electricity straight to my heart. I kiss her cheek and let my hand slither up between her legs. She doesn't yank it out but she squeezes it so tight I can't move it at all and I don't mind. I don't want to talk about other girls. I don't want to talk about anything. Everyone says you never talk about other girls you've had with the girl you have. It always ends badly, at least that's what all the guys say. I tell her it's not important, that there's nothing to say. Her thighs are hot. My hand feels like warm butter between them. She asks me a thousand questions and I answer them, telling her about my dream girl and the time I didn't sex her up but thought I had. My fingertips, all four of them rest at her vee. I tell Ingrid I slept with someone else, I just don't tell her who. If she wants to know, she can ask just about anyone else, cos they'll be happy to tell her the whole ugly story. Even though it happened ages ago, they still talk about it like it happened last weekend, and I still go all run-for-the-bridge red, ready to die cos of one stupid act every time someone brings it up. She unbuttons my pants.

"I haven't been with that many boys, you know?" she says. "Actually, just one, until you came along. We just broke up. We started going together in Grade Six. That's a long time to be with one boy.

"He was my first. My only one, so far," she says, then pulls down my zipper. "So, I hope you don't expect too much from me. Just know that I want you to be my second one."

"Really?" I unsnap her pants and tug at the zipper. My hands act as if they've just gotten a degree in doing it. She wiggles, helping me get her free of her pants.

I grab at her underwear. She yoinks free of my grabby paws. "I said you'd be my second. I didn't say do me right this second. What's your hurry? We have all night, don't we?"

"Sorry. I feel like a kid on Christmas morning. I want you real bad."

"Do you think I'm the best piece of cake you ever had?"

"Best everything," I say.

"I don't expect I'll see you after tonight. Will I?"

"I'll be driving in a year. But I could thumb out your way on weekends, maybe some week nights, too."

"I'm not looking for a boyfriend. I just lost one. I just don't want you to jump me and dump me."

"Not a chance. I real like you, Ingrid."

"*Really*," she says. "You *really* like me."

"Yes. I real, real like you."

She laughs. "I know that. It's just that you say *real* when you should be saying *really*."

"Same difference, i'nit?"

Our Grade Four teacher was a Nazi war criminal, at least that's what they say, and I believe it, too. Her name was Miss Swatunten and she wielded a yard stick like a nun and used it like one, too. A lot. She hated any word ending in *ly* so much that she'd club you with her yard stick if you said even one of them. She especially hated really. It was one of about sixty words I used, so it popped out almost every time I had to talk in class. What did I think of "The Fog?" It was a really good story. *Spank! Spank! Spank!* According to Miss Swatunten, it was an exceptional example of writing by a Canadian woman. To me it was just a story and a little bit scary. They say she passed me so I wouldn't be in her class again. If you ask some people, they'll tell you I coasted through school cos I was just a dumb half-breed, Indian, idiot, juvenile delinquent. I guess they were all right, except I'm not so sure about *dumb idiot*.

"Yes," she says. "Same difference. It's pretty clear to me you're neither dumb, nor an idiot," Ingrid says. "Maybe you're just lazy?"

Lazy (half-breed, Indian, idiot, juvenile delinquent). I hear that a lot, too. Hearing people call me names like that is pretty much the same as jumping into cold water, cos it shocks you at first but pretty soon you get used of it. I don't think Ingrid's calling me any of those names, it just feels like it. A little.

"I work hard, just not at school. I don't see what good it does, going to school, I mean."

"O, man," she says, "I dig that. Don't even get me started about school. Ugh! Who cares if Sally has four apples and gives three of them to her horse? Lucky horse, I say. And why do they make us find the damned topic sentence? If it was so damned important, you'd think they'd underline it or put it in plain language so we can find it easier. No. They hide the damned thing and ask you questions written in gibberish and then give you C-pluses because they don't know how to write a goddamned question a normal person can answer."

She laughs. She puts her hand on mine.

"Some things upset me. We could be learning so much about important things. Instead they waste our time with nonsense."

"What kind of important things?"

"Well, history. How our government works. How to feed the starving. How to distribute our wealth in ways that don't hurt anyone. Important stuff. How would we colonize the moon or Mars or Venus? I could go on."

Everyone says girls will latch onto you and start talking marriage and other scary stuff five minutes after you meet them. The guys always talk about sleeping with one foot out the door. They practice their leaving lines. I'm not gonna tell her I'll call or visit, not if I don't mean it. Maybe Ingrid'll want to be my girlfriend after we're done but prob'ly she won't want to see me ever again. I want her to want to see me again and again and again. For more than humping.

"You're staying for the dance tomorrow night? It's gonna be a good one. Maybe the best dance all year. Fast Freddy and the Frivolous Footnotes. The Footnotes? You know them?"

"I'm not big on popular music. Sorry. But, yes, we're gonna stay for the dance."

The Footnotes aren't pop music. They're a rock band. I say nothing. Ingrid wants to go all the way with me. That more than makes up for her small boobs and lack of musical knowledge. Anyway, I like the way she talks and most of what she says.

"Listen. The only reason I told you I was going to sleep with you is so we can just get to know each other like real people."

"*Really* people," I say. She slaps my arm. "And?"

"Well, we could talk and talk all night but all the while you're thinking about how you can get inside my pants. Don't deny it. You were, weren't you?"

"Not exactly. But yeah, I guess it was on my mind a little."

We talk and drink and sometimes we kiss. She lets me touch her crotch over her underpants. Moist. Warm. She doesn't let me put my hands up inside her top, won't let me anywhere near her boobs at all. Every time she slaps my hand away from her boobs, I want them more. I'm sure they're a mouthful and they say more than a mouthful's a waste. She tells me they're hers and she doesn't want me touching them. My hands have other ideas. She's winning, so far.

She asks me to kill the light. I put a fat log on the fire, turn off the Coleman lantern, then crawl under the covers with her. She pulls off my shirt and then my pants and underwear. Although it feels a little weird at first, it kinda turns me on, and when she touches my dink, it's not on accident. Her touch takes my breath away.

We've finished the Baby Duck and some of the whiskey. I'm naked and she's only wearing her top.

We have a bit of a hickey war.

My hands cup her boobs now and again, mostly on accident. She doesn't slap them down but she still says no. I kiss her belly button. She tells me not to put any marks on her down there, even though she has them just about everywhere anyone could see. We hickey each other up pretty good. My dink brushes against her, sneaks a little way inside her. She pulls it out and rubs it in a good way. A real good way. My little chief spits up. I groan. She giggles. I try to leave some hickeys on and around her parts. She moans. I didn't mean to hurt her, so I stop, but her hands find my head and kinda guide me back to what I was doing. She makes some happy sounds. I do, too. One of my hands finds its way up under her top and it closes on a round little boob and its dime-sized nipple. Ingrid says nothing. My other hand goes up there. Before I know it, my mouth is on one and then the other. Ingrid moans and squirms a bit. It's the sexiest sound in the world. I try sucking my initials onto her boobs. Anyone who says bigger ones are better has never given smaller ones a chance. Anyways, I might actually like Ingrid more than any of her body parts. I'm not saying I'll ever say no to a set of big ones—all of a sudden, my brain starts to sing something like "Hoochie Coochie Man": it's just that I'm a boob man, o yes I am. I'm a boob man, o, yeah. Big or small, I like 'em all, cos I'm a boob man. What a crummy time to come up with my first song. If I remember it at all, it'll be a miracle.

Ingrid's hands aren't all over me any more. One of my fingers worms its way inside of her and she moans a bit. Her breath isn't all hot and horny any more. I whisper her name. Her answer is gibberish.

And then she snorts.

Snores.

Ingrid's passed out on me.

I guess I was too slow, or too boring.

Great, I put her to sleep with my loving. Thing is, I'm more than hot and so ready to go again. My brain tells me she'd said I could do it to her, that we would do it, and we were well on our way. My brain also says she's not the kinda girl who'd leave me high and dry like this, that she's not a tease. I doubt she'd mind if I went ahead and put it in her. Then again, I was blacked out or passed out when Dolores Brown did it to me. I'm sure I asked for it, but I couldn't say and I can only guess that I had fun. I don't really want to do that to Ingrid, although I might never get this chance with her ever again.

I've drunk enough booze to sleep for a good long time, enough liquor to kill any shame I might feel, or may have felt, for what I may do, or may want to do but I—as naked as tall, beautiful, gently snoring Ingrid—toss and turn beside her, reliving the moment I awoke after Delores Brown sexed me up. At the time, I had no clue as to who took my boy cherry and not knowing for sure tore at my guts. Would helping myself to Ingrid leave her feeling as crappy inside as Delores had left me? I will probably never see Ingrid again. But I want to. Would helping myself right now mean she will never want to see me again? Wouldn't we both like it better awake? But girls don't like it, my father had said. They just do it for us guys, my father had said. Only sluts like sex, my father had said, so take what you want when you want it. But Ingrid is no slut. Why can't girls like it as much as us guys? The guys I know all talk about sex like it's the only thing worth living for. So why wouldn't a girl want to stay awake for sex? Why wouldn't she care about sleeping through it as much as I had? Ingrid's smells live on my lips, nose, and chin, and tickles my horny-bone like her perfume had.

She said she would give it to me.

She said she wanted to do it to me.

She said she wanted me to do it to her.

She said yes.

She finished me with her hand.

Does that count?

Is that what she meant?

It felt good. Real good and only a little embarrassing. My little chief spat up like a burped baby. Ingrid, already kissing me, kept kissing me, and didn't act all grossed out by the mess it made on her. And she let me kiss her down there. Made me kiss her down there. And I liked it.

They all said you never put your mouth there. Never. I would do it again. And again. And again.

Thinking about her and that thing I did with my mouth wakes up my dink. She moans, grumbles sour-Baby-Duck-scented words and slides away from it. I rock my hips back, keeping my upper body as close to her as she lets me. Even though my arm sleeps under her sleeping head.

Me. Lying next to tall, pale, blonde, perfume-haired Ingrid, a girl whose smile all but stops my heart. Me, all alone with a beautiful girl, a beautiful, naked, softly snoring girl. Her mouth hangs open. Drool dribbles out its corner. The most beautiful girl in my world. I want to hump her, to nudge her awake and flop on top her. Would that be okay? Can a guy go twice in one night, if whacking me off counts as the first time? Would she want to go again?

My hard one aches. It wags like a dog's tail and it's about to puke on her like a carsick dog—that dog who gets so excited about going on a ride it forgets it hasn't the stomach for car rides.

Eyes closed, painting pictures of Cow in her frilly underwear, dancing like those hippos in Fantasia, fails to erase beautiful Ingrid from my mind. Cow takes off her frilly bra and her boobs hang over her belly like limp windbags. She shakes them in my face. Her scratchy voice wilts me like day old lettuce. Kʷukʷscémxʷ, Cow. Kʷukʷscémxʷ. Cow chides me like I've forgotten to carry the ten again. She says: "X doesn't equal y. X equals Ingrid. If x equals Ingrid and y equals you then, Yyou? YnotArealMan-Boy?" Why me is right. This beautiful girl deserves more than me, a better guy than me. But she picked me. So, Cow, yme equals $e\ (410 \times 164) \div \sqrt{2}$. "Your math is, as usual, grotesquely flawed," she says. See Ingrid? In my bed? With me? We did it? We did it. Cow scoops up her frilly bra and fades. And for once in my life, maybe the one and only time, I want to show my father anything: "See, old man? My dink does more than shoot piss. So screw you."

Under the light thrown by my Zippo, Ingrid looks like an orange goddess from the golden age of myths and legends. This light makes her even more beautiful, if more beautiful is possible. Ingrid has all the same parts as other girls, but on other girls those parts don't touch me the same way, and not every girl is beautiful, and some, you wouldn't even think of as pretty, like Cow, who is so far from beautiful she can't even say the word.

Just one word, that never means the same thing the same way.

Ingrid, practically boobless and beautiful.

Cow, huge-boobed—uddered—and barely human.

Pixie, all her parts perfect and bursting with love, drives me wild, but her green eyes—them lovers that heat up your dreams—drive me wilder. Cow, saltpetre of a woman.

Beautiful. Four girls, well, three beautiful girls and Cow.

Bernie, the perfect girl, with Raquel Welch hair and boobs, whose eyes laugh at you and hump you at the same time. Funny, smart, cheerful, the most beautiful of beauties, and the one I could love a long, long time. If she would have me.

I lie with Ingrid and dream of sexing up Pixie and loving Bernie. Dreamy, hot movies with Pixie and Bernie form behind my eyes and those hot pictures fire up my mood, drive me to want to hump Ingrid, who already—all by herself—fires up my mood. I could hump her right now but she's asleep and I'd be jumping her with my body, not my mind, not my heart.

Cow comes back when I call. Dressed like Vampira, she remains Cow the ugly.

Cow chases away Pixie.

Cow the bad.

Cow chases away Bernie.

Cow the gorgon.

Cow chases away my hard one, twists my nuts till I feel like puking. Then she twists them tighter.

I kiss Ingrid's shoulder. She moans a drooly *don't* and scootches away from me. I cover her, turn my back to her. Our bums touch. I re-invent our sex—or whatever you call it—into stories I can tell my friends. I will take the first sip from a bottle, stab its mouth with my tongue, and then tell them how great putting your mouth on a girl's privates feels. Skinny will punch me. JimJim might punch me too. Cody will laugh. Bimbo will gag. And I will have sexed up a beautiful white girl from Ashcroft.

SATURDAY

4:30 AM

Her top, all bunched up above her boobs, looks like I'd ripped it off her. Her hickeyed-up boobs; her hickeyed-up neck, hickeyed-up thighs, hickeyed-up belly, in the flickering orange light of my Zippo she looks as though I've beaten her and left her for dead. A decent guy would cover her boobs up at least, not gawk at her like she's the first girl he's ever seen naked. A decent guy wouldn't've hickeyed her up the way I have. So what kinda guy does that make me? I can't see my neck but she put a hickey the size of a softball between my belly button and the top of my pubes. She didn't leave one on my dink. I don't know why not and I can't say I want to know. I haven't been in a hickey war since Grade Six and I never left any like the ones I've given Ingrid.

How can a guy feel horny and bad at the same time? My hand spiders her waist, inches toward her belly button. Ingrid swats my hand away.

"Stop it," she says. "No."

"O, honey, you know you got to start the day with a bang."

"Ugh, no. You have buzzard breath," she says.

"So do you. What's the problem?"

"Not when I'm like this. Can't you wait?"

"I could. But I'm not sure I want to."

"Want isn't need. Want can wait and so can you."

She rolls over and pulls her knees up toward her chin.

"Just let me sleep. One more hour. Okay?"

"Do I have a choice?"

"Nope. Now shut up and let me sleep."

Shot down. Even naked, lying next to a naked girl and I still can't go all the way. At this rate, I'm gonna die an almost-virgin. For a few ugly minutes I hate Ingrid and I want to take her the way a guy should. Whenever I think about doing it to a girl my dink jumps to life and starts pulling me toward her, or the nearest girl, but this time it sorta shrinks. I snuggle up beside her, careful not to touch her sweet little boobies or let my crotch touch any part of her.

"You know I told you not to go anywhere near my breasts," she says. There's no real anger hidden in her words.

"I thought you changed your mind about that. Just so you know, you got the nicest boobs I ever saw. I mean that. The nicest."

"Yeah, right." She covers them with her shirt. "What else did you help yourself to last night?"

"What you mean?"

"Don't play dumb. You took off my pants. Did you do it to me after I passed out?"

"You took off your own pants and you took off my pants, too. I let you take mine off. I almost did it to you but I stopped cos you were snoring. But at first I didn't know you passed out on me. I didn't."

"I'm not like that. I never just crawl into bed with any old boy." She makes a sound like choked off crying, I can't tell. "I should know what you did to me. A girl should know what's been done to her body. We're not stupid, you know."

"You could be the smartest girl I know. You are anything but stupid. Anyways, you should know I didn't touch you in that way. You do know I didn't touch you like that, right?"

"Touch? You mean screw me? I don't know you at all. I don't know what you would or wouldn't do," she says. "I really don't." Her body rocks like she has hiccoughs and she goes quiet for what feels like forever.

"Anyway, I suppose it doesn't matter much, because I said we were gonna do it. I know I said I was gonna let you screw me," she says, weakly.

"Yeah, you did, but I figured it'd be better if we did it in the morning. You know, when you weren't snoring and drooling all over me?"

"Eww. And who in their right mind wants to have sex in the morning? Not before brushing their teeth at least."

"Me, for one." Even if wanting to sex up this girl right now makes me wrong-minded, I'm pretty sure there was a way we could do it without killing each other with our morning breath. Man or monster, just what are you?

"Not me. Not ever. So you can just forget about it."

My shriveled dink says, "But you promised." Even in my brain it sounds like it's a big, fat whiny baby. Man or whiny monster? Maybe we'll get another chance, either here, or at the dance.

My shriveled dink puffs out its sunken chest: "I will get inside Ingrid's pants." Is my dink the boss of me? Man or monster?

Ingrid sits up. Her eyes pop open. She turns white and then pink and then red. She touches my neck, chest, and the hickey above my pubes.

"I didn't," she says. "I did, didn't I?"

"Did what?"

"Don't make me say it. Please."

"How can I, when I don't even know what you mean?"

Man or flesh-eating monster?

My mind paints pictures of me and Cyndi Wood in *Playboy*. She tells me she likes it when I look at her, all hungry for her. Not at all panicked and maybe-mad like Ingrid.

"You didn't put any of those disgusting things on me where anyone can see them, did you? Please say you didn't," she says.

"I can't say I didn't."

Monster. Definitely monster.

"All I asked of you, just one thing: Leave my tits alone. And look how that turned out."

Whiny monster.

Monster.

Flesh-eating monster.

Yéye? told me I wasn't ready for a girlfriend. Now I sorta see why. She said, at my age, girls were too much trouble. I thought she was just trying to keep me from putting babies in them. I'm pretty sure she won't ever have to worry about that, not the way things are going for me. I guess Yéye? was right, as always. But maybe she meant I was too young to understand them? Maybe I could start listening to her instead of trying to show her she has no idea how to be a kid these days.

"I thought," I stutter. "I thought. Never mind what I thought. I'm real sorry. Stuff happened. I guess I got carried away. And you never told me to stop."

"How could I? I wasn't just drunk—"

"Both of us were drunk."

"For crying out loud, I'd passed out."

"I guess maybe you did. I didn't know. It's not like you weren't doing stuff to me, too. I mean, you don't think I put them marks on my own spaeks?, do you?"

"Your what?" she says. Her eyes follow my arms down to my hands, covering my bits. "Uh, okay. Okay. It was all my fault. I asked for it and I got what I asked for. You happy?"

Vile monster. Monster. Evil monster.

"No. I didn't do anything wrong but I coulda, you know. And you didn't do anything wrong." She bats my hand away and pulls the blanket over her nakedness. It's cold. Goosebumps cover me and I've shriveled up so much it hurts like a groin punch. My brain kicks my balls, too, and tells me we're not gonna do it, not now, not ever, so I pull on my clothes.

"I'll build a fire," I say. "It'll warm the room up pretty quick."

"What's the point? I don't want to spend the whole day here." Ingrid doesn't say *with you* but I hear it.

"I real like you and I want to see you again," I say.

"Well, I don't exactly hate you. But I have volleyball and school and stuff. I'm not ready for another boyfriend."

"I mean *boy*. Friend. Not *boyfriend*."

"Just until I let you screw me?"

"I'd like that but no. I mean, not like a one-nighter or anything like that. We had a good time even before we started messing around. I liked talking to you. As I said, I *real* like you."

"You *really* like me."

"'Swat I said, i'nit?"

"Do you know what deja vu is?"

"Course I do. 'It's like deja vu all over again.'"

Her face looks as if she's just swallowed a lemon. I hope she doesn't puke. We drank a bunch of different stuff and finished off that whole magnum of Baby Duck, a wine that makes almost everyone puke until you get used of it.

"I put all those marks on you? I am so sorry. You have a turtleneck, right? You're not gonna let anyone see them? Are you?" she says.

"'Course I am. I like 'em." These hickeys will show everyone I got some. Last time I had any hickeys was during a lunchtime hickey war, back in Grade Six. Of us all, I was the only one who got suspended for a week. My father told me that the principal wanted me charged with something but couldn't cos I was too young to have charges put on me.

"They're disgusting. I never want you doing that to me again."

"You can give me as many as you want," I say. "Wherever you want." Saying those words paints a happy smile on me. Monster. Monster. Monster. My brain paints what it remembers onto its walls so I'll remember, too. Sometimes I like my brain, even when I hate me.

"If you tell anyone about what we did last night, I will kill you. My dad can never know about you and he cannot know anything about what we did last night."

"How's he gonna know? He's like two hours away."

"People talk."

People do talk, that's for sure, especially if it's bad or ugly. Stories about me come to life and pretty much tell themselves to whoever's listening, and then they get mangled up and retold and mangled some more. Before you know it, my story belongs to someone else, except I live on as its punchline.

"Okay," I say, thinking: I'll only tell my closest friends and no one else. I promise. Monster. Monster. Monster.

I build a small fire. It's early yet. Not even five in the morning, so there's no point in going back to the house, not with people passed out everywhere. You can bet at least one couple will be doing it pretty much in plain sight and I don't really want to see that. I doubt Ingrid will, either.

Ingrid squawks from the john. The toilet has no water; she can't flush. Her big, hairy conniption confuses me cos we went through this whole thing last night. I even went out and pumped two pails of water the first time she had to go. I guess I forgot to fill them again for this morning. She slides the pails under the curtain. Barefoot, I head to the pump.

What a mistake.

Of all the prayers to have answered, the Creator chose to make a dump of snow, just like I asked for. He hasn't answered my other prayer, the one I want more than any other. A good six inches of snow covers the ground and more swirls in Wind, as she carves it into drifts. "Serves you right, Monster," Wind says. She hisses, slapping my face with glass-sharp gusts of blowing snow. Walking back to town will take forever. I hope Wind hasn't blocked up the

Canyon to keep The Footnotes from giving us the dance. Maybe He did answer my other prayer. I mean, I wanted to be trapped with a beautiful girl and here I am, trapped with a beautiful girl. One who won't pee unless there's water for her to pee into.

Melting snow on the stove is a little slow cos there's only one dutch oven and the pails are plastic but I sit them close enough to the stove so they can feel its heat and not get cooked by it. When you live in a small place with a bunch of other people you learn to un-hear and un-smell bathroom sounds and smells. It's pretty plain to me that Ingrid doesn't live that way. She tells me over and over again the booze made her have the most unladylike accident in the toilet. Laughing at her right now should be okay. She acts like I've never seen a girl's poop before. Could she even use an outhouse or crap in the woods? Can't we think about other stuff? Sexy stuff?

What kinda monster thinks about sex when his girl's melting cos she had to poop? The little voice in my head that sounds like Yéyeʔ's says: xeʔłkʷúpiʔ Maybe. Maybe not. But yeah, probably just me.

She practically screams, "It still won't flush."

They could cancel the dance if The Footnotes got stuck in Big Town, or the snow caused part of Jackass Mountain to spill onto Highway One again, and she's ready for the rubber room over a stupid toilet. She's laid the tank lid over the sink so she could dump water into it. She has one knee on the toilet seat. Our eyes meet in the dirty little bathroom mirror. "I didn't ask you to come in here."

"Sorry," I say. "But how you expect me to help if I don't know what's wrong."

"No, I'm sorry. You have no idea how embarrassing this is for me."

I squeeze my lips together and nod. I can guess. I'm just a monster but not a (completely) stupid one.

"Listen," I say. "Just dump the water into the bowl. One quick pour."

"Into the bowl? You sure?"

"Yeah."

"It won't, you know, spill out?"

Not unless you went and made a crap the size of a damn brown bear. "It would take a lotta water for that. So yeah, it won't spill over. I promise."

She hefts the water pail like it's a glass of beer. I can't even carry it like that. She fills the little sink with hot water from the dutch oven and washes her hands a good long time.

"Have you ever had to use the Sears catalogue for, you know?" she asks.

I laugh. Who hasn't? "It's the good stuff, hey? Doesn't leave ink stains on your hands—and other places—not like them newspapers. And it's free. Anyways, the catalogue's better than using your hand, i'nit?"

"Ugh," she goes. "I don't know that I could ever get used to living like this. I'm gonna smell like smoke, aren't I? I don't like the smell of smoke."

"Think of it like nature's perfume. You could be kind of some Earth goddess or some other hippy-dippy thing."

"Great. So I should be happy to smell like a car freshener."

Ingrid might not be joking but I laugh. She could smell a lot worse. There's no way I'm saying that to her though, in case she thinks I'm talking about her bathroom stink.

We start talking about stuff other than what we did and didn't do to each other last night, or the toilet, or even the dance, cos I'd just talk about taking a girl onto the floor for the Home Waltz and how I still wished her to be that girl. Instead, we talk about the weather. She hates winter, especially snow. Like me, she thinks snow's fine until you turn twelve, a long enough time to live through every snow experience at least once. She thinks she'll spend her winters in Hawaii when she's done with college and working.

Places like that are so far way I can't even dream about them. They always end up being something like here, only worse. Man-eating plants. Man-eating, poisonous bugs. Even the land is out to get you, earthquakes and volcanoes spewing lava, and forests that grow so fast they'll bury you alive in ferns and paradise grass. A million different kinds of poison snakes and frogs. There are so many more ways to die in paradise and not one of them is the way I want to go.

I show Ingrid how to play crib. She's almost seventeen and has never played. Two years older than me. I guess maybe the Creator listens, so I should've been more specific about what I wanted to do while trapped with a beautiful girl. She can't believe I started playing crib when I was five. She can't believe how fast I can count a hand. Playing games, especially crib, rummy or gin, is the best way I know of to learn numbers. Not everything is as easy as fifteen-two, fifteen-four and there ain't no more: I mean, it is just a game, but keeping score and stuff has helped me sort out my newspaper money and make sure that crook at the corner store doesn't rip me off when I have to spend money there. She'll do that to little kids, just give them a nickel's worth of candy when they hand her a quarter. If you catch her, she gives you an extra marshmallow strawberry or a few more Mojos. We'd shop somewhere else, if we had another place to shop.

Ingrid catches on to crib pretty quick. She can make a good hand, maybe not the best one possible, but she's pretty good for a rookie. We laugh and joke after a bit, another good thing about games. What we did and didn't do last night gets forgotten. And she seems to like me the way she did when she was drunk. And I like her and want her in bed even more. She can't play the pegging game to save her life but I was about ten when I started figuring it out. We both like playing Uno but it's no fun with just two people. Anyways, I couldn't find an Uno set in the shack. One good thing about playing games is they help speed up time in a way drinking alone doesn't.

I pour myself a rye and ginger. Ingrid doesn't want one.

"I hate who I am when I drink," she says. "None of what we did, none of it, is who I am."

I like drunk Ingrid and I really want that Ingrid with me. Monster. Monster. Monster.

Morning- and whiskey-breathed and still banging each other's brains out: the best way I can think of to start Dance Night day.

8:00 AM

Around eight, people begin the walk back to town or wherever they call home. They grumble, groan, and laugh about the weather, about what great or crappy nights they had.

BANG! BANG! BANG!

The walls rattle. Stuff in the cupboards tinkles and claps. I jump out of my skin. Ingrid gasps and drops to the floor.

BANG! BANG! BANG!

"What's going on?" Ingrid hisses. "Gunshots?"

BANG! BANG! BANG! BANG!

"Nah," I whisper. "Just someone banging on the wall."

"Qʷóqʷésk̓ i?," shouts a ragged voice, deep as a bull's low. "Qʷóqʷésk̓ i? and you, tall blondy. I know you're in there. I guess the joke's on me, hey? But you still owe me ten bucks for the booze i'nit?" He falls silent. I don't recognize his voice and I don't feel threatened. "Hope you had a good time on my wine." He laughs loud and long and keeps laughing as he walks away.

All wide-eyed, Ingrid says, "Who?"

I shrug. Some bull of a guy will knock on my father's front door one day soon, 12-gauge tucked under his arm, demanding his money. Even my father has threatened to kill me, for far less than a magnum of Baby Duck. He will accuse me of running down his good name and beat me till I wished I was dead, then make me pay back the bull-voiced guy, double. Like I care.

Ingrid, all antsy, folds her hand back into the deck without showing me it first. "Do you need some money? I have a few dollars in my purse. If I can find it." She frowns. "I should head inside. Find my teammates and figure out what to do."

I gather up the cards and crib board and put them back where I found them and discover the Uno set crammed in the back of the drawer. Ingrid paces in front of the mirror a hundred times, at least a hundred times, fluffing and tugging at her hair, trying to hide her hickeys. Heck, I'd show mine on the CFJC evening news, if they let me. For me, these hickeys have marked me as a real man for the first time in my life. Monster. Monster. Monster. They pretty much tell everyone I got lucky with a beautiful girl so I don't have to fib about it.

"You got a choker?" I ask. "Lotsa girls wear chokers when stuff like that happens to them."

"Most girls my age shouldn't have to worry about 'stuff like that happening to them.'"

"No one cares."

"Uh, excuse me. My Dad will. And he'll kill you right after he kills me."

"Rubbing a little lemon juice on 'em's s'posedta work."

"Right," she grunts. "And just where the hell am I supposed to find a lemon out here, in the middle of nowhere?"

The middle of nowhere, my butt. "Nah, Nowhere's a day's drive from here. I could take you there one day. After I get my license, I mean." And a car.

"I'd like that, I'm sure," she says. Her hydrochloric acid words dissolve as they reach my ear. The stink of them burns my eyes and ears. She sucks in a harsh breath, softly squeezes my arm. "No, really. I'd like to go there with you." She kisses my cheek, then we wrap our arms around each other and kiss, not at all like we kissed last night, and not exactly like cousins, either. This moment might be as close to the Home Waltz as I get. Her hair, that smelled so good last night, smells a little like me mixed with stale blanket and dusty bed, mostly-sex and a shot of jism. Maybe not the sweetest smells but they're mine and my brain burns them into its Ingrid movie.

I hand her the blanket. "It's gonna be real cold out there."

"Really?" she snarks.

"Yeah. Real cold."

Ankle deep snow covers the ground. Wind's buffed a hard crust on top of it that cracks like glass under our feet. Shin-high drifts snake across the yard. Airborne snow flies at us like salt fired from a shotgun. Ingrid pulls the blanket tight and turtles inside it. I step in front of her, expecting her to walk in my footsteps so her feet don't get soaked. She steps beside me, leans into me. I feel her teeth chatter. I feel like a side of meat hung in a freezer but I try not to let on. Can a guy catch the frostbite on a hundred foot walk? Would Ingrid think less of me if she saw me all shivery and teeth-chattery?

I stop. "You know, if we stop moving we'll prob'ly turn into snowmen." I smile. Snow melts in my shoes and I can already feel my toes growing frostbite black.

She stamps her feet and nudges me with her shoulder. "You mean snowman and snowwoman, right? Now get moving or I'll go in without you."

The hundred-or-so feet feels like a ten-mile trudge, even after we step into the tracks left by people who'd already left. Six people huddle around the fire. Five had no business partying here and I don't know how they even snuck past Auntie. Three of them, way-older guys, spend a lot of time at Kami, the provincial prison. They don't even come from our res but hang out with Loretta and Candy John and some of our other Grade Twelve girls. The five pass a gallon jug of wine between them. Allan Billyboy, the sixth person, stands apart from the others, taking care of the fire. Anytime we have a shindig, Allan's the guy who makes the fire and watches it until it goes out. He only wears a black leather vest and white tee shirt (and jeans and black cowboy boots, of course), no matter how hot or cold it is. He never gets sick, not even with the sniffles. He doesn't talk much; they say he left the residential school like that. I didn't know him before cos he's a little older than me. Allan pops out his lower lip and nods. I flash him the peace sign as Ingrid and I trundle toward the house. When we get onto Auntie's back porch Ingrid wraps me in a giant hug and kisses me square on the lips. We brush each other's snow off. I let my hands accidentally brush her in places that don't need brushing. She harrumphs me but doesn't swat my hand away. I like this girl but even my booze-soaked brain doesn't paint happily-ever-after pictures of me with her. It does paint happy-tonight ones of us together, starting with the Home Waltz, then lots more, mostly too naughty for even *Playboy.* Walking into a morning-after house feels like a walk through your own morning-after brain. One body, covered in garbage, empties, cigarette butts, and who-knows-what-else, sits alone in my uncle's old easy chair. Its skinny white legs belong to Bimbo. I'd go get a closer look at Bimbo—and I'm almost certain it is him in that easy chair—but too many other bodies sprawl on the couch and other chairs and carpet the living room floor. Coughs. Snores. Farts. A couple screwing, or they've fallen asleep screwing. Morning-after zombies grunt corpse-eyed greetings as they slough around looking for smokes and drinks. Everyone complains about the snow. Auntie's carpet would've gotten ruined last night, if she'd got to put it in. Uncle told her a rug was a stupid idea on a working ranch and he refused to put one on their floors. If she has anything bad to say about Uncle, it has to do with the fights they had about rugs.

"How could they do something like that to that poor boy?" Ingrid says.

"He asked for it," I say.

I tell her about our game, about what happens when you pass out at a party. She thinks it's a cruel way to treat a friend.

"Yeah," I say. "It's kinda dumb, I guess. But it shows how much your friends think of you."

"How little, you mean?"

"Nah, we never do stuff like this to girls or guys we don't know. It's not usually this bad but it's Bimbo's first time. The kid never passes out."

Bimbo's the guy who draws spurting dicks and swears all over your face. On time he drew them on with indelible pencil. Skinny and them all laughed until Agnes told them what kinda trouble I'd get at home and school and anywhere else people gathered. She kicked us out of the coffee shop. Skinny cuffed Bimbo good, knocked him to the ground, making him cry. After my father stopped laughing at my marked up face, he belted me good, then made me wash my face with Varsol. I swore revenge on the kid. I'll shave off a patch of hair right down the middle of his head and either leave it white, or paint it yellow. If he wears a hat afterwards, I'll rip it off his head and feed it to River. Skinny specializes in shaving off one of your eyebrows. JimJim specializes in drawing on swears and dicks, but everyone draws dicks and swears, except JimJim's are art and almost always wash off easily. Mostly we just fill your pockets with cigarette butts, ashes, and bottle caps, cover you in empties and other trash—just to see how far we can go without waking you up. We have fun, until it happens to us, but we don't stay mad long. Until now, Bimbo's never passed out and he's played kinda dirty. No wonder he got it so good. For a second or six I kinda wish I'd gotten my revenge on him, then Ingrid rubs against me.

I tell her about what they did to me at the railroad tracks after lunch yesterday, about how Skinny and them de-pantsed me, and how instead of yacking off at them, I turned the joke back on them, by making them have to look away from or at my shrivel-dick. Of all the things you can do to a guy, de-pantsing him ranks up there with killing his dog.

"Anyways, I prob'ly asked for it. I guess I shoulda left with them."

Ingrid pushes away from me. "What do you mean, you asked for it? Were you all *o, please de-pants me and wipe your ass all over my underwear and make me wear them like a mask?* Well? Is that how it went?"

"No. No, nothing like that."

"You know, if you want your friends to treat you with respect, you have to respect yourself."

"R-E-S-P-E-C-T find out what it means to me," I go. I laugh: It's as fake as Sinister's moustache.

"Listen, I'm serious. Your so-called jokes are stupid and cruel and the complete opposite of funny. I'd call them savage and I'd call your friends savages. I don't like it one little bit."

My hands flutter over my thighs like wounded moths and my mouth dries up like Drake Creek in August. I can't look into her drooly eyes. She prob'ly won't even let me jump her now, let alone give me my first Home Waltz. Maybe I should've just dragged her into the bush and not wasted precious time talking when I could've been doing it to her, like my father always says real men do.

Ingrid and I step over and around the zombies to get to the kitchen. We should've stayed in the shack.

Auntie Max's kitchen is a refugee camp for empties and ashtrays. There's a huge pot of burnt Kraft Dinner on the stove, and on the burner beside it, sits a boot, with a bunch of raw sausages squished inside of it. Auntie won't like this one bit. It will take forever to get her kitchen clean, and another forever or two to clean the rest of the house. A beautiful noise rises from the mess. Alex, sitting at the table, plays his guitar with a wine bottle neck on his pinky finger. He sings low and strong: "'You better come on in my kitchen well, it's goin' to be snowin' outdoors you better come on in my kitchen.'" Ingrid slips her hand into mine and sways to the beat. Maybe one day I'll learn to play and let my music speak for me, instead of my stupid mouth.

"Hey," I say. "That one of yours? I never heard you play it before. Boss. Real boss."

He looks away, a small smile lights his face. "I play it all the time but usually for myself. Robert Johnson, one a them dead blues guys, wrote it. Clapton says he's one of the most influential guitarists ever."

"Clapton?"

"Eric Clapton?" Alex snaps. I shrug. "Holy, kid. You can't wanna be a rocker and know nothing about music."

I shrink into sweet Ingrid. "Sorry."

He hits an angry e chord—one of three chords I can sorta play—and slides the wine bottle neck down the strings, making that angry chord sing angel-sweet.

"Yardbirds." He slides a C. "Cream, for fucksake." He sneers, leans into his guitar, turning his head toward his left hand, then slides an A right back into his song. So much to learn. If I live a hundred years I'll never know all I need to know to be good at even one thing. Alex and them go to Big Town every month or two just to buy 45s from Sam the Record Man. One day I'd have to make it to Sam's, cos he'd have some of Johnson's singles. He's supposed to have at least one of every record ever made in his store.

"I didn't mean to sound so harsh," Alex says, now noodling. "Just makes me mad you guys think Creedence is all there is. And that's just wrong."

I swallow hard and gawk at him all bug-eyed. "You don't like Creedence?"

"O for fucksake, I love em as much as you guys. Maybe more. But we live in a time of musical revolution. Bands like Led Zeppelin, Black Sabbath, Deep Purple, Blue Öyster Cult, and some crazy fuck called Alice Cooper. That guy makes great music but eats the heads off bats and sings with a giant snake around his neck."

"Sick," I say.

Ingrid laughs. "A scaled boa instead of a feathered one. I love it!" Alex laughs.

"Look," Alex sneers, "Your sm?ém gets him."

"But if he's a guy, why they call him Alice?"

Ingrid sings, "Listen, Baby, you really wouldn't understand." A pout rises up in me, and before my four-year old brain gets to stomp my foot and shake vibrating fists at Ingrid and Alex and tell them I could understand if I knew what they were talking about, Alex laughs and breaks into another song.

Three or four chords into it, my brain and pout start to act my age. So boss. Ingrid sings along with Alex. I think she sounds good and you can tell Alex thinks so, too, cos he keeps playing and he points his lip at her and nods: "She struts into the room but I don't know her and with a magnifying glance I sorta look her over...."

Alex should be in Hollywood or Nashville: anywhere being a guitar king means something, but like most of the rest of us, he'll probably wait for weekends and get drunk around a bonfire, and do it every weekend until we're too old to lift a bottle to our lips, or else drop dead from this or that. Even though he doesn't drink now, he'll start one day. Everyone around here does.

Ingrid starts cleaning up the mess. I sneak into the cellar to see if there's any beer left. I need a beer, even a warm one. As I expected, they're all gone.

Alex shakes his head and frowns when I get back to the kitchen. He sings: "'Now I'm a drunken-hearted man, and sin was the cause of it all. Oh, play 'em now. I'm a drunken hearted man, and sin was the cause of it all. And the day that you get weak for no-good women, that's the day that you bound to fall.'"

I flip the bird at Alex. He tosses his head back and laughs. Then he becomes a guitar solo. You can't stay mad at a guy who becomes the song he plays. No matter how hard you try, you just can't.

Ingrid, up to her elbows in burnt macaroni, works in time to the music. Her hips sway, transforming her into my Home Waltz. But I'm in that twilight space between drunk and sober, between awake and asleep, between dreamtime and real time, both over-sensitive and senseless, so none of what I see and feel for her right now means much, not really. What will happen to Ingrid and me? Will she be my sm?ém? What if I try too hard and scare her off? It wouldn't be the first time. Even though the pot belongs to Auntie, I'd just dump it in the garbage and buy her a new one. I lift the fake-leather boot. It belongs to Bimbo. Even so, I give the sausages a sniff, not like I could tell a bad sausage from a good one, but it's what Yéye? does before she cooks any meat. They give off a bit of stink-feet smell.

I drop the boot into the big garbage can by the back door. "Waste of good meat, hey?"

Without looking at me, Ingrid says, "I suppose that's one of your little pranks?"

"Nah, especially not at Auntie's. She'll kill whoever did it."

"What about the poor guy whose boot you just threw in the trash?"

"Eh, just Bimbo's. No loss."

"Maybe not for you. But what about him? What's he gonna wear home now? I don't know about you. You can be so thoughtless. So cruel. Would you pull a stunt like that on me? I mean you say you like me and you say you like your friends and you pull stunts like this on them, so why not me?"

She gouges out clumps of macaroni with a soup spoon, sometimes stabbing it hard as we talk about the boot and other pranks. Bimbo's not a real friend. I wouldn't dream of pranking Ingrid like that or any other way. I've had my shoes filled with mud, and once, after de-pantsing me, some older guys put them in fresh cement the village workers put down to fix a crumbly sidewalk on Front Street. I didn't find those pranks at all funny. No matter how many different ways I tell her why the fact that the boot belongs to Bimbo makes it okay, she doesn't see the joke.

"Pranks like that are so childish and destructive. You're what, sixteen-going-on-five?"

"No, fifteen-and-a-half. Almost," I say.

"Then act it, for crying out loud. No girl wants to go with a child."

"I'm not a child," I say, sounding like one. "I mean, I'm not. I know that joke went a little overboard and that is a waste of two- or three-dollars worth of sausage." Still no good. Maybe I am just a child. I wonder if that's such a bad thing, if you can find a girl who doesn't mind you being a big child, not a big baby like Bimbo.

Most of the girls put empties on either the kitchen table or counter on their way out. A few girls hang around long enough to stuff a dozen or so into cases. Some of the guys help gather bottles too. But most of them just head straight out the door, moaning and grumbling about the snow, having no booze or smokes, and walking in the snow all four miles back to town.

James Charles kicks up such a fuss Ingrid and I race into the living room to see what's going on. James is bitching people out, calling them pervs for gawking at him and his jump—that mean-eyed Angelica. He blames everyone else for his decision to pass out on top of her in the middle of the living room. James, one of the older guys, is short, tough and mean. His grumping wakes Angelica. She screams: "Get off me, you pervert. Get off."

She pushes James off of her and sits up. Angelica has the kind of boobs that make *Playboy* so great. She pounds on James' chest—such a beautiful sight, until some of the other girls rush over to her and hide her under a blanket. James, with his pants around his ankles, laughs his butt off.

"O, my God, Ang. Why did you let him do that to your face?" Joanne says.

"It's covered in hickeys," Jennifer says. "Eww, you got them all over. Your father's gonna kill you."

Angelica's face, chest, belly, back and bum are covered in baseball-sized hickeys. One face hickey's okay, if it's on a cheek, but putting on any more than that is just mean. James has no marks on him at all, well he didn't have any before Angelica started laying the beats to him.

Angelica rubs her face. "What? What the hell did you do to my face?"

She turns redder than her hickeys. "Asshole! You asshole!" She rams through the girls surrounding her, loses her covers and ploughs into James. She whales on him and they both hit the floor, Angelica on top. Both of her fists flying like a mad Kung Fu fighter, not stylish or precise like Bruce Lee—just mad. Naked and mad. A hard one pops my pants: how often do you get to watch a naked, mean-eyed, beautiful girl beat the crap out of a guy? No one will look at my pants while Angelica pounds on James but you never know. I slip a hand into my pocket and shift it a bit. The girls try to pull her off and wrap the blanket around Angelica. She shakes them off. I've seen other guys fight back hard when their smʔém goes all batshit and whales on them. James only blocks Angelica's wild punches. I'm glad, too, cos I don't like seeing guys hit girls.

James' ribs heave laughter. He wheezes. Coughs. "O, honey, you know I like it rough."

The girls surround the scrapping pair. James chokes on a laugh as thick as phlegm.

Perry drifts away from the crowd. He stops, takes a good long look at me. "James get a hold of you, too?"

He laughs. He's supposed to look at my marks, then point at Ingrid with his lower lip and nod. He's supposed to say, "Good score," or something. Maybe he's just jealous. Ingrid joins Angelica and the rest of the Ashcroft girls. All of them except Pixie. They lead Angelica to the bathroom. Ingrid returns but not to me. She scrounges up Angelica's clothes. James leaves like a dog that just stole one of your chickens. I guess I would, too.

The lump of Bimbo hasn't moved. He could be dead. People drink themselves to death all the time. You think that would be the way to go but it's not. My uncle Ralph drowned in his own puke, a real ugly sight. My cousin Erica killed herself by taking a bunch of pills and choking to death in her own puke. Guys always drive their cars off cliffs, into River or a huge tree. Drinking leaves behind piles of bodies and all have closed-casket funerals.

Bimbo, all naked, wears his underwear like a hat. His skin's marked up with felt and ball point pen, charcoal and make-up. He's covered in cigarette butts, ash, paper, beer boxes, stale beer, bottle caps over his eyes and more cigarette butts stuffed into his ears. A sock hangs from his mouth like a lolling dog tongue. One of his eyebrows is shaved off. He looks kinda like a clown crawling up out of a dump. As much fun as I had last night and this morning with Ingrid, I kinda wish I'd helped decorate Bimbo. A half-sack box hides his spaeks?. They did a number on him. I lift the half-sack box. Someone painted it black. Even if I wanted to draw a spurting dick on him now, I couldn't, not without drawing over someone else's work. I tuck the half-sack box under my arm. I'll need it for the empties. I wish I had one of them home movie cameras. Filming him waking up would win an Oscar, for sure.

Most of the zombies have grumbled, mumbled, and farted out into Saturday. I will leave soon, too, hopefully before Auntie gets up (Why hasn't she gotten up already?) and after Bimbo wakes up. I'd head straight to Yéye?'s but I still have to deliver my papers: yesterday's *Vancouver Sun* and this morning's *Vancouver Province*, unless I got lucky and the Greyhound that brings them got stuck at

Hope. But if that Greyhound couldn't get through, The Footnotes couldn't, either. Now I sorta pray that my papers made it safely through the Canyon.

While I wait for Ingrid to come back to me and for Bimbo to wake up, I box empties and clean the counters and some of the floor's stickier spots. Perry's joined Alex at the kitchen table. They jam and sound way better than listening to a record. Music always makes cleaning up less like a chore. Skinny drags himself into the kitchen and plops into a chair at the table. He lifts beer bottles up to the light, one at a time, looking for one that doesn't have cigarette butts in it. He takes a small sip from one, lifts his cheek and cuts a rank fart, then downs the bottle of backwash.

"Ahh," Skinny croaks, weak-voiced. "Nothing like a shot of backwash to get your day started right, hey boys?" Alex and Perry, rolling their eyes, begin playing a little louder.

Sucking back your own backwash is gross enough; imagine drinking someone else's. I coulda given him a shot from my bottle of whiskey except I'll need it to get me through the day, so I decide not to mention it to him. So not like me. I only feel a little bit like a jerk.

"Holy! Look at you, hey. You nailed that little redhead? O, wait, I 'member now. You sneaked off with that giant séme?, i'nit? She looked like a goer. She any good? Do you even remember?"

Skinny laughs until he coughs. I hope he coughs up a lung, maybe both.

"'Course I remember." My smile tells the story my brain feeds it, a good story, well good enough for Skinny to grow all saucer-eyed.

"Good for you. It's about time, hey?" he says. Perry and Alex flash each other looks and start another old blues song I don't recognize. It's a good one. (Are there any other kind?)

Skinny goes, "I had two of the v-ball girls. Tried to get them together but they wouldn't go, so I took 'em one at a time."

He laughs and hunts for another nearly-dead soldier. He was with Henrietta and Belinda, and both, like every other girl on the planet, wanted his Golden Sceptre.

"So, I get Belinda on the bus. Backseat. And I whip out the Sceptre. Her eyes pop, wider than this table. And her jaw drops and she goes, 'that thing'll never fit inside of me.'" Skinny puffs up all big and proud and downs another leftover beer. "Once she got gobbling, man, o, man, she went all Linda Lovelace on me. I never saw anything like it before. She was good, maybe one of the best. I mean she sucked so hard and deep, when I blew my load, it shot straight out her butt." Skinny's grin's so wide it knocks stuff off the table.

"Yeah, right," Alex sneers.

Skinny frowns, swills stale beer around his mouth. "Ask her, if you don't believe me." He swallows hard and inspects empties. "Take a look at her ass. You'll see my shot spot on it."

Perry and Alex play "The Rotten Cocksuckers Ball," one of the filthiest songs ever written. Skinny bops along with the music but doesn't sing.

"What about the other one?" I say, mostly cos I feel like I have to. Really, the last thing I want to hear about is Skinny's scores, but you have to ask or he gets grumpy—and no one wants to see mad Skinny. Alex kicks my shin. According to Skinny, Henrietta has a nun's name and a devil's soul. She and Skinny did some wild things, stuff they don't even talk about in *Playboy.* He says they'd still be going at it but the snow started falling so she wanted to get back inside the house. He says he didn't catch a ride back to town with JimJim and a bunch of others cos he thought he'd go another round or two with Henrietta. I've never dreamed of doing that kinda stuff, mostly cos I didn't really know that sorta stuff even existed, but I'll dream, or have nightmares about it now—if you can even have sex nightmares.

Time stops when Bimbo yells, "What the fuck did you fucked fuckers do to me?"

Bimbo, his underwear bunched into a fist over his crotch, cursing everyone out, screams for his clothes. The few people left in the living room step out of his way and slap his skinny white ass as he stomps by them, telling them they're dead. He stops at the kitchen table. Perry and Alex, all google-eyed, stop playing. Bimbo spews a cloud of swears as thick as volcanic ash. No one laughs, not even Skinny. His face, his whole head, neck, and upper chest burn the deepest reds you've ever seen on a human—the first redskin I've ever seen, and the last one I ever want to see. *The Hope Standard*'s headline will read something like, ANGRY WHITE BOY'S HEAD EXPLODES, KILLING A HOUSEFUL OF INDIANS, and then they'll probably give his mother a medal or something to honour his sacrifice.

"I know you did this," Bimbo spits. "Gimme back my clothes or I'll kill you. Kill you dead."

He raises both fists. His dink, his whole crotch is covered with the words wee wee-wee. We all point and laugh. Why not? Bimbo brought all this on himself. He shrinks and drops his fists to his crotch.

"Kill you," he spews, backing away from us. He turns, spewing swears like a cow after eating a case of Ex-Lax. He sports strings of words like stink lines up his back, and a mushroom cloud over his butt crack. What a mess. It'll take him days to wash off all that felt pen, ink, and make-up.

Skinny nudges my ribs. "He won't ever find his clothes."

He laughs and laughs and laughs. My gut twinges something ugly and for a second I feel bad for Bimbo, and I hate myself a little more for simping out. Eyes all teared up, he huffs, "We burnt everything but his ginch and one boot."

Alex and Perry play "Woke Up This Mornin'." Again Skinny doesn't join in.

Bimbo bangs on a door and shouts ugly words about whoever's on the other side and demands his clothes. He rattles it, then bangs some more.

"Yeah, I saw 'em. Auntie Max'll kill us for wasting her food."

From what I've seen around the house so far, my aunt will kill us at least a hundred times, maybe a thousand.

"Nah," Skinny says, "the sausage was all her idea. She even stuffed it into the boot."

"Holy! She did?" I say. Alex and Perry stop playing mid-verse.

Skinny nods. "Yep. Idiot opens the front door and pisses all over her welcome mat, up the side a the house and that."

Alex and Perry pick up the song where they dropped it: " someone disliked him and shot him through the head. . . ."

"Kid's lucky to still have his spaeks?," I say.

Skinny sneers. "Lucky I didn't kill him for her."

Alex and Perry sing, "He's a bad, bad boy and his hog was gone. . . ."

Bimbo bangs on another door and shouts. He rattles it, then bangs some more.

Alex stops playing. "Skinny, shouldn't you tell him his clothes are ashes now?"

"Yeah," Perry says, "Maybe then he'll shut his foul mouth."

"Give us a bit of peace and quiet, too," I say.

Skinny sneers, "Nah. He'll figger it out soon enough."

Then he goes on about how my auntie got so mad she left her own party, and that's not my Auntie Max at all, not even close. My Auntie Max would've grabbed her shotgun and herded everyone—except her billets—out, no matter how hard the snow was falling. Then I realize this whole shindig had to have happened on Bizarro World, cos no way would my auntie have let any of what happened happen. Not even if the FLQ threatened to bomb us to smithereens. Skinny shrugs, fiddles with a dead soldier, and says something so soft the words melt before they get to anyone's ears. Two girls' voices break out of the bathroom. They shriek. Then Bimbo shrieks and thunders into the living room. Ingrid and Belinda hurry into the kitchen.

They look all ragged and dumbstruck. Pointing at the living room, Ingrid says, "Your naked friend scared the living crap out of us."

Friend rolls off her tongue wrapped in sarcasm as thick as Mohammed Ali's fist. The Home Waltz transforms into a nuclear war instead of a night of good loving.

Skinny turns grey and stands stone-still.

"I got to run, Squito," Skinny whispers out the corner of his mouth. "I need a beer and there ain't none here."

Alex and Perry break into "Going Down Slow." Skinny slips away as quiet as a shadow.

9:00 AM

The girls glare at Skinny until the door closes behind him. Belinda hisses, "Good riddance, you crumb."

"Yeah, good-fucking-riddance, a-hole!" Ingrid spits. She scans the kitchen. "You did this? You cleaned all this up?"

"Yeah," I say. Her hard edges soften a bit and she kisses my cheek. My grandmother wouldn't be happy with the job I've done so far—she'd chew me out for taking so long to get the job done. I should've finished the dishes already, even that hateful macaroni pot, and started on the floors. With a little help from just about everyone, almost all of the empties were boxed and stacked against a wall. I'd emptied all of the ashtrays and stacked them near the sink. I s'pose I could've kept working while Skinny yakked and sucked them dead soldiers, but I didn't want to be rude.

"I need some lemon juice and ice cubes to wash away those marks that awful boy left on Ang. Where can I find them?"

"She won't have real lemons," I say, trying hard not to sound too sucky. "Maybe a fake one in the fridge. Prob'ly no ice cubes, though. But I could go out and get a pail of snow. That work?"

"Clever boy. It should. Would you mind?"

"Not at all," I say. Mostly I mean it. It's not so much I expect her to drag me back to the hand's shack and do it to me. No, I want her to Home Waltz me into that shack and let me do it to her, or maybe we could do each other until the dance starts.

The clouds have cleared. Water drips off the tips of the icicles. Except for a few crows crowing and a snowplough grinding a path along the highway, it's quiet. I understand weather less than I understand girls: both can make you feel small and wreck your life in a second and both can fill you with hope. But only girls can fill you with hope and make you feel small at the same time.

Everyone has a plastic lemon or lime in their fridge, even Yéye?, but I doubt she's ever used hers. Auntie Max's still has the tag on it. Funny how they make that tag look like a cardboard leaf. I hold Ingrid's hand a little longer than I should've and she lets me. She grabs the lemon. I lean in to kiss her. She pulls away.

"O, no you don't. You're not putting those lips on me again, you vampire," she says. She chuckles but it feels as unfunny as her joke. Now I feel like I should apologize for James, too. One guy does something really bad and every other guy has to pay for it. I don't get it. Ingrid has a way of making me feel like such a little boy when she should be making me feel like a man. "I'm kidding." Ingrid kisses my cheek. "Really!"

"Anyone seen Pixie?" Belinda asks, her face as grey as Skinny's.

"I knew bringing her was a mistake. I just knew it," Ingrid snaps. She growls, low in her throat, like a cougar. "We need to take care of Ang. Then we'll find Pixie." Ingrid looks at me, "You haven't seen her, have you?"

Alex and Perry shoot each other sneaky glances. I shake my head. Thanks to Angelica, no—and I wish I did know where Pixie was, cos she sure made me feel like a man.

"Well, when you see her, send her straight to the bathroom. Okay?"

"Yes, ma'am," I say. The look she shoots hits me like a punch in the nuts. I wince.

After filling the sink with super hot water, I sneak out to get a glass of whiskey. I need it. It warms my belly, makes my girl troubles fade, and takes the sting out of cleaning Auntie's house. Alex and Perry noodle, every now and then breaking into another song, making it totally okay that they don't lift a finger to help me.

"Hey," I ask, "you guys know where that foxy little redhead is?"

Alex sneers a small laugh and Perry shakes his head.

Alex cranes his neck toward the kitchen door before whispering, "You mean the one Cody snuck off with?"

"Cody?" Anger like a puke-burp shoots up my throat. I swallow it. As much as I like Cody, I may have to kill him. I hope he didn't even get as lucky as me. Alex and Perry look at each other and stomp into a song they wrote: "Blue Balls Boogie." The kitchen looks filthy and uncleanable. I down my whiskey and slam my glass onto the counter like some dusty-throated Hollywood cowboy villain. Drowning my sorrows in whiskey while my hands wrinkle up in hot sudsy water. I got the drunken dishwasher blues.

The kitchen starts spinning by the time I get it clean enough to pass for what Auntie might consider clean and I'm only half-cut. Alex and Perry took off somewhere between the second and third pail of water I used on the floor. The Ashcroft girls and I are pretty much the only people left over from last night, except for Bimbo, lurking like a crybaby sċuwenáỷtmx behind Uncle's easy chair. The girls have taken over the living room, all mad about this and that, but mostly about what James had done to Angelica and about Pixie for running off (or disappearing?). I plop down onto the arm of Ingrid's chair, flash her a smile and offer her a sip from my glass—now more whiskey than sugar-water. She frowns, pats my knee, and turns her attention to Joanne, not their team captain, but their leader, however that works.

"Like I said all along," Joanne says, "thirteen's too young for the senior girl's v-ball team. Any seniors' team. Period."

"Who's thirteen?" I ask.

They look at me like I've just cut a huge fart—a gift I have but not one I ever asked for.

"Pixie, you idiot," Ogre-eyed Angelica says.

Pixie's only thirteen? She looks seventeen. At least seventeen, and I was pretty much sober when I first saw her. On top of all the other crappy things I feel, I could've been a statutory rapist. If I was a churchy, cos of all those thoughts and pictures of her that my brain had given me, I'd already be a rapist.

"Pixie's too good a player for the junior team, so they stuck her with us because it wasn't fair to the other junior players," Ingrid snarks. "That girl's been nothing but trouble since they put her on our team and we're supposed to look out for her." She giraffes my ear and whispers, "I feel so bad. I shouldn't have gone off with you."

"I didn't make you, did I?"

"No," she says, voice like a hammer just whapped her thumb. "I wanted to go off with you. I did. It's just that I shouldn't have. Pixie was my responsibility."

"Our responsibility," Angelica says. "We're all to blame for whatever's happened to her."

The girls, heads down, all nod and murmur. Bimbo breathes loud and obnoxious but doesn't show his face or any other part of himself. A door creaks open. Auntie's bedroom door. Only she, or someone she took in there to protect from something or someone, would come out of Auntie's room. She allows no one else in her room. Ever. The girls all look toward the sound. I take a small sip—my glass holds the last of the whiskey and I am so dizzy and so close to puking—and peer over the glass at Auntie's door. It's like the whole house holds its breath. I hope Auntie comes out. I'm sure the girls hope it's Pixie. They say their coach will forfeit the tournament and take them straight home. Ask the Magic 8-Ball if I'll have my Home Waltz tonight. It will answer, "Don't count on it."

Cody, wearing nothing at all, sneaks out of Auntie Max's bedroom. The girls gasp and quickly look away. I guess for some of them, seeing three naked guys in one morning is maybe three more than some of them have ever seen.

Cody holds up a hand, all five fingers spread wide. His face turns into a huge poop-eating grin. He holds up the other thumb. "Six times," Cody beams. "Six and counting."

Bimbo pokes his head over the top of Uncle's chair. "Bull. I call bullshit."

Cody smirks. Walking like a bull rider after being thrown from his bull, he hobbles back into Auntie Max's bedroom. The door clicks gently closed behind him. The deadbolt thunks into place. Bimbo again calls bull but says nothing else and slithers back behind the chair once he seems to sense all the girls gawking at him.

I'd wear that same indestructible happy grin if I got to do it even once with a girl like Pixie, but a Pixie-like girl who's of-age. Alex and them said that Cody went off with Pixie. If she's in there with him, they're both in trouble, Cody more than Pixie. They say fifteen'll get you twenty: What will thirteen (six times) get you? Cody'll prob'ly get life, cos he did it to a white girl. If Bimbo knows Cody's with Pixie he'd've told them Ashcroft girls already. The cops can't kill him more than once, so not telling him now won't make things any worse for him. Anyways, them cops'll treat him a little better than these Ashcroft girls.

"Who does it six times? That's gross," Joanne says.

"Must be a squaw," Angelica says, all teacher's-pet faced. Everyone looks at her. My body twists into a fist. "What? My daddy says they all have loose morals. Squaws'll do anything with anyone who asks. It's true."

My grandmother always says I shouldn't waste good anger on stupidity, cos that's the kinda anger that causes the cancer. She keeps telling me that we all say or do stupid things but that it doesn't make us stupid people—mostly I think she says that to keep me from killing myself over some of the stuff I do. Despite Yéye?'s words, despite the fact Angelica probably won't hear what she doesn't already believe, I want to chew her out and kinda feel like slapping her until she sees how stupid her thinking is. Stupid me, can't let her dumb words go. Through gritted teeth I growl, "Watch who you call a squaw."

Ingrid pulls me onto her lap and hisses, "Shh." And I shut up. Ingrid the tamer of monsters. Good thing, too, cos I just about blurted out that the loose-moralled squaw was just some white jailbait.

Angelica falls silent for a minute, draws in a huge breath. "Well, it is."

Nose all scrunched up, face a pale sneer, Joanne says, "Get a room, you two."

Ingrid slides out from under me, then lowers herself onto my lap, winks at me, and says to Joanne, "No thanks. We already had one." Every breath she takes makes me a little harder, until it feels like popping like a balloon with too much air.

"If she's not in the house, where could she be, Mosquito?" Ingrid says. I don't like that she calls me *Mosquito*—only some teachers and Mister and Missus Marshall, at the General Store, call me that—cos it kinda makes it feel like she's talking to someone else. The girls look at me like I should know. Every cell on my body screams, Run! But do I listen? No. Pixie might not be in there with Cody. People talk and they don't always speak any shade of truth. It'd be gross if he was in there with my auntie but I don't think that'd be breaking any laws. I hope he's in my aunt's bedroom with my aunt; a thought so ugly my brain can't paint pictures of it to show me. Thank you, brain. This time of year it's easy to get lost after a few; wander off into the bush for a pee, say, and get all turned around and then get killed by the cold night or something. I can't just tell these girls she dropped dead under a little snow, cos I don't know, and I don't want to make them feel worse before they need to, if they even need to.

"Maybe," I say. "Maybe she went back to town with that bunch before the snow started falling."

"Why didn't we all go back?" Joanne, says. Good question. No one knows. And some didn't even know people left last night or that going back to town last night was an option. That'd be some kinda record if all them girls got blackout drunk.

"Maybe we would've, if we coulda found Pixie and Ingrid," Angelica says. She burns Ingrid and me with heat ray eyes.

"We couldn't find you, either, Ang," Jennifer says.

"I was, well, I thought he was someone else."

"You looked like you were loving it," Joanne goes. Her smile is sweet poison.

"Funny, I never get that drunk on just one beer. And I don't remember any of it."

"You don't know how you wound up fucking that chug in the middle of a room full of people?" Henrietta says, defender of *squaws*, condemner of *chugs.* I forget my grandmother's words and stiffen into a fist, and just as quickly, Ingrid puts her hand on mine. Her hand's as soothing as Noxzema on a sunburn.

"Last thing I remember is we were headed to one of the back bedrooms. Just to talk," Angelica says.

"Just to talk," I snort. "Good one."

Henrietta sniggers. "Yeah, good one, Captain. You did way more than talk. And you're the one setting such a good example for the rest of us."

"Stop it, all of you," Joanne says.

Belinda pipes up for the first time in a while: "We all wanted this. Even you, Henrietta."

"Ugh, and who said getting some stray stuff would do us good?" Henrietta says. She cringes when the other girls point at her. "Any of you see me go off with that singer?" Some of the girls, but not Belinda, sorta swoon and tell her how lucky she was to go with Skinny.

"I got to tell you," Henrietta says, "what an ego. He takes me onto our bus—our bus—right to the backseat and as soon as I sit on that cold-fricking seat he whips out his giant prick and waves it in my face."

"Gross," Jennifer says.

"When? That bastard dragged me to the back of the bus, too," Belinda says.

"Eww," Ingrid says.

"I guess after he struck out with me he moved on," Henrietta shrugs.

"I'd have punched it right in it's squinty little eye," Angelica says. The girls laugh. My crotch shrinks back, as though her words are an uppercut to my parts.

I'm not so sure she would've, cos we're all so much tougher a mile away from trouble. Angelica is a roaring woman all covered in hickeys. Her beauty masks a mountain of shame or something far uglier. If she was less mean-mouthed, I'd feel sorry for her. I s'pose I should anyway but I still want to slap the stupid out of her.

"I know," Belinda says, "and I should've punched his dink into the next century but I didn't. I don't think I've ever met a tall guy who wasn't a world class prick. Have you?"

"Hell, no," Angelica says.

"O, please," Jennifer says, "That's the same as saying every big-titted girl's a slut. Are you a slut, Belinda? Are you one, Ang?"

"Shut up, Jen. Just shut it, okay?" Both Angelica and Belinda look as if they're about to fall into a hissy fit.

Henrietta picks up her story: "No matter how I say no, he won't stop. I'm slapping his hands off my tits. I'm just glad I wasn't wearing a button-down shirt because he'd have ripped all my buttons off. God, he was so rough."

"Desperate," Belinda corrects. "Desperate and lonely. He's just a sad, pathetic creature."

"Who wants to be around anyone like that?" Angelica asks.

"Apparently you two," Jennifer says. Their laughter fills the room with an icy chill.

"Well, he is kinda cute and man, o man, can he sing," Henrietta says. "Well, he can't get inside my sweater, so, get this, he whips out his cock, and then, get this, he calls his cock *the Golden Sceptre* and tries making me take it in my hands. And he begs me to kiss it, like it's the Pope's ring or some nonsense."

Henrietta stops for a breath. The girls gasp. I want to vomit. I don't want to know what Skinny does with girls, less from these girls than from Skinny himself. Still, she's telling a good story and my brain wants to hear it.

"I don't mind a cock in my face once in a while," Henrietta says, and my ears turn their full attention to her. Who knew a girl could actually like it? "But only if I ask for it and never a dirty one. Ugh! His was filthy. And talk about stink. I all but gagged and I swear if he waved it under my nose one more time, I'd have vomited all over it."

"Puke on a cock instead of having it vomit all over you. I like it," Ingrid says. She laughs but she's the only one.

"That woulda served him right," Henrietta goes. "I wish I had."

"How'd you deal with him? You didn't go all the way with him, did you?"

Henrietta squirms. She turns a thousand shades of red. "No. Well, almost, but no."

Skinny's story was so different from Henrietta's, and I think I like hers better.

"I didn't," Belinda snarls. "Not even close. I wrap my hand around it and right away he starts humping it. Like a fucking dog, only worse."

The girls laugh.

Belinda leans forward and in a low voice says, "Listen to this: he tells me his is the biggest cock I'll ever have and I should be thrilled that he chose me."

Again the girls laugh. I hear a soft groan from behind Uncle's chair. Bimbo had better not decide to come out now. I'd like to club him and drag him deep into the bush as an offering for the real sc̓uwenáy̓tmx, except I worry Sasquatch would be insulted and hunt me down like Clint Eastwood's character in *For a Few Dollars More.*

"It was the biggest one I'd ever seen but still not as big a prick as him." Even Belinda laughs. She tries to speak but chokes on her words.

"I squeeze it tight and yank it away from my face, look him in the eyes and say..." She loses her words in a stutter of laughter. She draws in a huge breath, looks at the ceiling and: "I say, you're right, it is a big one, the biggest I've ever seen. The goof just looks down at me and smiles. And then I go, it's so big, why don't you just go off and fuck yourself."

I laugh with the girls and they all turn murderous look on me. I shrink into Ingrid, hoping she'll protect me. Unless these girls kill me, I'll try that line on Skinny, once, just to see how he takes it. He might kill me but it'll be worth it just to see the look on his face. Belinda says Skinny yoinked his dick out of her hand and threatened to beat her into next spring. That doesn't sound like the Skinny I know. He beats up guys who hurt girls and has since Grade Six.

"He tells me to get out before he kicks the crap out of me," Belinda continues. "He didn't need to tell me twice. I believe he woulda, cos you could see murder in his eyes."

"You got off lucky," Henrietta says. "I don't even know how I got stuck with him. One minute I'm dancing with him—he is such a dreamy dancer, too—and the next I'm practically naked and shivering on the backseat of the bus. I suppose I'd have gone off with him anyway. I mean he is my type: all, dark, decent looking and I absolutely love his self-confidence. The thing is he has his dink poking out of his fly. The guy couldn't even take off his damn pants before lying with me. God, I just hate that. That's when things get fuzzy. I must've passed out or something."

My brain paints pictures of naked Henrietta and they are good. She's not quite as tall as me, not that me being shorter than Ingrid's been a problem. Like JimJim always says, on our backs, we're all the same size. Henrietta's boobs are a little bigger than Ingrid's, maybe not nicer. I guess I am just the sorta dog who would lie with any of these girls and love it. Monster.

"When I come back to myself, I feel him poking at my snatch and getting nowhere. I clench. This isn't how I want to get screwed, not by him. Not by anyone. And then he rolls me over and tries sticking that monster between my bum cheeks."

"O, sick," I say and wish I could've kept my mouth shut tight, cos the girls all see monster-me. "Sorry."

Henrietta looks at me and nods. She says, "I know. I guess I'm game for just about anything but not that. Never that."

"Eww. Definitely just about anything but that," Jennifer says.

"Maybe, with the right guy," Ingrid says. The girls look at her much the same way they'd just looked at me. "Well, if you're in love there's no harm in trying new things."

I guess Ingrid can say that cos she has the nicest bum on her team. I just hope she never asks me to do that to her. Just thinking about it makes me feel sorta sick.

"What'd you do? He didn't, did he?" Angelica goes. I guess she got off easy, going with James and not Skinny.

"No. I wouldn't let him. I just kept pretending to be asleep, clenched up so tight my cheeks were starting to cramp up."

"And he couldn't tell you were faking it, all knotted up like that?" Jennifer says.

"You'd think he'd have caught on, wouldn't you?" Angelica says. "He came on to me, too, all octopus-eyed. So I jumped at that

James-jerk, just to get away from his grabby eyes. I don't care how good he sings or dances. He's just a creep and I wanted nothing to do with him."

Henrietta nods, continuing: "You know, if he'd have taken off his clothes and laid with me like I was a human, I'd have let him do it to me. Not in my back door and not in my mouth. I hate having one of those things in my mouth. It feels so wrong." Henrietta shudders and I like her just a little more. "I kept my eyes closed real tight. I mean real tight. There's no way I want him knowing I'm awake or in any way interested in having him inside of me. So the prick jacks off on my crack. No matter how tight I clench, it's still not tight enough to keep his jism from oozing down into my crack. It's all I can do not to scream and run to the nearest hot shower. It'll take months to wash away that feeling."

The girls *eww* and *uck* and tell Henrietta how sorry they are. I am sorry, too, and would say so, except coming from me those words would prob'ly ooze into their ears like Skinny's jizz.

"Anyways, he wipes his dink off on my back and stuff. He says he knows I'm awake and that I can hear him but I don't move. He calls me a cockteasing bitch and leaves. I was fine until then. I burst into tears. I don't remember ever crying so hard. I feel so used. So dirty."

Henrietta bursts into tears. The Ashcroft girls, including Ingrid, surround her and smother her in comfort. I think about telling them Skinny's version of their stories. Would they call him a dirty liar? Would they want to kill me for saying anything? They would hate him more than they already do but I don't want to betray one of my best friends, even though he'd probably enjoy ratting me out if our positions were reversed. He'd use something like this to make fun of me for weeks, or months—no, years and years: prob'ly the rest of my life. I guess anyone would, cos it's juicy stuff, and I want to, but I don't know if I can or will, and it makes me feel weak.

They tell Angelica what she'd done last night. Angelica remembers none of it, or so she says. Blackouts trick you, cos they hide some stuff behind dark curtains and show bits of other stuff. But most of what they show you is somewhere between what might have happened and what you wished did or didn't happen. Usually, blackouts show you stuff you wished hadn't happened. Your blackouts never show you saving a kid from a burning building or sexing up the most beautiful girl in the entire universe. Not even close. You'll see a fist flying at your face but not the reason someone clocked you. Stuff like that. When your friends gang up on you and tell you what your blackout's hiding you get to relive it through their eyes—never a good thing.

Angelica, despite her hickeyed up face and neck, has turned as white as Bimbo's butt. The girls say she'd dragged James onto the dance floor and, in front of everyone, was doing the sorta stuff you do in private if at all. Skinny might have had a different kinda night, if Angelica hadn't hated him so much. If Angelica, and, I guess, Ingrid, had stayed with the other girls, Pixie wouldn't've disappeared and they'd have been on the first bus back to town when the snow started falling. Or its second trip. The third trip never happened cos most of the snow had already fallen. But here they are, eight girls—well, nine minus one—in a strange house, stranded, with no electricity and no phone. My brain had told me this would be my dreams come true. Paradise: me all alone with a bunch of pretty, horny girls. My brain lied to me.

Something makes Bimbo squawk like he's just realized that he's naked and covered in felt pen dicks in a roomful of girls. His moans kill the conversation. The girls whisper: "what's his problem? Is he okay? Who is he? What happened to him? Why is he there?" I don't know for sure but I could guess. Ingrid turns to ice on my lap as she tells the girls about our *little* game. None of them girls get the joke and they all think us guys are cruel, making anything I could say about it pointless.

Bimbo pokes his head up from behind Uncle's chair. "Those assholes went too far this time. My Mom's gonna kill me and put charges on all of them." He points at me and teary-shouts: "Even you, Moss-KEE-toe. You, the biggest asshole of them all."

The girls, all except Ingrid, burn me with the ugliest eyes I'd ever gotten burned by. "What? I didn't do nothing to him. Ask Ingrid. Her and me partied together all night. All night. Tell them, Ingrid."

"Stop lying," Bimbo yells. "You slipped me a mickey. I know it was you. You filthyfuckin'-'skin. Useless-fuckin'-'breed. Get my damn clothes, now."

Hold on a second. No one's said anything about slipping anyone a mickey. Some older guys have done it, mostly joking with their friends. No one I know would ever do something that mean. Not even Mad Skinny. Why Bimbo could think I'd do something that sick makes me want to break his face more than I've ever wanted to bust his nose and stuff before.

"Jeez, you," I blurt. "Why so rude?"

"Screw you, chugalug. Bring my damn clothes."

"Gettem yourself," I say.

"You took them. Now stop fuckin' around and get them."

"For the last time, shut up and gettem yourself." One more rude word from him and I will lay on him the beating he's asked for since Grade Three. Every part of me, clenched up like I've transformed to stone, itches to go.

"Where are his clothes?" Ingrid asks. I could tell her that Skinny says they burnt them up but they already hate him enough, and I don't know for sure that they really did toss them in the fire.

"Poor boy must be freezing," Henrietta says. "Shouldn't we get him a blanket or something? I mean it's so cold in here. And he's, well, naked."

"Finally," Bimbo says. "Thank you." He drops back down behind the chair. "And be quick about it."

The girls mouth stuff like "what a dick" to each other but they go to scrounge up a blanket or something anyway. They should let him find his own or suffer.

Ingrid climbs off me, pulls me to my feet. "You need to help him. He's your friend."

"I didn't do anything to him. Nothing!" I say. She squeezes my wrist and bends my arm back behind me, about as strong as any cop who's grabbed me. It hurts. "Let go, babe. I didn't do anything to the kid."

"First off, I'm not your 'babe.' Second, he's your friend and you will help him."

Yéye? always says your honey shouldn't treat you rough, just as you should never treat your honey rough. I guess Ingrid doesn't play by Yéye?'s rules but I want to give her one more chance, so another Home Waltz doesn't end with me alone in the dance hall's darkest corner. She yoinks a little more pressure on my arm. One more jerk like that and she'll break it.

"Well?"

"Let go. It hurts."

"You telling me you're not tough enough for my love?" She giggles as she lets my arm go. "I didn't mean to hurt you, hon." All red-faced, she kisses my cheek and pulls me into a hug. "I am serious, though. Get the kid his clothes."

I huff a sigh and focus on her toes. "I can't. They say they burned 'em. Everything but one boot and his underwear."

She grrrs. Before she can spout off about how crummy they've treated him again, Cody, fully dressed, grabs the door jamb with both hands. "Help me. Crisakes. We've gone seven times and she wants to go again. Squito, help me. Seven times. I can't go no more. You got to save me from this crazy woman."

I laugh. Cody doesn't. He drags himself out of Auntie's bedroom, slapping, and pulls the door closed behind him. "Crazy woman!"

A girl's voice, not my auntie's, pouts, "Hey, come on back." She sings, "Cody."

Pixie. Cody snagged Pixie.

"Pixie?" Angelica shouts. All eight girls push past Cody in their rush to Auntie's bedroom door. Cody yelps. The yelling, screaming, and crying start before Belinda slams the door.

"Hey, where's my fuckin' clothes, asshole?"

"Shut the hell up," I snap. I pull Cody by the arm and tell him, "You better run, cos them girls want to kill you."

"Run? Why? You are kidding, right? That crazy woman broke my damn balls. It's all I can do just to stand," Cody says.

"That crazy woman's thirteen and them girls want to kill you."

"The way she goes? No way she's thirteen. Has to be eighteen–nineteen, anyways. I never seen a thirteen-year old with a body like that. You?"

"They say she's thirteen going on thirty. I know. I think she fooled everyone."

"Damn. Thirteen?" I nod like I just told him he had the cancer and three months to live.

Shaking his head, he winces. "I don't want jailbait. I never do jailbait. Damn."

He dry heaves. His hands shake. "Thirteen?"

"Listen," I say, hunting my stupid brain for words that'll make Cody feel better, if that's even possible.

Monster-me, growls: "Better him than you, i'nit?" My brain cowers and loses the words it's gathered in in its apron.

"Listen. Everyone makes mistakes."

Cody says, "Doing jailbait is not a mistake." The red of his skin pools like blood at his feet. He hobbles away, mumbling, "Thirteen? Thirteen?"

One hand cradles his crotch. I guess he'll have to put his nuts on ice. What do you put on your head and heart when you find out you did something pretty bad? Me-Who-Looks-at-Me jeers at me-me from its cave in my brain: "Seven times in one night must be some kinda record, i'nit? But for you, one time would be a record."

A beer bottle zings past me and smashes against a wall. Another bounces off my chest. I duck just in time to avoid one targeting my head. Bimbo has a beer bottle in each hand, ready to wing them at me. I roar and run at him, a giant fist. He deflates and whimpers apologies and other nonsense behind Uncle's chair. I drag him out by his ankles. He kicks and squirms with more oomph than I figured he had in him. Almost since he moved to our town I've wanted to see him dead: at times, to kill him myself. All that swallowed black rage oozes up.

That black rage pushes me out of my own body, surrenders to the monster. Every insult he's sputtered and spewed; every indelible, spurting dick he's painted on my face; every stupid and mean thing he's ever said to me, or about me; each and every one of them lives, driving my fists into his face, head, and neck. My knuckles, raw and bloody from Bimbo's blood, my 'breed blood, my chugalug blood. Bimbo's tears, snot, and slobber thin our bloods. He whimpers and moans, *No. Stop. Please. I'm sorry. I'm sorry.* The black rage tries to punch him silent, punch him still.

I give. I give. I give. My black rage says he hasn't given enough.

I give. I give. I give. My black rage calls him a liar.

I give. I give. I give. My black rage punches his stupid face, his stupid neck, his stupid head.

I give. I give. I give. My black rage punches him, and punches him, and punches him, and punches him.

A bunch of voices outside my head scream at me to stop. They sound unreal. Tired and sweaty, my black rage's punches weaken. Its hold on me breaks, letting me back into my body. Hands close around my upper arms and throat and yank me off of Bimbo. My knuckles, elbows, and shoulders burn. Bimbo, as goggle-eyed as a spooked mare tries speaking through his tears, oozing blood and snot. A sick feeling shivers through me: what if the kid dies? I don't want to rot in jail for it—hell, he's not worth it. Now my knuckles sting as if salted, my heart drops like a boulder into the deep end of the pool.

Ingrid screams into my face. Her words make no sense. Ingrid and I, our Home Waltz is "Angie." Instead of dancing happily into a bed somewhere together, she has no love (for me) in her soul, and judging from the look of Bimbo, I have no love in me either.

The girls muscle me out of the way to nurse Bimbo. Angelica wraps a wool blanket around him. Ingrid slides under him, letting him use her body as a pillow. He nestles against her, a leer cracking his broken face. The black rage surges up, sloshing inside me like water in a bathtub. Henrietta and Joanne shove me back and tell me to screw off. Lucky me, I've replaced Cody as their new Public Enemy Number One.

Pixie, as much of a castoff as me, stands in shadows away from her teammates. She winces whenever she moves. She fidgets, looks near and around me, if she looks my way at all. Even though I know her real age, she still looks like a girl to die for, not that I would—now, I mean. I see why my eyes and other parts let her fool me. And yeah, I hear our Home Waltz: "The Midnight Special." All that whiskey I drank this morning rushes up. I go all swoony as my feet start to melt. I stagger outside, drop to my knees in a puddle of snow-and ice-covered mud, and blow black chunks. A little chunk of white glistens in the blackening blood on my pinky knuckle. Is it my knuckle bone? Did I hit him so hard I scraped away all my skin or break my own damn pinky? Did he bite me? Watery-eyed, I touch it, wiggle it, nudge it softly. Moving it around doesn't make me puke the way broken bones can and it doesn't hurt me any more than I already hurt.

One of the girls says they have to get him to the hospital cos I broke his nose and busted at least one of his teeth. Wow. Wow. Wow. I got myself almost sexed up in a good way and I beat the crap out of a guy. Okay, not a real guy, Bimbo, but that's got to count for something: I mean I broke his nose and busted off a tooth. Would it be cool to wear the tooth on a silver chain?

I heave myself dead sober, bringing up all the shame and guilt and even the good feelings—all of me, heart and soul, has spilled onto the slow melting snow.

Back inside, the girls nurse, clean, and coo over Bimbo, whose head rests between Ingrid's sweet little boobs. She holds a damp cloth over his forehead and strokes his greasy hair. Bimbo loves it. He whimpers and winces and rubs Ingrid's thighs. All the rage I'd loosed on Bimbo collects like quicksilver and crawls back inside of me.

I hold up my bloody fists and say, "Hey, I'm bleeding too."

Ingrid growls like a mama bear protecting her cub: "Get out. Just leave. Haven't you made enough trouble for one day?"

"Just make sure you clean this place up real good before my auntie gets back, especially all the glass that loser broke."

"Yeah, jutht fuck off you thtupid 'thkin," Bimbo says. That little loser just made my day, cos I did hurt him more than it shows. "And whereth my fucking cloth'th?"

"Don't encourage him, my darling," Ingrid coos, piling her affection on a little too thick. "He says he burned them."

"Burntem?" Bimbo tries escaping Ingrid's grip. She holds him back, daubing his face with the cloth. Angelica, Joanne, and Belinda crowd me like the Lions' offensive line and herd me toward the door. She kisses his forehead.

10:15 AM

Wind has let up but she never lets up for long. The snow seems to melt almost as fast as it falls, making the ground a partially frozen slushy mess. My feet are wet before I reach the end of Auntie's driveway. Every few feet I have to stop and bury my fists in what's left of the razoredged snow. A single set of tire tracks big enough to belong to a school bus, partially blown away, partially drifted over, head east from Auntie's driveway. A bunch more start or stop there.

The walk back to town will take forever. Every time my foot hits the ground, my right pinky explodes. Both hands burn, bleed, and throb. My right hand has transformed into a burning balloon. Its pinky jiggles and jogs, jabbing my guts, forcing me to lean against a tree and spew.

Wind hides, silent among the frozen trees. Still, except for the icy blowtorch she fires into my face. Wind doesn't make gooseflesh pop up like an acne. Someone, not Wind, insta-freezes the air around me and pulls the hair back off my face. I yelp, "Ai-ee!"

Erica punches my shoulder. "I'm just trying to help, you idiot."

All that time she's spent yelling at me hasn't hurt her voice.

"You think I was yelling at you?"

Her mom had her buried in her deer hide dress. Erica hadn't finished beading it yet but now it looks like it came straight out of an Indian Princess painting.

"You say that like it's a good thing, Qʷóqʷésk̓ i?. Should I feel flattered or should I kick your hungover ass all the way back home?"

Stomp a crust of snow. Kick my arse? Why? I just meant you look real pretty.

"Then just say I look pretty. I wish everyone just saw me for who I was."

Crunchy chunks skitter onto the road like pucks over lumpy ice. The soft snow under the crust bleeds pink around my knuckles. Pain bleeds into me, turning me into a shaky nugget of puke.

"Just stop it with your self-pity, Qʷóqʷésk̓ i?! I don't have much time."

Time?

"Time. Like tick tock I'm on the clock. Time."

I always thought that time stopped, you know, after.

"You did not! You just think being dead kills all your pain. Just like I did. That's just stupid thinking."

So you were just thinking stupid?

"I don't think about it much. I did what I did and it's done. But you gotta know. I did it to me. No one else, 'specially not you."

But I could've stopped you. I could've got someone to help.

"They'd have locked me up in a rubber room again. Fuck that. I wanted to die, Qʷóqʷésk̓ i?. Get that through your fat head. What I did, I did to myself. I'm sorry I drug you into it. I'm sorry. Now just let me go. Stop blaming yourself. Stop haunting my death."

Haunting her? Does that make me the dead one? It sort of makes sense, cos my life sure feels like hell a lot of the time.

Erica vanishes in a dust devil of icy blue flakes, scattering like sparks from a roman candle. The ground rumbles, hisses, opens up under me. Funny how the end of the world smells like dirty oil and diesel. Goosebumps as red and itchy as scabies bite into me. Tears freeze on my eyelashes.

Relief, as the shock of cold from the snow packed into the palm of my broken hand absorbs the pain thrumming from it. If I'm off to hell, this snowball goes with me.

Blinking away frozen tears unpaints the pale-redded blindness, paints in blurred mobs of pine trees in a grey, grey-blue, and yellow world.

Shaking my head doesn't focus my eyes any faster than blinking. After grinding them with the back of my less gibbled hand, the world takes shape around me. And let there be Elmer Lennart's school bus. And poof! there it was. Its door psssssshes open.

"Hey there, Squito. You all right? Let me help you up," Elmer says, his cigarette bouncing from the end of his lower lip.

Thanks, but no. I would rather die than go back to Auntie's house. "I'm okay. Really."

On my knees, swollen hands bleeding into snow growing crusty around them. Yeah, okay, all right.

Elmer grunts, hefts his planet of a gut toward me, then wobbles to his feet. "No bother."

"Really, I'm okay, just a little hungover's all."

He nods and drops back into the driver's seat, rocking the bus. "Well then, a little fresh air will clear your head." He adjusts his butt and belly and reaches for the door-closing-thing. "If you're not careful, that alcoholism gene inside of you will kill you."

Wobbly on my feet. My soaked feet will probably give me the pneumonia, as well as frostbite. My feet, nose, and hands will turn black and fall off but I'm okay. The door psssssshes and clumps closed. The bus lurches forward, rear wheels spinning before they get a grip. Miss Cloes, our Grade Nine science teacher told us all about the alcohol gene we had in us. If we drank any booze at all, she said, we'd be dead before we reached thirty. I asked Yéye? about the alcohol gene. "That's just stupid talk," she said. The next thing you know Miss Cloes packs up and leaves town. If anyone knows why, they won't say. The gym teacher, who also taught math, took over the science class. We watched NFB films for the rest of the year. And I still only got a C in Science.

And if I'm the dead one, why'd no one meet me at death's door and show me around. Why didn't anyone give me a map, or rule-book? And why does hell have snow?

10:30 AM

A chinook's landed, warming Wind and melting the snow fast. Walking the sloppy road slows me down as much as the pain in my right hand, which seems to swell up a little more with each step I take. At this rate, it will be the size of a blimp by the time I get to town. It won't take me much more than an hour to get back to town, add another three to deliver my papers: so begins the longest dance day in history. About a mile from Auntie's, Elmer pulls up beside me again. Everyone else is crowded in the back of the bus. Bimbo, dressed in some of my uncle's clothes, sits surrounded by Ashcroft girls. Not Pixie. As pale as sun-dried bones, she sits alone behind the bus driver. The pain in my hands pales next to the pain those girls will put on me if I get on that bus. Ingrid's eyes pull mine to hers. Ingrid smiles at me and my heart cautiously smiles back, wagging its little puppy tail. At the very moment I feel forgiven, she leans into Bimbo and kisses him on the mouth. Her sweet smile transforms into a black dagger and stabs me in the heart. Bimbo wastes her beautiful mouth, focusing instead on me, leering more bad words at me. You can't say that I beat him senseless cos he has no sense to beat. I swallow the urge to yell, "Hey, Bimbo, screw her. I did."

Ingrid, her black-dagger eyes deep in my chest, loudly says, "Hey, bus driver. Let's go. Nothing to see here."

Nothing me, that's for sure.

As the bus pulls away, the girls, including Bimbo, point at me, yacking and laughing. Englebert sings that the Home Waltz should last forever, bringing together two lonely people. With no sun, I don't even have my shadow to dance with.

12:45 PM

The nurse sews up my left hand. Seven stitches. My chest puffs up like my swollen right, which she can't sew up cos of the swelling. She says my right pinky's broken. Says I need to put it on ice to get the swelling down. War wounds. I feel tough and ready to scrap anyone, even Skinny. She straightens out my pinky and squishes it against a wide Popsicle stick and wraps bandages around it. Holy! I yelp like a kicked puppy. It hurts so much even my sweat screams as it soaks me with its fear stench. The nurse tells me to stop acting like such a baby. Who's acting? She tells me to take it easy and breathe as she ties a tongue depressor to my pinky. She may as well jam bamboo splinters up under my fingernails while she's at it. Tears blur my vision, which is a good thing, I guess. She tells me to come back and see her after the swelling's gone down, cos she wants to check for infections and x-ray my hand, then bandage it up properly. Then she gives me a tetanus shot but not the rabies shot, like I thought I'd need. She says the doctor will see me on Tuesday. She won't give me anything for the pain cos I couldn't promise her I won't drink while I'm taking her pain pills. I'll just drink until the pain doesn't matter. It's always worked before. And really, this isn't the worst I've hurt.

1:00 PM

Delivering papers without the use of my hands makes a slow day even slower and makes me late delivering Mister Testadicazzo's papers again. He ambushes me, cursing me out in English and Italian. Stupid. So stupid.

I hold up my hands, showing him the blood seeping through the left's bandages, and tell him, "I had an accident." I want to say: I don't see what the big deal is, cos by the time my newspapers get to town, they're old news. But I don't. The old jerk never tips me and sometimes refuses to pay his subscription. His wife seems nice. Whenever her husband chews me out, she gives me home-baked cookies and hands me a neatly folded dollar bill that she has tucked inside her apron, as always, with a little wink and her shush-finger at her lips. Today, Missus Testadicazzo meets me at their back gate, looks around and then slips me a whole ten dollar bill, just as neatly folded as the singles she always gives me. Her double sawbuck does nothing to stop the pain throbbing through me with every step and every beat of my heart but it helps me sorta dim it.

Darkness creeps into the Canyon hours before Sky pulls her black shade. I finish delivering my newspapers, drenched in sweat, melted snow, and slushy mud. Yéye? meets me at the door, wearing a scowl that flays me. She points her lip at a set of clothes draped over her wringerwasher, turns on her heel, and leaves me alone and very afraid on the porch.

Peeling off my soaked clothes takes forever. Showering and dressing takes even longer.

Yéye? points her lower lip and death-ray eyes at a chair opposite hers. A steaming teapot, two tannin-stained mugs, two spoons, a jar of honey, and a can of evaporated milk sit between us.

"Lookit you, Jeez," she says, breaking the choking silence that had filled the kitchen. I focus on the white enameled wood stove to keep from turning to stone. Silence fills the room again like strong hands crushing my throat. She fills both cups, stirs in some honey, and shoves one my way. "Drink," she orders. "Green tea. Good medicine." I drink. Aside from the occasional crackle of burning pine and the gulps and slurps we make swallowing our tea, the house remains silent. The green tea fails to ease my pain and fright. She tops up her cup and tips the teapot toward me. I shake my head. She drinks slowly, quietly staring straight into my heart.

"I did some stupid things," I blurt. "I'm sorry."

"I don't want to hear anything about what you did," she snarls. "The cops want to ask you some questions."

"Cops? Questions?" I say. If they really wanted me, they'd have snatched me from the street cos everyone knows my routes and town's so small that if you peed in the middle of Front Street at the east-end of town, then walked to the west-end, you would get there in plenty of time to see your pee drain into the storm sewer. The cops in this town wouldn't waste time talking with Yéye? if they wanted me, they'd have hunted me down and wild-rided me to a holding cell in Kamloops, or beaten me almost dead up past the dump. Yéye? knows this too.

"Yes, cops. Yes, questions. Someone spiked your auntie Maxine's drink last night. She's sworn to kill whoever did it."

"I don't know anything about spiking anyone's drink," I say, mouthful of cotton. Spiking Bimbo's beer, Auntie's Southern Comfort, something Angelica drank, and who else? Maybe Cody and Pixie? Sick, just sick.

"You look like you know or think you know who did it," she says, her voice the magistrate's gavel rapping his desk as he guilts me before sending me to juvie. I wish you'd stop reading my mind, damnit! I shrug.

"I guess Skinny mighta done it, to prank Bimbo, but I don't think he would ever do something to hurt Auntie. That he wouldn't do. I'm sure," I say, each word escaping my mouth like a ball of dried mud disintegrating into a little puff of dust as it hits the air.

"If he'd a done it to that Bimbo, what makes you think he wouldn't do it to someone else, hey?" Yéye? says.

Cos he knows better than to try anything on Auntie Max. My answer is so limp the last words fall out in a jumbled whisper. "I just know he wouldn't, I guess."

Drunk Skinny could get real careless and do stuff his sober self wouldn't dream of doing. Thing of it is, he does talk about pulling pranks like that on everyone.

"You know I don't like that crowd you go with," she says.

"Boys don't *go* with each other. We hang," I say, huffing out a grr sigh. "Boys go with girls. Boys *hang* with other boys."

"You keep going with them boys you'll end up hanging from the end of a rope. Cops don't like bad stuff like this. And they like it less when we do it." Her words bite into me like a willow switch. "Not to mention what you can expect to happen to you from those girls' fathers. And your aunt."

"But I didn't do anything wrong," I say.

"Don't matter. If your friends did this, you'll all pay for it."

"What makes you think it was us, anyways? There must have been close to a hundred people there. Some old guys, too. You know, them guys that go with the John girls?"

"Sheesh. Just cos a man's been to prison doesn't make him guilty of every crime committed. Them McAllister boys is a pretty good bunch and spiking drinks isn't their way."

"Skinny and them, they're good guys, too," I say.

She sighs, shakes her head, and says quietly, "Them boys are going nowhere except to jail or early graves. I don't want you following them down that road."

"Why do you always say that?"

"Always? Sheesh you. Always, my arse. And I'll keep saying it till you hear me."

All but thumping my chest, I stand up to Yéye?. "I heard you the first time and I hear you now."

Her rattlesnake-strike glare knocks the Tarzan right outta me.

"If I find out you had anything to do with drugging them girls, you will wish them cops put you in jail. You will wish you'd died."

I wish I had the guts to say, "I already do." She should be happy that I'm not a leper and that a few people actually like me.

Her words have sent me for a switch. Skinny and them, and me, we got some good in us, somewhere. Sure, we get a little crazy sometimes but we're just kids, and kids mess up sometimes. But slipping my auntie a mickey, or Angelica, or anyone else—except Bimbo, who prob'ly deserved it—none of us would do that, ever.

"Well?" she says, "What you got to say for yourself?"

"I dunno," I say. "I, uh, spent mosta the night alone. With a girl."

She snorts. "One a them sm?ém girls?"

"Yeah. It started out pretty good but ended up pretty bad, I guess."

"Long as you chase séme? girls it'll end up bad for you and her. Same thing if you snag a full-blood Indian girl."

"Why? That doesn't make any sense to me." You mean I'm not good enough for any girl?

"A séme? wants things a certain way and expects things a certain way. Same with an Indian girl. And they'll never understand you and what you need from a woman. You walk a different road, and those kinds of girls can't walk it with you."

"So I shouldn't ever have a girlfriend?"

"Sheesh, you! Stop that stupid thinking and listen to my words."

"I don't get it." I hurt. I need sleep. My stupid brain's as backed up as a shitty toilet. I mean, first a hot girl wanted me, then another one snagged me and we sorta had real sex together. And it was good, so good, she felt like my Home Waltz. Then she ran to her friends and practically ignored me cos of the things I found funny.

Then she fell for Bimbo.

The good thing about my broken pinkie? It keeps me from feeling my broken heart, till I realise that my heart didn't break. I just don't want the world to see me for the loser I am: the guy who lost a girl to Bimbo.

"I said," Yéye? grrs, "I said, when you're ready for a woman in your life, the right woman will find you. And I asked if you could stop thinking about your spaeks? for a minute and focus on something important, like what happened to your aunt and some of them səmséme? girls?"

What woman would want a guy who couldn't get girls? And what woman would want a guy who couldn't even protect his own blood?

"I'll find out who did that to Auntie and I'll make 'em pay for it," I say, all puffed up again, but more like Rice Puffs than Tarzan.

She snorts an unhappy laugh. "You'll just get yourself into more trouble. Promise you'll leave it to someone who knows how to handle things like this."

Promises are a spiderweb she lays out to trap my mosquito words. Back teeth mashed into each other, I nod.

She pats my weak fist. "I know, sínci? but trust the right people to fix it."

"Maybe I am the right people." Them words, all v-61 out the chute, throw me too fast for the rodeo clown to save me.

Yéye?'s mouth, a taut rope under eyes that crush me like v-61's fore-hooves, says, "No, you're not." Then, like the merciful pop of a .22 into a lame bull's ear, she says, "Promise me you won't drink tonight."

"Why you always got to blame the booze for the stupid stuff I do? Maybe I'm just stupid. Yéye?, you ever think of that?"

She has more to say to me but I'm done listening. Yéye? must sound madder than she is, or she would have followed me into my room. Instead she scolds me out through the door. A pillow may silence a gun shot, but it doesn't shush Yéye?.

Damn.

Maybe I slept a bit. Yéye?'s calmed, or talked herself mute. Or she's set a trap and waits to yip yip yip at me until I get out of earshot. Anyone who says silence is golden has never been around my angry grandmother. I brush my teeth and she says nothing. Putting on my shoes, she says nothing. Unless you count her glare choking me to death. I want to tell her, "Goodnight. I'll see you later, 'kay?' But I can't face her.

My hand closes on the doorknob. She says, "I'll send Walter out after you." She would've called him already but he's out past Gold River with the trestle gang. When he gets back to town he'll drag me by the ear out to his ranch and work me till I have even less will to live than I have right now. At least he'll pay me for my misery and won't make me listen to a bunch of words I've heard a zillion times already. Yéye? and Uncle mean well, I know that, but they just don't get it; it's like they were born old and have no idea what it's like to live in the modern world.

She sighs. "You may as well get a good meal into you and catch a few hours sleep before you run off and kill yourself." She puts on a pot of rice and sends me out to the root cellar to fetch a jar of salmon and some carrots. I fall asleep at the table and wake when she slams a plate in front of me. I eat alone.

4:30 PM

The stink of last night sticks to my teeth no matter how hard I brush. Maybe a good swig of lemon gin will wash it off. Stepping from the warmth of Yéye?'s kitchen into late Saturday afternoon gloom, the shadowy cold of early near-night darkness, sends shivers through me. Yéye? had handed me my winter coat and toque after I pulled on my boots. She didn't say a word. She didn't have to and I'm glad I listened to her. Moon slides over the mountains, followed quickly by the wishing star. Since most of the snow has melted or blown away, since I won't have my Home Waltz tonight, at the very least cos of my gimpy hands, I have no wishes left. Dull orangey-yellow light fills the front room windows of almost every house I walk by. The walk downtown is as silent as River ever allows. My right hand, locked in the crook of my left elbow, bounces pain like Keith Moon's kick drum drumming my marching song. A smart guy would've taken a few Aspirin and stayed in till the hand healed.

Front Street, all rutted tracks of ice-coated, grime-dotted snow, crunches under my feet. The side streets shine like frozen lakes. With only my face to break my fall, I step carefully.

Skinny, JimJim, and Cody, almost hidden in the hotel's shadow, hands deep in their pockets, hang at the corner, stamping their feet like skittish stallions.

JimJim chucks my shoulder, says, "Had yourself a night, hey?" Then he sniggers and taps my bandaged balloon of a hand. Pain shoots up my arm and stabs me in the brain. "Anyone seen Bimbo?" He laughs.

"We got that little bastard good last night, hey?" Skinny goes.

"I saw," I say. "Good one."

"But maybe not as good as you got him this morning," JimJim says.

Skinny, all up in my face, says, "Yeah. Didn't know you had it in you, tough guy." I flinch; the way he says "tough" means *so not tough.* For a second it feels like Skinny's gonna lay the beats to me cos I hurt Bimbo. After what they did to him? Just how gimped-up has my hand made my brain and its thinking?

Stepping back and bracing for Skinny's left, I say, "The kid went crazy and started smashing bottles in Auntie's living room, so I hadda put him down. I guess he got the worst of it. Them girls had to pull me off him, I guess, or I might've killed him."

Skinny and JimJim laugh.

Skinny scruffs my hair like I'm a good dog or something. "Our little mosquito stings again. Good for you. Even if it was just Bimbo."

Keeping Bimbo's tooth on a chain around my neck seems a stupider-than-stupid idea now. I did nothing heroic taking that kid down, otherwise someone would've done it years ago. The more I think about it the more I realize that all I'd accomplished was beating the crap outta our generation's Crazy-Thom-in-training. No one, except maybe Ingrid and them, will doubt he deserved to get the works after he passed out. Everyone, including Ingrid and them, will see everything wrong with the beating he took from me. I'd tattooed him with my right instead of a felt pen or make-up. Skinny and JimJim go on about who did what to Bimbo and the stuff the ring of people around them said they should do to him, including pinching his nuts with clothes pegs.

Skinny says, his voice patting him on the back, "Yeah, we got him good, hey?" He slaps my back. "You missed out on a good one."

JimJim nods, "Yup, best one yet. And the twerp slept right through it, too."

Skinny laughs. "Like someone put ludes in his beer."

"Ludes?" I ask.

"You know, Quaalude? Sleeping pills?" JimJim says. "But prob'ly just one or two. That's just enough to get the job done."

Skinny nudges JimJim's arm. "I don't know who'd do something so rotten but we owe him a huge kʷukʷscémxʷ, hey?" Skinny and JimJim laugh, lost in another of their private jokes. Cody snorts a sneer as he steps away from them.

I swallow and squeak out: "You guys slipped him a mickey?"

"Hear about them girls?" JimJim says, way too quickly.

I shrug and step away from my friends. They say everyone's talking about someone spiking all the girls' drinks with DA—MDA, the love drug—and downers like Ludes and sleeping pills, that both Auntie Max and the Ashcroft coach took some spiked drinks, then went off somewhere to lez out. I could see my aunt taking a spiked drink on accident but not on purpose and definitely not to go with another girl. She'll be so mad that she won't let anyone near her place ever again. She might even want me dead cos I was there. My friends won't think it's funny once they face Auntie Max. JimJim says he thinks James spiked their drinks but he doesn't know for sure. Skinny says the séme? drug pedlar from Kamloops gave the drugs to whoever pulled the prank. Maybe for the first time, I might see my best friends the same way as Yéye? and I don't like it.

I bite my lip and suck in a hard breath, then say: "You guys helped him?"

Skinny and JimJim look at each other, violently shaking their heads.

"As if!" they practically shout, "Jeez, you."

No one says anything. We fidget, looking at each other like one of us has cut a silent-but-deadly one and hopes someone else gets the blame. After a painfully long time, Skinny steps forward and throws up his hands, "Listen. Fine. I got a hold of a coupla Ludes. Two little pills. Just two. And I dropped them into Bimbo's beer. That's all."

"And," JimJim says, "we only put them in Bimbo's beer. To teach him a lesson."

"Yeah, just a lesson," Skinny goes, "and some payback." He points at me. "Like what you tried pounding into him. Just more sophisticated."

"Listen," I say, "my grandmother and them think we—all of us—did it. And she says the cops want to put charges on us."

Skinny purses his lips. "She's just running her mouth. Trying to scare you. That's all."

"Yeah." JimJim blurts. "We didn't do anything wrong so we got nothing to worry about."

I want to believe them. Slipping Bimbo a mickey, as dirty a trick you can play on anyone, is pretty bad and makes it way too easy for the cops and everyone else who hates us to blame all the rest of the drugged drinks on us.

It occurs to me that Pixie, then Ingrid, wouldn't've wanted me if not for the MDA, or whatever, in their drinks. But what if their drinks didn't get spiked? This morning them girls didn't talk like girls drugged into sexing us up. But how would I even know what those kind of girls even sound like? The guys say the Ashcroft coach yanked the team from the tournament and took them home. Pretty much all the out-of-town teams dropped out of the tournament and everyone at school's mad and want whoever spiked the liquor to hang. They prob'ly mean us.

The guys say Pixie had to be helped onto the bus and joke that she had to wear an ice pack on her snatch cos of the reaming she took from Cody, who walks like he needs an icepack himself. He snarls and his eyes flip them the bird. Skinny looks away. JimJim kicks the chipped plaster at the base of the hotel's wall.

This will be one more dance I don't get a Home Waltz, on top of every other thing that's gone wrong today. I feel like I'm about to bury another buddy and not groove with The Footnotes. On this, one of the supposedly happiest nights of the year.

Skinny wraps one of his long arms around Cody's shoulder, the other around mine, paints on his widest grin, and says, "You two look like you could use a drink, so let's go have a drink, boys." He looks over his shoulder and clicks his tongue at JimJim, then pulls us toward the bush and what's left of our weekend booze. "Maybe two. Hey?"

Skinny's cheeriness is sugar spooned into an abscess tooth.

"And you guys can tell us all about your scores," JimJim says.

"Not much to tell, " I say, slipping into full-on boast mode. "Just the best sex I ever had."

"I humped jailbait. What more is there to say," Cody says.

Together, Cody and I make up one whole donkey, with me as the back end.

5:00 PM

The air around us feels like a classroom just before a big test. Skinny talks and talks and talks but says nothing. JimJim, hangs back a little, humming the first two lines of "2525" over and over again. Cody, who has never griped about pain, groans with every step: so annoying. With me, even quieter than usual, all clenched jaw and white-blue lights flashing behind my eyes every time my feet tromp ground, we make a beaten gang of zombies: aware of each other but not a unit, not like we used to be until last night. We've all but killed the shine that The Footnotes bring with them when they come to town. A chance to hear The Footnotes play their music and see their tribute to CCR is all I have left to look forward to. Most nights that would be enough. That and hoping to have a real Home Waltz.

Skinny scrounges up some nearly dry sticks and starts to build a fire when we get to our spot. JimJim doesn't tell him the fire will attract the yardman and the cops. Cody tries lighting a thin pine branch with his Zippo. He knows better. JimJim, still singing the first two lines of "2525," has slipped into the shadows. I sneak to my stash and my last mickey of lemon gin, in the crotch of a cottonwood—the schoolmarm—a good ten feet above me. My gimped hands keep me from getting to my gin, the medicine I need. I try willing my gin down from the crotch. I try so hard it hurts my brain. No go. Leaning against the cottonwood, knocking the back of my head against it, I let the tears fall. But not for too long. Skinny calls me. Feeling hollow, I head back.

The boys passing a bottle of whiskey around a weak fire don't even look up. We usually have mickeys, not twenty-sixers. They don't seem to notice or care that I haven't brought a bottle into the circle. Normally they'd tease me till I filled up so full of shame that I couldn't take a drink at gunpoint. JimJim scootches off, returning with my lemon gin.

He holds it up, and says, "That old schoolmarm must have crotch-rot. Look what I found in it." He laughs. Skinny laughs. Cody turns away from JimJim, sneering. I hang my head. Why can't I find a hiding place my friends don't know about?

"For chrissakes," Cody snaps, "she crushed my damn nuts. I don't know how."

"What?" Skinny goes. "She grabbem and squishem? She bitem?"

"Shit, no. It happened right after I shot my sixth load. Like my left nut snapped off. Now when I try to pee it feels like someone's kicking my balls. Kinda like the dose, maybe?"

The fire pops, shooting a burst of tiny orange sparks.

"A dose?" JimJim snorts. "You can't get a dose from a virgin, It's gotta be something else."

"Most I ever done's like three in a night," Skinny says. "Who needs more than that?"

"Shit, I'da stopped after one but she couldn't get enough. All virgins wanna go like that?"

"All virgins? No," Skinny goes. "Now you know what I go through every weekend. Them girls can't get enough of the Golden Sceptre."

Aside from flames eating mostly dry wood and the sound of whiskey sloshing in a bottle: silence.

JimJim, after a long pull from the bottle, says, "Any blood in your piss?"

Even the fire's gone mute.

"Great," Cody grunts, "One more thing I need to worry about."

"Just one more?" JimJim says.

"They say she's just thirteen," Cody says. "Thirteen'll get you twenty. Right?"

"Meh," Skinny goes. "Jailbait's better than masturbate."

"But masturbate's better than jail," JimJim says.

"I wouldna done her if I knew."

He doesn't fool me. I doubt he fools anyone. Each of us would've boned her if we had the chance, except maybe me, cos I'd've found a way to screw it up before we got to the actual doing it. She looked like one of the oldest girls in the room and she made it so clear she wanted to go even I noticed.

"Thirteen. Seventeen. Ninety-six," Skinny goes. "They're just numbers. You got laid and you enjoyed it right? I mean, until you realized she busted your balls."

"Wait," JimJim says. "She bleed?"

Cody freezes, the whiskey bottle in front of his face like Pinocchio's swollen nose. "Bleed?"

"From her snatch, you idiot," JimJim says. "If she didn't bleed when you stuck it to her the first time, she wasn't a virgin. It isn't rape if someone already took her cherry."

"Really?" Cody says. "Not even statutory rape?"

Skinny snatches up the bottle, swishes it, and watches the whiskey swoosh. "Old enough to bleed, old enough to breed."

My father says that, too. I can't even look at Skinny, my best friend, right now.

Cody snatches the bottle from Skinny's hand. "That doesn't sound right to me."

"Jeez you. No one cares," says JimJim. "She put herself out there. She asked for it. Cops won't put charges on you for being all hormonal and stuff."

Skinny puts on his Sergeant Stadanko voice and says, "Boys will be boys. Now just remember to keep your pecker properly cleaned and holstered."

"Even Indian boys," I say. "An Indian boy with a white girl?

Uh-uh. They will put charges on you and they will send you to juvie till you turn twenty-one."

Cody groans a deeper pain than the groans from his broken-balls pain. Rocking, he mutters the eff-word like some sorta chant, his arms wrapped around himself like a straitjacket.

"Lighten up, jeez," JimJim and Skinny blurt.

"You ever do a young one? Hey?" Cody says.

Skinny, all furrowed brow, says, "'Course. Everyone does, well not Squito. He doesn't do anyone, except maybe the occasional grandmother." His eyes still frowning, he winks at me, wearing a hollow, big, monkey mouth-grin. "Reminds me, I got you something."

He reaches inside his coat and pulls out a brown paper bag wrapped bottle. Gilbey's lemon gin. A whole, perfectly sealed bottle. My first thought: Why? My second: What did you put in it, budz?

After examining the seal, I say, "K^{w}uk^{w}scémx^{w}."

Skinny sneers a laugh. "My uncle bought me the wrong stuff. I asked for a bottle of real gin—the panty remover, hey?—but he got me this crap. You don't owe me anything for it. My treat. This time, I mean."

"Thanks," I say again. Skinny's uncles never make mistakes like this when they run for us. You can't even say that they were too drunk to remember what to get, cos the liquor store doesn't sell to drunks. It doesn't feel like a gift. Cody seems to get quieter with each swallow, as if he's being pulled inside his whiskey bottle bit by bit.

"So, counting the two I snagged last night, I've notched my hundredth snag. That's one hundred pussies who've ridden my Golden Sceptre," Skinny says. His smile is glowing headlights. "And I'm only seventeen."

If his other ninety-eight are like Henrietta and Belinda, I wonder if any of them count as real sex. I wonder how many of them actually wanted his Golden Sceptre. I wonder if any of them asked him or begged him to bone them. My brain wants to ask him but my mouth swallows instead of spitting out the words. A shot of whiskey doesn't wash away my swallowed words' bitter taste. I wonder where he got my bottle.

"Some kinda record, hey? A guy your age doing more girls than most of us will by the time our dicks spit dust instead of jizz," JimJim says.

"You ever stop to think you got a hundred snags cos no girl wants to lay with you twice?" Cody says. "You're seventeen and still in Grade Ten and the only thing you got going for you is your mile-long spaeks?."

My breath stalls. You can feel Mad-Skinny rising up inside of Skinny. JimJim shrinks back. Cody looks Skinny square in the face. He doesn't back away, doesn't flinch, and doesn't take a defensive pose. Skinny's hands transform into fists of iron. His forearms bulge like Popeye's. Mad-Skinny is a death machine and no one's friend. He takes in a deep breath and shakes his head.

"Listen, cripple-dick, and listen good," Skinny goes, still a balled fist. His words come out like spit from a chew of snuff. "Almost every chick who's ridden my Golden Sceptre comes back for more. The only ones who don't couldn't handle it the first time."

Skinny stands. Facing Cody, he pulls out his spaeks?. Cody juts out his chin and stares straight ahead. Skinny slaps Cody in the face with his dink. Cody's face twists into a scowl but he doesn't flinch, move, or let his eyes flick away from Skinny.

"If I was counting coup, you'd be number one-hundred-and-one. But, nah. I ain't no homo. You're gonna get plenty of that in the can. They're gonna love you in jail."

Skinny puts his dick back inside his pants and tries to grab Cody's chin with his dick hand. Cody's hand zips out and locks on Skinny's wrist. He must be a lot stronger than he looks, unless Skinny's just playing with him, but that wouldn't be like the Skinny I know.

"Fuck off, Bernard," Cody says. I wince, feeling the pain Cody's about to get piled onto his broken bits.

Skinny will rip him apart for telling him to screw off, for calling him by his real name, and for grabbing his wrist. But Skinny doesn't even make a fist. Stuff this insane doesn't even happen in my dreams. Cody must have a death wish. Skinny would ignore a drunk Cody but Cody's practically sober. Skinny snaps his wrist free of Cody's hold and shakes it a bit before stuffing his hand into his coat pocket.

"A guy like you's gonna be queen of the tier. And that's what they'll call you, Tier Queen," Skinny goes.

"Skinny. Stop it. Let him be," I say. My words hang at my throat like a noose. Both he and Cody gawk at me, their quick-draw eyes ready to pull on me.

"Shut up, Squito. I can take care of myself," Cody says.

"Yeah," Skinny goes, "Stay out of it or I'll take back that bottle I gave you and ram it up your half-breed ass."

Stiff with fear, I swallow hard. I want to stand up to Mad-Skinny and take my lumps like a man, not a simpering rat like Bimbo. But I am more simper than man. Yesterday we were friends, best friends. We look way different today, not the tight group of guys looking forward to the best dance of the year, to a whole whack of new girls as horny as us. More than finally having my Home Waltz, I hope we can get over the bad stuff and be friends again.

"And fuck you, Skinny. Fuck you to hell," Cody says. He doesn't move to defend himself. What an idiot, a total idiot. Cody's begging Skinny to pulverize him, to kill him. I guess I'd rather be dead than jailed and maybe that's what Cody's up to now, cos if Mad-Skinny gets loose, it's all over for Cody, that's for sure. And if there's any of the madman left, I'll join Cody. It's not the way I'd thought I'd exit this world, except I'll be going out with my boots on, and maybe that's how they'll all remember me, if anyone remembers me at all.

Skinny laughs. His fists melt. His face softens. "I already said I don't do guys, so just fuck off, Cody. Fuck off and die."

Cody smiles. "I'd rather fuck on cos it's a lot more fun."

We all laugh, even Skinny. He tips the bottle at Cody, takes a swig, then passes it to Cody, who tips it at Skinny before taking a drink. Skinny leans into the fire, arms stretched out. He starts telling a story, using voices and words the Ashcroft girls said before we started to play last night. After a while, the stories Skinny tells erase the bad stuff and we laugh and joke and jabber on about how excited we are about the dance that's about three hours away. Skinny tells us again how he bagged two girls last night and would've had Annabelle, too, except that she left on the first bus, along with JimJim and them. JimJim laughs when Skinny tells his deep throat story, and about how, at first, those girls were afraid of his Golden Sceptre; about how they both chased him down and begged him to let them try to take all of it inside them. Skinny says he had to draw the line at going in Henrietta's back door, like she practically begged him to. He says Henrietta and Belinda wanted to tag-team him, too, and they would've, if the snow hadn't started coming down. Just hearing him say that makes me feel a different kinda sick inside as I swallow Henrietta and Belinda's versions of Skinny's story.

Cody wishes he'd gotten on that bus and never set eyes on Pixie. He's a shadow of himself. He says Pixie has the boobs and body of a nineteen-year old. At least nineteen. And perfect, like Cyndi Wood's, but not with the awe we usually have whenever a girl reminds us of Cyndi Woods. Is hating yourself afterwards a fair enough price to pay for a night with a girl like Pixie? He tells us what happens to statutory rapists in jail. He tells us how his Uncle William died of something like fifty stab wounds in the prison woodwork shop. But

William went around doing bad stuff to girls between four and six. Not just one, either. And not cos he was fooled. He hunted them like a poacher. William's story sucks all joy from the air.

All serious and silent, we drink, out of habit, and not for getting the happy buzz on three hours before the best dance of the year. I feel warm inside, a little calmer, but no closer to wanting all the good stuff that could come from a dance, even though, as I see it, all the bad stuff that could happen, happened last night. Despite being primed by the whiskey, my heart can't dance a joyous two-step and my little chief knows it has zero hope of snagging a girl. No Home Waltz for me. A part of me wants to drown in lemon gin's sweet oblivion but another wants to find a happy place where I can enjoy and remember Fast Freddy's show tonight, every single second of their performance. I would enjoy it more if I could drink while they play and the dancers dance. Sharing a good time with my closest friend: Gilbey's lemon gin. Anyone can sneak a mickey into the hall but no one can take a twenty-sixer. I have no idea what to do with my bottle, a problem that takes over most of my thoughts, until Skinny snaps me out of it with another one of his conquest stories. He always tells great stories.

Stories will change and grow with each telling and each teller has his spin. In Skinny's versions, he and his dink are heroes. In the girls', Skinny and his spaeks? are the villains. You have to wonder if truth or facts have any place in a story. Skinny's stories make me laugh, same as the girls' versions, but for different reasons. Now I won't see his stories the same way, cos I will never know the truth of them. He has something, something that makes girls like Annabelle and Muriel fight for him and want him. I don't get it. Is he a monster, too? What is it that makes him a monster to one girl and not another? Is it the same thing that makes me a monster to me and not Yéye? or Auntie Violet? I will go crazy trying to figure this stuff out.

“I hope The Footnotes have a new single for us,” I say, filling the silence following Skinny’s story. JimJim flashes me a quick look, smiling.

“Who. Fucking. Cares,” Cody growls. He looks ready to wing his whiskey bottle at my head. For a guy who doesn’t swear much, Cody’s spitting out a lot of them tonight. The only guy I know who swears less is JimJim.

“Yeah, who cares?” Skinny goes. “You think a new song’s gonna change a single thing about this place or make anything right in the world?” Maybe not the whole world but it’ll make mine a whole lot better.

“I guess not,” I say. “Think I’ll grab some chips from Bernie. Line my gut before pounding back this two-six. You coming?” I don’t look at any of my friends, hoping they’ll say no or just ignore me.

“You go on ahead,” JimJim says. “We’ll catch up with you later.”

Skinny and Cody say nothing.

I wave my bottle at Skinny and thank him again for getting it for me, then stuff it inside my coat and under my gimped arm. But thanking him seems wrong. Maybe them cops’ll leave me alone. After all, what trouble can a gimp, even me, get up to without hands?

5:45 PM

Despite the trees and nearby roofs, I can see the coffee shop to the west of me and the dance hall to the east. Two white vans have backed into stalls near the stage doors. No band who's played here has ever brought that much stuff, so this dance will be like a show at the Agrodome or Pacific Coliseum—not that I've actually seen shows in Big Town but I've heard a lot about them from the people who get to go. I need to see what they brought, maybe have a drink with Fast Freddy himself.

The band carries in their own stuff.

"Hey," I go, "Need a hand with that?"

Choctaw, the second guitarist, taps my gimpy hand and laughs. "Maybe next time, kid."

The Footnotes are so cool they've made me forget I'm gimped up. Watching them unpack their vans works on me like pounding back a mickey of gin in a single gulp.

Fast Freddy pops out the stage doors, waves, and says, "Hey, Squito." He smiles and slaps my shoulder. "You coming tonight?"

"Wouldn't miss it for the world," I say. "Hey, you got a new song for us? A new single?"

"We already put out two this year. What do you want from us?"

"A whole LP. You could do that, couldn't you?" I say.

He winks. "Might have a surprise or two for you tonight."

He grabs Rocky's kick drum and carries it inside the hall.

I can sing a little bit and can even sing in front of people when I'm drunk, not something I ever thought I could ever do, not in this lifetime, and prob'ly wouldn't have, if not for Skinny. But there's no way anyone would pay me to sing at a dance, not without Skinny and them, or make real records, like The Footnotes.

Andrew Moses pulls in and parks his pick-up right in front of the hall's main doors, taking up two whole spaces. He buys a new truck every September, mostly cos he's run the crap out of his old one and doesn't believe he'll get a second winter out of an old one. Sometimes he has to replace his truck cos he wrapped it around a tree or parked it under a falling rock. They say he drives so crazy he should just buy an old tank and be done with it. Yéye? says he should stay off the road and away from all living things. Andrew gets to be head of security cos he went to the States so he could go fight in Vietnam. He left our res on a warrior's boast and came back with a Vietnam Service Medal, Purple Heart and a Bronze Star, and, they say, without a single mark on his body. He wears a six-inch Bowie knife on his belt, along with a chrome key ring that holds a key to just about every building in town, and keeps a thirty-eight revolver in his right boot. No one's supposed to know about his gun but, like most secrets, everyone does. He worked security at the mill until they shut it down. Since then he's sort of made himself the town's security guard, patrolling the streets at night even though no one's asked him to and no one pays him either. No one seems to mind cos even the cops says crime rates have dropped a ton since Andrew started his patrols. Almost everyone, whether drunk or sober, listens to him.

He nods, his face hidden under the shadow of his ten-gallon hat. He doesn't even seem to look at his key ring before pulling the hall key up to the lock.

"You dancing tonight? Or drinking?" Andrew asks.

"O, you know," I say, shrugging. "Just gonna lay my trapline and see what I snag." With my chest puffed out, my words sound like they're being squeezed out of a leaking balloon.

Andrew nods toward the bushes at the end of the parking lot: "If you left anything over in them bushes, best move it or you'll lose it."

"Thanks," I say. Just as with Yéye?, there's no point in pretending you don't know what Andrew's talking about, or lying to him. He's spooky, cos he knows pretty much everything. I don't know if it's cos he's lived a long time and has seen just about everything, stupid or otherwise, that kids and most adults do. Like Yéye?, I believe that the grandfathers and grandmothers whisper our secrets to him. I figure they whisper our secrets to him when they think they need to, cos he always gets to the general store and liquor store, or wherever there's mischief to be foiled, before any harm's done. He always beats the cops to the scene of a crime, too, and sits on the bad guys until the cops finally show up. Unlike them cops, though, Andrew doesn't have to hold you down with handcuffs or a beating. I guess he's better than a cop, cos he can stop a crime with just a look, and he has a heart. He's let me go with a warning a few times, Skinny and them, too, but never for the same thing twice. No one's tried to break into the liquor store for a few years, not since the George Downey thing.

George Downey, drunk and thirsty, was the last guy to try to break into the liquor store, a smash and grab at two in the morning. Andrew grabbed George by the collar just as he was about to climb through the broken glass. George cut his arm, needing something like one hundred and eighty stitches—well, a lot of stitches, anyway—and tore some nerves and tendons. They say that George pretty much gibbled his own arm for life, even though Andrew squeezed George's upper arm until it stopped gushing blood. He held George like that until the cops brought the public health nurse over to patch him up. They took George away in a chopper, straight to the hospital in Kamloops and from there to jail, where he'll be for at least three more years. George's wife says saving his arm like that was a waste of time cos it doesn't work any more and neither will George when he gets out cos no will hire a gimped ex-con. She says she'll stick around until he's freed from prison and leave him the minute he takes his first drink. This time, she says, she means it. Thing is, she's shacked up with another drunk: Alex Cruickshank, a redheaded snake from around Hundred Mile. Alex could be another Crazy Thom, if anyone liked him.

"Yep," Andrew says. "And best not be trying to sneak that hip flask inside my hall."

I laugh. "My mickey got stuck up inside a tree. But I got a two-six of gin I need to stash."

"Gin? You drink too much gin and you'll turn into a damn woman. You should drink whiskey, a man's drink. Anyways, no safe place to stash it around here, not with all them outta town cops and rent-a-cops they brought in. If I was you, I'd put it some large soda cups from the hotel and try sneakinnem past me." He smiles, then closes the door behind him.

Dang, I like drinking in them bushes, cos you can see the whole parking lot, who's coming and going, and you usually see them cops before they see you. But if them rent-a-cops plan on watching this spot, I'll just stash my gin a ways up the hill, under the fallen tree near a stack of old railway ties. Walking up there every time I need a drink will help me keep my head tonight and maybe I won't drink so much. But with my luck I'll miss out on something cool.

It feels late. Some days I wish I had a watch, even though my grandfather always said a man who wears a watch is a prisoner of time. I worry they'll shut down the hotel coffee shop grill soon. As much as I want to hang out by the stage door and maybe get invited inside by the band, Town's almost as dead as it is early in the morning when I deliver my papers. A few people hang near the Ladies and Escorts entrance, joking and smoking. Dermot Black and Alphonse Charlie, a coupla young kids with zero brains between them, hang at the pub's front doors trying to get a runner. Brainless young twits, cos even Crazy Thom, who might have one working brain cell, knows you have to stock up if you want enough booze to get you through dance weekend. And no one'll get you off-sales, cos the bartender'll know the runner's running, or the runner'll use your money to buy himself a few more rounds. The liquor store always closes early on dance days, just like it does Wednesday afternoons, and the pub cuts off sales at noon, cos the cops tell them to. Unless you want to pay bootlegger's prices, you get your booze early. Unless you're already old.

Some old people step outside the Ladies and Escorts door. Sloppy drunk, laughing, trading stories, smoking, sipping draft beers they smuggled out. Old people get all the breaks, getting drunk in a warm room instead of outside in a night cold enough to freeze pop and people. And they get free pretzels, so they don't even have to stop drinking in order to coat their guts with a little food. I hope I live long enough to be one of them. On nights like this, it doesn't feel like I will, though: Not cos it feels like Death's stalking me or anything like that. Sometimes I just feel like my life is already over.

6:00 PM

Bernie. On dance night, near the end of her shift, Bernie, all bubbly smiles, dances through her closing chores, looking on the outside the way I sorta feel on the inside.

Bernie runs one of her long, slender fingers along the chain of hickeys around my neck. "Vampires get you? Finally get a girlfriend or did your gran's Hoover attack you?"

Her smile. If you can get eaten up in a good way, Bernie's smile just swallowed me whole. Warm as September Sun, I feel nothing but joy, like a Home Waltz should feel.

All trance-like voiced, I say, "A white girl. Closest one I could find that reminded me of you."

Her cheeks grow a little pink. Her smile gets chilly, as if November Wind has blown through her September Sun. She sneaks a squinty-eyed glance at the greasy guy sitting in Fat Elvis' seat at the lunch counter. She puts her hands on my shoulders, pressing her body against mine. I start to grow a hard one. I groan and try to push out the brain pictures of us dancing naked under stars before falling into the ultimate Home Waltz on a soft bed. Whispering, she hisses, "Listen up, Loverboy, don't ever say stuff like that around me again."

A little louder than I needed to, I say, "Sorry. I'm sorry." Sorry I lust you. Sorry I could love you. Sorry I'm three years younger than you. Sorry I don't have Skinny's dink. Sorry I'm just a 'breed. Sorry I'm not good enough for you....

My cheeks burn. Bernie winks as she pushes off me. What the hell are you saying to me?

What am I s'posed to think, or say, or do, or feel?

Tall, Brylcreemed black hair slicked back like a greaser outta

American Graffiti, some greasy guy watches us like a gunfighter ready to pull. With his alligator boots, tight black dress pants, and blue checked cowboy shirt, he looks like a gunfighter, and prob'ly rides bulls for a living.

"Watch yourself, kid," he says, voice as deep as a lowing bull's.

"Sorry," I say. Sorry I don't have fists of iron. Sorry I can't pound your head into the lino.

"O, Jack, leave him alone," Bernie gushes, all thick and sugary. "He's okay." She pats his hand and leans into him. A lot closer than she got to me. "Jack, meet Qʷóqʷésk̓ iʔ. Squito. Squito, meet my new boyfriend, Jack. Squito here is one of Margaret Bob's grandchildren."

"That bunch, hey?" He looks at my hand but doesn't accept it. Instead, he turns his attention to his cup like I'm not even there, then pushes it toward Bernie. "Where's my refill, Angel. And while you're at it, bring me another one a them doughnuts?"

Her bubbliness withers and her walk has lost its dance. She can't love that jerk. She just can't. I don't understand what she sees in him. Jerks like him always get the best girls and I have no idea why. My brain has me calling Jack out for treating Bernie badly and insulting my family. He could probably kill me with a single punch—he has that look to him. But even if I could take him, Bernie would rush to his bleeding hide and hate me for hurting the guy she loved. If I live to be a hundred, I'll never understand girls.

"Can I get you something?" Bernie says, her smile a faded daylight moon. "Grill closes in ten minutes."

"Just chips and gravy, please. O, and can I have a large Mountain Dew to go. Um, with two cups, too?" I don't like Mountain Dew but it goes pretty good with gin.

"Sure thing, Loverboy." She winks, but her words and smile are as appealing as a glass of warm, flat pop. I could drink the gin straight but it burns my guts and I don't want to get bleeding ulcers like my grandfather. They killed him slowly and left him in pain and broke from buying Tums by the case.

"Angel," Jack growls, "gimme a smoke." He glares so hard at the kitchen wall that it starts to melt. I don't know where this guy comes from but I wish he'd go back there and stay. We don't need him around here and Bernie sure doesn't need him wrecking her life. She runs out, fumbling in her purse for her cigarettes. She pulls one out, hands it to him, and lights it. He grabs her hand and clamps it on the countertop.

"No. Just leave it. And your lighter, too."

She drops her pack of smokes near his cup and hands him her lighter. He slips both into his shirt pocket and then lets go of her wrist. She rubs her wrist. There's no love in his look. I want to kill the quiet by playing the juke but I don't want to be any closer to Jack than I already am. Bernie brings me a large Pepsi.

"It's my mistake. You don't have to pay for it," she says.

Bernie's gone so fast I say thank you to her backside, a view that deserves its own thank you. She gathers up all the sugars, ketchups, salts and peppers, lines them up on the lunch counter and refills them.

"Shit, woman, you said you'd be done by six. No way I'm wasting any more time waiting while you piss around here. I'm going for a beer. Meet me in the pub when you get off."

"I said seven," she says, a warrior in her words.

"I know what I heard. Don't expect me to wait around for you all night." He leaves.

"I could put on some Creedence," I say.

"You could."

"'Lookin' Out My Back Door?'"

"'Travelling Band?'" she says, a bit of bounce tints her voice.

"'Kay. And how about 'Up Around the Bend?'"

"'Walk on Water.'" She laughs like her real self. "You need dimes?"

"Nah. I'll put in a silver dollar."

"Big spender, you," she says. In her way, she's made me feel like one and I like it.

Ten songs for a buck is a decent price, if you can spare a buck to play ten songs. I put on songs I think Bernie will like but no mushy ones, cos the last thing I want to do is make her all romantic for her a-hole boyfriend. She finishes refilling the salt and peppers and sugars before my chips are ready. She's so good at it I doubt she spilled a single grain of anything. She takes up some salt and tosses it over her shoulder. All the girls do it but they don't say why.

Bernie puts a mountain of chips and gravy in front of me, along with a small side of onion rings.

"Gladys says she made too many onion rings and thought you could use them. Got to fatten you up before you waste away to nothing, hey?" She puts her hand on my shoulder and I sigh. Those onion rings, all steaming hot and dripping fat, make my mouth water. There's no way Gladys made too many for someone else, cos she measures everything. I shovel them down and almost the whole mountain of fries. Bernie's filled all the ketchups and wiped down the lunch counter and all the tables by the time I'm done eating. I've shoveled in so much food that my buzz is gone. Normally, that would bother me, but tonight I see it as a good thing.

"Can I get the bill, Bernie?"

"Bill? What bill?" Bernie shrugs.

"For my chips and Pepsi and the other cup?

"G'wan," she says, pushing me toward the door. "Get out of here so we can finish closing up, hey?"

"Thank you," I say.

"For what? Have fun tonight. And watch out for them vampires." Bernie winks. She locks the door and flips the *Open* sign to *Closed.* I didn't even get to ask her if she'd be at the dance tonight. I kinda hope not cos that leech Jack will be stuck to her and she'll look unhappy and so will I, or she'll look happy with him and that would make me miserable. Bernie's not my girl, so I have no right to be jealous of Jack, but I guess I am. I wish bad things would happen to him and I don't even feel sick about it. Anyway, I'd feel the same way if any guy treated any girl the way he treats Bernie.

7:00 PM

I'm pretty much the only one walking the street, though loads of cars and trucks line it, most headed to the dance hall. Wind, all fired up, blows through me like I'm naked. I'd be happier in any one of them cars. I doubt one of them fancy winter coats you see in the Sears catalogue would warm me up. I'd have been smart to put on my long johns, even though they'd turned pink in the wash. I'm usually pretty good about keeping colours and whites separate but the one time I forgot, I let my father's new, red cowboy shirt in with our underwear and sheets. That shirt's now as pink as a baby blanket, same as my long johns and other underwear, and our sheets and pillowcases. It cost me twenty dollars to replace the shirt. Yéye? leant me enough money to buy him new bedding, which we needed anyway cos ours was so thin it ripped a little every time you cut a fart. Only my father is stupid enough to spend a whole twenty dollars on a shirt he'd wear maybe twice. Yéye?, Auntie Violet, and I could eat for two weeks on less than that and we usually do. I see why they say "mad enough to make my blood boil", cos being mad about having to buy my father that new shirt has made me angry all over again and now I don't feel so cold. I walk faster, too. Sweat beads and then freezes on my forehead and Wind huffs over it, icing my brain. I need gin's fire to warm me in a happy way.

Cars, trucks, and even two horse and buggies cruising for parking spots crawl along the road. Barnaby Nixon paces the space in front of his house, a shotgun tucked in the crook of his arm.

"Hey, Squito, howzit going?" Barnaby says, through a huge two-toothed grin. He says losing his teeth is just part of getting ready for his second childhood.

"Good, I guess. You?"

He pats his shotgun. "Got sweet Alma here. Tonight we're a no parking sign." He chuckles. Poor guy, dance night magic must have skipped his house.

Even with their windows rolled up, I can hear each private little car party. Girls saying no and giggling. Guys talking about the moose Johnny John bagged up past nk̓úxʷ, a monster of a bull that everyone's talked about for days and days. No one offers to let me in—not like any of the vehicles has room for anyone else. The ones who see me hold up their drinks and oww whooo. I wave without howling back, cos that always gets me tossed in the 'tank for causing a disturbance or being drunk in public. "Walking while intoxicated," Skinny always says in his Sergeant Stadanko voice. The gin pulls me to it. After pouring half of the Mountain Dew into the other cup, I top them both with gin. Swigs of whiskey or rum would've made me puke but the gin, sweetened by the Mountain Dew, lights me up a little. I down the first one in three big gulps.

Andrew opens the hall's main doors. Their rattle, like a dinner bell, makes everyone crowd toward them, everyone except me. Some of the crowd cheer. Some clap and whoop. Clinton Adams shouts, "It's about damn time." I walk, real cazh, holding the second cup between the heels of both hands. The ground, all dry, snow and ice free, seems to slip under me. My heart pumps like it did during that first feet-melting kiss with Ingrid. My nipples tingle but that's all.

No wood, nothing like that, just the same sorta feeling I get when Della d'Angelo belts "Amazing Grace."

"Get in line," Andrew shouts. "Act like humans. Not damn cows." Just then, Constable Bailey pulls up beside the hall. As far as I'm concerned, he really shouldn't even be on the res and I'm not the only one who thinks so. We don't have much say in when or if cops should be allowed on our land. I slip a little deeper into shadow and watch Bailey walk over to Andrew.

Alfred John, usually quiet and polite, growls, "C'mon, Andy. Just let us in. It's freakin' cold out here."

Andrew slowly shakes his head. "Longer it takes you to toe the line, the longer it's gonna take you to get inside the hall. I got all night."

Small voices tell Alfred to be quiet and behave. In almost no time at all, people are lined up around the corner of the hall. Andrew lets them in two at a time, stopping anyone he thinks is carrying a bottle or packing a knife. He confiscates a lot of knives and almost as many mickeys.

Two of the cops I saw in Snook's lobby yesterday join Bailey and Andrew. One of the new cops elbows Bailey's ribs, and says, "Looks like we're partying hard tonight!" He laughs. Bailey and Andrew do not.

We all know how stupid it is to try sneaking anything past Andrew. We all know he could pour you a drink from the bottle he took as easily as he could bar you from entering the hall. We all know he won't turn you over to the cops unless you do something wrong, like beat someone up. Growing older should make you smarter, but some of these people, even my own relations, act worse than us kids after they've had a few. After the last person goes inside, there's a green garbage can half-filled with mickeys of whiskey and even a couple of jugs of wine. He put maybe a dozen knives and a blackjack into a box that sits between his feet. On Monday or Tuesday he'll give the knives back but the cops'll take the blackjack. They'll ask him who he took it from and Andrew'll shrug his shoulders and say he doesn't know. He knows his family and he knows them cops and what they do. I guess Andrew takes his job pretty seriously and does it well enough that almost no one gets mad at him for taking away their booze or knives.

But there's always one or two and tonight there are two: Marlon Jack and Esther Black. Bailey puts them in the backseat of his cruiser, so they're pretty much guaranteed to stay in the drunk tank until Magistrate Perkins shows up for work Monday morning. They're old—in their forties at least—and should've known better. Constable Bailey doesn't take people up past the dump to teach them lessons like most other cops, but if Marlon doesn't shut his mouth, he could be Bailey's first.

Esther's no better. She's bitching out Bailey and punching Marlon, who's doing good at not hitting her back. If she keeps it up, Bailey will put charges on her and she'll end up in jail for a good long time. Esther's not one of us. She says she's Indian but she doesn't know from where or who her family is. She came to town as Frank Turner's sm?eméc̓e and stuck around after he let her go but she never left town. She says she stays cos she likes it here. But almost everyone says she stays cos she has nowhere else to go, which must be true cos she doesn't really live anywhere here, either. They say she shacks up with anyone who'll let her stay and one day she'll leave with a trucker and never come back. All the old women dislike her, even Yéye?. They say their men pass Esther around like a jug of wine. The women say she'll go with anyone who offers her a drink or meal or whatever. Some guys at school say Esther's let them do it to her for one beer or a half-pack of smokes. I may be desperate but I'm sure not desperate enough to pay an old woman to let me do it to her. Not yet, anyways. And if I ever get desperate enough to do it to Esther, I'll never tell a soul. Those old guys have it all: vehicles, homes, money, and they're allowed to drink in bars and stuff, so it's no wonder they get all the girls, even if they're just like Esther. But being old seems a high price to pay for all those good things. If there's a way, I'd like all that good stuff to happen to me before I get old, so I could enjoy it.

Bailey grabs me by the shoulder so hard that my drink sloshes over my hand. I let it splash to the ground.

“Hey,” I say, maybe meaner-voiced than I meant. “You made me spill my pop.”

As he drags me toward his car, he says, “That’s not all I’ll make you spill.”

Guys in the crowd laugh, another, whose voice I don’t recognize, shouts, “Busted!” JimJim shouts, “Run, Squito run!”

I could die right here.

A few seconds ago I thought Marlon might be the first guy Bailey takes up past the dump, now it looks like I will be first, my guts spilled on the road and left as food for coyotes and wolves. My Home Waltz and swan song all at once.

I’ve never run from Bailey so I have no clue how fast he is or if he would even chase me. If I did get away, I’d have to run uphill and I run uphill about as good as a dead rabbit—I guess I pretty much run like a dead rabbit downhill and across flats, too. The only cop I ever outran was Spotface. But next time we crossed paths—something that always happens in a town this small—he cornered me and batted me around like a cat on a catnip mouse. Most guys would take their licking first time, cos it won’t hurt nearly as much as the next one, or prison time when he puts resisting arrest and maybe other charges on you. I sorta hope he hits me now, in front of people who could tell the judge he started it. Only in some of my dreams would the court believe me.

My breaths stop and I start going limp. They call cops bears but they won’t leave you alone if you play dead. My brain whispers, “Lighten up. You didn’t do nothing wrong. Act guilty and you’ll miss the dance. Lighten up. You could wind up dead.” They call cops bears but they don’t look out for you or help you when you get sick. They call cops bears but they act like sharks: always hungry, looking for something to eat. Bailey squeezes my arm tight enough to make my pinky grow numb, and gives me a shake, not a brain-rattling shake, just hard enough to rip me from my head.

"'Kay. How come?" I say.

"Just a few questions about a matter I'm looking into. Nothing to worry about," Constable Bailey says. Right. When a cop tells you not to worry, you'd better worry, and think of a good story fast. Bailey could arrest me for whatever he thinks I did last night. My Home Waltz dances off the dance floor and out the doors without me.

I shouldn't have to fake casual and innocent, cos I am. Mostly. Still, Bailey's already made me feel like a criminal. You have to think cops took courses on making you feel guilty in order to get their cop license. Bailey, who's the closest thing to a good cop I've ever seen, is a master of making you feel like you've done something wrong. You have to wonder how cops can sleep at night when they spend their time putting crimes on you that you never committed. I wonder how people who've done bad stuff feel when they have to face cops. I guess if I feel guilty when I'm not, I'd feel guiltier when I was, so one thing's certain, if I choose a life of crime, it will be short. One of the new cops pulls his nightstick and the other rests his hand on his holster, one on each side of the window framing Marlon's screaming face.

Nightstick taps the window at Marlon's nose and, in a voice loud enough for everyone outside the hall to hear, says, "Quiet down or I'll give you something to cry about." Nightstick sounds just like my father. I shiver.

Over his shoulder, Bailey says, "Time to separate those two. Put the woman in your car."

Nightstick and his buddy try to pull Esther by her hair from the backseat.

Marlon, trying to grab a hold of Esther in his cuffed hands, yells, "Hey! Let'er go. She's my sm?ém. Let'er go or I'll fuckin' kill yas."

The cops drop Esther on her butt and Nightstick pokes and bops Marlon with his nightstick. They shout at each other, Marlon and

Nightstick, until Marlon yelps and quiets down, probably laid out on the floor and hopefully not dead.

The crowd sighs and gulps, then falls as silent as a funeral. Andrew scowls at Nightstick, his hands balled into sċuwenáy̓tmx-sized fists. Four more cops from out of town screech to a stop near Bailey's car. They pile out, one cradling a shotgun. We outnumber them by at least 40:1 but none of us runs at them. I want to but I am petrified. I guess we all are, except the women.

Some women and girls try running to Esther and Marlon. Their boyfriends and husbands hold them back. I won't be the only missing guy tonight. Poor Marlon. I feel bad for Esther, all spread out face-first on the ground under that cop's foot. Nightstick makes Marlon sit up. He can't or won't lift his head but he can't hide his already swollen eye and lips.

The other three cops drag Esther by her arms to another cop car. Her pants slide off, showing everyone who looks her big bum and pink underpants with the stretched-out elastics and Thumper painted on them. She has the kinda bum no one but Marlon could love. I gawp at it anyways. When they drag her into the backseat she flashes her bush and bitty pink slit. The cops laugh but don't cover her up. One of them drives off with Esther, another takes Bailey's key and drives off with Marlon. He calls Marlon a disgusting pig. He starts the cruiser. He drives off like a kid learning to drive stick. Peels out. Slams on the brakes. Punches it. Slams on the brakes. Punches it. First time I ever seen old people get shakers. You just know Marlon and Esther are being slammed around that backseat like a canoe in white water. I can't say they didn't ask for it. I kinda hope they pee in the backseats. It would serve them city cops right.

Under his breath, Bailey grumbles, "He'd better clean up all that blood. Or else."

The taste of fear thickens the air, so thick Wind can't carry it away.

"Let's hope," Constable Bailey says, "we don't have a repeat of that with you, Mister Bob."

"No sir."

"Good," he says, smiling like my best friend in the world. He flips open his black-covered notepad. "What can you tell me about Mister Bimbo?"

"I think he's out of town. Doing something for the Village, right?"

He shoots me a look like a nightstick upside the head. "You know I'm asking about your friend Thaddeus Bimbo. I'm not in the mood for games. Understand?"

"Yes sir. What about him?"

"His mother has filed a complaint. She says her son was assaulted last night and that you were the principal assailant."

"She what?" Anger at stupid-Bimbo's stupid mother trumps my fear of cops.

"What do you know about the incident last night?"

"What incident? No one assaulted that kid. No one laid a hand on him."

"I have evidence to the contrary. His girlfriend says you brutally attacked him."

"His girlfriend? He doesn't got a girlfriend."

"Ingrid Sorrensen. She says she's Mister Bimbo's girlfriend. Why would she lie about something like that?"

"Ingrid said that?" A cancerous lump forms in my throat. She did this to me cos I put a few hickeys on her boobs. I didn't realize I'd made her so mad she'd try to put charges on me and go with that poor-excuse-of-a-human-being, Bimbo.

"Does that surprise you?"

"Yeah, I guess. I thought she was going with me."

"O? Did something happen between you two?"

"No. We made out a little, is all."

"You made out with Mister Thaddeus' girlfriend."

"No. I made out with Ingrid. She was my girlfriend before she was Bimbo's."

"If she was your girlfriend, why would she say she's Mister Bimbo's?"

I fight back a tidal wave of tears. I don't know what's making me feel worse, that I lost a girl to Bimbo or that she's trying to put charges on me for smacking him around a little. Dance weekend does not go like this, not when The Footnotes are playing. Again my Home Waltz feels like a funeral march.

"That's what I'd like to know."

"Is that what you and Bimbo fought about?"

"We didn't fight. Not really. He tried smashing a buncha beer bottles on me and then he jumped me. For no reason. I just defended myself."

"You broke his nose and two of his teeth. That sounds more like assault than self-defense." I can't stop the smile from cracking through my nervous face. Despite being grilled by Bailey, I puff up with banty rooster pride. Like Skinny said, though, it's too bad it was just Bimbo, cos winning a scrap in that way, with anyone else, could make a guy famous.

"Honest. The kid went crazy and wouldn't stop. It was him or me and I wasn't gonna let it be me."

"How did this altercation start?"

"I don't really know. He was off in a corner, pouting. Like usual. And then he started trying to boss me around and calling me names in front of my girlfriend. Ingrid, I mean."

"Is that when you attacked him?"

"I never attacked him. No. Is that what he said?"

"What did you do then?"

"Ignored him. What else would I do?"

"And that's when you broke his nose and smashed two of his teeth?"

"That came later and it was on accident."

"How do you accidentally do that much damage to someone's face?"

"I mean I didn't set out to break anything. I was just protecting myself."

"Why did you say you accidentally did all that damage to Mister Bimbo's face?"

"Like I said, I didn't set out to damage him. I mean the kid's already seriously damaged. You know?" I make the cuckoo finger sign. "I just punched him a coupla times."

"Just a couple? Are you sure? You must have quite a punch."

"I just got lucky. Everyone knows I'm not much of a scrapper. You know it too, right?"

Bailey cracks a smile and chuckles. I feel eyes on me and know every tongue in town is wagging. There are some people who think I should've been sent to juvey as soon as I turned twelve, and not counting Bimbo, at least two who think I should be executed. But those two are just elementary school teachers, so what they think doesn't really count for much.

"Mister Bimbo has a glass jaw? Is that what you're saying?"

"Glass? I don't know. He's just weak. And mouthy."

"Can you tell me why Mister Bimbo was so mad at you?"

"Yeah. He was mad cos I wouldn't jump and find his pants for him."

"His pants? He was naked?"

"Jeez, no. He had on his gonch."

"His what?"

"You know. His underwear."

"He was naked except for his underwear?"

"Yes."

"And you felt threatened by a nearly naked boy?"

"He was acting crazy. I thought he was trying to corn-hole me or something."

Bailey laughs. He nods and closes his notepad. "Well, no wonder young Mister Bimbo himself had nothing to say. That's all I need, Mister Bob. For now."

Bailey's eyes lock me in a chokehold. "Those two just now taken to lockup? That's you in five or ten years if you don't change your ways. This the kinda life you want?"

"No sir," I say.

It's the answer Bailey, well, every adult, wants to hear. I guess it makes them feel like they're doing their jobs. Letting them have the answer they want saves you a lot of grief. And they all think we're stupid anyway, so they don't mind repeating themselves. I doubt I will live long enough to become anything like Marlon or Esther.

Clarence Black, no relation to Esther, walks by. His stitches are still in but his bandage is gone. A few weeks ago, he took his fists to a knife fight in Kamloops and won. Except it was a screwdriver, not a knife, and it wasn't so much a fight, just some crazy man stabbing him in the cheek with that screwdriver. Clarence wasn't even at a bar, or party or anything; he'd just left McDonald's with his kids. Over coffee at the hotel, he told Skinny, Bimbo, Agnes, and I all about it a few days after it happened. He pulled back his bandage and showed us his stitches: ten on his cheek and a dozen inside his mouth. He also showed us the ragged remains of two teeth. Agnes didn't look away from Clarence's sore, all black, scabby, and oozing yellow gunk. Bimbo gagged. I looked away so I wouldn't gag. I just don't have the stomach for such sights.

"I couldn't just stand there and let that goof get away with stabbing me," Clarence said. "Not in front of my kids. What kinda lesson would that be? I ain't raising no victims, hey? What I really want to do is smash his skull in but I can't do that in front of my kids, either."

"So, what'd you do?" Skinny said.

"I yank that screwdriver outta my face. Like this," Clarence said, acting it out. "And punch him. One of them one-inch punches? *Whap!* Fucker flies back two feet. Right into a brick wall."

I shot a quick look at Agnes after Clarence said the eff-word. She acted like she never even heard it.

"Got my fist wrapped around the screwdriver. Blood gushing out my face." Everyone's eyes grew as big around as Moon. Clarence, his voice as huge and strong as he is, tells at least as good a story as anyone. "My kids're screaming their heads off and I'm just about ready to kick this guy's balls into his adam's apple." Clarence stopped talking. He sipped his coffee and looks each of us in the face.

"But he's the one crying his eyes out. Hiding his head behind his arms. He goes, 'I thought you were the guy who's been banging my wife. I'm sorry. I'm so sorry.' Then he drops to his knees and begs me not to hurt him." Clarence laughs.

"All I can do now is laugh at him. He's just a weaselly little Poindexter. Like you, hey?" Clarence poked Bimbo in the chest. Bimbo shrunk and then bantied up, making us all laugh. Bimbo transforms into a hen of many colours, just reds, but every single shade you could imagine. He's not smart enough to be a Poindexter, or a weasel for that matter.

"O, yeah? Well, I'd have killed him," Bimbo says. Clarence sneers. Skinny punches Bimbo's shoulder. He yelps, rubs himself, and whines, "Why you hit me so hard?"

"Shut up, or I'll give you hard," Skinny goes.

"In front of your kids?" Clarence says.

Bimbo peeps, "Well, maybe not."

Clarence slips his coffee cup toward Agnes. She refills it and tops up ours. "Maybe he deserved to die. Maybe he didn't. I still want to punch the loser into next year but he ain't worth hanging for and I sure don't want to scare my kids even more than they already are."

Clarence looked at me in such a way that I felt I should've been taking notes.

"Anyways, that's about when the cops show up. Two of 'em. Revolvers drawn and pointed at me. They order me to drop my weapon and turn to face them good and slow. It's just like you see in the movies but these cops are scared and yelling at me. So I drop the screwdriver. No point in arguing with a drawn gun, hey? Especially when it's in Mister Chicken's hands." He shook his head and took another sip, looking nowhere, at none of us.

"Last thing I want is these two yo-yos opening fire and maybe hitting my kids." Clarence's cup rattled on its saucer. He went quiet, like Grandfather falling asleep at the dinner table before the apple pie. In a voice quieter than a whisper, he said: "So, as I'm turning around, cop goes: 'What the hell happened to you?' and that's the last thing I remember. I guess I blacked out, dropped like a rock off Jackass Mountain. Next thing I know I'm at Royal Jubilee with this honking huge bandage on my face and a headache bigger than the worst hangover you can imagine."

"They put charges on the other guy?" Skinny said.

"I doubt it. All I know's they didn't put none on me. They even paid my hospital bill and they're paying to fix my teeth, which is where I'm going now."

"Who?" Agnes said.

"Couldn't tell you. All I know is it's taken care of so I'm not gonna make any waves." Clarence wiped his mouth with the back of his hand and, before leaving, counted out thirty-five cents in nickels, slid them toward Agnes.

Now Clarence nods my way and I nod back. He and Andrew shake hands. Andrew pulls a mickey of Five Star from his bucket of confiscated booze and offers it to Clarence.

"Naw. I'm off it. For a while, anyways," Clarence says and heads toward the stage door.

"What about you, young Bob. Come have a drink with an old man?"

He cracks the mickey and lets me have the first drink. He takes one and hands it back to me.

"What'd Bailey want you for?" Andrew says.

"Just wanted to ask me about Bimbo."

"O?" Andrew nudges my elbow and hands me the whiskey. "Haven't seen him all night. What's up with that séme??"

"I guess I hit him a few times last night and his mother wants to put charges on me."

"They stick?"

"Don't know. I don't think so." He asks me what happened and I tell him everything except the part where Ingrid dumped me to go with Bimbo. No one else needs to know about that. After I'm done Andrew tips the Five Star my way.

"Come see me a little later on and I'll buy you another one."

"Thanks," I say. He takes my ticket and stamps my wrist.

7:30 PM

Cigarette smoke as thick as orange Jell-O shrouds the packed hall. Groups of people clump together around the outside of the dance floor, line the walls near each bathroom, and a chunk of guys crush up against the stage, filling maybe a third of the dance floor. That's probably where I'll find Skinny and them. The Stones blast from the PA, "Factory Girl." The music vibrates my busted hand. The hall vibrates too and it feels like a party, as if that stuff with Marlon and Esther never even happened. Only a dance by Fast Freddy and the Frivolous Footnotes has that kinda power. No wonder I love them so much. No wonder the cops fear them so much. I push through a crowd of hey, how-are-yas and back slaps, shoulder taps, winks, and hey-make-room-for-the-studly-guys, and stand behind Skinny and them, talking like kids seeing their first *Playboy* centrefold. Except they're talking about The Footnotes' gear. No wonder. I stand invisible behind them.

Rocky Valentino's massive drum kit, maybe the biggest one I ever saw, takes up a good chunk of the stage. I bet The Ventures' Mel Taylor would kill to have Rocky's drums. I bet Buddy Rich would drool over them. I bet Keith Moon would ravish them and beat them to pieces. Ever boss! Rocky and Fast Freddy are the original members of the band. They've had trouble keeping bass players and second guitarists.

Freddy says every bass player he's ever known—except Denver "Denny" Hayes, who's played bass with the Footnotes since I started going to dances—thinks he owns the band and everyone should do as he says. Denny's a short little guy and plays a fretless red Fender Jazzman that's almost as tall as he. Second guitarists, says Freddy, seem to think that they should get solos and sing once in a while. He laughs, then tells us the story of their first second guitarist, Juby Janesse, a short-fingered, tone-deaf guy who sang like a beakless chicken and played his guitar like a drunk accordionist. Them days the band wasn't called Fast Freddy and the Frivolous Footnotes but Clouds in My Sunshine, and Freddy says they stunk so bad they couldn't even get sock hop gigs at their high school. They fired Juby from his own band and Juby cried like a little girl, Fast Freddy said, for days, maybe weeks. He said they couldn't get a gig until they changed the name of the band. By that time, Fast Freddy was at college. I never believed The Footnotes could be bad, no matter who played second guitar. Fast Freddy just laughed and told me, "Kid, you don't have a clue about what you don't know." You can't say something that confusing to a kid and then just walk away. Fast Freddy did just that.

I've only known the Footnotes' second guitarist, Choctaw a while. He plays an ancient Telecaster that has almost no finish left on the body. He sings sometimes, and sings pretty good too, and sounds a lot like Deep Purple's Ian Gillan. No one knows whether his real name's Choctaw, and if any of his bandmates know, they won't say. Sylvester "Sylvie" Silverstream plays a scarred up Hammond organ and a Moog that makes real weird sounds, and he sings a bit. He's only played with the band a few years. He usually dresses up like an Indian—painted face, buckskin leggings and apron, ribbon shirt, choker, and headband. The girls that can't get with Fast Freddy try to get with Choctaw. He says he and Freddy never fight over a girl cos they have so many to pick from.

And of course there's Fast Freddy Gandolpho himself. Freddy plays every instrument you could name. Tonight he's set up a saxophone and four guitars. One's a black and white Flying V. Skinny and JimJim argue about whether it's a real Flying V or a Hamer copy. I could care less, cos it's still a boss guitar and the coolest looking one a guy can play on stage. Fast Freddy's set up alone has me just about walking on air. Ever boss. Seeing the rest of their gear just about blows up my head.

They have two strobe lights, one on each side of the stage, and at least three smoke machines. Most bands use one, if they have even one to use. Three smoke machines out-cools cool. I don't even think The Rolling Stones use that many. THREE! The Footnotes even brought their own lights.

The stage gives off a low hum. It will explode as soon as The Footnotes hit the stage. The band laughs loudly backstage. "Roadhouse Blues" starts and my feet leave the ground. I accidentally elbow Skinny in the back. He whirls, fists up and ready to kill me dead.

"O," he says. He chuckles. "It's just you."

"Hey," I go. Cody raises an eyebrow. JimJim does nothing, like he wants to be invisible to me, or something.

His fists melt into the pockets of his jeans. "Whenjoo get here?"

"Just now," I say. Cody scowls at me, shaking his head.

"Cool," Skinny goes. "Check out the stage. What'd you give to have gear like that?"

Cody, still all scowly, grunts, "Says he'd give his left nut. Thinks that'd make him more like me."

Skinny laughs. "Got a little surprise for you, boys," he says. "Snuck in a bottle of Five Star. 'Sin the john. Wanna take a hit before the show starts?"

JimJim shakes his head, "Someone's gotta stay and keep our places."

Cody says nothing. I follow Skinny, zipping through the openings he's cut through the crowd. Sometimes I think he's a ghost or has powers like the Invisible Girl cos he gets away with stuff no one else can. Ask him how he did something and he'll answer with a pasted-on cheeky monkey grin and a shrug.

8:45 PM

The gin and whiskey have quieted my hands' pain. Cody and I, pretty much abandoned by Skinny and JimJim, sulk in the shadows at the back of the hall. Skinny, all grab-hands and kissy-lips, begs Muriel to forget what he did last night. He tries to convince her that the stories (that he'd started) about what and who he did last night were nothing but a pack of lies and gossips. Muriel has the scariest "as if" in the world. It cuts through BS like a chainsaw with a new chain through dry pine. Her "as if" carves his words to bits. Instead of backing off, he doubles down, angling her towards the parking lot.

"Lookitim," Cody sneers. "Thinks she'll give in to his giant prick. He goes on like he's a one-man tag team." Maybe Cody's right about Skinny but Muriel doesn't look like she wants to play Skinny's game.

Muriel slips away. Skinny gives her a step or two then corals her again. I can't watch. I don't want to see him shot down by his own girlfriend. I don't want him to win her over, either.

A bunch of guys flirt with Annabelle George—Skinny's sure thing, his not-so-secret side jump—near the door down to the ladies room. She laughs with those guys but her eyes flit to Skinny and Muriel. Hope, a pretty girl from Spuzzum, almost never comes to town. JimJim stands real close to her, talking into her ear. She steps back, giggling, hand on his upper arm. JimJim looks too cazh to be putting moves on her but with him you never know, not like nothing-but-moves Skinny.

Andrew calls me over. He hands me a can of Pepsi and motions me to sit beside him.

"Listen, kid," he says. Holy! My Pepsi's at least half-whiskey. I almost spit up the first taste of it. Andrew laughs. He hiccoughs,

"Not ready for a man's drink, hey? I could take that one back, give you a glassa pink lemonade instead?"

"No. No, it's a good one. Just took me by surprise. A little." I take another mouthful and cringe as it burns down my throat. I couldn't take another drink right now if he put a gun to my head.

"I'm gonna say something to you and I'm gonna say it only once." I nod. He slaps my thigh. "Good." He leans into me like he's gonna plant a kiss on my cheek, except Andrew isn't that kinda uncle. All serious, his eyes grab mine. "Girls'll come and go in your life. That's the way it is. So don't ever get your guts tied in knots over one. Don't ever think about jumping off the bridge. Nothing stupid like that. Hear me?" I nod. "Good." He slaps my thigh again but not so hard this time. "Okay, git. Just remember what I said, all right?"

I git, as dazed as though I'd just taken a shot to the head.

"What's the old fart want?" Cody says without looking up at me. I shrug.

"Gave me a pop. Wanna hit?"

He takes it, sniffs the opening, then takes a giant gulp. "Least he knows how to make a drink, hey?"

"Yeah," I say, shaking the half-empty can. "He sure does."

The PA blasts songs by Deep Purple, The Doors, and Jimi Hendrix. The songs and crowd chatter blend together, turning beautiful music to mud in my ears. Cody's turned as black as the shadows we hide in. He's stopped whining about his broken nuts and bitching out Pixie for tricking him into doing it to her. At least five girls ask him to dance. Five more than have ever asked him, and five more than have ever asked me to dance. Each of them would give a guy a Home Waltz. Skinny, of course, has Home Waltzed them all. Well, he said he had.

"Hey, you think they'll play 'Wipeout' first?" I ask.

"Nah" Cody says. "Prob'ly 'Smoke on the Water?' Maybe 'Tequila' but no one ever starts a set with 'Wipeout.'"

"Bet?" I challenge.

"I don't bet with suckers: I buy them at the store."

"That's so original."

"Whatever."

"You know," I say, like the best playlist maker in the world, "I think they should start a set with 'Wipeout.' It gets everyone on the dance floor."

"Exactly," Cody says, "and that's why it's always near the end of a set. Lookit, just about everyone's outside, so they'd miss dancing to it. And you know some of them'll be mad, cos that's their best song to dance to,"

"I never thought of it like that. I guess you're right."

"Still wanna bet?"

"Why not?" I say. Cody's laugh is as fake as the Cow's.

"Man's drinks," Andrew says out the corner of his mouth. "Make sure you boys grab partners and hit the dance floor before the enda this set." He hands each of us a Pepsi, then continues to circle the dance floor.

Cody takes a long drink. He hunches over, crushing the pop can in his hands. "I'll never dance again."

He drinks from his crooked can. What he needs to do is get so hammered that last night's erased from his brain, but I can't make him do anything he doesn't want to. I feel like I should say something to him, tell him everything'll be all right, or some other bull crap. But I got nothing. Not a clue. Not a prayer. No words. Just a lot of nothing.

You either win the Irish Sweepstakes or you don't. You lose a girl as fine as Ingrid to a kid like Bimbo, that is *losing.* And the sting of losing The Ingrid Sweepstakes to Bimbo burns like a hand held over an open flame. I tell Cody about the cops hunting me down and wanting to put charges on me for smacking Bimbo around. Instead of telling me that beating Bimbo meant nothing, Cody shrugs and tells me I had no choice but to beat him and that I should let it go. I almost tell him that beating Bimbo felt good. If they hadn't pulled me off of him, I'd have beaten him to death. I wanted to.

What kinda monster wants to kill another kid, even a Bimbo? My father's called me a little monster for as long as I can remember: how'd he know? Am I the same kind of monster as my father? Nicer? Worse? What if I am a worse monster than my father? Do I have the right to live? Maybe I should've known when I attacked those two old guys who wanted to hurt Auntie Violet back when I was eight. Only a real monster would try taking out two old giants and think it could win. Maybe that's what the judge at Auntie's trial saw in me and that's why he said all those mean things to me. Maybe my father hasn't wanted to kill me all these years; he's just tried beating that monster out of me, to make me a good person. Maybe Yéye? could make me good but not my father. Definitely not my father.

But guys like Bernie's boyfriend and my father always have girls chasing after them, so maybe I'm not a real monster, or just not very good at it yet.

My pop's too strong to gulp down. The whiskey tastes like the cheap stuff, the kind that gives an ugly buzz, the kinda buzz where you see things that aren't real, or that tricks you into pissing your pants. Even small drinks go down like turpentine, not that I've actually swallowed turpentine.

Cody looks hollowed out.

I lean toward him. "You know," I say, "Pixie had me fooled, too. I wanted her but you got to her first."

"No kidding," he spits. "The blonde you went with? A fox like her should have guys lined up around the block just waiting to be with her but she went with you so you wouldn't get with Pixie. Why else do you think she'd settle for someone like you? You got no money. No car. And like the rest of us, no future."

"At least I still had a little fun."

"Spare me the details. I don't want to hear about your romp with her. Or anyone else for that matter."

Lucky for him I have no details and no lies ready to tell. Instead of notches on my bedpost, I have demerits. Something everyone might know but not something I want to spread around. The PA fades out with the house lights. The crowd bubbles toward the front of the stage. I tingle as I count five flashlights bobbing across the blackened stage. In the darkened hall, the emergency exit lights cast spooky red light over the murmuring shadows watching the stage.

Clinton Adams shouts, "Ow-whoo! It's about time."

Over crowd noise, three smoke machines hiss to life and inch by inch, the crowd is swallowed in fog. I jump and punch air and shout out, "Yeah!" so loud it scares me a little.

"Smoke on the Water" cuts through the fog and red-tinted darkness. At first, we hear Freddy and his guitar alone on the black stage. Eight bars later, on the still-dark stage, Rocky and Choctaw kick in. Fingers of smoke poke the back of the hall. Sylvie's bass booms to life. Every note he hits fires purple spotlights, spilling creepy light over the band, silhouetted under a curtain of fog. The Footnotes hit their groove.

Red, yellow, and blue spots paint the thinning fog. Freddy, armed with his Flying V, steps up to his mic.

He growls.

Everyone except Cody cheers.

People near the stage wave their lit Zippos over their heads.

Freddy starts to sing and even the dead rise up and dance. My feet move. Cody slouches in his chair, as stiff as a corpse. He should be dancing in place, like me, safe in shadow. It's easy to dance like no one's watching when no one is. Right now, I wouldn't care if anyone saw me. Sylvie rips an organ solo near the end of the song. Right in the middle of it, Clinton Adams shouts, "China Grove. Chiiiiiiiiiiiii-naaaaaaaaa Grove!" Sylvie fires a quick look into the crowd and then ends his solo with the opening notes of "China Grove." Fast Freddy and Choctaw crank out a few chords with him and then they stop. People grump and clap and shout for The Footnotes to play. "China Grove." Something. Anything. "Wipeout." "Highway Star." Freddy trades his flying V for his S-G. He tunes it. Rocky counts them in and they blast into "Fast Freddy's Stomp." They play super fast. I dance like a Russian ballet guy in lead shoes but I break into a mad sweat, dancing anyway, alone in my dark corner. As long as The Footnotes play, I am free. Happy. Glad to be alive.

9:00 PM

The band stops playing about halfway through the set. All five guys, under two burning white lights, huddle together at Fast Freddy's mic. They sing like a barbershop quartette, except good: "Fast Freddy and the Frivolous Footnotes bringing you some news. We love you lots so don't get those cryin' blues. We're goin' away but don't despair. LA beckons and our first album's on the way." The boys step back. Fast Freddy steps up to the mic. The boys doo-wop behind him. Ingrid sorta broke my heart. The Footnotes shredded it with .50-calibre machine gun fire. The liquor's spell on my hands breaks and my broken hand throbs like Fast Freddy's snapped my fingers at the third knuckle, then ground them under his heel. Right now I hate them all and want to rush to Yéye?'s and smash their 45s, tear up their autographs, then burn the works, but I can't move, as if the old witch who tries dragging me to hell-or-wherever when I sleep has grabbed me by the ankles, forcing me to hear and see the best night of my year transform into the worst night of my life.

The crowd stands in stunned silence, except Clinton Adams: "Home Waltz! Hooooooooooooooooome Waltz!" Clinton squeezes his honey, a girl from Deadman's, a friend of one of my cousin's cousins, or something.

A few guys, including Fast Freddy, laugh. All crooked-smiled, Fast Freddy points at Clinton and says, "O, buddy, if you're in such a rush to go to that happy place between the sheets, don't let us stop you."

The doo-wopping stops, replaced with laughter.

Freddy turns to his bandmates, "Should I tell'em now or keep it a surprise?"

Clinton shouts, "Now! Now! Now-owwwwwwwwwwwwwwwwhoooo!"

His girl pumps her hands like she wants us all to shout with him. Woots, hollers, cheers, clapping, and foot stomps shake the hall. Clinton kisses his girl, then lifts her onto his shoulders. The band stands around, waiting for the now!-now!-nows! to die down.

"You know that we love you, too," Fast Freddy says.

You don't leave someone you love.

"Of all the halls we play in western Canada, Washington, and Oregon, this one's our favourite. And you're the best group we play for."

He stops until the cheers and clapping die down.

"You guys are the best! Give yourselves a round of applause."

And they do. The Footnotes are breaking up with us and these idiots—my friends, family, and just about everyone else in the village—don't get it.

"Okay, okay," Fast Freddy says. "We got a real surprise for you." Freddy stops until Clinton and them quiet down. Don't those idiots realize that every second they outshout Freddy, the less time the band has to play? I could scream *shut up*, if the old witch would unhex my throat. Fast Freddy finally spills his big surprise for us: No CCR set tonight. Instead, they'll play some of the songs from the album they're recording. Like everyone else, the band has to go away to make good things happen. They'll be way too big to play for us any more. I hate Fast Freddy and the Frivolous Footnotes more than I've ever hated anything in my whole entire life.

I hadn't noticed the band grab their instruments while Fast Freddy gave us their break up speech. The lights go down, then a green spot paints Denny alone. Fast Freddy's sneaked off stage. The crowd falls silent. Denny never sings lead. Never. He sings, "I've Been Loving You"—bangs a hand-jangling A, followed by two more that have my hand vibrating like a tuning fork—"too long to stop now…"

Groovy: a break-up song for me and the whole town and I thought I couldn't hate Fast Freddy and the Frivolous Footnotes any more than I already did.

Denny's singing's put Ingrid front and centre in my brain and on my heart. He had no right to put the before-Bimbo-Ingrid there, making my pain worse, cos the after-Bimbo Ingrid stings like fresh road rash on my heart already. As soon as the old witch lets me go, I run from the hall, past Andrew, trying to flag me down.

Some bands, like Slipped A Mickey, use "I've Been Loving You Too Long" as their Home Waltz. Until tonight, it made sense to me. I even thought it might be mine, until I heard "Angie." Now even "Angie" seems wrong.

I figured I'd run toward my bottle, but no. I screech to a halt at the hall's side door, in front of Freddy and Clarence yacking and laughing. If I had fists, I'd jump Freddy and pound him into the ground. I mean if I had fists and was Superman, I guess. Fast Freddy could kill me with a flick of his pinky. He'd dropped Clarence, the king of one-inch punchers with two quick punches. Now they're like best buds.

"Squito!" Fast Freddy says, "Just the man I wanted to see."

How can you stay mad at a guy who greets you like a long lost brother? He puts his arm around my shoulder and leads me to one of their vans. Clarence walks a few steps behind us.

"I'd planned to keep this a secret till we'd done finished playing tonight," Fast Freddy says. "But now seems like as good a time as any. Right?"

I shrug. Considering I don't have a clue as to what he's up to, I can't say.

"I'm so excited. I wanted to tell you when you first asked but I couldn't. I'll tell you now if you promise not to say a word to anyone, all right?"

I nod. Taking in one more secret shouldn't kill me, I hope. Still watching over us, Clarence backs slowly away.

"Great," he says. He turns to Clarence, "Get back here, you big goof. I want you to hear this too." He laughs. Clarence steps forward like a guy testing lake water before diving in. He tells me to close my eyes and put my hands out. Usually when someone tells me to do something like that after telling me they have a big surprise, they dump fresh dog crap into my palms.

Clarence barks, "Do it. He ain't got all night."

I do it. If Fast Freddy gives me some kinda crap, I'll smear it all over Clarence's windshield, then run far and fast for the rest of my life. Fast Freddy puts a 45 onto my bandaged palms.

"Go ahead. Open your eyes, Squito. Open them!"

I open them. He steps aside so the parking lot lights shine enough light on it so I can read it. I just about crap my drawers. The red sleeve protects a brand new single from the band. More than that, they wrote on it:

Hey, Squito!

Thank you for your support over the years.

It's fans like you who keep us loving our jobs and keep us playing.

And the whole band signed it. The A-side is a new song: "Home Waltz," and the B-side's another new song, "Johnny's Song." And cripple-handed me won't be able open it for at least a week.

This Home Waltz makes my night, makes it the best dance night ever. I have my own Home Waltz! I could cry real tears—happy tears.

"It's the first single off our new album," Fast Freddy says. "It should be out in April or May. If you like, I can send you a copy?"

Even though he's a guy, I could kiss Fast Freddy right now. He takes Yéye?'s address and promises me he'll send it. I promise to tell no one about the single until the band announces it in their last set. Clarence grins wide and winks. He points his lips at my 45 and reaches for it. His lips moves as he reads it. He nods again as he hands it back to me. My backbone clacks against my ribs when he slaps me on the back.

Fast Freddy hands Clarence a signed one, as well, and then hands him a boxful of the new singles.

At the stage door, Freddy stops, rests the box on his thigh, raises the shh! finger, then disappears into the rocking hall. I slip the record into my secret pocket. Making the pocket was the best thing about being forced to take Sewing in Grade Nine. JimJim showed us how to make secret pockets in our coats, making it easier to lift chocolate bars and stuff.

People, trying to turn their backs on Wind, stand in clumps in front of the hall. Wind whips around them, stealing the huffs of smoke and air they exhale. Duane Black and his sm?eméc̓e Alice scrap in the backseat of his Valiant. No fists fly but they roll around with their hands on each other's throats. No one bothers them, not any more. Those two scrap like drunk loggers every weekend but always wind up humping each other right where they scrapped. They look gross doing it. If the church and school really wanted kids to stay off the sex, all they need to do is put those two humping maniacs on a poster, with the words: "This could be you!"

Everyone says, "Hey, Squito " as I pass them, my feet a good foot off the ground. Well, they either say, "Hey, Squito" or "How's your grandma?" Mostly older guys and women. I repeat the same tired wave and ?éx k^w ń̓—one of the few words I know—and tell them Yéye?'s fine and that I'll make sure to tell her hi, cos that's the way she taught me.

Uncle Angus bellows my name and I practically jump out of my coat. He calls me over and hands me a half-empty gallon jug of wine. A real drinker can cradle a gallon jug on his arm and bring it to his mouth without spilling a drop. Not me.

I hold up my injured paws. "Kʷukʷscémxʷ, Uncle, but I can't even hold it."

All of Uncle Angus' friends laugh.

Jenny Jack, from Chilliwack, pinches my cheek, pulls me into her, plants a wet, toothless kiss on my cheek and says, "Let me bottle-feed my sweet baby."

"Then how 'bout you tit-feed me after, hey?" Henry Thomas leers. He laughs. Uncle Angus laughs. Bill White Laughs. Terry Thom doesn't. Liam McNeil doesn't. I don't.

"Ha!" Jenny says. "It's called breastfeeding. Breastfeeding, you dummy. And the only one sucking on my tits tonight's Liam. I'nit, hon?"

Liam glares at Henry. Henry shrivels up small enough Wind could carry him off if she wanted. "You got that right."

Jenny puts the bottle to my lips and tips the jug. More dribbles down my chin than into my mouth. She licks my chin and plants her sloppy lips on my mouth. If you ever thought you couldn't grow a hard one in a strong winter wind, I got news for you. Jenny rubs the front of my pants. "Look boys. My baby's all growed up!" Great, one more old lady's given me a hard one. Jenny and the boys laugh, but not really at me, and not the way my friends'll laugh when they hear Jenny Jack gave me a hard one.

Cody, locked in what looks like a dry-land deadman's float, hasn't moved from where I'd left him. I could never sit still that long, cos everything below my neck would be sound asleep and it would take me hours to straighten out.

I put a hand on Cody's shoulder. "You okay?"

"Compared to what?" Cody grumbles, without looking at me.

"I dunno," I say. I chuckle. "Your nuts?"

He brushes my hand from his shoulder. "Funny guy." His words sound like they came from a ghost.

The house lights dim as people pile back into the hall. Clarence stands behind a table stacked with 45s. I pat my secret pocket. Everyone'll get a copy but not like mine. I have my Home Waltz and no one can ruin it for me. Not tonight, anyways.

The stage is black. Fog hisses from the smoke machines. Green spotlights colour the rolling fog. The band said they weren't doing their CCR show tonight but the fog and the lights are always how they start "Born on the Bayou." I shoot a quick glance at Andrew, then climb up onto my chair, ready to flick my Zippo.

Green and blue spots light the band.

Choctaw poses like Conan at Freddy's mic, his Tele strapped to his back like the Barbarian's sword. Freddy, holding his Flying V over his head, stands with his legs spread wide apart, a few feet to the left of Choctaw. Sylvie, his hair hiding his face, is hunched over an acoustic guitar, kinda like Igor. He never plays anything but keyboards. My heart pumps. Oww whoos, as loud as I'm able, burst from me. Two flicks of my thumb and my Zippo flares. Waves orange flame. Denver stands as still as a statue of a bass player. Rocky sits holding his drumsticks in the form of a cross over his head. If it weren't for the fog coiling around their knees, you'd think you were seeing a still image of Fast Freddy and the Frivolous Footnotes. If this was their album cover and I didn't already know who they were, I'd buy their album anyway, knowing their music would blow my mind.

Freddy scissor kicks the air. Spins. Drops to his knees in front of an amp. Everyone, except Cody, hoots and cheers. Choctaw whips his guitar into place. Rocky counts them in. Freddy's guitar wails a longing moan. Choctaw and Sylvie join in. Wow: three guitars. What a sound. Denny and Rocky join in as Choctaw, growls, "O, Johnny, a man at thoiteen, a bigger, better man than me...."

The fog, the lights, Choctaw's sleazy growl, the way the band plays, put me in a mangrove swamp. The stage lights glow green.

Purple lights flash with each moan of Freddy's guitar. The room sways to the rhythm. I flick my Zippo open against my thigh and whip the wheel across the thigh to light it. I'm the only one holding up a lighter and right now I don't care.

All is right with the world.

"Holy crap, Cody!" I shout. "They never done this before!"

Cody shrugs, "So?" It doesn't matter what crawled up his butt, he should be digging this super boss moment.

"Sick," Cody says. "You got wood. What the hell's wrong with you, anyways?"

"I do not." It's not even halfway hard but I drop my busted hand down in front of it and shift my hips, trying to jiggle the little chief back into place. I jump off my chair, lean into Cody and say, "Hey, I didn't know you liked me in that way."

The Zippo heats my palm. I flip the lid closed and drop the lighter into my shirt pocket.

"As if. What makes you think I like you at all?"

Cody jumps to his feet, knocking over his chair. He stomps out with blinders on. A couple of old guys at the edge of the dance floor watch him leave. They watch Cody leave and then go back to watching the real show.

They play one of their older songs after "Johnny's Song."

Clinton shouts, "Down on the corner. Down on the corner."

Freddy mixes the riff from "Down on the Corner" into his solo. The guy's a magician. The house lights come up as the song ends. This never happens.

"Outta my way," Andrew shouts. "Goddamnit, clear a path."

10:45 PM

Andrew waves his arms and almost immediately a path appears.

The words: *There's a body in the men's room* roll through the crowd like the fog machine's hiss. My first thought makes my gut gurble: Cody lying dead with a knife stuck in his throat. A ridiculous thought, really, cos he went toward the front doors. And why would he sneak in a side door to get to the john? I guess a body in the john's a good enough reason to stop a dance but whoever croaked could've waited until after the dance. Clarence pushes through the crowd to guard the stairway.

Andrew slips past him, says something to Freddy.

"I need y'all to leave the hall," Freddy says. "Just wait outside while the man fixes the plumbing, or whatever."

Andy Whitacker screams like a baby and runs for the doors, yelling about bombs, or something.

Aside from Andy and the people he shoves past, no one moves. They say Andy has a screw loose. But I think most of his screws have fallen out. He's about our age and a different kinda nuts to Crazy Thom. When we were little, JimJim, Skinny and I would sneak up on Andy and yell in his ear cos it made him pee in his pants. It was the funniest thing in Grade Three and it stayed funny until Grade Seven, when Principal Fish saw us scaring the piss out of Andy and strapped each of us, including Andy, I guess for peeing in his pants. I got fourteen on each hand, the second-most number of whacks I ever got. Seeing Andy now, I feel sorta bad for him, cos it's not his fault he's a mental case. We were young and stupid. I guess now we're just stupid. I can't even tell him how sorry I am cos Andy doesn't go to school and almost never comes out during the day. When you do see him, he runs if you try talking to him. He never ever comes to dances but I guess The Footnotes are a big deal, even for kids like Andy.

Andy charges at me but I doubt he can see past the blood dripping from his hands. Did the kid finally snap and kill a guy in the john? You hear about stuff like that sometimes but you don't know how scary it is till you stare it in the face. I step aside and Andy zips past me, mumbling something like "Wasn't me. Wasn't me. Dammit, wasn't me." Then he crashes through the front doors, out into the night. A coppish voice shouts coppish words. Soon after that, Andy howls like only Andy can. Then the coppish voice shouts, "What the hell's wrong with you?" You just know Andy's pissed in his pants. Coppish sounds. Andy shouts. Coppish words. Andy screams. And screams. And screams.

Now muffled, Andy screams.

Nightstick and Hand-On-Gun barge in, barrel through the crowd, straight to the men's room. Instead of heading outside, the crowd shoves its way toward the men's room doorway. Cody has to wait, cos I need to see what'll happen next, so I stand tippy-toe on my chair and try to see through the throng. Andrew, now on the stage, yells into Freddy's mic: "Everyone. Out now." Everyone moves toward the exits like a kid you just sent to bed without his supper.

Andy bawls for his mommy from the backseat of a city-cop car. Skinny and JimJim are nowhere. Cody, sucking on a bottle, hangs in shadows at the back of the parking lot. Everyone else hangs near the doors waiting for the cops, for news of what happened. Clinton shouts, "Home Waltz. Home Waltz. Home Waltz." Hand-on-Holster tells Clinton to put a sock in it, and all red-faced, Clinton shuts up, about as quick as he's ever shut up. Cody waves me over. I raise a wait-a-sec finger.

Wind, all fired up, shoots us with slivers of icy rain, and stories about who died in the john and how he died shoot shivers through me. No one knows anything but that doesn't stop them talking. Andy, all bloody-handed, went berserk and stabbed someone in the john. And they add, "Someone shoulda locked that mental case up years ago." My gut snags a knot of sick that staggers me back a few steps. One story has the dead guy passing out and smashing open his skull against the sink, something that happens more than you might think. Another story has him getting into a fight and being stabbed in the heart, or liver, or kidney, or throat. Wagging tongues whipping up stories, adding more chilliness to this already cold night. Wind takes all their tales and whips them together into a stew of gibberish.

For a long time, nothing happens.

The bush offers some cover form the rain and maybe a little from the cold, too. So I back away from the wagging tongues and wild stories. A hit of whatever Cody has will settle my guts, or make me puke. Either will do.

"What happened?" Cody asks, as soon as I get to him. I reach for his bottle—Anisette, for some stupid reason. If anything, a swallow of this tiny-arse water'll fuel the sick already holding my guts hostage.

I pull my grabbing hand back. "What the?"

He shakes the bottle at me. A drink's a drink and I guess I've swallowed worse plonk and lived. I sip. Sweet. Liquorice. Burn. I take another.

"Holy," I say, "Not too bad, hey?"

"It does the trick. 'S'going on?"

I tell him what I think I know and what I think I saw. "So, yeah, looks like Andy went and killed someone in the men's can."

Cody says, eyes all bugged out, says, "You really saw blood?"

"Not like he'd bathed in it but his hands were pretty much covered. And I saw a knife. Some kinda jackknife, maybe a four-inch blade."

"No!" Cody says.

"Yeah."

A ruckus erupts at the hall. Waves of gossip smash through Wind as soon as Crazy Thom, filthier than usual, bursts through the front doors, one shoe gone. Who knew that crazy old drunk could sprint like a running back? I guess we all gain an extra step when we got two cops after us. Cops yell for him to stop and that old drunk yelps, the jets going into overdrive. Nightstick almost trips over his feet zipping his billy club from his belt. Crazy Thom crashes into the bushes. He waves a bloody hand as he zooms past. Like Andy, his hands are thick with blood and fresh blood darkens his thin coat, pants and one shoe. Did those two nutbars scrap each other? Did they team up and kill some guy in the john? This dance will go down in history. Our kids' grandkids will talk about it.

The cops crash around in the bushes. Cody turns away, lifts the anisette to his lips and chugs it back, then tosses the bottle deeper into the bushes.

"'S'go see what's the what," he whispers. He puts a fist to his lips and swallows hard. He shudders. "Jeez, that stuff goes down hard."

Cody belches, groans.

Two out-of-town cops question everyone hanging at the hall's front doors. No sign of Bailey or Andrew. An ambulance siren cuts through gossiping gossipers, Wind's wail, and River's roar. Thom cuts through a tear in the chainlink fence, then dashes behind The Footnotes' vans. A normal person would run far away, not return to the scene of his crime.

Behind me and Cody, Nightstick and Hand-On-Holster mumble from the bushes, Nightstick clutching his belly, his billyclub dangling from his thumb by its leather strap. We speed up but not enough to make us look like we're running from them.

Nightstick straps his club to his wrist as he pushes past us.

As he huffs past us, Hand-On-Holster grumbles, "Slow down, goddammit. Slowdown."

We stumble back toward the hall. Cody says that Skinny found almost three cases of hard stuff: lots of gin, some twelve-year old whiskey, overproof rum, and a few different liqueurs, and a bottle of vermouth—not the kinds of booze most normal people get.

"He say where he found it?" I ask.

"'Course not!" Cody says. "You know him."

"Yeah, I guess."

"Rumour goin' around that someone broke into the liquor store."

"Holy! The liquor store?" I say. If that's true, how'd the burglar get past Andrew? Man will Andrew be mad.

"I know, hey. Idiot, if you ask me," Cody sneers.

It sounds like something Skinny might do, I guess. But that's not really fair, cos I have no idea what the kid's capable of. Him lifting booze, especially gin, makes sense cos he's never actually bought me anything before tonight.

"Take some kinda guts to rob the liquor store," I say.

"B'n'E, maybe burglary. But not robbery."

"Same difference," I say.

"No," Cody growls, "you got to be nuts to rob a store and just an idiot to break into a liquor store, 'speshly this one."

"Even with Andrew stuck here all night?"

"That old bastard's spooky. Prob'ly already knows who done it and who drank the stolen booze. He'll get us all. You watch. You'll see."

"Be careful, hey?" Cody says, "if you don't stand up to Skinny and them, they'll try to pin the break in on you."

"Robbing the liquor store?"

Cody slaps his forehead and growls. "Get it straight. Breaking into it and taking three cases of the good stuff."

"What makes you think they'll do something like that to me

and not you?"

"Skinny's a coward. He won't mess with me and it wouldn't matter, anyways."

"Why not?" I ask. What makes you so special, anyways?

"Cos it won't."

"We don't even know Skinny pulled the B'n'E," I say. We don't, so why hang the kid before anyone knows anything?

"You seen him since the dance started? Or JimJim?"

"Sure," I say. But really, I don't think I have.

"So ask him what he was up to next time you see him."

Ask him? Right. And have him beat me to a pulp to teach me a lesson?

"I wouldn't want to make him mad," I say.

"You got no reason to fear that kid," Cody says. "None."

"'Course I do. Everyone's afraid of what Skinny'll do to them if they touch him."

"Everyone? Do I look scared of him? They're just as scared of you, too, Qʷóqʷésk̓ iʔ: the kid who goes batshit if you push him hard enough. The only one of us everyone likes is JimJim."

Only my grandmother calls me by my name like that. Something's up with Cody. If he wanted to force me to fight him, he'd have called me Dolores or something else I'd never live down.

"And he's Skinny's best friend."

"Maybe. You ever think that's what Skinny's trying to do? Make you crazy enough to beat him up?"

"I'd die trying. You know that."

Cody laughs. Deep from his guts. It's insane to think I could beat up Skinny; even passed out or dead, he'd still kick my butt. He's that good.

"You're just another Bimbo. You do know that? You're not so much a friend as you are Skinny and JimJim's pet."

"I'm no one's pet. Anyways, what's that make you?"

"I'm a big fat nothing. Maybe more nothing now that I'm also a rapist."

"You're not."

"Not what?"

"Any of that. You're talking crap."

"Was Pixie over sixteen?"

"No, but you aren't either. And she wasn't a virgin. And she wanted you. You know that. Anyone woulda done it to her."

"But I did. Not anyone else. Me. And you heard Skinny: They're gonna send me to jail and make me everyone's bum-buddy. I don't want that."

"Yeah, but you did it to her seven times. That's a record no one's gonna break anytime soon."

"Cos no one's gonna be stupid enough to break their nuts like I did. Anyways, no one cares about that stuff. No one."

"I don't know. I mean, we talked about it all afternoon. What it must've been like. Stuff like that."

"That's today. By tomorrow? Today'll be forgot and everyone'll be yacking about something else, like that liquor store B'n'E."

"I guess. But no one's gonna forget what you did."

"They'll remember who I did. They'll remember how young she was. Not how many times I did it to her."

Why beat yourself up so badly? He's had more sex in one night than I've had in my whole life, maybe more than I'll ever have. I wouldn't do it to a young one, not if I knew she was jailbait. I guess I'd make sure she was old enough. Thirteen's too young, no question about that, but how can you stop it from happening when it's already started? You could check her ID or something, but fake IDs are easy to get a hold of. Pixie's friends knew what she was up to and they failed to make Pixie keep her pants on. They should've told everyone

Pixie was too young to mess around with, even though she looked way older than thirteen, way older than most of the other girls on the team. She was good to go, more than good to go, and she had all of us guys fooled. Ingrid and Angelica saved me from Pixie. I guess Angelica saved her from Skinny or someone else. Still, anyone who wants something bad enough will find a way to make it happen.

But a guy can't just walk up to a girl and ask her to do it to him. He'll get a slap in the face or words that sting as much as one. Then she and her friends will talk about him and laugh at him all night. That's how it happened for me, anyway. I walked up to Belinda Brown and asked her to go to bed with me except, cos of the vodka, I asked in a rude way. She used that same rude word on me and hit me so hard lightning fired behind my eyes and made my ears ring. But Belinda didn't stop there. She slapped my face with her left and then her right hands, then she punched me in my solar plexus. I went down like the Creator'd cut my strings. Instead of kicking me, she looked down with her hands on her hips and said: "I wouldn't sleep with you if you were Robert Redford. I wouldn't sleep with you if you were Donny Osmond. No one will ever sleep with you cos you're ugly and stupid."

I'd rather have been kicked but I learnt my lesson: never use the eff-word when you want to do it to a girl. Everyone says Belinda goes with anyone who asks, so I asked. Every guy you talk to says he's done it to Belinda, that she's a sleeper car of a girl. Maybe if I'd asked nicer? Skinny says if you can't do it to Belinda Brown you may as well turn homo, cos no girl in the world will ever let you do it to her. That might be okay for some guys but it's not for me. I kinda hope there is a girl for me, just like that song says. That could be a long way off and I know I'd rather be dead than wait that long.

Even Ingrid didn't want me much, and maybe wouldn't have wanted me at all if it weren't for the drugs in her drink, and I guess that explains why she went off with Bimbo. On top of that, she just wanted to keep me from going off with Pixie. In the end, you know you're not much of a guy when, despite the happy drugs inside of her, the thought of being with you makes her jump into the arms of the world's biggest loser.

Learning this about myself should make me sadder than Cody. Maybe I'll be that sad tomorrow. Sunday's only good for feeling sad and regretful and stupid about what you'd done on Friday and Saturday nights, which is why the Creator set up his white church as places to go and whine and grovel for His forgiveness. I'll never really understand why we even have churches, cos everyone who goes is quick to see the ugly in you and the rest of the world but not any of the good—not unless you wrap it in a page from the Bible. I don't see how doing this or that and rubbing some beads makes things okay. I don't see how lighting a candle or putting a little money into a pot makes anything better. Me, I just thank the Creator for letting me live another weekend, and then I ask Him: *Why me?* Yéye? says He's teaching me lessons and lets bad stuff happen, like that thing with Belinda Brown, so I'll grow a little smarter, a little more like a man should be. Humiliated, beaten, and miserable is how I feel. Yéye? says I'll be a good man when I feel humble, wise, and respectful.

An ambulance siren grows louder, still barely audible under Wind's howl. The closest ambulance station is about twenty-seven miles west of us. They don't call an ambulance for a dead guy but that won't stop the stories. I guess they didn't call our volunteer firemen cos Andrew's sorta the captain of it already and the rest of them are here and prob'ly half-cut. I turn to ask Cody what he thinks. He's vanished. Nowhere in the crowd in front of me, nowhere in the parking lot, Cody's simply vanished. Part of me says I should go find him but it won't tell me why, and another part tells me to find out who got stabbed and how he lost so much blood and hasn't died yet.

"Band gonna play an extra set?" Clinton, all grumpy-voiced, shouts. "We paid for four sets and haven't even got three."

You sure can't blame him for getting mad. No one died. No one brawled. They know who prob'ly did it, so why punish the rest of us? No disease made anyone else crazy; Thom and Andy were born nuts. None of us has turned into a zombie or anything, except maybe Cody.

Nightstick holds up his club and shouts over the crowd, "Shows over. So just go home. The hall is an active crime scene and the perpetrators remain at large. So go home."

"You giving me back my money, then?" Clinton barks.

"Take that up with whoever commissioned this event," Nightstick says, each word a pistol shot.

"I won't leave without my refund," Clinton says, his words fired from the same gun. A chorus of "yeahs" ricochet. Everyone knows they don't refund tickets before, during, or after a dance.

Nightstick nods at Hand-On-Holster. He and two other out-of-town cops—one cradling a shotgun—step toward the crowd. "You can leave now, on your own, or we can escort you to the station house, where you'll be our guests for the rest of the weekend."

We shut up like someone's choked us quiet. Almost everyone turns, grumbling, away from the hall, even though we probably outnumber them 40–1. Shotgun, all finger-twitchy, watches Clinton and his crew pile into his pick-up. Clinton's death-ray eyes blast Shotgun backward a full step. That whole pack of cops will probably hunt him down later. Yéye? always says pick your battles carefully. Clinton should've picked better.

The Footnotes have started loading their gear back into their vans. Clarence stands between the band and about a dozen girls. What a life those guys have! Girls panting all over them all the time and they get paid to play music and even paid not to play. If I had a life like theirs, life would be worth living. Could a guy in a band just pick out a girl, maybe more than one, and say come with me and have them girls fall into line behind him? Can a guy take more than one girl to bed and not go totally crazy? The girls—some of them relations—and I transform into a writhing mass of nameless, faceless, naked bodies, doing the things you only read about in the kinds of coverless books my father hides in the garage. Wind slams her icy hand between my legs, snapping me back into my own body.

I guess I should be glad we don't just whip our dicks out and whack off whenever we feel like it, like monkeys. Well, most of us don't. Take a guy like Chappie Smith, our old magistrate, who liked to whack off in his car when the primary kids had recess. Every school day at ten Chappie'd pull into the parking lot and whack off—*just spanking me monkey*, he'd say. I knew that was no monkey in his hand; we all did. I guess he didn't mind being seen, at least not by us kids, but he sure didn't want us to tell anyone else he was whacking it in his car. We didn't tell on him either, cos he was an adult and our town's magistrate. He had the power to send us or someone in our families to jail, or he could've had us taken away from our families, and other stuff like that. One day he told Margaret O'Reilly—then just a kindergartener—to pet his monkey for him. Some say she did. Some say she didn't. Everyone says Margaret went straight to her teacher afterward and told on Chappie. No one believed Margaret, because magistrates know better. Everyone teased her so much afterwards that her family sent her to school far away. No one's seen her since. Her parents moved away a few years later.

JimJim and Heather MacDonald tumble from the backseat of her father's '62 Impala. Something from his hand lands like a wet slap on the pavement. Head down, Heather half-runs toward town. JimJim, walking to me like the Duke after he's just taken down the Cherokee nation singlehandedly, raises a hand and smiles.

"Not seven times for me," JimJim gloats. "Just one good, long screw. Yep. That's the way, long and slow."

With my track record, how would I know? I couldn't even get short and quick right, squirting my load pretty much as soon as my spaeks? rubbed against Ingrid's naked thigh.

"So I'm not normal, I guess?" I say, trying too late to swallow my words.

With some grumpiness in his voice, JimJim snaps, "What's normal, anyways?" He smiles and says, like he would to a Third Grader, "Whyjoo even care what I or anyone else thinks?"

"I don't."

"Yeah. You do. You're so afraid of being laughed at you don't think or say nothing that might make you look dumber than any of the rest of us. You need to grow up, Squito. Stop being such a coward."

"Coward? I am not!"

"Yeah, you are. You coulda bagged that white chick last night. Instead you kissed her ass and let her run off with Bimbo."

"I did bag her. All night. In the hand's shack. Ingrid was great. Best one I ever had."

"Might've been, if you'd nailed her. But you didn't."

"Did so."

"Nope. Guys got a way of walking after they're done. You don't have that walk. Not even close."

"Then what's my walk like?"

JimJim, shaking his head, says, "You walk like a guy who got a good whiff of love just before it closed its legs up tight." He slaps his thigh and laughs.

"I don't really look like that?"

"You got that right," he says, before laughter chokes out his words. "Nah, you look worse. Like a guy who'll spend the rest of his life spunking into a hankie."

"Sick. I'd rather die than let that happen."

"You'll have to. Keeping all that nut-juice insida you'll kill you, cos it's poison."

If I had something to drink I'd drink it, then punch his face in for saying that.

Feeling all Grade Three, I say, "I won't. I'll get lotsa girls. Maybe as many as Skinny."

"Sure, you will. You'll have a new one every month, when your copy of *Playboy* comes in the mail. And you'll spend every other night drunk and calling out Cyndi Wood's name as you jerk it into a tissue." No one should know I sometimes whack off with her and I've been real careful about not spitting jizz on the magazine.

"Who doesn't?" As much as I want to run far away and hide from him until one of us is dead, I swallow a breath and wait. "Everyone says she's the best Playmate ever."

"Not everyone. I only spank it to Claudia Jennings."

"Really?"

"'Course. We all got our secret crushes. We just never talk about it," JimJim says. I haven't really admitted to any secret crush but everyone knows Cyndi Woods makes tents pop up every time she walks into a room fulla men. You can't even open her gatefold without popping one.

"Why her?"

"Stupid as it sounds, Claudia was my first. You know, the first one I jerked off with. And you know what? It wasn't even one of her titty pictures. She's a beauty like none I'd ever seen."

"Still?"

"Almost never have to any more, not since I started doing it to real girls. But I still got a copy of the November, 1969, *Playboy* she's in."

"Can I see it?"

"I don't carry it around with me. Jeez, you," JimJim says. He doesn't laugh, not that I'm joking.

"I didn't mean right now."

The ambulance pulls up to the front doors. Me, JimJim, and a few stragglers sneak in as close to it as the out-of-town cops let us. Three ambulance guys pour from it, two pull a gurney from the back. The third talks with some cops, then goes inside the hall. Nightstick and Hand-On-Holster shoo us away. Town lock-up has only two cells and they're already full. If they haul us in tonight, they'll have to take us all the way to Ashcroft. Taking a shaker that long's almost as bad as a trip up past the dump. Nightstick's the kinda cop who'd rather take you up past the dump and leave you there all but dead.

A gang of older guys tease Cody in the street near the far end of the parking lot.

I grab JimJim by the shoulder and say, "C'mon, Cody's in trouble."

JimJim shakes free of me, and hisses, "Forget him! Pussy deserves whatever he gets."

"He's our friend."

"Leave him alone. We're his friends, not his mother. A little ribbing never hurt no one. He'll be fine."

JimJim swaggers into the night like an old bull rider. I need to practice that swagger. He and Cody told me to stop acting like a coward, so I rush the gang of guys yelling at Cody.

"Hey, Cody," Albert Sam, a guy my father's age, says. "I hear you let a youngun break your nuts. That true?"

Albert's gang make up most of the guys picking on Cody. Cody tries to push his way free of the crowd but they push him back. Guys with kids Cody's age, yipping, crowing, and acting all tough and child-like just makes you sick inside. These guys are loggers, miners, and railroad gang workers. Each one of them could punch the crap outta Cody with just their eyelashes. And piss-drunk Cody can hardly stand, making him an even easier target. They sing-song "jailbait's better than masturbate" and call him kiddy diddler. They say Albert does his daughter's friends. Every one of them guys has done a young one, or so they say. What gives them the right to tell Cody not to do something they've all done and most have bragged about?

A little anger mixed with booze makes you feel tougher but doesn't make you stronger or a better fighter. Sober, you know this. A little drunk and you forget.

Instead of a booming threat, my voice decides to go through the change again. "Hey, leave the kid alone."

They focus on me, as well as a bunch of old drunks can focus. Albert laughs a deep, rich laugh. Lorne Two Feathers slides into a fighter's stance, clenching and unclenching his fists. He's not as tough as he looks but I'm just a skinny fifteen-year old who can't fight his way out of a wet paper bag.

Lorne grunts, "You look like a mad grandma, kid." He takes a careful step toward me. His friends move aside and close around me. My first fight since Grade Eight. The fight ring's always made me feel sorta woozy. "You gonna send me for a switch?"

Albert pipes up, "Careful you don't wake up the mad mosquito, there budz. He could beat you up."

"Beat me off's more like it," Lorne sneers. "Or try, i'nit?"

Now blind with anger, I snarl, "Blow me."

Lorne takes another step forward and spurts, "How 'bout you gum me after I punch your teeth out?"

I smile and hold up my gimped hands. "See these? They sent a kid to the hospital last night. Hurt'im so bad they almost sent him to that hospital in Big Town."

Some guy behind me laughs. Another snorts, "Yeah, Too-Big-For'iz-Britches here, beat the living shit outta Thaddeus Bimbo. Real man, hey?" A poisonous chorus of oos and ahhs closes in on me. Then a poisonous round of jeers and jabs drowns out the oos and ahhs. I shrink faster than that guy in *The Incredible Shrinking Man.* In seconds, I am no one, a nothing. I've transformed into a Bimbo.

On the plus side, Cody's slipped away. On the non-plus side, he left crying for real and he didn't head home. Also on the non-plus side, these old drunks are about to kill me. If Lorne thinks I'll let him put his dink in my mouth, toothless or not, he'll have to shove it into my severed head. Lorne holds me in a headlock before you can say, "Lorne holds me in a headlock." He squeezes and squeezes, and guys kick my butt, just hard enough to let me know I've been kicked: not hard enough to break me. Then they stop and Lorne frees me.

Clarence puts one of his huge paws on my shoulder. "You all right, kid?"

"Yeah," I say. "Just goofing around with Lorne and them."

"Your buddy said you and the mopey kid were in trouble."

"We was just joking around," Lorne says.

"Yeah," Albert chirps, "just some friendly teasing and rough-housing. You know how it is, i'nit?"

"Sure," Clarence says. "Maybe you boys want to joke and rough-house with someone your own size, hey?"

"Hey," Lorne says. "We didn't want to make any trouble. It's late. We should head'er."

From a smile so cold even the devil would step back, Clarence says, "Yep."

Lorne, Albert, and them pile into three cars.

"Go straight home," Clarence says. He squeezes my shoulder, a pressure point, the place Spock pinches villains.

I have no spit, no air, and my heart beats like I just ran a hundred miles across Death Valley at noon. My body acts like it just realised that how scared it was. I'm fifteen and having a major heart attack. My tombstone will read: *This loser, the one buried right here, just scared himself to death.* One more for the plus column: I haven't crapped myself. Yet.

"I mean it," Clarence says. I have no reason to doubt him.

"Yes, sir," I say, my voice, a laryngitis-whisper.

Nightstick bellows, "Get down!" at some guy on the dance hall roof. He waves his billy-club, barking threats. Shotgun points his gun at the chimney. Hand-On-Holster rushes around a corner, waving his pistol. Clarence and I run to the hall. How does a guy built like that move like a ballerina?

I don't see Bailey but Constables Spotface and Howe have shown up. We call Spotface and Howe the Indian killers. Howe even scares the səmséme. You got to wonder what we did to deserve the meanest cops ever made. All the cops, except Shotgun, shine their flashlights at the roof, trying to light up the chimney's night-shadow and whomever it hides: Crazy Thom.

Crazy Thom punches the light beams. "Back off, scoundrels!" He tosses bits of roof tiles at Nightstick. "Take that. And that. Shame on you, persecuting an old man. Begone! Begone, I say!"

He tosses more roof junk: an old Frisbee, sneakers, a bra, some panties, twigs.

"Listen to me," Thom says, "and not those voices in your head. I tried to help that pour soul, not kill him. You have the wrong man. The wrong man, I tell you!"

The ambulance, siren blaring and lights flashing, speeds east toward the real hospital in Kamloops. Only a helicopter or ambulance plane ride out of town is more serious. Bailey finally shows his face. He tells the out-of-town cops to take a breath, orders Shotgun and Hand-On-Holster to put their weapons away. He speaks quietly to Nightstick, who taps his club in his hand while Bailey speaks.

"O, for fuck-sake, Bill," Nightstick says, "the subject's a suspect in an attempted homicide and has fled from a peace officer, resisted arrest, and assaulted peace officers. The subject clearly has no interest in surrendering and poses a clear and present danger. We need to take him down."

Bailey, all pursed lips, shakes his head. Everyone knows Crazy Thom wouldn't hurt anyone. Thom scoops up bugs and spiders and frees them outside. He hold funerals for roadkill.

"Let me handle this," Bailey says. "I know how to deal with old Thom."

Backing off, Nightstick says, "Anything goes wrong, it's on you."

"Yeah, yeah," Bailey says, then tells the cops to shut off their flashlights and keep quiet. He waits till everyone quiets down a bit, takes a step toward the hall, and says, "Thom? Thom, it's me, Bill Bailey?"

"I'm a nut-bar, not a blithering idiot, Billy-boy."

"Yes, Thom. Allow me to apologize for my oversight, good sir."

"Apology accepted, sirrah. Now take a moment to tell me what troubles you, and what has so rattled your cohort."

"Would it not be prudent of you to come down so we might talk as equals?"

"Nay, sirrah. I trust your goon squad naught. I would, however, welcome you up here. Won't you meet me in my inner-sanctum? Would you?"

"Alas, I don't have a ladder that tall," Bailey says. "Just come down the way you climbed up there."

"I'll not fall prey to your ruse, sirrah. You only wish to uncover my secret path."

As Thom and Bailey talk, two cops wrestle a ladder from the hall, plant it, and climb up. A cop's head pops into view over the roof's peak. Thom scrambles to his feet, then disappears behind the chimney. The cop creeps across the eave. Another shouts, "Got him. He's descending the northwest corner of the building."

All the cops stampede the hall's far corner.

Thom cries out, a muffled cry for help. Two cops drag him toward the parking lot, one holding each of Thom's limp arms. His pants hang like a wrinkled curtain around his ankles. His boney, white arse blows a bunch of huge, wet-sounding farts all the way to the cruiser.

He cuts one that lasts a good five seconds as they shove him into the backseat. As they slam the door, he says, "And that, sirrahs, is my last and final word on the matter."

11:15 PM

After tossing Crazy Thom into the back of a cruiser, a cop starts it, then jumps out, yelling, "That crazy fuck just shit himself."

Thom, his face pressed against the window, smiles a squished up smile. Crap-Car punches the glass. Thom sticks out his tongue and laughs, like he has a death wish or something. Thom'll be lucky to live through the night. The other cops, including Bailey, laugh. Crap-Car rolls down the front windows before grumping into the driver's seat. Nightstick and Hand-On-Holster get into their car. Spotface starts his.

Howe taps on Crap-Car's door, saying, "Take two deep breaths and you'll be fine."

Crap-Car says something low and poisonous. Howe laughs all the way to Spotface's car. Crap-Car guns it. Thom whaps against the back seat. Slams on the brakes. Thom splats against the glass between the front and back seat. If Thom isn't dead by the time they get him to wherever they plan on taking him, he will be soon after. Poor guy.

The other two cop cars follow Crap-Car. Bailey watches the little convoy head toward town, biting his lip.

He checks on The Footnotes. Each one of them guys has a girl. Funny how some people can have a great time and party while someone else nearby dies, or will be dying soon. Thom's just crazy, not stupid, even though he'll do stupid things for drinks sometimes. But you gotta wonder, what if he's stupid enough to think getting the cops to kill you's a good plan.

Using cops to kill you is like Russian Roulette: the odds are good but not a sure thing. Sometimes I think I'd be better off dead and that the world would be better off without me. But I'd jump into River, cos River swallows everything you drop into it. For the millionth time, Yéyeʔ asked, "Think killing yourself will solve anything? Think your father would give a shit?" And for the million-and-first time I snapped, "Nothing would. You know that!" And for the million-and-first time, I regretted opening my mouth, cos Yéyeʔ mad is far scarier than a shaker with a dozen Spotface and Howes. Anyways, no one would come to my funeral, if I even had one. I mean Cody even skipped his older brother Francis'. Everyone says they saw it coming and should've done something to stop it. Even me. Like when my cousin Erica killed herself with wine and sleeping pills.

Clarence taps my shoulder, rattling me back into myself.

"Hey," he says, "I don't think your bud's okay. Seen'im headin' towards the bridge a while back. Couldn't say nothin' in fronta them cops. Know what I'm sayin'?"

"Crap," I moan. "O, crap."

"Look, I'd run you down there in my truck but I gotta guard them fuckin' vans all night."

"K^{w}uk^{w}scémx^w, anyways. I'll find him." Hopefully alive, or mostly alive. If I could use my hands, I'd just jump a few fences, then zip down the hill to Bridge Road, maybe even beat him to the bottom. But even before that, I check his house. He might have just wandered around a bit before going home to pass out. Their chihuahua, Bull, is the only one in their house. He growls, shaking all goggle-eyed, with his tail between his legs as I close the door behind me. Whimpering, he refuses to jump into my outstretched paws—one of the few tricks he knows. He ducks out from under them when I try to pet him. He sniffs them a bit, then licks them like tasting a new colour of Popsicle. I ask him where his human is. He whines. I don't speak dog but Bull speaks human. So, yeah, even dogs are smarter than me. Bull almost trips me before I get to the door. He transforms into a ten-foot rope, snaked around my ankles, slowing my exit. Their backyard overlooks River. About a hundred years' worth of footsteps have stamped a trail down to the highway, but drunk or sober, I have trouble following a trail. Even if sċuwenáy̓tmx had left this trail, I couldn't pick it up without a flashlight and a guide.

Cody, about two-thirds the way down the hill stops, rubs his crotch and stretches. I could yell for him to wait up but he's a lot closer to the bridge than me. We've had landslides quieter than me scrabbling down the trail but I don't spook Cody cos he's a good quarter mile away. I sweat about as much as I would under a hot August sun and suck in cold air that slashes my throat and lungs. My sweat freezes on my forehead and tips of my hair. At least he doesn't scoot off, so maybe I've no reason to worry about him doing something stupid.

I clunk to a stop in front of Cody. He pouts, "Leave me alone."

"Thought I'd walk with you awhile," I wheeze.

"The fuck?" he says. What's with all the foul language, kid?

"I just don't think you should be alone right now," I say, once my breaths slow down to something close to normal.

"Why? You think I'll find another thirteen year old to rape?"

"Don't talk so stupid." Now I sound like my grandmother.

"Everyone hates me for what me and Pixie did. They think I raped her."

"No one thinks you raped her. And no one really cares, except you."

"None of you raped her. I did, so yeah, I care."

"Look," I say, huffing. "It's real shitty what happened. But you got nothing to worry about with the cops. You know they won't do anything. They never do." To their own, sure, but with us, you can't be certain and Cody probably knows it, too.

"Then why'd Skinny say I was going to jail and tell me I was gonna be treated bad, like a kiddy diddler?"

"You know better than anyone you can't let Skinny get to you like that."

Less than an hour ago, he told me pretty much the same thing. What's changed so much in just an hour? Stupid question. He probably feels like less than crap.

"He got everyone in town ripping into me."

"Teasing you, just. No one meant anything by it. They were just having fun. Anyways, it's not like it fell off, or anything." Those same guys have teased me to the point of wishing for death, buried so deep in the ground I can't hear their voices any more. Cody seems as hurt by the teasing as I but he's never shown it before. Just when I think I should get him to St. Jude's, he smirks. Then he laughs. Uncontrollably. Madly.

He wipes away a laugh-tear then pats my upper arm. "Now where've I heard that before?"

At different times from him, from Skinny, from JimJim. I feel sick inside.

"You know me," I say, "genius of the human condition."

"Not so much a genius of the English language, your mother's tongue."

Smiling dumbly, I shrug. "Then you should hear me mangle my grandmother's tongue."

"I have. You're better at porking grannies than speaking their language."

"Yeah, I am the most famous granny-porking virgin around."

We both laugh. Then, as Wind scatters our laughter, we go all quiet.

"The only one around."

"Let's hope it stays that way," Cody says. "Granny-porking virgin." He laughs.

I'd like it better if someone took my title from me. I'd like that night with Delores Brown erased from my mind, from my history, from everyone's history.

"You the granny-porker, JimJim the musical genius, Bimbo the sad clown, Skinny the giant dick, you all got something you're famous for. But me? I got nothing."

"You don't have less than anyone else. Except Skinny's spaeksʔ, but no else has one like that. And almost everyone wants one like it."

Cody says, "You want one like his?"

"Jeez, no. You?"

"Nah. I'd prob'ly trip over it every coupla steps."

We both laugh.

"I guess you could learn to pole vault with it, hey? Maybe then Coach would let you join the track team."

"When'd I ever want to be on the track team?"

Without thinking much, I answer, "I think maybe once, in Grade Never."

We laugh some more.

"Knowing that coach, he'd try to make me do bad stuff to him," he says.

"See? Just talking about having one like Skinny's and you already think everyone wants to do it to you."

"Sick."

We laugh.

"Wanna go for one last drink before headin' home?"

"Sure." He smiles like I'd just offered him a hundred bucks. "As long as it ain't lemon gin."

"Nah, Skinny gave me a bottle of the good stuff," I say. "It's up near the hall. C'mon."

He offers me his hand. I hold out my bandaged paw. He clamps onto my wrist and, thankfully, doesn't shake it. He holds onto it for a good five-ten seconds, a thin, tight smile stretching his face. "You're a good friend Qʷóqʷésk̓ iʔ 'Squito' Bob. I'm glad to know you."

"Thanks. Me, too," I say. Nothing strange about drunk friends getting a little mooshy with each other when they're drunk. Words. Just words. "Let's go."

"'Kay," he says. "I got a bottle of Southern Comfort stashed near here. It'll take me a few minutes to find it, so you go on ahead. I'll catch up with you."

His smile and the dance in his voice let me know he's okay. Maybe I am a genius of the human condition, even though I have no idea what I did, or how.

"Prob'ly a good idea." I hold up my hands. "These slow me down a lot."

"We could star in our band," Cody says, "Snail-Boy and Rock-it Man." He laughs.

His face lights up. He pats himself down, pulls a wad of papers from an inside pocket.

"I know you say your English sucks but I'd like you to read these. Tell me what you think."

He wouldn't leave his songs with JimJim and Skinny. I feel more important than I have a right to.

"Really?"

"Yeah, really. I know you'll do the right thing with them." He shoos me away. "Now go. I'm right behind you."

Like an obedient dog, I head to town, thrilled that I'd managed to please my master. Wind screams through telephone wires and trees, scrambling River's roar.

Then Wind stops screaming.

River roars, as if from under four-feet of ice.

A splat, like someone smacking a sunburnt back half a block away, fills the nearly silent night.

Cody has disappeared. Maybe over the bank to grab his stash?

"Cody?" I say. No answer but for River and Wind's muted duet.

Walking toward the bridge, I yell, "Cody!"

Running now, I shout, "Hey, Cody! Cody!"

He's not over the bank, not on the CN tracks. He could be under the bridge, out of sight, and almost away from Wind.

Scrambling down the bank sets my hands on fire. The broken bone vibrates like chattering teeth. But that pain smashes into nothing when I scan the foot of the bridge. Like an idiot I run to the bank, shouting for Cody. River never spits out her dead and she swallows the living whole. Like that idiot nine-year-old me, I let someone sucker me into letting them die on me. Cody looked fine. Cody looked *happy*. Who looks *happy* when they know they're about to off themselves. No one, that's who. Erica didn't look *happy*. Far from *happy*.

But maybe he just slipped and fell down among the rocks. Maybe he needs help. Maybe I'm not too late.

By the time I get to the hotel's lobby doors, I am one ice-knife-breath shy of dying. My hand feels re-broken. My knuckles ooze blood as black as the lobby. I rattle the door. I bang on the glass with the flat of my unbroken hand. I yell for Snook, someone, anyone, to open the door and let me call the cops.

A cop car creeps up from the alley behind the hotel, freezes me mid-bang in its spotlight. I flap my arms, squawking, "Over here! Here!"

Its spotlight locked on me, the cruiser glides to a stop beside me. Facing the shadowed cop with my hands up, I pray it's not Howe or Spotface.

"Mister Bob," Bailey says, all chagrin-tinted voice. "Haven't we spent enough time together for one weekend."

A lifetime, more like.

"Sorry. Sorry. It's just." Words leave me. I bawl.

I bawl.

I bawl, unable to think thoughts or speak words, just point dumbly toward River. He shuts down the spotlight. No matter how hard I blink, my eyes still see it burning into my brain.

"Get yourself together, lad," Bailey says. "Nothing can be that bad."

Sinister, dressed in something like Henry Higgins wears in My Fair Lady, with a sleep-toque and shiny goo on his little moustache, stands in the doorway like a mouse's long shadow.

"Well," Sinister snaps, "arrest the little hooligan. He's interrupted my nocturnal ritual and wakened every guest in the house."

Shining his flashlight in Sinister's face, Bailey, with no hint of a smile, says, "Hold your horses, Mister Snook. I don't think we have a statute specific to the interruption of one's nocturnal ritual."

"Good lord, man! Have those heathens corrupted you already?"

Like the grief that exploded from me, anger tears through me like a rip tide. "Shut the fuck up. Both of you. Just shut up. We need to save Cody. He fell into River."

They stare at me like a plop of poop they'd just stepped in. The eff-word stumbled from my mouth like a bear just released from a trap.

"When?" Bailey asks.

"I dunno. Maybe five minutes ago?"

"O," Snook squeaks, "that's different."

"Hmm," Bailey says, "Time's not our friend."

The clock over the hotel's front desk shows 2:30.

Snook huffs, "Well get on with it then."

He pulls the fire alarm. Within minutes the out-of-town cops, some still dressing, gather in the lobby. Seconds later, the town fire alarm out-screams Wind. Bailey tells me to get to my grandmother's, says he'll take care of it. Once inside, he points at the phone and tells Sinister to call someone. Then he talks to the other cops.

Agnes, in her waitress uniform and her hair up in curlers, comes downstairs. She nods as Sinister gives her orders. He hands her some keys. She heads toward the coffee shop.

Pick-ups and cars speed through town, some toward the volunteer fire department, others down to the CN station. And soon after that, a pair of speeders putt the tracks between the station house and the train trestle. Then our volunteer firemen push the firetruck to the lobby entrance. Before long, cop cars loaded with cops and volunteer firemen zoom toward the bridge.

I don't see the point of going to Yéye?s and I don't see the point of sitting on the hotel's porch. At the lookout, I can watch the rescuers and stay out of their way. And sit.

Something sadly hypnotic about the search lights bobbing along the shore and the steady sweep of the larger lights from rescue boats lulls me into near-sleep—a place I can talk with both physical and spiritual beings, the place Grandmother Bear or my grandfather sometimes find me. Not a place I feel safe and not one I visit on purpose. Shadowy Skinny and JimJim run toward the point. Breathless, they drop onto the bench on either side of me.

Skinny, smooth as a slippery-tongued alderman, says, "Sorry. We came as soon as we heard. What happened? You okay?" He hands me a bag-wrapped bottle of whiskey. The smell of it gags me. I sip, shuddering. Habit, not need. Do I look okay? I just let another friend die.

"What a stupid fucking question!" The eff-bomb explodes like Little Boy. Skinny and JimJim shrink from me like I just let a radioactive fart. Winter-like silence falls over us.

Wordlessly, we drink.

Then JimJim laughs. "Sorry, just thinking 'bout that time you, Cody, and I went down Spences. Fishing."

Now Skinny laughs. What the hell is wrong with these two? Skinny puts the bottle down, says, "O, yeah. That time. We tried running off them geese—"

Skinny chokes off his words with laughter. Where was I? Why don't I know this story?

JimJim continues, "And that big one hisses and chases us up the bank."

"Yup. And Cody trips on a rock. Falls flat on his face. He don't say a word till that darn goose bites his arse."

Both JimJim and Skinny laugh, once more trapping the story in their throats.

He manages to cap the bottle and make it disappear somewhere in his coat. "I guess we should save the last of it for Cody, have one last drink with him."

JimJim nods. I don't, not cos I don't think we should have a last drink with Cody, but cos I fear the bridge and the cold spot that will cover the place he last stood. And River. How will I answer if River calls to me? I can't think about that, not right now.

"Anyways," Skinny goes, "So that goose bites Cody's arse. The poor guy jumps up, both hands on his butt, yipping and yowling at the goose. 'Fuck off, duck! Get the fuck away from me!'"

JimJim interrupts: "First time I heard him say anything stronger than 'darn,' i'nit?"

"Last time, too, hey," Skinny says. "Until tonight." JimJim gets to his feet.

Skinny stands. He pats my shoulder, "C'mon, Squito, 'sgo."

"I can't," I say. "Maybe I'll catch up with you later."

They disappear around a corner, still talking and laughing like nothing's happened to the guy they laugh and talk about. He calmly told me he wanted one last drink before heading home. And I believed him. Like a coward, I listened to Skinny and JimJim tell funny Cody stories. Like a coward, I fear standing where he jumped, in case his spirit taps me, or the cold spot it left flings me over the railing. He chose River as his Home Waltz partner. Who will I choose for mine?

Home Waltz. One of two secrets hidden in my coat. I study The Footnotes' autographs, squint to read the liner notes, hoping they include the words to "Home Waltz." In this dull yellow light and through my watery eyes, I can't tell.

Cody's songs. The other secret hidden in my coat. The lyrics, written in black ink, blue ink, and pencil, and a mix of cursive and block letters. Some I can read easily. Some I can't. Why'd he give them to me? Why not JimJim or Skinny, guys who could make them live off the page? What does he want me to do with them? I read Cody's songs under the faint yellow streetlight.

Sometime after Skinny and JimJim have gone, Cody's mother, wailing and pulling her hair out, shows up, all in tears and barely able to hold herself up. Her death-ray eyes burn hatred into me.

She rushes me, slaps, punches, and shoves me but doesn't knock me over. "You're dead. You killed my son. I'll kill you."

I stand square to her but can't look at her. Right now I'd welcome death. But her words have way more power than her slaps, shoves, and punches. Her words have the power to slap me to the bridge and heave me over its railing. She slips in and out of the language like some of the old men and women on the top floor of the old folks home, the ones whose souls and minds have left their bodies confused and hollowed out.

"You shoulda stopped him."

Is she right? I should've learned from Erica.

"You shoulda seen it comin' and done somethin'."

Should I have seen it coming? What lesson did Erica waste on me? How could I be an expert at reading sad people's minds, when I can barely read my own? He never said that he'd be better off dead, never said he wanted to die, or kill himself. Could I have stopped him if I knew? If I knew for sure. Maybe I did know, and maybe I thought a quick death is better than living a hopeless life. Maybe I envied his courage for doing what I only think about doing. Maybe I should've forced him to sit with Yéye?. She would've changed his mind. How many of my uncles and cousins has she lost to that bridge? Or Erica's ghost. She would've shown Cody that the afterlife doesn't strip away the pain of living this life.

Constable Bailey screeches to a stop alongside us. Cody's mom screams for maybe the hundredth time since she got here: "What kinda friend watches someone die and not even lift a finger to stop him? Are you even human? What kinda monster are you? You belong in River. Not my little boy."

Bailey barges between us. "Stop!" He waves me back. She wails and raises her fists against Bailey. Maybe quicker than Skinny, he grabs her wrists. "You do not want to assault a peace officer."

"I don't care for shit. You're in my way. Let me go. It's my right to kill him. He killed my baby."

"We don't know for certain what happened to Cody. He may be out there alive, sleeping it off. So, I'm sure you don't mean any of that."

"Damn right I do. He killed my boy and if you don't put charges on him, I'll take care of it my way."

"This must be a very difficult time for you. I understand that. But threatening to hurt Mister Bob will not help you in any way." He stays so calm. Why?

"Forget you, Pig! It's not a threat. I swear I'll kill that little shit for what he done."

"Stop, Missus John. I know you're upset but getting yourself locked up will not help Cody, you, or the rest of your family."

"I got no one left. Cody was my whole family. And now I got no one, so it don't matter what happens to me. I don't care what you do to me after I kill that monster."

She breaks away from Bailey and jumps at me. Bailey grabs her and pushes her back a yard or so.

"Listen, I will not charge you with anything if you calm down and walk away. Go home. Have a cup of wine and try to rest." Bailey should know Cody's mom doesn't drink wine or any other sorta booze. He ought to know better. That's his damn job, right?

"You're gonna put charges on me and not my boy's killer? There's no justice." She screams, "No justice at all!" If a breaking heart makes a sound, her heart just made it.

Cody's mom wrestles free from Bailey and rushes at me, her hands balled into fists. Bailey spins, locks her in a chokehold, taking her down like wrestled steer. Her chin hits the pavement, sending her uppers skittering across the ground.

Bailey hefts her to her feet, handcuffs her. She yells threats at us both. He stuffs her into the back of his cruiser.

He says, "Go home, Squito. Just go home."

I wave and nod. I'll go home when they bring Cody back to town, shivering in a wool blanket, or wrapped, dead still, in a canvas tarp. River never releases anything she's caught. Cody won't be back, I know this, but xeʔłkʷúpiʔ, you expect someone who loses a kid to go a little crazy. Cody's mom has the right. Bailey should know that. He shoulda just taken her for tea and let her rant and cry. But what can you expect from a cop, even a good one like Bailey?

Once she cries herself out, she'll have a chance to see clearly that Cody hurt so bad he thought only River could cure him. She won't want to see me dead, at least not as badly as she does now.

One day she may forgive me.

Despite my promise to Erica, I let Cody jump. I replay those last minutes with Cody over and over and don't see a single thing I could've done to make him stay. I was there and should've seen what he was gonna do. I didn't. He looked fine, all smiles, happy, and joking. He'd agreed to have a last drink with me. He wanted to form a band with me, even gave me his songs to protect. If I'd known he wanted to end it, could I have stopped him? Like Erica, if I'd known, could I have stopped her? I've asked myself that question a million times since she died and I still don't have the answer. Can I ask the question once for both Cody and Erica? They died at different times, for different reasons. Or maybe the same ones. All they have in common is me, the last person they saw before their deaths. Does that make me their killer? Do I drive people to their deaths?

Maybe Cody's mom's right; I am a monster. Death in the flesh. I stab my chest with my fingers. I want to rip out my cold, dead heart.

I hate Cody for putting his death on me. I hate Erica for putting her death on me. I hate the world. I hate xeʔłkʷúpiʔ for putting me in front of them before they died. I hate xeʔłkʷúpiʔ for not showing me how to stop them.

I pick up Cody's mom's teeth. Aside from some bits of sand and dirt, they seem okay. I brush them off and slip them into my coat pocket with Cody's songs. She'll need them soon enough.

ACKNOWLEDGEMENTS

I started life believing books were magical objects that just were, until I read Ethel Wilson's "The Fog" in Grade Four. The story, set in Vancouver, showed me stories could be set in rather mundane places, such as Vancouver, a place in which I had once lived. Then I believed writers lived solitary lives in lofts, sweating out masterworks, and plagued by demons only whiskey assuaged. Ah, the whiskey! Special (and unendorsed) shoutout to Wolfhead Distillery in McGregor, ON. Then I started to write, and learned different.

First of all, k^{w}uk^{w}scémx^{w} to my partner Susan for pushing me to write again, and who has supported and stood by me for the past eighteen-or-so years.

And now in almost chronological order, people who have helped me improve as a writer and/or human being.

From the early days, before I knew I could write, instructors at Capilano College (now University):k^{w}uk^{w}scémx^{w}, Jean Clifford, who suggested I take creative writing classes in the first place, and asked to keep a poem I wrote for a class assignment. I thought she was nuts for thinking I could cut it in a creative writing class—I sure didn't think I could.

K^{w}uk^{w}scémx^{w}, Pierre Coupey for your patience and prodding, also for introducing me to the need to develop a thicker skin. Classes with you were not so worse, not so worse at all.

K^{w}uk^{w}scémx^{w}, Dorothy Jantzen for teaching me disciplined writing and the importance of getting MLA citations correct.

Then we jump ahead a bazillion years....

K^{w}uk^{w}scémx^{w}, Lynn Coady, UBC-O's first writer-in-residence, for your considered comments on this story's troublesome sex scene. I had no idea on your thoughts of them in stories, for that I apologize. Kʷukʷscémxʷ, Fred Stenson, for your valuable input of the same sex scene Lynn Coady dealt with. The scene is the story's pivot point, and it had to be correct. You both helped me get it there.

Although I wasn't a University of British Columbia—Okanagan student (I would have completed my education there, had I not moved to Ontario), I owe a shit-tonne of néxʷm kʷukʷscéyp ?es kncémxʷ to the Creative Writing department for continually short-listing my stories in the Okanagan Short Fiction Contest, notably Nancy Holmes, Michael V. Smith, Anne Fleming, Sharon Thesen, and your students. Kʷukʷscémxʷ, too, for making me feel like a part of the Okanagan writing community.

Kʷukʷscémxʷ NaNoWriMo (National Novel Writing Month) for providing me the impetus to write this novel in November, 2008. The first half has largely stayed intact, but vastly improved. The second half was a shit show I had to revise four different times.

Kʷukʷscémxʷ, Gerald Kematch, for teaching me to be a better Indian and showing me the power of hope in a story.

Kʷukʷscémxʷ, Shuswap Association of Writers, for your kindness and generosity, your hard work, and the Blue Pencil sessions during Word on the Lake, with Diana Gabaldon (kʷukʷscémxʷ, Diana), Kelsey Attard, Managing Editor at Freehand Books (kʷukʷscémxʷ, Kelsey), George Bowering (kʷukʷscémxʷ, George), and the delightful English instructor from Okanagan College, whose name escapes my Swiss cheese mind (kʷukʷscémxʷ); your exuberent response to that very same troublesome sex scene—have I mentioned how pivotal it is to the story?—encouraged me to keep working on the story at a time I needed encouragement to stick with it.

Kʷukʷscémxʷ to the University of Windsor, where I completed my BA (Honours) almost exactly thirty years after I started at Capilano College. And my MA in English Literature and Creative Writing, immediately thereafter. Néxʷm kʷukʷscéyp ?es kncémxʷ to Dr. Susan Holbrook, Dr. Karl Jirgens, Dr. Andre Narbonne, Dr. Mark Albert Johnston, Dr, Katherine Quinsey, Dr. Suzanne Matheson, Dr, Richard Douglass-Chin, Dr. Carol Davison, Dr. Sandra Muse Isaacs, Dr. Nicolas Papador, and Marty Gervais. All y'all helped me immensely. Your willingness to share your wealth of knowledge and the love of your specialties fuelled my desire to learn. Who knew that ecocriticism, walking, post colonialism, and cross-dressing characters were actual topics of study?

Also, a huge double néxʷm kʷukʷscéyp ?es kncémxʷ to Nino Ricci, a fantastic writer and an incredible Creative Writing instructor. I workshopped parts of this story in his novel writing class and taking it was the absolute right thing to do. I learned a lot from him while he was my creative writing instructor and the Uni's writer in residence.

Special shoutouts and kʷukʷscémxʷ to Karl and Sandra, I had no idea how much serious criticism was dedicated to Indigenous writing and writers. Along those same lines; kʷukʷscémxʷ Richard, post-colonial works and criticism sure opened my eyes to a bunch of shit we (still) need to change.

And kʷukʷscémxʷ Margaret Atwood, for your incredible encouragement during your masterclass at the Pelee Island Book House.

And kʷukʷscémxʷ Dorothy Jane Kavanaugh, my writing buddy whose insights revealed story elements I didn't know were there.

Also, ginormous kʷukʷscémxʷ to Molly Philips and Bridget Heuvel, a pair of Creative Writing classmates whose criticisms of my submissions were both insightful and helpful. Your talent and brilliance awed me in the biblical sense.

Lastly, kʷukʷscémxʷ Palimpsest Press: Aimée, for taking a chance on this story, and your staff for their support; Jamie Tenant for his delicate approach to editing the manuscript; and Dawn Kresan for your cover design, typesetting, and book layout (and kʷukʷscémxʷ for whispering good things about my story to Palimpsest).

And lastly, this time for reals, kʷukʷscémxʷ Susan, because you're worth mentioning twice.

Blessed I am, ye-es!